# ELEMENTAL STEAMPUNK TALES

## A COLLECTION

### ANNE RENWICK

# A TRACE OF COPPER

CHAPTER ONE

*Aberwyn, Wales*
*Spring, 1885*

"IT BIT ME," the young woman informed Piyali, hiking her skirts and rolling down her woolen hose. "Right through my stocking." Miss Price, the shopkeeper's daughter, plopped down on a chair and propped her foot upon a stool, pointing. "And now it's blue."

Dr. Piyali Mukherji leaned closer. As insane as Miss Price's words sounded, they rang true. Her ankle was indeed blue.

Well, part of it. There was a decided lesion approximately two inches in diameter above her fibular protuberance. Piyali pressed two fingers against the blemish. She would describe it as an infection. Except it didn't appear inflamed, and it wasn't hot to the touch.

And it was *blue*.

Unheard of. But that was why she'd accepted the Crown's commission, taken on the added duties of a Queen's agent. The Duke of Avesbury, the gentleman at the head of this small, select group, had offered her a chance to be on the forefront of

3

investigations into strange and unusual medical conditions. This certainly fit the bill.

"A frog bit you." Piyali's eyebrows rose, hoping she'd heard wrong. "A blue frog. With teeth." Did frogs have teeth? And frogs—at least in Britain—were supposed to be green. Or brown.

Miss Price bit her lip. It didn't bode well that she needed to consider her story.

Hoping for an explanation, she looked to the man who loomed beside her taking up far too much space in the small parlor. Time had turned familiar into foreign. Mr. Evan Tredegar wore his dark, tousled curls longer, no cravat wound under his collar beneath the rough shadow of his beard, and a small, curved scar cut through the edge of his right eyebrow. Under her study, a muscle twitched at his jawline, and his lips pressed into a thin line. He refused to meet her gaze. Perhaps it was just as well, for his eyes never failed to ignite a slow burn beneath her skin, and she needed to focus.

Still, a certain unease gave her pause. Once she'd been able to read his every mood and would have labeled his expression as concerned. Except the man she'd known wouldn't withhold information vital to a patient's treatment. What wasn't he telling her?

"Miss Price?" Piyali prompted.

The young woman nodded. "Then it hopped away and disappeared into the woods." Sticking her lower lip out in a pout, she looked up at her mother. "Is this really necessary? Besides, she can't be a real doctor. How can a *woman* hold such a degree?" With a sidelong glance at Piyali's clothing, her voice dropped to a whisper. "An *Indian* woman."

A real doctor. Piyali resisted the urge to roll her eyes. If she had a shilling for every time she'd heard that sentiment... Instead, she lifted her chin and replied, "I attended medical school at the Université de Paris where women have been accepted since 1860."

Never had Paris seemed so far away. Four of the best—and worst—years of her life. She'd earned her place there by being twice as good as the other students, most of them men. Any who had sneered at her inclusion swiftly adjusted their opinion as she collected one award after another, graduating first in her class. As to the prejudice, she no longer felt the need to justify the traditional clothing she wore. If a person could not appreciate the richness and intricacy of Indian designs, then it was their loss.

With an unsteady hand, Mrs. Price patted her daughter on the shoulder and threw Piyali a nervous look. "Lister University's choice of medical practitioner is alarming. No doubt Dr. Mukherji was all they could spare, but I have every confidence in Mr. Tredegar's ointment. The blue stain has barely spread since you first applied it. In fact, I think it's grown smaller." From the pinched expression on her face, the woman clearly wished Piyali elsewhere. "But your father worries and wanted to consult a board-certified physician in case amputation becomes necessary."

"Amputation!" Miss Price's chest began to heave, her eyes growing wide, her fingers digging into the cushion of her chair. "It's just a spot!"

"A very unusual spot." Evan finally spoke, though his words were tight and strained. "One that must be examined by someone with more expertise than myself."

Resentment sparked. His defense of her skills was unwelcome. Both by her and, judging from the deep frown upon her face, Miss Price.

Piyali glanced again at the blue lesion. Could it be no more than a stain of blue ink? Had she interrupted a hoax, a bizarre courtship trick designed to lure a handsome, young pharmacist into this parlor? For upon her arrival, her purported patient had been fluttering eyelashes and casting Evan glances drenched with unfulfilled longing. Or—she narrowed her eyes—did the fault lie squarely on Evan's shoulders? Did he toy with the young shopkeeper's daughter, making promises he couldn't—or wouldn't—keep?

For once he'd made her promises, ones she'd clung to for four long years abroad. Promises he'd failed to keep when he returned from his overseas voyage some three months ago. Upholding her own vow, she'd sent him a message, then pounced upon the daily post for days—weeks—hoping for word of his imminent arrival, but... nothing. Save a devastating silence.

Heartache must have shown upon her face, for her mother had hunted down coconuts and banana leaves before taking herself down into the kitchens of their London townhouse to personally oversee the preparation of Piyali's favorite dish, *bhetki macher paturi*—marinated steamed fish—in an effort to coax her to eat something... anything. Food wasn't her mother's only crisis response. Gentlemen of all kinds had begun to appear around the dining table. At first they were Bengali, then merely Indian. She knew her mother grew desperate when a six-foot-four, blond Swede had joined them.

"Choose a husband, Piyali," Ma had begged, reminding her that if her father were still alive, he would even now be arranging her marriage. Even Piyali's British stepfather conspired to assist Ma, making noises about grandchildren. But no other man, no matter how accomplished or handsome, could mend the rift in her life.

An acidic pain had lodged itself beneath her heart, slowly corroding all of her hopes and dreams. Though she'd buried herself in her work, establishing a research program in her laboratory while training to become a Queen's agent, nothing eased the ache.

Which was why she'd cringed when Mr. Black, the duke's

right-hand spy, had handed her this first assignment. "Aberwyn, Wales?" she'd read. Evan lived there.

"Two birds, one stone." The agent's eyes had sparkled with mischief. "A competent research pharmacist and a specialist in infectious disease reconnecting over a mysterious and peculiar illness." He'd laughed. "What could go wrong?"

Though she'd wanted to cry, orders were orders. She'd packed a trunk with the essentials and boarded the first train to Cardiff, enduring lewd stares and bawdy speculations about the bedroom predilections of *exotic* young women. Aether, how she hated that word. In Cardiff, she bought a ticket for a rickety steamstage, one that had broken down twice en route to Aberwyn. There, despite her exhortations to be careful, the driver had tossed her trunk from the roof onto the muddy street where a grumbling stable boy had dragged it—bumping up each step—to a small, cramped room above the town's only tavern, *Yr Ysgyfarnog Wen*—The White Hare. Later, a short walk along the rutted main street had brought her here, to the shopkeeper's cottage.

"Are you all right?" Evan's voice was soft and considerate.

"Merely contemplating treatment options," she lied.

The long hours spent traveling had jarred every joint and coated her with a film of dust, all while doubts gnawed at her mind. But deceitful hopes kept whispering that perhaps Evan's missive had gone astray and so, though exhausted, she'd taken special pains for their first meeting in five years.

Shaking the travel wrinkles free, she'd donned a favorite green lehenga—skirt—with a simple, paisley embroidered border edging the hem. Buckling her corset atop the matching half-sleeved choli, she'd brushed her long, wavy hair to a shine before twisting a green, satin ribbon into a plait over her shoulder. But his eyes hadn't flashed with desire, his pulse hadn't jumped in his throat, and his fingers hadn't twitched—as they once had—with a need to touch her skin. Evan had barely looked at her at all.

The ache settled back into her chest. It was no use, clinging to the past. She kept her gaze fixed upon her patient, trying to anesthetize her response, for it hurt too much to gaze upon Evan's once familiar face, to fight the urge to smooth his unkempt curls and drag her palm over the roughness of his cheeks.

"Ointment?" she asked, pulling a decilamp from its loop upon her leather corset, shaking it to activate the bioluminescent bacteria within. She bent over Miss Price's foot, directing a beam of light at the lesion. There. At its center, a tiny, curved, pink line. A scratch—bite? —that had already healed. Possibly the entry point of whatever organism had invaded her skin.

"An ointment of *khu-neh-ari*," Evan replied, speaking a foreign word that likely originated deep within the Amazonian rainforest, "made from the *Caniramon divaritum*, a climbing shrub."

She glanced at him out of the corner of her eye. "Have you encountered this particular ailment before?"

"I've been unable to identify it." He shifted on his feet. "Though the outward progression of its margins is reminiscent of a fungal infection. Hence the ointment."

"Infection!" The older woman yanked her hand from her daughter's shoulder.

"Fungus!" In a move worthy of Drury Lane, Miss Price threw herself backward upon the chair and tossed an arm across her forehead.

"Possible, but—" Piyali shifted the beam of light and the lesion… sparkled? She flicked the light away, then back. For a second, the skin shimmered, flashing pink and silver. Then, once again, it was blue. Not good. "I'm going to need a biopsy."

"Biopsy?" Miss Price's voice quivered, and she squirmed on her seat. "What's that?"

Turning to her bag of medical equipment, Piyali extracted a

glass aetheroscope slide, a few eyedropper bottles of stain and a sterile razor, arranging them all upon the small side table. "I'm going to shave away a tiny portion of the surface of your skin so that I might analyze it beneath my aetheroscope. You should feel no more than a slight pinch."

Miss Price whimpered.

With a long-suffering sigh, Evan reached out to take Miss Price's hand. Odd that he wore gloves inside the parlor. "Squeeze as tight as you feel you must."

Minutes later, the skin sample was prepped and loaded within her small, portable aetheroscope. Once the light source was activated, Piyali screwed in a pressurized canister of aether, listening to the gas hiss as it filled the chamber of the device. Perched on the edge of a chair, she bent over, peering through the eyepiece to adjust focus and magnification.

"Interesting," she murmured under her breath, then changed the angle of illumination. The color shifted.

A brush of feet on carpet. The faint disturbance of the air around her as Evan crossed the room to her side and leaned close. "What is it?" The heat of his breath swept across the bare skin of her neck and sent uninvited shivers across her skin.

How was it one man could affect her so?

She took a deep, steadying breath before answering. "A pearly luster." Still, her voice caught. He was much too close. "One that tends toward iridescence of the pink and blue variety. It could be…" She dialed in to the highest resolution and stifled a curse. As feared, the jolting of the steamstage—or the tossing of her trunk—had indeed broken valuable equipment. Shaking her head, she stood and stepped back from the aetheroscope—and away from Evan. "My objective, the one with the highest resolution? Its crystalline lens is cracked."

She could guess, but she wouldn't. Not even for Evan. Especially not for him. He knew something, and he wasn't sharing. Childish of her, but now that she too knew something, she wasn't sharing either. Resolve stiffened her spine. He could wait —they all could—until she confirmed her findings with cold, hard evidence.

"Piyali?" Evan prompted.

Mother and daughter drew offended breaths at his overly informal address of an unfamiliar and unmarried woman. Even in a small Welsh village, propriety must be maintained.

"Dr. Mukherji," she corrected him, her voice cool and clinical. Unless Evan decided to share whatever he concealed, there was nothing more she could do today. She was tired and hungry and irritated. And a report was due to Mr. Black. "I can't say for certain. Further tests are required."

---

A LIGHT MIST of rain dampened Evan's hair as he stood in the street staring at the door of *Yr Ysgyfarnog Wen*. If only he could turn back time.

Five years and she was still as beautiful as ever. He had no right to look, no right to steal glances. But he had. Of dark eyes he'd once stared into. Of long, wavy hair he'd once twined about his fingers. Of deep pink lips he'd once kissed.

He'd done his best not to stare, not to notice how the graceful arc of her collarbone peeked from beneath the edge of her neckline, how a short corset clasped her narrow waist beneath its tooled, leather surface, how her skirt flared outward over generous hips, or how its raised hemline revealed ankles encased in laced boots.

Her corset was studded with metal loops, hooks and chains to which she'd clipped all manner of essential devices and tools. Including a government-issued TTX pistol that gave his pulse a jolt. Was there anything more alluring than a strong, competent woman? But it was the familiar, amber glass vial dangling from a chain beside her hip that focused his gaze. Wondering, he'd bent close to peer through the aetheroscope and inhaled. Essence of orange blossoms. All these years she'd kept it, the same essential oil still scenting the water that rinsed her hair. Long-suppressed desires stirred.

He closed his eyes. He had no right to such thoughts.

Not one week after he'd returned to Britain's shores, a skeet pigeon with rust-tipped wings had alighted upon his window sill, a brief note tied to its jointed ankle with news of her degree and the direction to her family's London townhouse. To speed his reply, she'd even included a punched return card for the clockwork bird.

With stars in his eyes, he'd sat down in his tropical greenhouse to put pen to paper. Halfway through his letter a small, blue frog had leapt onto the back of his hand. A stowaway upon one of the many lianas—climbing vines—he'd brought back from his voyage to the Amazonian rainforest. He'd thought the shimmering creature cute, adorable, delightful.

Until it bit him.

Evan rubbed his thumb and forefinger together, the soft black leather of his gloves reminding him of the moment everything went wrong. He'd never sent that letter. Or any letter. One didn't ask the woman he loved to share a slow descent into madness.

Time passed, and the vine of his silence slowly twined itself about his throat, growing so thick that only a machete could cut it free. Too late to ask her for help now. Not only did she likely despise him, she was a Queen's agent.

Nonetheless, he must speak with her. Her aetheroscope was broken and that meant she would want to return to London on the morning's steamstage. That couldn't happen. He couldn't allow her to leave, not with a sample of Miss Price's skin in her possession. Here, in Wales, things could be kept under control.

Stopping her meant entering The White Hare where one Miss Sarah Parker, the tavern's daughter, would be lying in wait.

He willed his feet to move, to cross the rutted road, willed his hand to wrap around the iron handle of the tavern's door and pull it open.

"Evan!" Sarah cried, her voice a confection of icing and spun sugar. Wiping her hands on her apron, she rushed to his side.

Out of the proverbial pan and into the fire.

Three months ago, Sarah and Miss Price—Tegan, she insisted whenever her mother wasn't around—had begun fighting to gain his attention, all in a futile effort to secure a marriage proposal. Their bickering was a constant reminder of what he would never have, a thorn that pricked at his conscience.

Tegan found any remotely credible excuse to throw herself in his path. Unchaperoned, she regularly dropped by his cottage—a three-mile walk into the countryside—to request more packets of headache powder and throat lozenges for the shop. Chances she sold that much were close to zero.

And Sarah? She pounced on him every time he stepped into The White Hare, always ready with a pint of his favorite ale, begging for tales of his time in the rainforest even as she tugged the bodice of her dress scandalously low. Worse, her parents aided and abetted, turning a blind eye to her blatant flirtations and not calling her to task when she ignored the other customers.

"Miss Parker," he replied. "Where is Dr. Mukherji? I need to speak with her."

Wrapping her arm about his, Sarah urged him closer to the peat fire burning in the grate. "Upstairs," she admitted, playfully pushing him into a chair and dropping into his lap. "But I'm right here."

"Sarah," he warned in a low voice. "I've asked you not to—"

She leaned forward, pressing generous breasts against his chest while twisting a finger into his curls so tightly it threatened to rip his hair from its roots. "Oh, *please*. All these months you've been without a woman to warm your bed. You need a wife, one who can help you run that pharmacy of yours in Cardiff. Tegan might know business, but she's far too uptight to keep you satisfied after hours."

"Stop," he snapped, grabbing her hips and shoving her away. "I've no intention of taking a wife."

Laughing, Sarah caught her balance on the sticky tabletop. "No? Then you'd best be careful. The Indian princess can't take her eyes off you." The lift of her chin redirected his attention.

*What?* He whipped his head about, catching Piyali's narrow-eyed gaze from across the room as she descended the stairs. Guilt stuck in his throat. He'd not been unfaithful and didn't want her to think... Did it matter? Her eyes slid away, and she turned her back, climbing onto a stool at the bar. A deliberate move to avoid any and all private conversation.

"She's not a princess," he said.

"Oh?" Her voice rose in a teasing lilt. "Then why do you stare at her as if she wears a crown of gold and precious jewels?"

Evan glowered. "Please, just bring me a pint."

"Of course," Sarah said, then winked. "And I'll see what I can do about a little something extra." She sauntered away, swinging her hips with each step. Tossing a quick word to her father, she jerked her head in Evan's direction. Then, sliding onto a stool, Sarah turned her bright eyes upon Piyali. Her lips moved, and Piyali laughed. Not good. Sarah's interference was akin to swatting a bee hive with a stick. The dull, throbbing beginnings of a splitting headache began to hammer away at his skull.

Glass banged on wood as Mr. Parker dropped a pint of frothy ale onto the table before him. "The way you've been handling my daughter? I think we ought to speak about calling banns."

Evan dropped his head into his hands.

"SO TELL ME, is the all-too-precious Miss Tegan Price going to live?" The blonde, blue-eyed serving girl dropped onto a stool beside Piyali and leaned close. "Not that I wish her ill," she hastened to add, "just that we've been at each other's throats fighting over Evan." She waved a dismissive hand in the air. "Tegan's always fabricating one ailment or another, any excuse for Evan to formulate her a new potion." Her voice dropped to a whisper. "Not only is he the most handsome man for miles around, he has a shop in Cardiff, and both of us want out of this dismal village." A deep sigh slid from her lips. "Not that he wants anything to do with either of us."

Piyali blinked at the sudden onslaught of unsolicited information. "I'm sorry, I can't discuss a patient's health," she said. Then, reminding herself she was an agent tasked with collecting information, forced herself to sip the bitter ale and plaster on a conspiratorial smile. "But please, feel free to share any and all gossip about her with me."

A wide grin split the woman's face. "We're going to be great friends," she announced, slapping a hand upon the bar top. "I'm Sarah Parker, daughter of this humble establishment. Sorry about the shameful display of overt flirting you had to witness. What *is* your trick? Evan can't seem to take his eyes off you."

"It's not what you think," she began, but a discordant note rang in her answer. "We knew each other once, long ago."

"And now find yourselves forced to work together to cure Tegan of whatever it is that ails her." Sarah held up a hand. "Which you can't talk about, but it's good to know you're not added competition." She leaned forward, eyes wide, waiting. "So tell me instead, are you from India?" She continued before Piyali could draw breath. "I love the embroidery on your skirt. I've always wanted to travel, but the only other place I've ever been —not counting Cardiff—is London." She sighed. "I miss London."

Sensing an easily won ally, Piyali shared a bit more than she would otherwise. "I was born in northeast India, but moved here as a young girl with my stepfather and mother. Aside from the four years I studied in Paris, I've lived in London." After an epidemic of diphtheria tore her family to shreds, her mother had resisted remarrying, choosing to support them by selling the stunning *kantha* shawls she hand stitched, until a chance encounter with a British textile importer had brought her stepfather into their lives. Ignoring the many yelling and pleading aunties and uncles, they'd married and moved to England. Her mother had found a second chance at love... could she?

"Paris!" Sarah's eyes grew hazy. "I'm so jealous. It's awful here, but my father lost his job over a bar fight and decided he'd open his own tavern. Here. In Wales." She rolled her eyes. "I've no idea why. It's so remote. And forget about learning Welsh! It's impossible to wrap the tongue about. Just try to say the name of this tavern."

Piyali made her best attempt, and they both dissolved into tears of laughter.

"See?" Sarah said, then lowered her voice to a whisper as she waggled her eyebrows. "Thing is, I understand it just fine. Makes it fun to listen in on all the gossip."

"Sarah!" Mr. Parker yelled, beckoning his daughter. "Enough. Back to work."

Feeling as if she'd struck gold, Piyali pressed a hand atop Sarah's. "You'll tell me more about this town later?" Perhaps it was a path to nothing but renewed pain, but she needed to know about Evan, about what he'd been up to since his return.

"Only if you tell me more about India. And Paris."

"Agreed."

Sarah hopped onto her feet and turned back to the customers.

Sensing Evan's stare between her shoulder blades, Piyali took a deep breath and turned. Sad blue eyes met hers. Why hadn't he answered her message? Perhaps he'd fallen in love with another? Her chest constricted. They *had* been apart far longer than they'd been together.

Her heart had almost healed. Almost. Not that she would be giving him a chance to tear another hole by squabbling with Sarah and Tegan. It didn't matter what kept him silent. He'd made his choice.

His eyebrows drew together. Good. He ought to feel guilty about never answering her message. If he'd changed his mind, it was simple decency to inform her that she no longer fit into his life plans.

Difficult as it was, she needed to speak with him. She needed to know what he knew about the blue lesion and, to meet the bare minimum requirement of her mission, she needed to deliver Mr. Black's invitation.

She spun on her seat to face the bar and waved Mr. Parker over.

"Hungry?" he asked.

"No." She placed a punch card, a rolled parchment in a tin canister and two coins upon the bar. "Rather, I'd like to charter your skeet pigeon." The clockwork bird didn't look particularly airworthy. She frowned. "If it's in working order."

"Tends to malfunction," he warned, his voice suggesting she wasted perfectly good money. "Even on a good day, doesn't make it much past London."

Worth a try. It was the only bird in town, and she hadn't seen any telegraph wires. If Mr. Black couldn't arrange to have a new crystalline lens objective shipped, she'd take her sample back for analysis in her laboratory at Lister University. Waiting a few days for an answer would give her time to keep an eye on Tegan's lesion. "Good enough."

He pocketed the coins and, as he turned to tie the tin canister to the bird's ankle, his wife burst through the door, a bloody rag wrapped about her finger. Glaring at her husband, she pushed past him and plunged her hand into a bucket of soapy water all the while muttering under her breath about stupid plans and unreasonable men.

"What happened?" Sarah asked, handing her mother a clean cloth.

"It's nothing." Mrs. Parker dried her hands. "I scratched myself on some thorns by Seren's Well."

"The fairy well?" Sarah hissed. "You didn't. Tell me you didn't."

The steam in her mother's answering stare could make the nearby copper teakettle whistle. "I did it for you," she snapped.

"You can't," Sarah spat back. "That's the whole point. Do you know what the other girls will say if they find out?" She stalked away.

As Sarah's mother struggled to bandage her finger, Piyali offered, "I'm a doctor. I can look at it if you'd like."

Mrs. Parker's head jerked up. For a long moment, she stared at Piyali, her face expressionless. "More than a doctor, I'd say. Everyone knows what the Price Family is up to, pulling strings to drag you all the way here from London." Her mouth twisted. "Bet they were mightily disappointed when a woman arrived. And a foreigner at that. Nothing they'd like better than to see their precious daughter wed to a man of influence."

Piyali sucked in a sharp breath of air. She *was* a citizen, granted as a royal prerogative when she joined the Queen's agents, an offer only extended by special invitation. By working as a British spy, she had done—and would do—far, far more to serve this country than most natural born citizens. All this, however, was not something one announced, particularly in a Welsh tavern.

"Elena," her husband growled in warning, "there's no need to air the dirty laundry of others."

"*Hmphff.*" Mrs. Parker snatched a rag and set to wiping the far end of the counter.

A hand touched her shoulder, and Piyali jumped.

"It's me." Evan's voice was hushed. "We need to speak. The rain has stopped. Perhaps a walk?"

Given the hostile glances the tavern owners hurled at each other like poison-tipped darts, Piyali was all too happy to flee. "I'll grab my overcoat."

———

"WHAT'S THIS ABOUT A FAIRY WELL?" Piyali asked him.

Lines of irritation pulled at the corners of her mouth. Insulted by the Parkers, most likely. They were experts at open hostility and masters of harsh insults. How they'd managed to conceive a daughter, he'd never know.

"*Ffynnon Seren.* Seren's Well. A bit of local tradition and legend," he answered, happy to let more serious topics wait until the dark cloud lifted from her face. "A pretty little spot just outside the village. Come, I'll show you."

Evan didn't offer her his arm. He wasn't a gentleman, and

she wasn't a lady. Besides, it was better if they didn't touch. He wouldn't want to let go.

Despite all they had to say to each other, they walked in silence beneath the gray sky, following a narrow, winding path into a wooded gully. As they neared the well, he waved her ahead of him, not wanting to obscure her view of the ancient holy site. A small pool edged by rocks collected the upwelling of water beneath an old tree. Its roots had twisted and turned, invading the crevices of the ruins that stood beside the well. Overhead, scraps of cloth tied to its branches fluttered in the wind. Rough stepping stones led downward to the cool, clear water.

"It's beautiful. And so very peaceful. Like a *pabitro pukur*..." She trailed her fingers over the moss-covered stones of a low wall. "What was this?"

"An alter? A shrine? A chapel?" He shrugged. "No one recalls. But," he couldn't suppress a smile at the ridiculous legend he was about to share, "tradition has it that one can cure epilepsy by bathing in the pool at midnight while holding a duck beneath one's left arm."

"A duck?" Her face lit up as she laughed. "Are there any other odd traditions?"

"Too many to count. All invocations involve an offering of a bent steel pin to the water-sprite who lives here. Most requests are for healing various ailments. Warts. Leprosy. Toenail fungus."

Her eyebrows rose. "Skin lesions?"

Ah. It seemed they were done with pleasantries. "I've no idea what causes it."

Only a partial lie, but it wasn't like he could hand her the frog. The blasted critter had leapt from his workbench and disappeared into the tropical plants and vines that grew in his greenhouse. He'd searched for hours—days, weeks, months— but had never seen the creature again. He cancelled all visitations to his greenhouse, all the tours he'd promised of the strange, wonderful plants he'd shipped home, unwilling to expose another person to its bite. Now he was a recluse, fast becoming the village eccentric.

Unfortunately, forbidding anyone to enter his greenhouse had the opposite effect, generating ludicrous rumors that he'd brought home man-eating plants and snakes that could swallow a child whole. Soon adventure-seeking boys had arrived, peering through the condensation-fogged glass, trying to catch a glimpse of whatever lay hidden inside.

He'd ordered a lock—the 3XR CinchBolt—but it arrived too late. A little over a week ago, Evan awoke to find the door to his greenhouse ever so slightly ajar, the plants nearest the crack struggling to endure the cold spring morning.

Though nothing obvious had been stolen, his first thought had been of that blue frog. Had it escaped? It seemed so. For not three days later, Miss Tegan Price had knocked on his front door, begging an ointment for a strange rash. This time, she'd not been pretending an illness.

Plying Tegan with questions, he'd discovered that the frog had bitten her while she walked upon the foot path that led to his front door. After compounding a jar of ointment and sending her home with promises to call on her soon, he'd searched the path, the shrubs lining it, turning over every rock and fallen log he could reach, until finally resigning himself to failure. Instead, he turned to the desperate hope that the tropical frog had perished with the early morning's frost.

But he couldn't be certain. And now Piyali was here—the last place he wanted her.

"I owe you an apology," he said, speaking past the lump that blocked his throat. "I wanted to write... but things changed. I'm not the same man I was when I left." A gross understatement. He wasn't sure exactly what he was anymore, but according to the folklore the *Kayapo* shaman had shared, eventually he would no longer be human. Myth? He hoped so, but he couldn't be certain. With Tegan now facing the same fate...

"Did you meet someone?" Hurt shaded her voice as she searched his face. "Another woman?"

"No." His hand rose, reaching for her, but he forced it back to his side. "There will never be another woman for me, Piyali. I'm simply... unfit."

"An injury?" She glanced at his groin.

Blood rushed to his face, and he nearly choked. "Not that."

"Then what?" She placed a hand upon his arm, sending a fierce jolt of hunger through his body. "What is it that you feel you can't tell me? Once we shared... everything."

His eyes fell upon her rosy lips. He wanted nothing more than to pull her soft curves against his chest, to thread his fingers through the curls of her midnight-black hair that seemed to shine with its own light and pull her mouth to his. Kissing her would solve everything. And nothing.

The air between them shimmered with memories. At a fateful symposium—*Herbal Extracts and Their Use in the Treatment of Parasitic Infestations*—held at the Pharmacological Society of London, he'd lost awareness of all women but one. The attraction had been mutual, and a courtship had begun. Shared glances, touches, whispers over the course of several lectures, all culminating one fateful day in the shadowy recesses of the society's cloakroom. His pulse jumped at the memory of his mouth moving over her smooth skin, of linen and silk sliding to the ground, of her legs wrapped about his hips urging him closer, deeper.

He'd proposed the very next day on bended knee, asking her to come with him to South America. But her own dream had become reality, and with tears in her eyes, she showed him an acceptance letter granting her admission to medical school. In Paris.

Unwilling to let her go, he'd promised to ask her again in four years and begged her to wait for him.

Looking now into the twin dark pools of her eyes, he knew that with a few words, with a simple touch, she could be his once more. But at what cost? Her career. Possibly her life. He'd given her an apology, but he could not give her an explanation. Under no circumstances could he allow the British government to become aware of what had transpired. Nor would he inflict his future upon her.

The air was thick with regrets, making it hard to breathe.

"Evan?"

He dragged his eyes away, forcing himself to study the dappled light that filtered through the leaves above the surface of the spring. "You saw something through the aetheroscope," he said. "If it's not a fungal infection, the ointment I compounded won't cure her. Perhaps you ought to excise the lesion."

"Perhaps." Piyali moved out of reach, her boots tapping softly across the stepping stones. "Her skin, the basal layer, is blue. While that's odd enough, it also color shifted when I changed the angle of illumination." She lowered herself onto the low wall beside the water. "I've sent a skeet pigeon to London requesting my laboratory to send a replacement aetheroscope lens without delay. Before I set a course of treatment, I want to collect more data."

"Why not simply excise the lesion?" he asked, hoping she didn't find his insistence too presumptuous.

"Excision would prevent its spread, but once removed, the tissue—and anything that has invaded it—will die."

Exactly as he hoped. But she intended to investigate. Already, she'd dispatched a skeet pigeon to London. As his plans crumbled before him, Evan struggled to present her with a blank face. So much for his hopes of sending Piyali back to

London without a sample. Still, if he could locate that blue frog, this disaster could be contained.

"Bet I can catch it first!"

"I'm faster!"

With a shout and a laugh, two boys ran up the pathway, skittering to a stop in the leaf litter at his feet.

"Simon," Evan greeted one boy, then the other. "Aron. Glad to see the skin's clearing up." He glanced at Piyali and murmured, "I've written a paper and plan to send my findings to the Pharmacological Society soon." They'd have to publish it, for he wouldn't be speaking in public.

The boy yanked his collar away from his neck. "Almost all gone," he said. "And no more itching." His face twisted as he stuck out his tongue. "But the tea is... blech."

Piyali stood and nodded a greeting. "Pleased to meet you both." She peered at the boy's face and neck, both impressed and incredulous. "You found a treatment for eczema?"

"From a shaman in the rainforest," Aron answered, his eyes wide and sparkling.

"If you're already cured," Piyali replied with a smile, "what brings you to the fairy well?"

"Mr. Tredegar told us all about how the natives hunt in the rainforest. With blow guns and poison darts," Aron said, snapping a branch off a nearby tree, whittling its end into a sharp point. "We're gonna do the same, soon as we find that blue frog."

"A blue frog," Piyali said. "What a coincidence." Her voice told him she knew it was anything but.

Biting back a curse, Evan closed his eyes. The creature's skin secretions might not be poisonous—not like the boys foolishly hoped—but its bite was a different matter. He had to catch that frog. Now.

# CHAPTER THREE

*E*VAN HAD BUNDLED her back toward the tavern, reaching its door just as the sun slipped over the horizon. He'd refused to enter, refused to discuss the frog situation, muttering something about stoking the greenhouse stove as he turned away.

Bewildered, she stood there in the street as his form disappeared into the twilight. That he'd found an effective treatment for eczema was... amazing. Test, analyze, report. Since his return from Brazil, he'd sent a number of groundbreaking reports to the Pharmacological Society of London, and its members were all enamored of him. When this paper arrived, they would extend him a speaking invitation, but given he'd yet to visit London, she doubted he'd accept.

Was it because she lived in London? Or did it have something to do with this frog?

He'd almost kissed her there by the spring. She'd read the intent in his eyes. Dark and intense, it was the same stare he'd fastened upon her that first day their eyes caught in the lecture theater. Not the stare of hostility most women who dared step into the male stronghold received, but one of intrigued attraction. One he'd underscored by taking a chair beside her own. Then, as now, desire had rushed like liquid heat throughout her entire body.

If there was interest, was there still hope? Possibly. But this infection—and apparently a frog—stood between them. Love thwarted by an amphibian. Absurd.

Stomach growling, she stepped into the smoky tavern, hoping Sarah might be inclined to indulge in a bit of gossip. Perhaps she might know something about this elusive frog. Alas, she was busy carrying pints of ale and side-stepping the wandering hands of men who believed a compliment was best delivered by pinching a woman's rear. That they dared to do so in her father's presence said something about the man, casting him in a most unpleasant light. A father ought to defend his daughter's honor, *consistently*.

Among this cohort of men, one particular set of eyes with an arrogant gleam turned in Piyali's direction as she strode to the bar—back straight and chin held high—but the man's vanity refused to recognize her discouraging demeanor. His mouth widened in a manner suggestive of all kinds of improprieties as he rose from his chair.

A woman alone. An Indian woman alone. A young Indian woman in a skirt with a hemline that exposed her booted ankles… and escorted by no man.

Somehow this was an invitation. Once, such blatant interest unsettled her. Now, she viewed it as an opportunity to realign his priorities.

As he approached, his gaze shifted downward, raking over her body with an air of speculation, and she pulled back the edge of her overcoat, giving him a glimpse of her government issued TTX pistol in its holster. *That* snapped his drifting eyes back to a more acceptable location, and he dropped back into his chair, scowling. A most gratifying response. She allowed herself a small smile.

"Hungry?" the innkeeper asked as she settled onto a stool. "Got stew and Welsh rarebit."

"Rabbit?" she asked, her brow wrinkling.

A long-suffering sigh escaped his mouth. "Cheese on toast."

She could see the stew bubbling on the stove. Gristly beef and overcooked rutabagas in a fatty broth. Her throat constricted in protest, and her stomach also threatened to rebel. "The rarebit, please. And," she stopped him as he turned away, "the skeet pigeon?"

"Liftoff went as expected." He raised a shoulder and stepped aside as his wife slammed a pint of frothy, overflowing ale onto the bar before Piyali.

"Don't even think of drawing your weapon in my establishment," Mrs. Parker warned with narrowed eyes. "Next steamstage leaves at sunrise."

"I need to keep the room a few more days," Piyali said, ignoring the unnecessarily strong hint. "Bit of a problem with a frog, I'm afraid." She leaned forward eyeing the bandage wrapped about Mrs. Parker's fingers. "Is it infected?" Recalling Sarah's reaction to her mother's visit to the fairy well, and Evan's comments about offerings to the water-sprite, she added, "Did the bent pin you stuck yourself with happen to be rusted?"

Mrs. Parker stiffened. "What do you know about Seren's Well?"

"I know much about many things, such as a duck is a useful fowl. That two boys are on the hunt for a blue frog."

"Blue?" The innkeeper snorted, setting a plate of rarebit before her. "That's but a fairy tale to go with a fairy well." He gave his wife a hard stare. "What were you doing out there? Dipping your fingers in the sacred waters to rid yourself of warts?"

With a glare, his wife turned on her heel, tossing a few final words over her shoulder, "Keep it up, old man, and you'll find yourself outside sleeping in the steam cart."

Sarah leaned close as she passed behind Piyali. "See why I'm so desperate to marry? It's a rare moment they're ever in agreement about anything. But what's this about a blue frog?"

So much for her source of gossip.

---

HER MIND UNSETTLED, Piyali tossed and turned all night on the lumpy mattress and, by morning, she was convinced it was stuffed with hay—not feathers—and infested by creepy-crawlies with an inclination to bite. She'd had sleepless nights before, but always—even in Paris—her fingers had been able to trace the embroidered motifs of her *kantha* quilt, the various flowers and birds stitched into the fabric by her *dida's* very own fingers. During such restless nights, she allowed herself to remember a very different life, one she'd lost long ago. Such memories were the force that drove her to study infectious disease.

Before the sun had fully crept over the horizon, she was dressed—this time in a subtle coppery-orange *lehenga*—and pacing the rough boards of her room. A mythical fairy well, a blue frog and two boys on a quest to locate it in the undergrowth surrounding the pool. All had sounded like nonsense until Evan had turned her around and marched her away from said spring as fast as their feet would carry them, a muscle jumping in his clenched jaw.

Grounds for further investigation.

She glanced at the pocket watch that hung from her corset on a silver chain. The general store would be open by now. Miss Price, pampered daughter though she was, might be minding the counter with her mother. Perhaps if Piyali could draw her aside, she might coax forth more details.

With a quick check of her TTX pistol—men waking from a drunken stupor were often irate—she shrugged on her overcoat, picked up her doctor's bag and stepped from her room. She exited the tavern into the cool, fresh air that promised a beautiful spring day.

"I'm Dr. Mukherji, here to check on your daughter," she said, nodding a greeting to Mr. Price as she entered the store. He stood behind a gleaming brass till, tying on an apron as he prepared for the day's business.

"Heard about you." Mr. Price stared back at her, his eyes flat and unwelcoming. "Heard you were a woman. Trained in Paris, no less."

Would she always be greeted with such venom? Quite probably. Not that she would let that stop her. She pulled back her shoulders and met his gaze directly. "With a specialty in infectious diseases." She stood silent, letting that detail sink in, waiting to see if he was prejudiced enough that he would risk his daughter's health.

His jaw slackened. "Is it..."

"I've no idea," she answered, happy to have his complete attention, his grudging respect. "But I want to monitor her condition carefully."

Miss Price was presented without delay.

In a snit, Tegan flounced into the room. "This isn't necessary," she whined. "Mr. Tredegar is a renowned pharmacist."

"So he is," Piyali agreed, quietly wondering if anything more than the promise of financial security drove her interest in Evan. "But all men and women of science consult their colleagues. What two minds can accomplish together is far more than the sum of their individual work."

"Sit," her father commanded.

With a huff, Tegan sat upon a nearby chair.

Piyali knelt to unwind the gauze from Tegan's ankle. Much to her relief, the blue lesion didn't appear to have spread. Neither, however, had it decreased in size. Perhaps Evan's ointment had had some effect. Except, without an untreated lesion for comparison, no true scientific conclusion could be reached.

Not that this was something she wished to test on a young woman. Or any other person.

"Where in the woods were you bitten?" If she could catch the creature, the minute her lens arrived she could analyze its saliva beneath her aetheroscope.

Tegan shrugged. "On a path." But her eyes slid away.

Piyali dropped her voice to a mere murmur. "Might this unfortunate event have occurred beside Seren's Well?" A soft gasp from her patient. "The location of the attack—" A frog attacking. The very phrase sounded ludicrous. "Shall remain between us. Doctor-patient confidentiality."

"You—an outsider—have no business at our fairy well." Tegan crossed her arms and pursed her lips. "Who told you about it? No. Let me guess. Sarah. She'd do anything to win."

"Win?" What on earth could the spring have to do with the two women's matrimonial designs upon Evan?

"Don't pretend you don't know," Tegan huffed. "Your flashy dress and exotic, dark looks might draw Evan's glances, but he won't marry you." The spiteful use of his given name was not lost upon her, and it stung, the implication she was nothing but a pretty plaything to be used and tossed aside. "You wouldn't fit in. Not here. What he needs is a true Welsh woman to look after him."

Tegan thought her the newest competitor for Evan's romantic attentions. While Sarah had all but welcomed her to join the game, Tegan refused her admission outright. Yet once, Evan had asked Piyali to share his life. Not so these village girls, not even after months of shameless pursuit. "You'd rather lose a limb than confide the location of the frog?"

Hard eyes glinted at her and, when she spoke, her voice was hushed, staking an intimate claim. "If you *must* know, I was bitten on the path just outside Evan's front door whilst returning from our usual rendezvous." Her patient leaned closer.

"We have spent time together behind closed doors. Frequently. His mother's opal and diamond ring *will* be mine."

That did it. She would not tolerate such disrespect. Slamming shut her bag, she stood. She was under no obligation to coddle Tegan's misguided hopes. And so Piyali left her there, perched like a queen upon her throne, to reapply Evan's *miraculous* ointment on her own.

Striding down the street, fingers clenched about the handle of her bag, Piyali searched the edge of the woods, hunting for a break in the vegetation, for the path that would lead her to Seren's Well. Either Tegan was lying or the frog had hopped through the woods until it found a likely location to establish a new home. She would find it, and she would analyze it, dragging it back to London as her small, blue hostage if necessary. With or without Evan's approval.

Evan. Good grief. Sarah and Tegan were poised to claw each other's eyes out over the man. But neither of the young woman knew—or cared—anything of his heart. Tegan wanted nothing but economic security attached to a handsome man. Sarah wanted all that and escape from her parents with the promise of a touch of adventure.

Piyali wanted him for himself.

Yes, Evan's physique was impressive. Particularly after spending four years deep in the rainforest. He had sharper edges now. His body was tougher, harder, as if his muscles were forged from steel. She couldn't help but wonder what it would feel like —now—to be wrapped in his strong arms. His gray-blue eyes held a depth that hadn't been there before, and yet his gaze still sent blue flames ablaze across her skin. Yet she craved more than his physical touch. She missed his impressive mind, his advanced thinking, his adventurous spirit, his kindness, his directness... though that last trait now seemed lacking.

She sighed. He was holding something close to his chest and —setting aside her hurt, anger, jealousy, and disappointment—

she was nearly certain he was trying to protect her. She frowned. But from a frog?

Her eye caught upon a break in the underbrush. The packed dirt of a path. She ducked beneath a branch and entered the forest.

Whatever ate at Evan's conscience, it must be serious, or even now his ring would be on her finger. Opal and diamond. His mother's ring. The ring he'd presented her on bended knee all those years ago. She'd wanted to accept, to announce to all the world that they would be husband and wife. But the dreams they both pursued were about to drag them into separate hemispheres for four long years. Any number of things could happen to drive a wedge between them.

And, indeed, something had.

EVAN HAD NEARLY CAUGHT the blasted amphibian twice. The first time he'd been too slow, the second time his net had snagged upon the underbrush. Half the night he'd sat awake upon the cold, hard stone wall, staring into the bubbling spring. Pointing his bioluminescent torch at one likely crevice after another, he'd tried to search out the wee beastie's new home. Then, like an ember jumping from a freshly stoked furnace, it struck him hot and burning between the eyes. He was an idiot.

*Tree frog.*

He'd turned the beam of his torch upward, searching the overhanging branches. The frog must have been snoozing comfortably, tucked within a cluster of dew-damp leaves, for it wasn't until the first rays of sunlight fell upon the leaf canopy that he caught a glimpse of something blue and shimmery.

Scaling the tree, he wriggled out onto the branch, holding the handle of his net tightly as he stretched his arm ever so slowly and carefully toward the frog. But despite his stealth, the amphibian turned about, blinked at him—once, twice—then launched itself into the pool.

Grumbling about frogs and trans-Atlantic voyages to vacation at a mineral spring in Wales, Evan dropped back to the ground. The cold shock of the water must have been too much, for the critter now hopped about in the weeds edging the water. Evan lunged, almost catching him.

Now the blue frog was somewhere between the stones of the low wall. On hands and knees, he crawled through dew-damp grass, peering into one crack after another.

"Much as I can appreciate the posterior view you present," Piyali said behind him, her voice full of smothered laughter, "wouldn't it be easier to admit you need help catching a certain blue frog?"

Evan scrambled to his feet, nearly pitching himself into the pool in his haste. He dragged a gloved hand over his hair, then cursed silently, remembering he'd just been on all fours in the dirt. Closing his eyes a moment, he swallowed his pride. It was for the greater good. "Will you help me?"

"Fine." She set down her bag and picked up a long stick. "But if I find him first, I won't share unless you tell me what's going on."

"No." Absolutely not. Under no circumstances could the frog be allowed to leave Aberwyn. The poor creature would have to be destroyed.

"No?" she scoffed, poking into a crevice. "You'd rather see the frog dragged back to London, poked, prodded, its every secret extracted? That lesion of Miss Price's? Still there, your ointment notwithstanding. What becomes of her if I don't discover the cause of her skin infection?"

"The lesion needs to be excised," he stated. The ointment would only slow the spread of the discoloration, not eliminate it. Better a doctor perform the surgery, but if necessary he would lift a scalpel and do his best.

"Oh?" She threw a challenging glance over her shoulder. "What brings you to that conclusion? Such a surgery risks an infection of another kind."

The sunlight filtering through the leaves overhead accentuated her thick eyelashes, the curve of her cheek and the graceful arch of her neck. *The pistol at her hip.* She was a Queen's agent now. Even if he told her everything, her loyalty was to Britain first, him... at best, second.

But if he didn't tell her, she was going to keep digging. If that frog bit her... if what had happened to him, happened to her... His gut twisted. He couldn't bear it. She could help. Together, they might just be able to solve—

The air shimmered. Odd. Nothing sat there upon the rock wall. Or did it? He swept his net across its surface and felt something catch in the mesh. A small weight, about that of a small, shimmering tree frog. Quickly, he tied off the opening.

"Did you catch it?" Piyali asked, crossing to him to stare into his net. "There's nothing—"

There was. Tiny and thrashing and barely visible, the once-blue frog reflected the light of the forest around them. A near-perfect camouflage. No wonder he'd had such a difficult time locating the creature.

"I've a glass terrarium," he announced, partly to her, party to the frog. "No more hopping about biting the ankles of young women."

"Evan," Piyali's voice was soft as she wrapped a hand about his wrist. "You have to tell me what's going on. Don't make me summon Mr. Black."

"Mr. Black," he repeated. He'd met the man only once, but once had been enough to cement the man in his mind. If Mr. Black was involved, the situation was worse than he thought. "He sent you?"

"He did. I'm to solve the mystery of the blue lesion and evaluate your competence."

"For?" Worry twisted in his stomach.

With a deep breath, she dropped an artillery shell, exploding his calm resignation to his fate. "Mr. Ranunculus has taken ill and is not expected to recover. They're searching for a new Director of Tropical Plants to work in the Lister Botanical Gardens and Greenhouse. Your name was put forth."

"Mine." The depth of resources they possessed alone was enough to turn his head. To be a member of that institution—one that collected the greatest minds and the most obscure botanical specimens from all over the globe—would be an honor. To become one of its directors? He hardly dared hope they would ever consider him. His pulse jumped despite the impossibility.

Piyali shifted closer and the silver, metallic threads sewn into her bright skirt shimmered. Only then did he realize how over-dressed she was for a walk in the woods. The moment he'd met her, his life had exploded into vibrant color. Without her, the intensity had slowly washed away... until now. He yearned to accept the offer, both her unspoken one and the directorship.

"I'm told your papers on the medicinal value of Brazilian flora are groundbreaking," Piyali cajoled.

They were, but he would never pass the interview process. They would note his reluctance to remove his gloves, to dig into the dirt with bare hands. No, he'd not be offered the position. Instead, he would find himself installed in the biological research laboratories as a specimen himself.

His stomach churned. He could not allow them to discover his secret. Notes scribbled as the shaman spoke about the curse indicated that Evan had a year. Perhaps two. In that time he needed to make arrangements for the support of his sister and grandmother, to explore the medicinal properties of the eighty-one novel plants he'd so carefully transported to Wales. To publish his results. He would not survive the intense scrutiny of Lister Laboratories.

As if she read his mind, Piyali said, "I'm afraid the clamor for one particular pharmacobotanist is loud. If you refuse, they may insist."

Imagining an entire suit-clad committee arriving in Aberwyn to inspect both him and his greenhouse painted a grim picture. His secret would be discovered. Better to trust one particularly insistent Lister University physician. He barked a laugh. Was defeat inevitable? "Come then, Piyali. Grab your bag."

# CHAPTER FOUR

HE MOMENT PIYALI entered the greenhouse, humidity began to curl the tendrils of hair that had escaped her braid during the frog hunt. Moisture gathered at her temples. "It's amazing."

She'd stepped into a traditional Welsh cottage of stone, through the large room—kitchen and living space—barely taking note of a large desk stacked with texts and papers, of a table and shelves covered with glassware and plant cuttings and chemicals. She'd hurried through to the back of the cottage, intent upon seeing the greenhouse Evan had described when they'd strolled the streets of London beneath the moonlight, speaking to each other of their pasts, of their hopes to balance careers and family in the future.

Slowly she turned about, staring in amazement. Great sheets of glass supported by an iron framework let in the fading beams of afternoon sunlight, and in the center, a leviathan of a stove burned large blocks of peat, churning out heat, intent upon defying the chill of a Welsh spring day. All about her, trees stretched their branches upward as vine upon vine twisted about their trunks, also stretching toward the sun. Exotic bushes and shrubby plants covered every inch of the ground, all but a narrow walkway that meandered between them. It was a lush, tropical paradise. Particularly as it came without the usual accompaniment of biting insect life. Her enthusiasm was dampened only by the knowledge that this must be where the blue frog with the toxic bite originated.

"It's far more wonderful than you ever described." She reached out with gentle fingers to stroke the soft petals of a beautiful, orange flower.

Catching her fingers, Evan shook his head in warning. "This one is safe. But remember my assignment was to collect potent flora. Not everything here is harmless, even to touch."

"Much like its curator." Her heart jumped as her eyes fell on his rumpled cravat, and her fingers ached with the memory of the last time she'd untangled its knot, pulling on its loose ends to bring his lips to hers. Did she dare? She lifted her gaze to his face. The corners of his mouth twitched with a suppressed smile. Progress.

"You smell of orange blossoms." His gloved fingertip touched the glass vial that hung from a loop on her corset. "You kept it."

Now was the time to revisit the past, before darker topics stole the moment. "Always," she said, moving closer to rest her palm against the hard plane of his chest. "It's my favorite scent. Ever since you gave me my first vial and informed me it was an aphrodisiac." She tipped her face upward. "Is it working?"

"Too well." His gloved hand tightened about hers. "It's driving me insane."

"Once you wouldn't hesitate." They'd shared stolen kisses in shadowed alcoves at any and every opportunity. She walked her fingers up his chest. "What happened? What could possibly be so awful that you would rather chase me away than confide in me, a woman you once asked to share your life?"

"Piyali," he growled. "I can't make promises anymore."

"I'm not asking for one." She slid her hand over the rough stubble of his cheek, its rasp triggering a flood of cherished memories. "Just a confidence, perhaps a kiss."

Something deep inside him seemed to snap. Cupping the base of her skull with both hands, he dropped his lips to hers. Soft, warm, sweet. A gentle kiss that spoke of a longing ache finally satisfied. Then she parted her lips and reminded him that for too long, their hunger, their thirst for each other had gone unsatisfied.

His tongue dove into her mouth, devouring her, consuming her. Wrapping her arms about his waist, she pulled him closer, moaning encouragement as she pressed her breasts tight to his chest until she could feel his heart pounding.

Sparks flew. Five long years with an ocean between them. Not a single man compared to Evan. Not one of the many men who once pursued her had managed to hide his horror at the idea of a working wife. Not one had eyes that saw into her soul, causing her breath to catch, her heart to race in anticipation. *This* was why she'd waited.

"God, I've missed you," Evan rasped as his mouth left her lips, trailing kisses along her jaw, her neck, sending shivers across her skin and a rush of warmth between her thighs. He slid his hands down her back to fall on her hips, yanking her tight against his own. Whatever it was that had kept him from her, it wasn't a lack of attraction, for there was *firm* evidence of that.

Encouraged, she smiled against his neck. "We've waited forever," she whispered, "to be alone like this." She nibbled his earlobe. "Perhaps we could try a bed this time?"

A low rumble sounded in his chest. "Piyali, it's near impossible to refuse you."

"Then don't."

His hands loosened on her hips as he took a step backward, refusing to lift his eyes to meet hers. "We can't. Not until—"

A loud knock sounded, and his head swiveled. Piyali wanted to scream in frustration. Not merely because she wanted to explore the advantages of a feather mattress with Evan, but because he'd been about to tell her what was wrong. If she knew what was broken, perhaps she could make repairs. She caught the edge of his chin in her palm. "Tell me. Until what?"

More knocking, this time louder and more frantic. "Mr. Tredegar!"

"Don't," she pleaded even as he turned toward the door connecting the greenhouse to the more traditional Welsh cottage.

"It's Tegan," he said. Regret softened his voice. "I can't ignore her. The frog bite, it's my fault. Or perhaps there's been some injury to another within the village... Stay here. Don't let her see you."

Her face burned. "I won't have what's between us hidden away, Evan. Not this time."

"I'm not ashamed," he said. "I never was. But she's a spiteful girl, always has been. Would you have the whole village know of our past before we sort out if there's to be a future? It would compromise your entire investigation."

*Bang. Bang.* "Evan!"

*His fault.* He'd said the frog bite was his fault. "You'll tell me everything?" she asked.

His mouth opened, then closed. "I promise."

*For all that was worth.*

Managing a tight nod, she conceded his point. "Fine." She spun on her heel and moved deeper into the foliage, hiding like a shameful secret.

---

Evan opened the front door, and Tegan pushed past

him, stomping into the small cottage. "What can I do for you, Miss Price?"

"A headache powder for Mrs. Lewis," she answered, pacing about the room, stopping before his worktable to stare at the miscellaneous equipment—flasks, alcohol burners, glass distillation tubing, among others—gathered together, along with a number of various compounds extracted from tropical plants, ready for his next experiment. She waved at a mortar and pestle. "No, make that two." Tegan pressed her hands to her temples.

Worry flared. He closed the distance between them to study her face. She seemed rather flushed, her eyes shadowed. What if the infection had spread to her blood? "Are you sick? Feverish? Does your ankle pain you?"

"I'm fine." She waved a hand. "What pains me are the games we play, Evan."

A whisper of worry snaked its way down his spine at the use of his given name. Rouge, not fever colored her cheeks and lips —and was that coal dust upon her eyelashes? Immediately, he regretted unlatching the door. "Games?" he repeated. "Miss Price, this is most improper."

"It wouldn't be improper," Tegan fluttered her eyelashes in what must be an attempt at seduction, but only served to remind him that she was barely old enough for long skirts, "if you'd drop to one knee and offer that opal ring to me."

He bit back a curse. "I—"

"I know you intend to offer for me." She lifted her face. "You've been so patient, so solicitous of my fragile health, rushing to my side with a special ointment when that awful creature assaulted me in the woods."

*The bite of a frog was an assault?* It sounded ridiculous, but given how the blue blemish would spread...

A strangled snort from the greenhouse had him reaching for Tegan's shoulder to steer her away from its entrance. "I'm sorry, Miss Price, if I've given you the wrong impression, but—"

"I'll make you the perfect wife, Evan." She lunged, flinging herself at him, and he was forced to catch the girl in his arms. "We shall run the most prosperous pharmacy in all of Cardiff. The sooner the banns are read, the sooner we can be together."

*Aether*, he'd sorely misjudged the love-sick glances she'd tossed him, chalking them up to a youthful infatuation that would pass. Gripping both of her shoulders firmly, he pushed her away. "I've no plans to marry. We cannot be together. You ought to go now, unless you still require headache powders?"

Her eyes filled with tears. *Tears!* How could he fix this?

"No," she sniffled. "No powders. Unless you've one for heartache?"

"Er."

Tegan ran for the door, flinging it wide. "When you realize your mistake, I'll be waiting. Waiting for you." With that dramatic aside, she ran from his cottage into the woods.

Strangled laughter burst from the greenhouse. Two dark eyes peeked around the door frame. "Oh you cruel, cruel man. How could you turn down such an impassioned plea?"

"Not funny." He ran a hand over the back of his stiff neck. "How am I to ever present myself at the town store again? Let alone examine her lesion?"

"You won't have to." Piyali glanced about as she stepped into the one large room that served as kitchen, living space and laboratory. What must she think of his primitive cottage? Of the uneven flagstones upon the floor, the cast iron stove crammed into an ancient hearth, little furniture beyond a desk, a rough wooden table and chairs? "I'll examine her lesion," she said. "And you need not stay in Wales. I hear there's a position available for a pharmacobotanist in London. That it's practically his for the asking."

She looked at him from beneath long eyelashes, and his mind flashed to his thick, feather mattress. There was nothing he'd rather do more than slide an engagement ring onto Piyali's finger, carry her upstairs to his bed. Then leave with her for London on a hunt for a special license followed by a visit to Mr. Black to accept the invitation to interview. Once she saw his hand, however... His stomach hurt as if he'd swallowed a solution of quicksilver salts.

Two paths lay before him.

Refuse to confide in her, and Piyali would summon Mr. Black. That would bring him under intense and unwanted scrutiny. It would, however, leave him time to excise Tegan's lesion and destroy the frog.

Or he could reveal his secret and beg for her help and silence. He lifted his eyes to meet her watchful gaze. Trained at the Université de Paris in infectious diseases, handed her own laboratory at Lister University and recruited to the Queen's agents, she was an expert in her field. If anyone could solve the mystery, he had no doubt it would be her.

He gave a stiff nod and, eyeing the terrarium where a certain shimmering frog crouched, tugged off his leather gloves. First the left—nothing unusual to see there—and then the right.

"It's blue!" Piyali gasped. "Your hand, the entire thing. Blue!"

That was the color of the moment. He rolled back the cuff of his shirtsleeves.

"Schistosomiasis!" Her hands clapped over her mouth as her impossibly wide eyes took in the disaster that had transpired. "How far has it spread?"

"Far," he said, yanking off his cravat and unbuttoning his collar. He tugged it aside so she could see how its tendrils crept across his shoulder toward the base of his neck.

"Does it hurt?" Her hand darted forward, then stopped, fluttering, uncertain if she should touch.

"No." Not physically. The anguish was entirely mental. "The infection is completely painless. A tiny bite by our tiny blue nemesis, and the next day I awoke with a lesion a half-inch in diameter. A day later, one inch. It had encompassed my entire hand and wrist by the time I compounded an ointment—the one I shared with Miss Price—that slowed its progress."

"Slowed," she repeated. Grief and heartache mingled on her face.

"So far I've only managed to delay the inevitable. There's a myth among the natives I studied with, it translates roughly as the 'Tribe of Invisible Devils'. Once bitten by the blue—sometimes invisible—frog, the curse overtakes the body, one limb at a time. Legend claims that when the disease consumes them, madness sends a man—or a woman—running into the rainforest never to be seen again. Many choose to take their lives rather than face that fate."

"And when it… consumes the entire body?" Piyali pressed a shaking hand to her throat as the full implications of his situation registered.

"Banishment." Wisps of a black fog began to cloud his mind as he stared down at his hand, at this now alien piece of himself. It was a daily struggle to reconcile himself to his future. "They can't allow a man—or woman—to remain within the tribe because with extreme or heightened emotion, the skin begins to glimmer, to color-shift and reflect the world about it."

"Making him—or her—invisible."

She had a beautiful, quick mind. "Exactly. And the tribe won't tolerate something it can't see. Ghosts. Devils. Call them what you will, they can no longer be a member of society. That is my fate. And the reason we can't marry. I may last a year, two." He lifted a shoulder, not wanting to upset her further by revealing his distress. "Perhaps five. But once the blue crawls up my neck, I'll no longer be fit for British society."

"Can I touch it—you?" she asked, reaching out again. "Is it contagious?"

"If it were, I'd never have allowed you to examine Miss Price." He held out his hand.

She cupped it gently in her palm, turning it over to study it from all angles. Determination injected steel into her voice. "I'll find a way to fix this. We'll find a cure. Together."

Hope had long since died. It lay, black and shriveled in a dusty, forgotten place. All that was left was to save others from a similar fate. He kissed her on her forehead, then dropped the other shoe. "You can't tell Mr. Black."

Jerking back, she released his hand, taking away the comforting warmth of her touch. He dared not reach for her. Not now. Emotion needed to be set aside. "But—"

"Imagine what Britain would do with such knowledge. Men —agents—would be purposefully infected, sent across borders. God forbid the technique fall into enemy hands. All because a small, blue frog hitched a ride on one of my plants. I'm begging you, Piyali. Better to destroy the frog and leave me—and Miss Price—to our ends."

"Ends…" Wrapping her arms across her chest, she shook her head, unwilling to accept such a scenario. "It could take years. How do you propose to cope as whatever this is overtakes the both of you?"

"Excision of her lesion would be my first choice. Failing that, I could marry her." Tegan would find it a bitter life. There'd be no romance, no pharmacy in Cardiff, no social interactions of any kind. Eventually, even her family would not be able to visit. "Hide her from society. You heard her, she's amenable and already considered in fragile health."

Piyali's mouth tightened. "Yet you declined her."

"I did." Tegan was a constant thorn in his side. The only woman he *wished* to marry was Piyali. "But if it saves lives…"

---

"Unacceptable," Piyali cut off his words. If anyone was to marry him, it ought to be her. How dare he suggest such steps?

Tegan's overt manipulations had been amusing until Evan raised it as a feasible option. But such messy emotions must be shoved aside; there was no time for them. They needed to take advantage of every moment left. "I refuse to abandon you to an uncertain fate."

She spun on her heel to face the scarred wooden table that served as his workbench and studied his makeshift laboratory. A scale. Boxes and jars and tin containers filled with powders and oils and emollients. Bottles and flasks. Tubing and corks. All manner of titration and distillation equipment. An excellent chemistry setup, but not conducive to microbiology.

Evan followed her and began to clear one end of the table, his features set in stone. "Tell me what you need. If it's not here, I'll find it."

She thought of the frog inside the terrarium. Calm, in safe and secure surroundings, it had returned to its lustrous blue color. She *had* to find a cure; the alternative was unacceptable. Gears spun in her mind. If infection was transmitted through a bite, that meant the contagion was contained within its saliva.

Ducking into the greenhouse, she retrieved her black bag and dug into it, pulling out a number of glass aetheroscope slides and cotton-tipped sticks. "To begin, we'll need to swab the inside of the frog's mouth—and biopsy its skin. Given its camouflage capabilities, I suspect the amphibian harbors the infectious agent throughout its entire body."

"I'll do that," Evan stated. "Carefully. While wearing heavy gloves."

So like him, always looking out for the welfare of others, putting her safety above his. But today it left a bitter taste in her mouth. If only he'd answered her message with the truth of his terrible situation. "I'll set up my aetheroscope here." She moved to the large desk, setting aside stacks of books and papers to claim a corner. "We'll also biopsy your skin. Near the initial bite, further up your arm so that we might see if cell morphology alters over the progression, over the spread of the disease. And for comparison to Tegan's biopsy."

"The broken objective?"

"Will hinder our progress." She pressed her lips together. Odds that Mr. Black would be able to send one in their direction any time soon were low. He'd made some quip about selkie trouble in the north and needing to travel to Scotland. His mission could take a day... or it could last for weeks, and she hated to leave Evan alone lest he take some drastic action. "Is there any chance of finding a replacement in Cardiff?"

"There is," Evan answered. "Today, we collect evidence and, tomorrow, we'll travel to Cardiff to gather necessary supplies?"

"Agreed."

Piyali turned away, her grip tightening upon the swab she held. Conflicting loyalties battled in her mind. In Cardiff, there would be reliable skeet pigeons to hire. As a Queen's agent, she was bound to report this development to Mr. Black, but what did she have beyond a fanciful tale of a rogue Amazonian frog prone to bite? Besides, this was Evan, and Mr. Black was likely still in Scotland. A few days of investigation would provide her with more data, more evidence. Her report could wait a few days.

CHAPTER FIVE

IYALI'S WIDE SMILE set Mrs. Parker grumbling. Despite Evan's revelation, the prospect of spending a day at his side—this time in the open air and beneath the sunshine—had floated her mood into the upper aether, as if a curse placed upon them by some wart-nosed witch had lifted.

Yesterday, their heads together, they'd taken turns staring through her aetheroscope at slide after slide after slide, until their eyes began to cross. The frog's saliva provided no answers. No visible micro-organisms writhed or wriggled beneath their view at which they could point fingers. All skin biopsies appeared—more or less—the same. Including that of the frog.

Nonetheless, they'd set up a number of cultures, using what was available from Evan's meager bachelor's kitchen stores, in an attempt to coax any infectious agent to grow and multiply.

Piyali had a favored hypothesis, but until she could obtain a higher resolution with her aetheroscope, it was no better than wild speculation. If the organism responsible was intracellular, a replacement objective—along with a few additional specialized stains—would disclose its presence.

A grunt of irritation jerked her back to the moment, and a

plate of oatcakes was slammed onto the table before her along with the tavern's ubiquitous ale. Mrs. Parker's expression suggested she hoped her breakfast guests would choke.

"For breakfast?" Piyali asked, eyeing the frothy, unfiltered drink.

"I suppose you're used to drinking *tea*." Mrs. Parker snarled the last word as if the beverage derived from a chamber pot. With a sneer, she dropped a copper tea kettle onto the range with a loud clang. "We aim to serve."

"Well, yes. Thank you." It was then that Piyali noticed Mrs. Parker's bandage was no longer confined to her fingers. It now wrapped about the entirety of her hand. Moreover, she pressed her hand to her waist as if its use pained her. "Perhaps I should look at your injury?"

Mrs. Parker's answering glare vibrated with barely-suppressed hostility.

"Mother." Sarah's voice cajoled as she crossed the room, "let her look. She *is* a physician. If it's infected, her attentions are better than Father's." She rolled her eyes. "Though I'm certain he exaggerated when he offered to lop off your finger."

The villagers seemed overly concerned with amputation, though the Parkers needled each other at every possible opportunity. Why on earth they'd chosen to marry was beyond her comprehension.

"I'm sure amputation won't be necessary," Piyali began diplomatically, "but infections shouldn't be left untreated. Mr. Tredegar is a competent pharmacist, Mrs. Parker. Today we are traveling to Cardiff, to his store. If you require an antibacterial—"

"Cardiff?" Her eyebrows arched toward her hairline. "Together? Alone?"

"Yes," Piyali answered. "I'm in need of supplies."

"No. That will not do. Sarah, get your bonnet. You must accompany them for propriety's sake."

Sarah's eyes brightened, but she glanced at Piyali and demurred. "I don't think my company is desired, Mother."

"Nonsense." Mrs. Parker waved her bandaged hand and winced. "I'll draw up a list of required items." She strode away before any further objections could be voiced.

"I'm sorry," Sarah sighed. "She pressures me daily to win Mr. Tredegar's regard. I promise not to be too obnoxious. Would it help if I promise to make myself scarce once we arrive? There's a book I wish to purchase at the booksellers and—wafts of aether—what I wouldn't do to escape Mother if only for a day." A mischievous look lit her face, and she leaned close, adding in a conspiratorial whisper. "I have to admit Tegan's jealousy would sweeten the trip just that much more."

Only rigid determination kept Piyali's shoulders from slumping. To invite Sarah along meant hiding—yet again—her rekindling relationship with Evan. A relationship that wouldn't have a chance if they couldn't concoct a cure. She wanted time with him, but maintaining Sarah's friendship and good graces was important. Particularly as her mother had acquired her infection at the fairy well before the Amazonian frog was apprehended. How else would she be informed about village affairs? And she had to admit, she liked the young woman. "Very well," she conceded, "but only if you answer one question about your mother."

"Oh?" Sarah looked as if facing her mother's irritation might be preferable. "What is it you want to know?"

"Nothing much. I'm a physician and can't help but care." More she was curious. "Her wound, is it blue?"

"Blue?" Sarah's face scrunched up as she thought. "No, not exactly, but it is spreading rather quickly. Her skin has taken on a rather odd appearance. I only glimpsed it, but I'd say it was pink and shimmery. The wound itself has mostly healed."

That fit. Mrs. Parker was nearly always in a foul mood. Shimmery and pinkish when feelings ran strong.

"Is that what's wrong with Tegan?" Sarah leaned closer. "The reason you're here? Is she—for once—truly sick?" She gasped. "Don't tell me her ankle is *blue!*"

Secrets in a village. One in exchange for another. Sharing that information went against all her medical training, but not necessarily that of the Queen's agents. "Cultivate the locals" was one of Mr. Black's favorite expressions. She needed to play along. Besides, Sarah had guessed. Was it wrong that deep in a corner of her soul she was enjoying this moment?

Pressing a finger to her lips, Piyali too leaned forward. "*Shh.* I never said a thing. Don't let this become public knowledge."

"Sarah," Mrs. Parker bellowed. "Your bonnet. No daughter of mine shall freckle in the sun."

Sarah winked, then hurried to her mother's bidding.

A few minutes later, after forcing down a dry oatcake with weak tea, Piyali waited as Evan handed Sarah into the crank wagon. Resignation and reproach tugged his lips into a frown as he glanced at her sideways.

"I had to," she whispered, noting how Sarah sat in the middle of the rough board that formed a seat. "An exchange of favors." She pretended to stumble, bringing her mouth to Evan's ear. "She doesn't realize it, but her mother has also been bitten by the frog."

He cursed under his breath. "You have Sarah spying for you?"

"A necessary step," Piyali breathed back. "Mrs. Parker is refusing any and all treatment." She hesitated. Much as she wished to dismiss this professional duty... "We ought to check on Tegan."

"Already done," Evan replied, taking Piyali's medical bag to place it inside the cart. "Her condition remains unchanged. Now up, we've a long day ahead of us."

As they drove away, a curtain twitched, and Piyali caught a

glimpse of Tegan's vexed face pressed to the window of the village store. Her pursuit of Evan was far from over.

---

THE ROAD to Cardiff was rutted and rocky, and Sarah—who had planted herself between him and Piyali—took every advantage to bump against him. Shoulders, hips, legs. Even her hand slid from her lap to press the side of her pinky finger to his thigh. Evan supposed he ought to be grateful that she didn't outright climb into his lap. So much for enjoying the pleasant spring day with Piyali. His fault, he supposed, for refusing to reveal their relationship. From the amused press of her lips, she knew exactly what Sarah was up to. At least Miss Parker wasn't demanding a proposal.

Relationship. He swallowed hard. A mistake. But with that kiss, a seed of hope had germinated. The oppressive feeling of doom and gloom had lifted—ever so slightly—as he unburdened his secrets. Still, there was a lingering feeling of melancholy, a certain pessimism that even if they managed to uncover the cause of his infection, they wouldn't be able to formulate a treatment.

All night, he'd worried about bringing her into his confidence, not at all certain he had made the right choice. Now, with the unwelcome revelation that the frog had another victim, the situation threatened to grow out of hand.

He forced himself to listen to the women's chatter.

"What book are you hoping to find in Cardiff?" Piyali asked Sarah.

"Well, I'm not certain." Sarah fiddled with the ribbon at her chin. "Not exactly. Though I hope to find an intelligent husband," she fluttered her eyelashes at Evan, "I thought I might follow your example and become a self-sufficient, career-minded woman."

"Oh?" Piyali raised her eyebrows.

"I adore babies," Sarah said, then addressed her next comment to him. "While I work to convince a handsome, young man to start a family of his own," her eyelashes fluttered again, "I'm aiming to attend a woman's college. There's a school opening in Cardiff, and I mean to apply. Perhaps someday I might manage medical school. I hear there's an entire field of medicine involving childbirth—obstetrics and gynecology." Her brow wrinkled. "But first, I have to pass an entrance exam."

Evan cleared his throat. "Hence the bookstore."

"Yes. I won't keep you from your errands, but perhaps you might recommend a few titles?"

Piyali rattled off a few, and it brought a certain measure of relief to know that Sarah was taking control of her future, beyond plaguing him with endless flirtations and shameless suggestions. Even though his ears began to burn as the two women discussed childbirth with much candor and detail. He squirmed on his seat.

He dropped Sarah off at the booksellers—with great relief—before continuing to his own store. "Was that necessary?"

She smiled and fluttered her eyelashes in imitation of Sarah. "Better than discussing the making of babies, was it not?"

Now he could think of nothing else. Could his face grow any hotter?

Ears burning, he redirected the conversation. "I hope you don't mind, but I do have customers who will wish to consult a pharmacist. And, if you're willing, a physician."

"Of course."

They rattled to a stop behind his store. Several long weeks had passed since he'd last visited his sister and *mamgu*, his grandmother. It was hard making constant excuses for his gloves but, when the worst came to pass, the business must support them, and for that, more preparation would be required. Only when he had no choice but to confide in them, would he reveal his blue appendage.

The moment his sister Megan realized it was him, not some delivery cart, she rushed from the service door. "Evan!" she exclaimed, throwing her arms about him. "And who is this?" she asked, knowing damn well exactly who Piyali was.

He hugged his *mamgu,* then performed introductions. "This is Dr. Mukherji, who has agreed to see a few patients. But don't waste her time, make certain first that they are willing to trust in the expert advice of a woman."

"I'm happy to assist in any way I can," Piyali said.

His grandmother's gnarled hands gripped Piyali's. "*A'i hon yw hi?*" she asked. *Is this her?* His *mamgu* had insisted they learn the Welsh language when she came to live with them after diphtheria stole away most of his family. "The woman whose hand ought to wear opals and diamonds?"

Evan cleared his throat, replying in the same language. "Yes. Perhaps. There are complications to resolve first."

His sister's eyes widened.

Piyali turned to him with raised eyebrows. Unfair, using Welsh to speak around her in this manner.

"We have much to talk about, Dr. Mukherji," Megan said, switching the conversation back to English. "The moment word gets out, our shop will be overrun today by people seeking your combined expertise. Evan, did you bring more of that miraculous eczema cream? One child in particular is in desperate need."

"I did. Among other things." He reached into the bed of the wagon and handed her a jar. "Before I tie on an apron and set to work, I need to escort Dr. Mukherji across town. She's in need of a specialized piece of medical equipment that might prove difficult to find."

"Oh, no you don't, Evan," Megan chided as she untied her apron and pressed it into his hands. "The list of items you need to attend to here is longer than my arm. Step to it. I'll take Dr. Mukherji to Colonel Pickering's. If anyone's likely to have medical devices, it'll be him."

His sister would spend the entire trip quizzing Piyali about… well… all things related to that opal ring. He opened his mouth to object, but Megan gave him no choice. She slid her arm through Piyali's and dragged her down the street peppering her with questions.

Though Piyali glanced back at him over her shoulder with pleading eyes, she was a trained Queen's agent. With a pistol on her hip. He had every confidence she would survive the interrogation. Better her than him.

"WHILE WE HUNT down this aetheroscope attachment piece," Megan said, her arm tight, offering Piyali no illusion of escape as she turned into a delightful shopping arcade, "might we discuss weddings?"

Her stomach dropped. If Evan had mentioned her, that he planned to marry, that conversation lay far in the past. A wedding was not at all a certainty now, though she desperately hoped to one day call Megan her sister.

"You're engaged?" Piyali deflected, as a touch of panic crept its way up into her throat. "Many congratulations! Who is the lucky man?"

"Not me," Megan laughed. "Though I've suitors aplenty, I've yet to find one who makes my heart beat faster." She squeezed Piyali's arm tighter. "Yours. To my brother. He teased us before leaving for Brazil, telling us only that his future bride was an Indian woman born in Calcutta. I've studied the wedding traditions. A red gown—a *sari*—embroidered in gold is traditional, correct? Will you arrive in a *palki*?"

"A sedan chair? Through the streets of London?" Piyali

cringed in horror, though she wouldn't put it past Ma to try to arrange such an event. A quick simple ceremony in the front parlor would suit her much better. She looked at Megan's face, so full of excitement, and sighed. Perhaps a small, traditional ceremony. Oh, who was she kidding? Small meant hundreds of people, even if her mother was forced to confine the event to the ballroom of her London townhouse. None of which would happen if she couldn't save Evan. "I'm afraid we've rather a serious obstacle in our path. I can't share the details with you. Suffice it to say we need that aetheroscope objective badly."

"Are you ill?" Megan's eyes widened. "Is Evan?"

"Something like that. I'm sorry. I'm sworn to secrecy." By the Queen's agents, by Evan himself. Pulled in two directions, Piyali had a nagging suspicion her loyalty to both would soon be put to the test. Always, her career was a wedge between them.

She pressed her hand against a Babbage card tucked into a pocket, a card that could send a skeet pigeon winging in the direction of Mr. Black. Guilt weighed heavily upon her, but to send a message so soon would be disloyal to Evan. Three months he'd struggled on his own. She could give him a few more days. Then, if they still had no answers, she would have no choice.

"I'm doing my best to help him. If all goes well…"

For several steps, Megan was silent. "I can't lose my brother. He hates to speak about it, but illness is what carried away our family."

Evan had confided the story to Piyali one dark night as they walked through Hyde Park. Her heart squeezed at the memory of his tale. He'd been fourteen years of age when his father, mother, two brothers and a sister all died within the space of a month. He, Megan and his grandmother alone had survived.

"My family suffered a similar fate. I lost an older sister, a younger brother, and my father to diphtheria as well." *Baba.* She'd been so young—all of five years—that they were no more than a fuzzy memory. Was it better—or worse—to have crystal clear memories of how it had once been? "For a while, it was awful." She remembered Ma's grief. "Then my mother met my stepfather who brought us here. He's given me everything, including two little sisters, and the love of a father."

Megan reached out and squeezed her arm. "I'm sorry."

Piyali gave a tight nod. Their losses were the reason for both Evan's chosen profession and for her own, for the drive that pushed them both to seek to cure all manner of infections. She changed the subject. "How did you convince Evan to accept the grant to travel to Brazil? He almost turned the committee down, he was so worried about leaving you and your grandmother behind, unprotected."

"Yes, always worried for my future," Megan scoffed. "How? I threatened, at the age of sixteen, to wed a man twice my age to ensure my so-called security. As he did not care much for Mr. Jones, after much heated discussion, he agreed to leave me with Grandmother." She rolled her eyes. "For the sake of appearances, a cousin looked in on us during his time abroad, providing that all-so-necessary male authority."

They shared a knowing look as they came to a stop before a shop. Emblazoned across the storefront in gilded lettering: *Colonel Pickering & Company's Scientific Gadgetries and Curiosities.* Dusty, dark and dimly lit. Piyali squinted through a window pane and came face to face with the stuffed head of a quail sewn onto the neck of a squirrel. The chimera wore a miniature tiara. Such... décor did not provide her with much hope for scientific equipment, at least, not equipment that *functioned.*

"He keeps the legitimate items in the back, away from sticky fingers," Megan said, reading her mind. They stepped inside. Useless oddities of all kinds were mounted upon display counters, the better to lure in the gullible. But in the back, boxes upon boxes were stacked from floor to ceiling. Perhaps there was some hope. A man emerged from a back room. "Colonel, we have need of a…"

"Crystalline aetheric objective," Piyali finished.

"Right this way, dearies." The colonel's eyes twinkled behind a mass of grizzled facial hair, and she suspected he grinned at the thought of lightening her pockets by several pounds.

CHAPTER SIX

ᴀFTER ᴀ ʟᴏɴɢ ᴅᴀʏ of patient consults of ailments ranging from croup to toenail fungus—during which mild suspicion of her origins had been overcome by the promise of pain relief and treatment—Piyali was exhausted and all too happy to climb back onto Evan's crank wagon and head for Aberwyn. This time, he arranged for her to sit between him and Sarah.

Not that such a maneuver stopped the other woman. Setting down a stack of thick, paper-wrapped textbooks, Sarah exclaimed, "Oh, no! My gown!" Her fingers fluttered over a dark smudge upon her bodice, drawing attention to its low-cut neckline. "Mother will have a fit!"

Beside her, Evan sighed. He tugged a handkerchief from his waistcoat and passed it to Piyali. "Here. Save her from her mother's wrath." He kept his eyes carefully focused upon the road before them. "Please."

"It's probably only a touch of dust, most likely from the bookstore," Piyali said, using the square of linen to brush at the smudge, but her efforts only seemed to grind the dirt into the pale, pink fabric. "Um."

"Let me." Sarah snatched the handkerchief from her and made far better progress. "Did you find what you needed?"

"We did," Piyali answered. In a dark, dusty recess of Colonel Pickering's storage room. She'd all but given up hope. Just as they'd been about to try another store, the wizened old man had stumbled—coughing—out from among a pile of dusty boxes holding aloft a small box. Inside, an older model of the objective lay nestled in cotton batting. With luck it would be adequate. She clutched it in her lap now, wrapped and padded against the rigors of traveling over rock-studded roads.

After a few more awkward moments during which Sarah made several unsuccessful attempts to flirt with Evan, Piyali—tired though she was—attempted to buoy her spirits by suggesting a tutoring session. Gleefully, Sarah unwrapped one of her books—a chemistry text—and by the time they arrived at the tavern, they had explored John Dalton's atomic theory, the periodic table of the elements, and the concept of whole-number ratios forming chemical compounds.

"I predict a successful admissions exam," Piyali said, impressed. "You've a sharp mind and will go far."

Sarah drew her shoulders back at the compliment. Had anyone ever praised her for her mind? Given her buxom milk-maid appearance and the bar's clientele, the likely answer was no. "Mother would be furious if she learned of my plans, so tell no one. Better she believes I'm reading penny dreadfuls. You go in first, I'll scurry behind and hide these textbooks away."

Evan, who had been largely silent the entire ride home, spoke. "Dr. Mukherji shall accompany me to my laboratory." He walked about the wagon to offer the young woman a hand down. "We've a bit of a mystery to unravel."

Sarah tipped her head. "As in experimental?" Piyali nodded and Sarah's face grew somber as she hopped from the cart. "I admit, I'd love to see Tegan fall face-down in a mud puddle. But not die from some obscure infection. Is it serious?"

"It is," Piyali said and pressed a finger to her lips. "*Shh*. Not a word to anyone." After moment's hesitation, she added, "Keep an eye on your mother."

Frowning, Evan climbed back onto the cart. He gripped the steering wheel and released the break, setting the crank wagon lumbering along the road. "She's a terrible gossip."

"She guessed," Piyali defended. "And knows nothing about the frog."

They drew up before his stone cottage with its moss-covered slate roof. She barely spared it a glance as she waited for Evan to unlock the door before hurrying to her aetheroscope at his desk. Time was of the essence. A remedy was desperately needed, and, if she could solve this quickly and present a cure, perhaps Mr. Black wouldn't relieve her of her weapon and consign her to her laboratory.

Conscious of the Babbage card she'd elected not to employ, Piyali wasted no time replacing the broken objective. She had a glass slide prepped and ready before she noticed Evan was not at her side. She looked up to find him frowning at the shelves that held jars and boxes of his chemicals and concoctions. "Is something wrong?" she asked.

"Someone has been here in our absence," he stated, gloves clutched tightly in one hand. "The *nah-puh-de-ot* ought to be next to the *o-ko-ne-de-kuh*, in clear alphabetical order. Look," he pointed, "this jar, it's been rotated such that the label is not easily readable."

"Theft?" Piyali had no idea what those plants were, but if he was concerned… "But the cottage is locked." Her forehead wrinkled. She'd seen the advanced lock he'd installed, both on the greenhouse door and the cottage door. "Quite securely." An agent might be able to break it, but it wouldn't be easily cracked by someone in search of free medication.

"So it is." Evan lifted each jar, examining its contents, replacing it upon the shelf. "I've not a clue who would go to such lengths. I've always reduced—or outright refused—payment if a client couldn't afford it." He set down the final jar with a grimace. "The minute a medication proves successful, I provide as much product as the plant's growth will bear."

"Has anything like this, anything unusual, occurred before?"

His brow furrowed.

"What is it?"

"Last week, the night before Tegan was bitten, I found the door to my greenhouse ajar. I installed the lock the next day, but I expect it's how the frog escaped."

"Frog!" Piyali jumped to her feet and ran into the greenhouse, Evan following close behind. The frog still crouched in its terrarium, safe, happy and blue. "Thank goodness." The frog was not involved. She dug for an explanation. "You have a number of projects underway, all experimental. Have you boasted of initial success to anyone in so much as a simple letter?" Piyali went still as her words loomed between them, a specter from their past. She swallowed nervously.

"I'm sorry," Evan said, his gray-blue eyes softening as they focused upon her. "I didn't know what to say… I didn't want to drag you into this disaster, and then I decided it was best if I didn't write at all. I should have replied, I should have said… something. Can you forgive me?"

Could she? All too easily. But if they couldn't solve this… problem, if she reported it to Mr. Black, could he forgive her? "Of course," she whispered.

His hand glimmered with heightened emotion, and he reached for her and caught her hand. Heat shimmered in his eyes. "Come with me, upstairs."

"Not yet." Her entire body—ablaze with heated anticipation —objected to her words, but her brain insisted. "First, I want answers." The question would nag at her until it was answered. She smiled coyly. "Only then can I give you my *full* attention."

"Work before play." He stroked his thumb across her palm,

sending a shiver down her spine. "I gather the new objective is installed and ready for use?"

"All I need is a fresh biopsy," she stuttered.

"Then grab your razor." His voice rasped across her skin. "At the moment, there's only one thing I'd like better than a definitive diagnosis."

Minutes later, perched on a chair before the desk, she slid the prepared slide into the aether chamber and screwed in a canister of compressed gas. The seal popped and a low hiss indicated the chamber was filling. Staring through the eyepiece, she first brought his skin biopsy into focus using the lower magnification objectives, finally spinning in the new high-powered lens and carefully adjusting focus.

*There* lay the answer. But only part of it. She stared, not quite able to believe her vision wasn't playing tricks upon her. This shouldn't be possible, not in a mammalian species.

Evan cleared his throat, then spoke with an unsteady voice. "What is it?"

Piyali lifted her gaze to his. "It's your melanocytes."

He shook his head. "I only know plant histology."

"Your epidermis, the top layer of your skin, is comprised of several layers dominated by keratinocytes—layers upon layers of flattened cells. Tucked among the cells in the basal layer—the deepest layer of the epidermis—are cells known as melanocytes. These are the cells that produce a protein responsible for skin pigmentation called melanin. Normally, the pigment is of a brown or black color."

Understanding dawned on Evan's face. "Are you telling me that my affected skin has blue melanin?"

"Not exactly," she hedged. "It's iridescent, and I wouldn't call the pigment melanin. In any case, that's not what the cells are making, not anymore. They're producing an entirely different substance."

Running a finger beneath his collar, he asked, "Do you know what it is?"

"Yes. I've seen this before, but never in humans. Guanine crystals appear to have replaced your normal pigment."

"Guanine crystals." Confusion creased his brow.

"You've seen the effect before, in fish most likely," she said. "The silvery flash of scales as they swim. More tropical varieties can produce stunning shades of a variety of colors—blues, reds, yellows. It's also common in reptiles and amphibians. Normally, however, the colors are static. In your case, however, the angle of the crystal can change, altering the color of light that is reflected back."

Evan swore and stabbed his fingers into his hair. "I'm a bloody chameleon?"

"Of course not. But your comparison is apt in that you do possess the ability to color shift. Some scientists hypothesize that the flat, plate-like crystals are stacked, one upon another into a kind of lattice that can be actively adjusted."

"Which would explain why the infected members of the tribe, when angry or upset or afraid, would *disappear* into the rainforest." He threw a hand in the air and began to pace. "They were simply mirroring all the colors around them."

"I expect so." Her mouth tugged into a frown. How to break it to him?

"I don't like your expression, Piyali." He closed his eyes for a brief moment. "I'm not going to like this, am I? Maybe I should just look."

"Wait." She put her hand over the eyepiece. "There's good news and bad news." Evan groaned. "I've found the organism responsible. You have an intracellular parasite. It's not transmissible because it's creeping along beneath your skin at the basal layer."

"A parasite?" He grimaced, rubbing his shimmering hand. "Please tell me that's the bad news."

"I'm afraid not," she said. "The bad news is that I've never seen—or heard—of anything like it. But now that we can *see* it, we'll be able to quickly determine if any of the chemicals and drugs are taking effect."

"Let me see if I have this straight." He pinched the bridge of his nose. "An intracellular parasite entered my skin via a frog's bite. This tiny creature worked its way into my melanocytes, somehow altering the chemical makeup of my melanin—or replacing it, turning it blue."

It was more than simple replacement, but the description was apt. "Unless you're affected by strong emotion as you are now," she reminded him, recalling the first time she'd seen his hand color shift. It was the moment she'd realized there was still hope for them.

"At which point I shimmer pink and silver like a soap bubble." His lips twisted and his voice was wry. "How very lovely. If we manage to kill this parasite—"

Reaching out, she placed her hand on his arm. There was nothing she wouldn't do to solve this, to find a way to stop this parasite. "We will."

He raised an eyebrow in doubt. "If. Will my skin return to its normal color?"

"I don't know," she admitted. "Perhaps, if the presence of a living parasite is necessary to provide the melanocyte with whatever code is necessary to produce guanine crystals... or it might be permanent. Either way, if we stop it now—"

"At least my face won't turn blue."

As long as he was hers, Piyali didn't much care what color his skin turned. Not that such a declaration would bring him any relief. If brown skin placed one on the edge of respectability, blue skin... Well, who wanted to be treated like a carnival side show?

WHEN EVAN finally peered through the eyepiece of Piyali's aetheroscope, he could hardly believe that such small, cigar-shaped creatures were the cause of all his problems. The biopsied melanocytes collected from his hand contained but one or two parasites, but those cells collected closer to his shoulder—where the infestation continued to spread toward his neck—were teaming with the creatures, all creeping toward the front edge poised for migration.

He imagined them crying out, "Onward and upward!" It seemed the only thing slowing them down was the ointment he'd concocted. Some component of that compound contained toxins. If they could isolate it, then concentrate it, perhaps there was a chance of ending—if not completely reversing—this nightmare.

Only then could she again be his.

Grabbing a machete, he stalked into the greenhouse to cut down one of the many *khu-neh-ari* lianas tangling through overhead branches.

"Evan," she said quietly, following him. He could tell from her voice that she was about to broach an uncomfortable topic. "I know you wish to keep this secret—and why. I've not contacted Mr. Black, but if we can't devise a cure and soon, I'll need to let him know. With all of Lister University's resources, with all their chemists working on this, progress will be fast."

She wanted him cured. Given how his heart ached at the thought of a life without her, he understood. Not enough, however, to place a powerful, infectious biological agent into the hands of the government. It would be misused. Of that he was certain.

"A few days," he hedged, slicing through the fibrous vines of the climbing shrub, a liana, and handing her a segment. With luck, perhaps they could avoid this argument. "This is the *khu-neh-ari* plant, the one I used to make the ointment."

As she studied the leafy vine in her hand, lines of worry carved themselves between her eyebrows. "How do we go about this?" she asked. "Sorting one component from another."

"Chromatography. Extraction and isolation of components. Distillation. Testing—over and over and over until we find the right dose, the right combination." He cut free another branch and handed it to her. "I was taught to boil the leaves for two days, adding a handful of large stinging ants. I have a limited supply of those in dried form."

Piyali gagged. "Along with eye of newt and wing of bat?"

He grinned. "The ointment works, doesn't it?"

"Not quite well enough." A determined look was back in her eyes. Cure him she would.

*God, I hope so.*

A glimmer of moonlight fell upon her cheek. Instead of reaching for another branch, he stroked her skin, that silky, smooth slope, with the back of his finger. "I never stopped loving you, Piyali, not once. Every night I would climb into my hammock beneath swaths of mosquito netting and think of nothing but returning to you."

Pressing his hand against her face, she looked up into his eyes with such sadness. "Then why hide this from me?"

"I didn't know if it was contagious. I didn't know how fast it would spread, how quickly it would consume me. Like me, you watched your own family die, one person at a time. I didn't want you to have to endure that again, watching a loved one die, unable to do anything." It was why he'd tossed his reply to her into the fire, abandoning all hope of a wife and family. "It was hell."

"But you wouldn't have wanted to be anywhere but at their side. When you didn't answer, when the skeet pigeon didn't return, I thought..." A tear slid from the corner of her eye and Evan's heart almost broke, and his lungs felt heavy, as if they might fail to inflate. "I thought you'd realized I was a mistake, that you'd come home to find a Welsh girl from your childhood had grown into the woman of your dreams."

"Never." He threw aside the machete and brought his other hand to her face. "You are everything to me. I thought it better if I simply disappeared from your life." His thumb brushed aside a new tear. "You have so much potential, so much talent, hiding here—with me—in the forests of Wales would be the world's loss. I was so proud when I heard you'd won a laboratory of your own at Lister University." He smiled. "And now you're a Queen's agent with a pistol on your hip... it makes you irresistible."

An answering smile tugged at her rosy, full lips. "Irresistible?"

The experiments could wait. Evan pulled the cut branches from her hands and tossed them in the general direction of the cottage door. He hauled her up against his chest and kissed her exactly as he'd dreamed about doing all those nights alone in the rainforest. She tasted soft and sweet—of everything that meant home.

Moaning, Piyali parted her lips and ran her hands over the linen of his shirt, making appreciative sounds as she explored the shape of his muscles. As his tongue delved deeper their kiss grew hungrier, touching a match to dry tinder.

Heat shot down his spine, gathering low. Kissing her wasn't enough. He needed her silky, bare skin sliding against his own, and there would be no focusing on anything else until such primal demands were metHe dragged his mouth from hers. "Not here."

"Why not? The cloakroom didn't stop you." Her voice held a breathless note, as her fingertip traced the blue tendrils that radiated from his shoulder across his chest and about his neck. "You've no need to hide anything from me."

Even at his most vulnerable, laid bare before her eyes, she made him feel whole. Scooping her into his arms, he carried her back into the cottage and up the stairs. "Those walls weren't glass, and this time I want to see everything."

# CHAPTER SEVEN

*E*VERYTHING.

Nervous embarrassment hovered in her eyes, but she was no innocent. Their encounter in the Pharmacological Society's shadowy cloakroom—their joining desperate and frantic and wonderful—had seen to that. He'd clung to that memory, a memory he'd unsuccessfully tried to cram into a dark corner of his heart and lock away. His groin throbbed with need, but as much as he wanted to be inside her again, this time he wanted to *see* her.

He set her down on the edge of his bed and knelt before her to unlace her knee-high leather boots, but the way she bit her lower lip made his fingers pause as conflict gripped him. "I can only promise you today. If that's not enough, we'll stop." Though he might explode with the effort.

"I'm not asking you for forever." Piyali threaded her fingers through his curls and tipped his face upward. "Don't stop. Even if everything falls apart, I want this. Here. Now."

"Good. Because I don't think I can manage to wait much longer." He yanked the boots from her feet and threw them aside. His own shoes joined them. Without bothering to fully unbutton his shirt, he dragged it over his head. She shifted to unbuckle her corset, then, unclasping hooks, she slid her *choli* down her arms, leaving herself bare to the waist.

He let out a low whistle. "I knew I was missing out last time. So beautiful," he murmured, sweeping his palm over her breast as her nipples puckered under his gaze, "and begging for attention." Dipping his head, he caught the tight bud between his lips and sucked. With a moan, she gripped his head, holding him close.

Her back arched. "Oh, Evan!"

Cries of pleasure that had haunted his dreams fell from her lips, and he lapped in each one even as an unwanted thought crept into his mind. She was not his to keep. Not yet. Perhaps never. This explosion of longing, these shared moments of intimacy might be their last. All the more reason to treasure every one. Inhaling her sweet scent, he sent his hands wandering over the dips and curves of her body.

Hands. Hers were on his shoulders now, sliding over his biceps, then gripping his muscles. With the edge of his teeth, he scraped the tip of her nipple and was rewarded with a tight gasp —and the sharp bite of her nails into his skin. A heartbeat later and her fingers trailed over his chest, landing on the top button of his trousers, loosening it. He wanted this to last, but it wouldn't. Not if she wrapped her hands around his hard length. With a gentle push, he sent her falling backward onto the thick, down-filled mattress.

"You first." Bending over, he slid his hands over her soft skin, catching at the drawstring of her *lehenga*. A quick tug with his fingers, and the garment loosened. With a gentle kiss to her navel, he whisked away the satiny garment and lay her bare to his view. But before he could return his mouth to her skin, she rolled onto her side, propping herself on one elbow. Her long braid fell over her shoulder, and she toyed with its end, unfastening the tie that held the plaits in place.

"Take them off," she said, her eyes slightly unfocused. "You're not the only one who wants to look." She ran her fingers through her hair, freeing its long, silky lengths. "Take them off and join me."

All too happy to oblige, he yanked his trousers off and climbed onto the bed, stretching out beside her and skimming his hand over the curve of her hip. "So soft."

"So long," she said, her voice sultry as she traced his length. He clenched his jaw, wanting her touch but desperately trying to maintain control. His member throbbed as her slender fingers wrapped about him. "So thick and hard." Her flashing eyes teased. "Remind me how we fit together, for it doesn't seem possible."

"No?" He caught her wrist. Much more of that and he wouldn't last long enough to slide inside her. Encircling both wrists with one hand, he rolled her onto her back—then lifted her arms above her head, thrusting her gorgeous breasts upward. "Let me remind you." He brushed a finger across the soft curls at the apex of her thighs, then slipped a fingertip along the seam of her wet heat. Her well-kissed lips parted and her breath came faster as he circled her center. "Remembering now?"

Eyes closed, her dark lashes fanned across her cheeks. "A glimmer," she breathed, tipping her hips and parting her knees. "But I recall a bit more *depth* to your explorations."

Nipping the delicate skin of her neck, he laughed against her skin, then slid a finger deep inside her hot, wet channel. "Like this?" he asked, pushing slowly in and out of her. He watched, greedy for the vision of her pleasure. Their first time together had been one of touch and taste—he'd missed the sight of her hips flexing against his hand, her back arching, her heels digging into the mattress.

"More," she gasped. "All of you, Evan. Fill me."

In no frame of mind to deny such a plea, he rolled, dragging her with him, across him, crushing her heavy breasts to his chest. Her hips to his. Needing to be inside her, he guided her leg over his hip.

"You want me... on top?" She rose up onto her knees, straddling him, lowering herself onto his throbbing member. Long, dark hair fanned about her face and over her shoulders, its ends a gentle tease against his hot skin. His breath caught as she flexed her hips, gliding her wetness over his arousal. "Like this?"

He groaned, and his answer was strangled, but he managed a retort. "Exactly that way, but with more depth." It was her turn to laugh as he reached for a paper package upon his bedside table and pressed the sheath into her hand. No good pharmacist should be without one. He'd snatched a box at the store, hoping... "Cover me, then take me inside you."

Sweet torture, her soft hands moving over his stiff rod. He dug his fingers into the sheets, fighting a need to surge upward. At last, she notched him against her opening and took a few inches of him inside. Slowly, she pulled away before easing him back into tightness and wet heat.

"Oh, yes," she said, spreading her thighs wider, sinking onto him and finally, finally, finally taking him fully within her. "This is the delicious fullness I remember," she said, her voice a low purr.

With a growl, he jerked his hips upward. "There's more moving involved."

"Is there?" she teased, holding perfectly and painfully still. She leaned forward onto her hands and took his lips with hers. A deep, soul-shattering kiss. He let go of the bed and pulled her face to his. As they kissed, her hips began to move, slowly at first, rising and falling upon his length until he tore his mouth away on a groan.

Reaching between them, he pressed a thumb to her swollen bud, and her hips bucked, taking him deeper. "Yes!" She threw her head back. Waves of hair tumbled over her shoulders as her back arched, tipping her breasts upward. Piyali, wild and beautiful. An image he'd never forget. "Oh, God, Evan. Don't stop."

His body tightened, tension coiling at the base of his spine, but he held back, wanting to wait until she found her pleasure. He clenched his jaw, trying to hold on, but he wasn't going to last much longer. She was so perfect and it had been so long. Too long. He gripped her hips, his fingers digging into the soft flesh of her buttocks, and buried himself in her.

"Yes!" she cried.

Her hips jerked against his, and her sheath clenched about his shaft while her face contorted with pleasure. At last, he let himself go, diving deep to bury himself within her. His climax tore through him, his heart pounding wildly as he plummeted over the edge.

She collapsed onto his chest, her hair falling about them like a curtain, shutting out the world so that only the two of them were left. He wrapped his arms about her waist, holding her tight as their ragged breaths slowly returned to normal.

"I love you so much, Piyali," he whispered, brushing a strand of hair from her face. Long ago he'd professed his love, and he'd not hold it back from her now. Not when it was the only thing he could give. He couldn't promise her forever, not yet, but she should know that she would always have his heart.

---

SHE LOVED HIM TOO. But the words wouldn't pass her lips. Suppressed anger that he'd not called upon her for help the moment he'd known something was wrong? Or the nagging feeling of disloyalty to the Crown? It was a most uncomfortable position. She ought to report her findings concerning the origins of the blue lesion. But to do so was to betray Evan's confidence.

Or was it simply that she could only offer such words to

someone who promised her forever, no matter how short forever was? A promise he would not make. Not yet.

Lying here curled in his arms, body and emotions laid bare, she couldn't bring herself to speak, to destroy the illusion that all was well. But even now, even as his glimmering fingers traced a slow, seductive path over the dip of her waist, the curve of her hip, her mind puzzled over how the infection might—at the very least—be stopped in its tracks. For it had to be stopped. This intracellular parasite could not be allowed to steal away her heart's desire.

"We need to get back to work," she said, breaking the silence. She rolled away, reaching for her discarded *lehenga choli*. "At some point, Mr. Black will take note of my failure to report." While she was willing to delay that particular missive, she would not compose an outright lie.

Evan groaned, but he too pried himself from the mattress and stood, discarding the sheath. "The minute we solve this problem, I'm dragging you back to bed—and we're staying there. For hours, if not days."

Glancing over her shoulder, she treated herself to one last glimpse of his toe-curling physique. Her heart leapt at the dark and sultry look he cast in her direction, a contemplation of all manner of erotic activities. The muscles of his broad shoulders, of his defined pectoral muscles shifted as he tugged on his shirt. Tempting, to reach out with her fingertips and trace the ridges of his stomach that marched downward toward a resurging interest in bedroom activities.

"Then let's begin." After dressing, she padded down the stairs and crossed to the iron stove, adding a block of peat to the fire and setting a pot of water onto the range. "Boiling leaves and dried ants. Primitive. My mentors would recoil in shock and horror." But not her *dida*. How many times had Piyali watched her grandmother boil *methi*—fenugreek—to make tea for settling her stomach and balancing her blood? Though in this particular case, *dida's* bottle of neem oil might prove more useful as an anti-parasitic.

"Back to the basics, with refinement to follow." Evan's voice rumbled over her skin, a sensual distraction she forced herself to ignore—until he caught her in his arms for one last kiss, leaving her breathless, her determination to resist his charms cracking and crumbling. "I'll gather the *khu-neh-ari* branches," he said, then took himself off to the greenhouse.

Fanning her hot face with her hand, Piyali examined the shelves of his supplies, contemplating a variety of options. Pharmacology was not her specialty, but she knew the basics, and so —braiding her hair and knotting a string about its end—began to gather any and all supplies that held even the faintest promise of a cure. Bottles and jars accumulated: black drawing salve, boric acid, calamine, castor oil, chaulmoogra oil, copper sulfate, gentian violet, iodine, mercurous chloride, sulfur, turpentine...

Hours later, glass Petri dishes covered the table's surface. Each held a small sample of biopsies of Evan's blue skin to which a variety of treatments—botanical and chemical—had been applied. Including the leaf and ant concoction. Conditions weren't perfect, but it was the best they could do without a fully outfitted laboratory. The heat of the stove would keep the cultures warm, if not exactly at body temperature. Piyali clung to the hope that one of their makeshift experiments would yield results.

Now they waited.

"Evan," she said, slipping behind him to wrap her arms about his waist and press the side of her face to his broad back. She choked out words her heart advised against. "It's nearly midnight. I need to go back to the tavern." By now Sarah—and the entire village—would have taken note of her failure to return, and she did not wish to antagonize them.

"Stay." He wrapped a strong hand around hers.

"I shouldn't. You know as well as I that gossip will be bubbling. If you want to conceal our relationship, that isn't the way of going about it." Agreeing to the here and now hurt, but if it was all they'd ever have, she would grab it with both hands. However, there was his sister to consider. Though she hesitated to broach the topic, she forced the words past her lips. "Without a wedding on the horizon, gossip will wend its way to Cardiff and impact Megan's future."

He sighed, but nodded. "I'll walk you back."

Ignoring the ache in her heart, Piyali lifted her bag and followed Evan out onto the moonlit path that wended its way down the hillside. Halfway, a flickering glow illuminated the forest glen and the fairy well it cradled.

Swearing beneath his breath, Evan came to a sudden stop. His arm looped about her as she stumbled into his solid form.

"What is it?" she whispered into his ear.

"It's Seren's Day." He turned her around. "We'll need to take a different path."

"Wait." Curiosity pricked, and she stepped past him, creeping closer to the well, taking care to stay well-hidden behind a nearby tree.

A number of young women—including Sarah and Tegan—gathered in a circle about the pool of water, looking remarkably serious. Each held a flickering candle in their left hand and pinched something between their right forefinger and thumb. With a glint of silver, one girl tossed her offering into the well, murmuring something—Welsh from the sound of it—and peered into the moonlit pool. There was a collective inhale, a holding of breaths, then a giggle, a blush and the announcement of a name. "Aled."

"What on earth are they doing?" Piyali whispered as the next woman stepped forward. A time-honored ritual, but to what end?

"Tonight's the night when a maiden can toss a bent pin into

the well to ask the *gwragedd annwn* to show them the face of their future husband."

"*Gwragedd annwn?*" Piyali tried to wrap her tongue around the strange Welsh words and failed.

"The water-sprite, a kind of fairy, that lives in this well. A few would even have you believe that a woman can—with the right words and offerings—coax the water-sprite into delivering the man of her choice into her arms." He scoffed. "Sheer nonsense."

"They seem quite serious," Piyali observed, intrigued by the age-old custom and the seriousness of the ceremony.

"Mmm," Evan answered.

Sarah's turn arrived. She mouthed the words, tossed the pin, but instead of bending over to look, tossed in a scrap of cloth.

"That's cheating!" Tegan accused, rounding on her. The harsh tone of her voice shattered the sacred silence. "You stole that handkerchief from him."

Him. *Evan's* missing handkerchief.

Smirking, Sarah gave a half shrug. "*You* snuck up here days ago, trying to coax the *gwragedd annwn* to do your bidding. *That* is cheating. At least I'm open about my wishes."

"I did not!" Tegan pointed a finger. "You sent your mother to appeal to the sprite on your behalf."

There was a collective gasp from the group of women. "Shh," one admonished. "You'll frighten the *gwragedd annwn* away."

"At least I'm not creeping about Evan's greenhouse," Sarah said, "peering in windows or throwing myself at him with any number of ridiculous and fictitious afflictions. I hope your entire leg turns blue and falls off."

With a howl, Tegan launched herself at Sarah, grabbing her by the hair and dragging them both into the shallow water. Both of them screamed, clawing at each other with their fingers, splashing and thrashing, each trying to hold the other's face beneath the water.

"Stop!" The women cried out, leaping away from the brawl. A few—those who had yet to make their appeal to the water-sprite—burst into tears.

"That's enough!" Evan bellowed as he stepped from behind the tree. "Stop this nonsense immediately. Home, all of you." There was a slight hesitation as horrified faces turned in his direction, and then the women began to move, running down the pathway. He reached over the low stone wall and hauled Tegan away from Sarah.

"Ow!" Sarah cried as she crawled to the muddy edge of the pool, clutching at her lower leg. "I think it's broken!"

"Now who exaggerates!" Tegan yelled.

"That's enough!" he barked, scooping Sarah into his arms and leaving a sour-faced Tegan sitting half-submerged in the pool. "Once you manage to control your temper, Piyali will assist you."

Reluctantly, Piyali extended a hand, but Tegan only narrowed her eyes. Several long gashes reddened where fingernails had streaked down her face. "You," she spat. "You've ruined everything." Thrashing about, the young woman dragged herself from the pool, and set off down the path behind Evan.

# CHAPTER EIGHT

 VAN KICKED THE tavern door open and stepped into its smoky, alcohol-steeped interior. A number of men whooped to see him carrying Miss Sarah Parker, her arms wrapped tightly about his neck and her face pressed to his chest. Picking her up was a mistake he'd immediately regretted, but what was the alternative?

"What are you doing with my daughter?" Mr. Parker barked. "That's it, I'm calling the—"

"I'm *not* marrying her." A statement he made *every* time he walked through this door of late. He plopped Sarah's sodden form down on the nearest chair and pried her arms from his neck. Her torn bodice gaped. "Dr. Mukherji and I found her—and others—at Seren's Well. Miss Price and Miss Parker had an… altercation. Miss Parker has injured her ankle."

This announcement drew forth another round of whoops, including table slapping along with a number of ribald comments and speculation as to who had won the catfight. Congratulations were called out to Sarah, who wore a satisfied smile at all the attention.

"What happened to Tegan?" he asked Piyali softly.

"She refused my hand," she muttered. "And called you a number of creative names as she stumbled home."

He cringed. "I'm sorry, but we shall have to pay her a visit later." It was the last thing she wished do, but it was the *right* thing to do.

She jerked a nod. "Let me see to Sarah's leg first."

Dragging up her wet skirts, a whimper escaped Sarah's mouth. "There's a reason we call her two-faced Tegan." A deep, bloody gash cut through her stocking and into the skin of her calf.

Piyali set down her bag and bent to examine the wound. "That's going to require stitches." Painful ones. "Where is your mother? You should change into clean, dry clothes before I employ my suture kit."

"She's not available," Mr. Parker said, placing a hand on his daughter's shoulder, pressing her into the chair. "Stay." He nodded at Piyali. "Much obliged if you'd sew her back together."

"Your wife, is she ill?" Evan asked, recalling the accusation Tegan had hurled at Sarah—and Piyali's report that Mrs. Parker had also been bitten by the blue frog. Much as he disliked the woman, he couldn't ignore the possibility that she too might have need of treatment. His initial "rash" had spread all too fast. "I've heard reports that she's favoring a hand. Shall I take a look at her injury?"

"She's fine." Mr. Parker's words were gruff, leaving no doubt in Evan's mind that he would never, ever, under any circumstances be allowed to attend his wife. His daughter's injury, however, couldn't be dismissed.

After much drama involving screams and tears and shots of gin to calm a much-distressed patient, Mr. Parker carried his now-contrite, inebriated daughter to her room.

A heavy sigh met his ears as Piyali followed him out of the tavern. It was well past midnight. "Tegan?" she asked. Her hand sought his, and he grasped it tightly, squeezing. A small comfort. But it wasn't enough.

"Her injuries were minor," he answered. "Better to call upon her in the morning." With a tug, he pulled Piyali into his arms and out of sight of the tavern's dirt-streaked windows. He slanted his mouth over hers and kissed her until she melted against him, until he nearly threw propriety to the wind and hauled her back to his cottage. Gossip be damned. Reluctantly, he released her. "Go. Sleep. We've much to do tomorrow. Today."

"We do." She lifted a hand to drag her palm across the stubble on his cheek. "I've missed you so much, Evan. We will solve this..."

The silver embroidery upon the hem of her skirt glinted in the moonlight as she stepped back into the tavern. She'd left a few words unspoken, but he'd read her unspoken thought in her eyes, and they sent a shaft of pain deep into his chest.

*Whatever the cost.*

The cost might very well be calculated by Queen's agents and the scientists who kept Britain's security at the forefront of their minds. Even Piyali struggled to rank him above her loyalty to the Crown. He'd know the minute she tossed a skeet pigeon toward London; guilt would scrawl itself across her face as if written in red ink, for she'd be unable to hide such a decision from him. At which point Tegan's lesion would be excised, and he—and the frog—would disappear from Wales and from her life. Forever. He desperately hoped it wouldn't come to that.

---

LONG BEFORE THE first rays of sun lightened the sky, Piyali tapped softly at the door to Sarah's chamber. Something about the young woman's wound nagged at the back of her mind.

Only examining it, studying its ragged edges and finding nothing abnormal would put her at ease.

The door cracked open and a pair of sleepy eyes set in a drawn face peered out.

"May I come in?" Piyali asked. "I want to make certain there's no infection." Of *any* kind.

Sarah waved her in, dropping back onto her bed and stretching out her leg. "It hurts, but only a little."

"Was it worth it?" she asked as she unwrapped the gauze.

"Even if Evan wants nothing more to do with me, he's at least met the real Tegan. Such a brat." Satisfaction stretched Sarah's lips wide.

Agreeing with her mildly vindictive patient seemed unwise, even if Piyali's heart hummed a happy tune at Evan's inability to resist her charms. For years he'd waited. For her.

"No sign of excessive redness," she said. But neither had Tegan's ankle shown any normal signs of infection. That stray thought had her reaching for the torch at her waist. Not possible. Was it? Better to know than to leave any lingering doubt. Shaking the decilamp, she pointed the beam of light toward Sarah's calf.

A glimmer, a flash and a nightmare unfolded. The edges of the wound—a tiny fraction of an inch—were iridescent. Guanine crystals.

An iron band tightened about her chest; air scraped its way in and out of her lungs. This was a disaster. With the frog in captivity, it could mean only one thing. Whatever parasitic organism lived in the amphibian's salvia, it did not require its host to survive. Despite its tropical origins, the parasite had managed to colonize the cold waters of Seren's Well, entering Sarah's skin via the open wound.

*Tegan.*

Piyali's stomach clenched. Sarah had dragged four fingernails —four *wet* fingernails—down the side of Tegan's face. *Her face.* "Keep it clean and rest today," she said, careful to keep her voice steady as she wrapped the wound once again. "I'll have Mr. Tredegar prepare a salve. Be certain to use it."

Outside Sarah's room, Piyali fell against the closed door, pressing a hand to her chest. Her heart pounded against her ribs. What to do? Stepping back into the common room of the tavern, she searched out the rusty skeet pigeon, perched once again upon its shelf, returned from its last delivery. Hers. Odd that Mr. Black had sent no reply. He must still be in Scotland, her message languishing among his extensive correspondence. Not that her note mattered. More than an objective was broken now. An entire well was contaminated, one frequented by the local population. Disaster loomed.

She could delay one more day. If the experiments didn't provide a cure within the next twenty-four hours, she'd have no choice but to write to the head of the Queen's agents, the Duke of Avesbury himself.

---

THIS WAS A COMPLETE CATASTROPHE.

Evan stared at the four blue streaks that raked down Tegan's face. Tears ran from her eyes as she blew her red, puffy nose. "I'm going to die!" she keened.

As always, Tegan was completely self-centered. She offered not a single word of apology for instigating the fight, nor showed any concern for how Sarah might have fared. *Sarah.* He ran a hand over his eyes. If Tegan's scratches were so affected, what of Sarah's wound?

Her mother stood beside her, wringing her hands, looking to him with pleading eyes, but all he had to offer her were false promises and an imperfect ointment. Tegan might not die, but the quality of her life was definitely on a downward spiral unless he and Piyali found a cure and soon.

In the doorway, Mr. Price cleared his throat. "Dr. Mukherji has arrived."

Mouth open, Piyali stepped into the room, yet her expression wasn't one of surprise, rather one of horror at the verification of her worst fears.

A ball of lead dropped into his stomach. "Sarah?"

A grim nod was her answer.

There was nothing more they could do here; their time was best spent searching for a cure. Mouthing useless words of encouragement and instructing Mrs. Price to continue to apply the ointment, he grabbed Piyali by the elbow and steered her toward the shop's door. "We'll be back to check on her tonight."

Piyali shook her elbow free. "If I might purchase a jar, Mr. Price?"

"A canning jar?" Mr. Price's voice was incredulous.

"Yes." She dropped a coin into his hand as he handed her the glass container. "Thank you. It'll do."

Evan kept his lips pressed tightly together until they had traveled several feet down the rutted road, exiting the village. "It's not the frog this time."

"No," Piyali agreed. "It's not."

"The experiments are a failure." Ice slid through his veins as he presented a cold and bleak report. "As you predicted, without proper incubation the cultured skin cells died. Even more worrisome, I examined a drop of the culture media beneath the lens of your aetheroscope and," he took a deep breath, "the parasites broke free from the dying cells and are now free-swimming."

Pain, not surprise, crossed her face as she lifted the jar. "In the water of Seren's Well too. It appears they require a wound, a laceration of the epidermis for direct access to the basal layer. Sarah's fingernails digging scratches into Tegan's face. The sharp edge of a stone wall cutting Sarah's ankle." She dragged in a ragged breath. "Evan, I need to write to Mr. Black. The water is contaminated. If anyone seeks the well's healing waters, anyone with so much as a tiny scratch, they too might become infected."

An entire town slipping into madness. There would be no hiding such a crisis. No longer could this be kept a secret. They turned off the main road, following the narrow path upward into the forest, winding their way toward the fairy well. Soon the small, sleepy town of Aberwyn would be overrun with agents of the Crown.

He, Tegan, Sarah—and quite probably her mother—would be quarantined, his sister and grandmother notified. He cringed. For the mental and physical safety of them all, separate—locked —cells would be required. Once the government realized the potential powers behind the side-effects of a blue frog's bite... No, he could not allow himself to contemplate such a bleak future. Not yet.

"One more day," he pleaded, stopping before Seren's Well. Its once innocent waters now teamed with tropical parasites that had colonized an entirely new habitat. "One more day to find a cure."

FROM THE SLIGHT sag of his shoulders, Piyali knew it would cost him much to relinquish control. Though it was time to summon assistance, neither was she ready to admit defeat. A small concession was in order. "We'll sample the water," she said. "Confirm our suspicions. We'll set up another round of experiments, and then I'll compose a report. Maybe the parasites will prove easier to kill outside a host."

She lifted a stick from the ground, threading it through the wire handle of the canning jar, and dipped it into the water. Sample collected, she stepped back onto the path, careful to hold the vessel steadily before her.

"Let's hope so," Evan said, his jaw set with determination.

Once the Queen's agents became involved, quarantine was a strong possibility, and they might well judge the situation a security risk, refusing to inform his family of any specifics regarding his health or whereabouts. "If it comes to it, I'll see to your sister and grandmother." Whatever it took.

He managed a stiff nod.

They returned to his cottage in painful silence, neither one of them wishing to speculate as to what the future held.

Soon she was perched once again upon the chair at Evan's desk and bent over to peer through the eyepiece of the aetheroscope. Her skin crawled. Wriggling in the water droplet on the glass slide were hundreds of microscopic organisms.

Evan took one glance and cringed. "Perhaps we ought to consider a more toxic approach, with the primary intent of cleansing the well."

"Chemicals?" she said. "Sodium hypochlorite would bleach the well. It might work, but it will also kill anything else living there. And once the bleach breaks down..." She shook her head. "The well would need to be monitored on a long-term basis. We don't know the life-cycle of this parasite. If it forms a cyst—a tough, protective capsule—in response to environmental insult, it could return the moment conditions are once again favorable."

"We would need to go back to Cardiff to obtain sufficient quantities of bleach to begin treatment. I've only enough here to destroy these samples. As to the problem of potential cysts..." He ran a hand through his hair. "We could post warning signs at the well, inform the entire village, but it won't stop a determined individual from sneaking there in the dark of night and making offerings to the *gwragedd annwn*."

Reaching out, she took Evan's glimmering hand. Frustration had shifted the guanine crystals. She squeezed. "We proceed as planned." She lifted her gaze to his tight eyes and pulled her shoulders back. "Now is not the time to concede defeat, but to redouble our efforts. You were up all night. What components did you manage to extract from the *khu-neh-ari* plant?"

"You're right, of course." Evan drew himself straight. "I've evidence of naphthoquinone…"

They gathered together another collection of plant extracts, chemicals and organic compounds. She reviewed each Petri dish, each test they'd assembled the night before, hoping to find something they'd overlooked.

She didn't.

Piyali set up a dilution series, testing the effectiveness of the few extremely toxic chemicals Evan kept on hand. At last, weary from work and the previous night's events, there was little to do but stare at each other across the table, across a wide selection of Petri dishes, containing well water and a new range of potential anti-parasitic pharmaceuticals. With luck, a few hours from now re-examination would reveal a solution, a chemical and its necessary concentration to eliminate any and all life stages of the parasite. But neither their diligence nor their patience was rewarded. Bleach killed off the parasite, but only when used in unusually large quantities.

"Scrofula!" She slapped her forehead and jumped to her feet. Lack of sleep had fogged her mind. "Sarah! She has no ointment. And, really, I must see if there's a way to convince her mother to allow me to view the bite to her hand."

Evan handed her a small container of his ointment. "She needs to apply it four times a day."

He kissed her forehead, and she wanted nothing more than to wrap her arms about his waist, lay her head on his chest, close her eyes and listen to the steady beat of his heart. Instead, she rose on to the tips of her toes and gave him an all-too-brief kiss. "I'll be back soon," she promised.

CHAPTER NINE

$\mathcal{B}$ACK AT THE WHITE HARE, Piyali found Sarah up and about, hoisting trays laden with stew and ale. She tsked. "Eleven stiches warrant a day off."

"Father says there's no place for loafers in our family." Her eyes lifted to the blackened overhead beams of the ceiling, and her next words were louder. "Not that I've seen hide or hair of Mother since I was gravely injured doing *her* bidding."

"*Her* bidding?" Piyali tipped her head.

"I told you the first night you were here." Sarah swatted a hand in the air. "They want me to marry Evan. They've been plaguing and pestering and nudging me in his direction ever since he returned from Brazil." She wiped down a table. "Handsome as he is, wealthy though he might one day be, not once has he offered me any encouragement. Still, I dutifully stole his handkerchief as instructed and tossed a bent pin in a pool of water, mangling some ancient Welsh blessing. And what happens? Tegan, mad as a hatter, drags me into the water, and I end the night with you sewing my leg back together."

"How is your leg?"

"Crusty and sore, if in a sparkling sapphire kind of way."

Sarah tipped her head and lifted an eyebrow. "You could have told me. I'm not the type to faint or fret. I do, however, expect you and Evan to provide a cure."

No one could sum up a situation quite like Sarah. With a bitter laugh, she handed Sarah the ointment and gave her instructions. "Your mother ought to use the ointment as well."

"It'll hardly be enough," Sarah said, pulling a face as she slipped the jar into her pocket. "It's spread clear up her arm now. I told her to let you look at it. But no—"

"Sarah!" Mr. Parker yelled from behind the bar. His lips were a harsh, bloodless line and his eyebrows formed a sharply pointed V. "Hush your mouth. I've raised you better than to gossip about family."

Sarah opened her mouth, thought twice, and snapped it shut. Piyali touched her elbow in silent sympathy. With a sidelong glance that spoke of the trials she endured beneath the thumb of her father, Sarah hefted a stack of dirty dishes and wound her way through the tables and chairs to the kitchen.

Curious that Mrs. Parker pushed the centuries old Welsh custom upon her daughter. Wanting Sarah to marry well was understandable, but Piyali wouldn't have pegged Mrs. Parker as the superstitious type.

Now was clearly not the time to press for a visit with Sarah's mother, so Piyali made her way to her room. She'd compose that letter to Mr. Black, then approach Mr. Parker about sending another message. Perhaps that would be the best time to inquire after his wife.

In her room, she placed pen to paper, then stopped. *A frog attack?* Her account read like a fairy tale gone horribly wrong. There had to be a better way to relate the odd events that had occurred in Aberwyn. She scratched out her words and tried again. And again. Tossing aside her fountain pen, Piyali fell backward upon the lumpy mattress. Describing the process by which the man she loved was slowly turning invisible simply was not possible in the small square of parchment a skeet pigeon could carry. Her mind was too muddled. She'd rest her eyes a few minutes, then make another attempt.

The sun was low on the horizon when she pried her eyes open. *Schistosomiasis!* She'd slept away the afternoon. No more time to dally, the evening rush would soon be upon the tavern, and Mr. Parker would only grow more taciturn and gruff without the aid of his wife.

Hastily scratching off a report to Mr. Black containing nothing but bare facts—and trying not to reflect upon how ridiculous it all sounded—she rolled the note into a narrow cylinder, slid it into a tin casing and sealed the end. She bent over her trunk, hunting for another skeet pigeon punch card.

Gone. They were all gone. Her hands stilled as she scanned her belongings. Nothing seemed out of place, and the trunk had been locked. Though, admittedly, her lock was not particularly secure, a mild deterrent. Someone wanted to keep her from contacting headquarters. But who?

Only one person knew she possessed such punch cards. He also happened to be the proprietor of this tavern and inn. Was it Mr. Parker? His wife?

Sarah?

Had her first missive ever reached London?

She slid the message into a pouch hanging from her corset and took a moment to inspect her TTX weapon. Overreacting? No. Her training had taught her it was better to take precautions when one's nervous system sent out an alert, and from the way the hairs on the back of her neck quivered... The Parkers were an odd bunch, but Piyali could think of no obvious reason they would wish to interrupt her communications.

Hand loosely poised by her hip, she slid down the stairs. Only a few bleary-eyed regular drunks occupied a dark corner beside the peat fire on the hearth. Sarah leaned on the window sill, staring out at the street. Her parents were nowhere to be seen. Careful to move silently, Piyali ducked under the countertop and crept on her toes toward the Parkers' private quarters. If challenged, she would insist Mrs. Parker required medical evaluation. For now, she listened at the door, to the cadence of what became increasingly hostile voices. Ever so carefully, she nudged the door ajar.

"What more do you want me to do?" Mrs. Parker grumbled. "I have it."

"What of the plant?" the innkeeper challenged.

Mrs. Parker huffed. "A cutting."

"Not good enough." Contempt laced his voice. "We need roots."

"They've killed every live sample we've sent," she snapped. "What good are roots? This time will be different. *We* take them the vine. *They* send a botanist to the rainforest to dig up an entire plant. We need to go. Now."

"No. Not with Sarah injured," he objected. "Besides, there might be further instructions."

There was a long silent pause in which Piyali imagined they glared daggers at each other.

"You want her cured," Mrs. Parker accused. "Yet you're quite happy to leave me to my fate. After all these years together, you'd sacrifice the queen to save the pawn?"

"I'm not the one who declined treatment."

"I overheard them. The ointment merely slows down the inevitable. Excision is the only cure. With that woman set upon recruiting help from London, we need to leave."

"Then shall I sharpen the knife?" Bitterness honed his words. "For amputation at your elbow is now your only opinion. The more natural joints you preserve, the better the prosthetic will function."

Mrs. Parker snarled back, her words too guttural and mangled for Piyali to understand. No, she realized, not distorted at all. The Parkers now argued in Russian.

*Scrofula.* They were both spies. Russian spies! Here. Living in the countryside of Wales—according to Sarah—for some years, establishing a cover, raising a daughter, biding their time. Realization dawned. If Mr. Black and Lister University wished to recruit Evan, so too would the Russians. Encouraging—*forcing*—Sarah to pursue him as a husband was a most excellent strategy.

Mrs. Parker must have been the one to break into Evan's home, leaving the greenhouse door ajar, rearranging shelf items. Sloppy of her. But what, exactly, had they taken? They'd had three long months since Evan returned from Brazil. The list could be quite long, even if they'd taken pains to steal only small samples of his specimens and tiny fractions of his supplies.

Piyali swallowed hard. They must know she was more than a physician. Why else steal her punch cards? This cast Mr. Black's silence in a different light. Had the tavern's rusty skeet pigeon ever taken flight?

Slowly, carefully, silently, she backed away. Evan's worst fears were about to become reality, but not at all via the channels he'd expected.

She needed to tell him. Now.

---

EVAN SCRAPED his hand through his hair.

Over the past several hours, a gnawing sense of desperation had overtaken him. The latest development—free-swimming parasites infesting Seren's Well—had escalated the situation beyond anything he could hope to control. If he couldn't produce a solution, a cure, there would be no choice but to agree to summon Mr. Black and his agents, a most unwelcome conclusion to his struggles. While Lister University might be able to develop a cure, his secret would be in the hands of the British government.

He tried to imagine a positive outcome, but none of the scenarios his mind constructed ended well. Blue-skinned men—or women—with the ability to become invisible, an uncontrollable ability that was entirely subject to the whim of their emotional state. The government would ignore this unfortunate fact and try to mold such individuals into agents, to employ them for the greater good of the British Empire. But when inevitable madness resulted, what then? These agents would go rogue and disaster would result.

No. There was no alternative. A remedy had to be found.

"Copper," he announced to the empty room as a flash of insight struck.

Turning on his heel, he stared at the bottle of blue vitriol—copper sulfate to be exact. Though it was a substance often used to treat skin diseases, it hadn't proven equal to the task of eradicating the parasite. Neither had a *khu-neh-ari* preparation optimized for maximum naphthoquinone content.

However, analysis of the *khu-neh-ari* vine had also revealed the liana possessed an unusually high copper content. What would happen if he supplemented, rather than reduced the copper content of the new ointment?

Minutes later, an alcohol lamp burned at the base of a ring stand beneath a beaker containing the *khu-neh-ari* preparation, a yellowish, gel-like substance. Above the flask, a clamp held a glass volumetric burette filled with blue copper sulfate.

Evan stirred the ointment in the beaker with a glass rod until it melted. Then, slowly, he turned the burette's tap, allowing a drop of the blue liquid to fall into the yellow solution. Drip by drip, the *khu-neh-ari* absorbed the blue vitriol, gradually turning a reddish-brown as the mixture became more acidic.

Time to place his hypothesis to the test. After pipetting a

measure of this new mixture into a Petri dish containing contaminated well water, there was nothing left to do but wait.

Staring at the hands of his pocket watch, he paced the flagstone floor—and lasted all of ten minutes. If this worked, if he could exterminate the parasites in the fairy well, then Mr. Black would not need to be summoned. That would win him additional time for further experimentation, time to determine a method by which to kill the creatures that crept beneath his skin.

But he was getting ahead of himself. First things first.

Recalling how Piyali had operated the aetheroscope, he prepared a slide and slid it into the aether chamber. A hiss. A process of focusing upon the specimen, gradually increasing the strength of the objective until the parasites came into focus.

For a moment, he forgot to breathe. Not a single one of the unicellular parasites moved, all floated motionless inside the small drop of fluid. A number of the wee creatures had lysed—burst—and fragments of their intracellular organelles were strewn about the field of vision.

Heart pounding, he leapt to his feet, knocking over the chair behind him in his haste to return to the solution-filled beaker. With a shaking hand, he lifted an eyedropper to extract a single drop of the anti-parasitic solution. He forced himself to take several long, steadying breaths—in and out—until his shimmering hand returned to a regrettable, yet familiar, blue.

He touched a drop of solution to the skin on the back of his hand and stared intently, praying, hardly daring to hope that it might penetrate the many layers of his skin to eradicate the creatures that burrowed within. Shock, then euphoria, rippled through him as a circle of blue color began to fade, slowly returning to a more normal, flesh-colored shade.

Whooping, he leapt to his feet, a wide grin stretching across his face as he strode across the room toward the door to snatch his coat from its hook. He needed to find Piyali, needed to pull her into his arms, spin her about and make plans for their future.

But before his hand could wrap about the handle, the door burst open and Piyali herself rushed into his cottage, wide-eyed and frantic. Her clothes were rumpled and several strands of hair had pulled free from her normally sleek braid. She slammed the wooden door behind her and fell backward against it, dragging in long, ragged breaths.

"What's wrong?" Worry shoved excitement to the floor.

"Spies," she panted, staggering forward. He caught her by the shoulders. "You've been living in a nest of them."

"Spies?" He lifted an eyebrow. "In Aberwyn, Wales?"

"The Parkers," she said.

As he listened to the rush of words that poured from her mouth, Evan began to pace. Her discovery reframed every interaction he'd had with them these last three months. As the proprietor of The White Hare, Mr. Parker had received and signed for every single item he'd shipped from Brazil during his expedition. Many of those crates had arrived before he himself even set foot on the dirigible that had carried him home to Britain. He'd not have noticed a few missing grams of dried Tawari tree bark or a few milliliters of Wasai extract. And his plants... Once he'd begun to propagate them here, a missing seedling or two he would have overlooked as a failure to germinate or root in British soil.

Evan turned on his heel. An inventory of his stores, of his plants, might reveal discrepancies, but how could he—at this late date—hope to pinpoint exactly what was stolen? "Wait." His mind finally caught up with Piyali's words. "Did you say they pushed Sarah to seduce me?" Her constant flirtations, her wandering hands and the ever-present overflowing bosom accidentally brushing against him at any and every opportunity.

She nodded. "Though I don't think she knows her parents

are Russian. I think she went along with the plan to wriggle out from under their thumb."

"Instead it would have tightened the noose about my neck." He strode to the tabletop, slapped a small square of paper upon it and lifted a fountain pen. "We need to send Mr. Black a message. Inform him of the spies and request backup. But whatever you do, don't mention the frog."

"What? We can't. Weren't you listening?" Her voice rose in volume.

"I'm sorry. Too much, too fast." His mouth fell open as she repeated herself. "Even if we trusted Mr. Parker to toss the clockwork contraption into the air, he has stolen all my prepunched direction cards."

He looked pointedly at the pistol strapped to her hip. "Then we handle this ourselves."

"I suppose I could shoot them both, then bind them hand and foot," Piyali grumbled. "Heave them both in your crank wagon and haul them to Cardiff. From there I could contact headquarters, send them a cryptogram over the wire."

He snorted. "Dr. Piyali Mukherji, bounty hunter."

"Oh?" Her eyebrows rose. "You don't think I could?"

"I don't doubt it for a minute. I'll help. But first we ought to cure this infection."

"Evan," she said, shoving a few loose strands of hair behind her ears. "We're out of time. If they escape your village and turn this over to their handlers—"

"Let me rephrase," he interrupted. "While you slept the afternoon away, I found the cure." He no longer felt as if a spotted jaguar hunted him in the night. Once again the future held promise of happiness.

"A cure!" She rushed to the table, but its surface was clear. "What is it? What worked?"

"Copper," he answered, pointing to the aetheroscope upon his desk. "Take a look." As she bent over to peer into the aetheroscope, he explained. "You were right to suggest chemicals. Blue vitriol added to a *khu-neh-ari* preparation optimized for maximum naphthoquinone content. Neither works alone, but together, the copper multiplies the effect of the ointment."

She straightened. A wide smile lit up her face, her eyes. "This means we can treat the fairy well."

"Not quite." He waved a hand at his shelves. "I've not a fully-stocked pharmacy here," he reminded her. "Just a small bottle of copper sulfate. We'll need to make more."

"Simple enough. A couple copper farthings, some sulfuric acid, hydrogen peroxide, a little electricity courtesy of a strong battery..."

"Exactly. For now, the resulting preparation is rather watery, more of a tonic than an ointment, but there's more." He lifted the eyedropper. "Watch."

Holding out his hand, blue but for one small spot, he touched another drop of the solution to the skin on the back of his hand. Piyali stared intently, her eyes widening as a second circle of blue color began to fade, slowly returning to a more normal, flesh-colored shade.

"A biopsy," she demanded, breathless. "We need unambiguous confirmation. Have you performed one?"

"Not yet." He handed her a scalpel.

Piyali took a deep, calming breath, performed the procedure and inserted the slide into the aetheroscope. A moment later she pressed a hand to her heart and looked up at him with tears in her eyes. "Cured," she announced, then flung her arms about his neck, hugging him tight.

*His—their—entire future, saved.*

He wrapped his arms about her waist, ignoring the various attachments of her stiff leather corset that jutted into his skin. "With the entire fairy well infested, we'll need more of it than I have on hand in this bottle, but I've copper and acid and the *khu-neh-ari* liana grows quickly... with a touch of effort, we should be able to generate enough for our needs without traveling to Cardiff." He slid his hands lower, spreading his fingers wide over the curve of her backside. Her soft breasts pressing against his chest made it impossible to concentrate. "Perhaps, before we set to work, we could celebrate."

CHAPTER TEN

"OH, IS THERE something in particular you'd like to do?" Piyali kissed the rough edge of his jaw in encouragement. Now was not the time to speak of their future, but instead to celebrate that they once again had one, one that they would share together. Applying her fingers to the buttons of his shirt, she spread the coarse linen wide and hummed in appreciation as she ran her palms over the strong muscles and crisp hairs that lay beneath.

"As if you need to ask." He unfasted the metal buckles of her corset and stripped away the leather barrier that encircled her waist. Sliding his hands beneath the hem of her *choli*, he skimmed his palms over her rib cage before pulling the garment down her arms and dropping it to the floor. "I've not been able to stop thinking about you, about us."

She stood still as he caught a loose strand of her hair between his fingertips and drew its silky length forward across her shoulder. The backs of his fingers caressed the curve of her breast and her nipple tightened under his appreciative gaze. Then something in his eyes shifted. "I should have written sooner. The time we've lost…"

Brushing the pad of her thumb across his lips, she said, "I should have sent another skeet pigeon. And another. Until an entire flock pecked at your windows and compelled a reply. Forgive me?"

"Always."

Catching his lips with hers, she poured every ounce of her love into her kiss. Barriers crumbled between them, but Piyali refused to allow the tears that pricked at her eyes to ruin the pure joy of this moment. She held still as he pushed her away, tugging the string free from the end of her braid. He ran his fingers through her hair until it fell in loose waves, covering her shoulders and cascading down her back.

Only then did she step forward to peel back the collar of his shirt and press her lips to the soft skin of his neck where his pulse throbbed and tendrils of blue skin glimmered. "I've a request," she said, her voice once again light and teasing.

"Anything." His hands encircled her waist, urging her closer until the hard column of his shaft pressed against her stomach.

"A final request of sorts."

Worried eyes lifted to hers. "Final?"

"A final… performance for your hand." Her face burned at the erotic image that rose to mind. "I want to see it—or not—as it moves over my skin." Watching and not seeing, as if surrendering to a sensual dream.

His answering laugh was a low rumble. "Look down, then. Watch."

She lowered her gaze as his work-roughened left hand—in all its iridescent beauty—slid upward over her ribs to lift the weight of her breast in his palm. Something scraped the tip of her nipple—his fingernail—but she saw almost nothing. Everything was pure sensation. The roll of her flesh between his invisible thumb and forefinger. A delicious pinch sending a jolt of heat through her core.

"Evan!" she cried out as heat flooded her center, and her hips bucked against his. Then his mouth descended upon her other breast, sucking its tip deep into wet heat. "More," she demanded.

His hands left her breasts and cupped her buttocks. In one smooth motion, Evan lifted her into the air and strode across the room. Her backside landed upon the scarred, wooden table. He yanked the slippers from her feet and dragged off her skirt. "Not once did I ever imagine you spread like a feast upon my table." His eyes glinted darkly as they raked down her body. "But now that you're there..." He spread her knees apart, a glint of mischief in his eyes. "Don't forget to watch."

An unseen hand swept across her thigh, his finger slipping along her wetness, gently circling her nub. "Aether," she whispered, falling back onto her hands and arching her back when he plunged an invisible finger inside. In. Then out. And in. Her eyes fluttered shut.

"You're forgetting to look," he said, dark laughter in his voice. She forced her eyes open. The pressure inside her increased—a second finger joining the first—and then the base of his hand pressed hard against her mound.

Her hips bucked. *Enough.* Clawing at his waistband, she unfastened his trousers and shoved them down over his hips. "I want you inside me."

"So soon?" he asked. "I thought—"

"Now." Encircling his thick, hard length with her fingers, she drew forth a groan.

The pressure from his fingers slid away. A moment passed as he dug into his pocket, then a paper wrapper tore, and he covered himself. Rough hands dragged her hips to the edge of the wooden table. She lowered herself backward onto her elbows and wrapped her legs around his bare backside, urging him closer.

The head of his cock notched against her center. He gripped her hips and took her with one powerful thrust of his hips. *Yes.*

*That.* That was the pressure she craved. Filled, stretched. Claimed by the man she loved.

"God, you're perfect." He retreated, then surged forward again. Over and over.

It wasn't enough. She wanted him closer. Needed him. She caught the free edges of his shirt and dragged him down on top of her. The crisp hairs of his chest rasped against her nipples, sending a tremor across her skin. The table beneath her grated against the floorboards, shifting with each passionate thrust, a potent expression of desire.

"Yes, Evan," she cried. "Don't stop." She lifted her knees higher, tipping her pelvis and twining her legs about his thighs to pull him deeper.

He grasped her hips, increasing the angle of his thrusts to rub harder against her center. His hot mouth fell against her neck, a gentle bite that left her mewling.

"Piyali," he rasped. "Come for me."

Her nails dug into his backside as a desperate tension built inside her and at last burst free. "Evan!" She cried out as tremors rolled over her, muscles clenching around increasingly frenzied thrusts. With a yell, he stiffened, driving himself into her one last time.

Sense returned slowly. Slowly, lazily, she opened her eyes and smiled. "How many feet did we travel?"

Laughing, he stabbed his fingers into her hair and gave her a long kiss before straightening. "Three?" Lifting her into his arms, he carried her upstairs to his bed, laying her upon its soft surface. "Tables might have their points, but beds…" He climbed in beside her, and she draped an arm across his chest, resting her head on his shoulder. His fingers trailed through her hair and she let her mind drift away as he murmured into her hair. "Once we eradicate this parasite, the Queen's agents never need know about any of this."

On the edge of sleep, his words shattered her euphoria.

"What?" She bolted upright, clutching the sheet to her chest. "You still think there's no need to inform Mr. Black?"

"Exactly that," Evan replied.

"It's too late to hide what happened. Besides, he has ways of making people talk. When I bring them in, the Parkers will tell him everything. As will Tegan and her family. I'd look like a fool." Her career would never recover. How could he ask this of her? She climbed from the bed, wrapping the sheet about her. "Impossible."

***

"WHY?" he countered, missing her warmth, even though the blaze of her narrow-eyed stare threatened to incinerate him. "Without the parasite, there's no risk of further infection. Once we treat the pool..." He trailed off, knowing they were at an impasse.

"Not so. Even after it's treated, the contaminated well water will need to be monitored on a regular basis to be certain the parasite does not take on a cyst form. Some unicellular organisms can survive months in cold water in such a state. To do that, my laboratory will need to know what to look for and how to identify the particular organism involved. I've no choice. Mr. Black must be informed."

She was right. Even if she agreed to hide the events of the past few days, Mr. Black would learn of them during an interrogation of the Parkers. He asked her to jeopardize both her career as a Queen's agent and the laboratory she'd been granted at Lister University. Not something he had the right to do.

"No." Piyali sliced a hand through the air. "I'll have no part in concealing this." She shot down the stairs.

The sheet from his bed made a soft *swoosh* as its loose end trailed downward. He yanked on a pair of trousers, grabbed a clean shirt and followed. "If we can wipe it out entirely, it won't fall into the wrong hands," he entreated.

Already she was half-dressed and pulling on her slippers. "Better to make a full report in the event that someone—hostile or friendly—encounters this infection again."

"Government has a way of abusing scientific advances," he countered, buttoning his shirt then reaching for his boots.

"True." She buckled her corset about her waist. "But who's to say the Russians haven't already been informed of this blue frog and the effects of its bite? Or whether or not they take the Parkers' reports seriously? Even if they don't have a sample yet, they're going to know where to send their people to look. Tracking your movements through Brazil can't possibly be that difficult. We take the frog into custody and record the cure. Better to be prepared, than to be caught unawares."

Evan pressed his lips together. They would never agree. Though he didn't relish the task, better for the blue frog to die, than to fall into the hands of Lister's research scientists. Not that that would stop herpetologists from hunting out more of its kind in Brazil. Perhaps he could simply soak the creature in the cure and deny this entire incident? He grabbed the flask of copper and *khu-neh-ari* extract. Pouring a generous amount into the palm of his hand, he began to rub the solution over his arm.

Piyali lifted an empty, lidded jar and strode into his greenhouse.

"Leave the creature here," he objected, following in her wake. "You can't possibly apprehend two Russian agents and keep the frog safe at the same time."

"If I leave it here, will you guarantee the frog won't disappear for good?" she asked, her expression growing suspicious.

Guilty intentions made him glance away. He'd make no such promises.

"I didn't think so." She bent before the terrarium squinting through the glass, searching for a hint of the frog. Unable to locate it, she heaved a sigh. "Can *you* see it?"

"Rather the point of being invisible, isn't it?" The greenhouse door was closed, secured with the 3XR CinchBolt. Still, he too stared through the glass. Not with the intent of handing it over but worried the frog had somehow escaped once again despite the heavy pharmacology textbook he'd placed on the terrarium's lid. He saw nothing blue. Nor was there a telltale pink and silver shimmer. Not even a frog-shaped blob reflecting the green of the terrarium's plant life. A cold tendril of fear wrapped around his spine.

"Stand back." If anyone was going to be bitten again, it was going to be him. Setting aside the textbook and shifting the lid, Evan reached inside. He felt nothing. When was the last time he thought to look for the frog? Yesterday. Before he plucked Sarah from Seren's Well. "What *exactly* did Mrs. Parker claim she'd taken?"

A faint knocking began at his cottage door, one that grew more frantic by the moment.

"A plant cutting. But she also said, 'I have it.' Do you think she meant the frog?" Piyali clamped a hand across her mouth, her eyes wide. "*That's* why she was unavailable last night to attend her daughter. If they've been watching you—us—then they know our every move. Mrs. Parker must have stolen the frog while we dealt with the aftermath of the fairy well altercation."

A trained agent would able to pick his lock. It was a probable scenario. His heart crashed into his ribs, then took off at a breakneck speed. "Yes." Sweat gathered at his temples. "I've no intention of handing over this frog to the Crown so they might seek out more of its kind. But I won't have the Russians run away with it either, and I'm ninety-nine percent certain it's not in this terrarium. They must have it already."

A face pressed up against the window of the greenhouse

wall. Sarah. She slapped her palm repeatedly against the glass, shaking the metal frame. "Help!" she yelled. Tears streamed down her face. "You have to help me!"

Evan darted to the greenhouse door, unlocking and yanking it open. "What is it?"

Sarah fell into his arms, sobbing against his chest.

"Beginning to be a bit of a pattern, all these girls throwing themselves at you." Piyali's lips twisted as she reached out and pried Sarah free, steering her by the shoulders into the cottage. "Come sit. Mr. Tredegar has a new treatment to apply, a guaranteed cure. Your ankle will be fine." She pushed Sarah into a chair. "In the meantime, I have questions." She reached for Sarah's foot.

For months, the flirting had been relentless. Sarah and Tegan were too self-involved to realize his heart was sworn elsewhere. But Sarah wasn't one to cry crocodile tears. "It's not her ankle," he said with gut-twisting certainty.

"It's my mother," she keened, dragging in great gulps of air. "He killed her."

"Excuse me?" Piyali's hands froze on Sarah's stocking. "Explain."

"My father," Sarah cried, dashing away tears that would not stop falling. "They were fighting. It was awful. Worse than usual." Large glistening eyes blinked up at Piyali. Gasping for air, she struggled to control her breath enough to speak. "My mother was yelling about you being more than just a doctor. About how they were going to be locked away and tortured. She grabbed the teakettle from the kitchen range, shaking it at him and said something in a strange, foreign language. I've never seen my father look so angry. He raised his fist and struck her." A fresh deluge of tears poured down her cheeks. "Her head hit the corner of the table." A rattling gasp. "Blood. There was so much blood. And she didn't move. Father yelled at me to ready the steam cart, but I ran here instead."

"He needs to be stopped." Piyali's hand landed on her TTX pistol. She tugged it free, checking its readiness, before returning it to her holster.

"First we treat her ankle," Evan ordered as he lifted the bottle of copper and *khu-neh-ari* extract. The situation was escalating out of control. He wouldn't have this infection leaving his village. In any form. "It will only take a minute."

Piyali threw him a narrow-eyed glance, but yanked down Sarah's stocking and unwrapped the bandage about her ankle to reveal a glittering laceration. He soaked a cotton ball with the copper-liana tonic, then swabbed the liquid along the length of the suture. Corking the bottle, he shoved it into his pocket and yanked Sarah to her feet. "Grab the gauze," he ordered Piyali. "We'll bandage her later."

After running from the cottage to a nearby shed, Piyali jumped into the passenger's seat as he heaved Sarah into the bed of the wagon. Furiously, he cranked the vehicle to life.

"Hang on!" he yelled. Then, leaping into the driver's seat, he jerked the break free and rammed the driveshaft into full forward. The crank wagon took off like a shot, its wheels clattering over the many stones that studded the packed-earth lane that led down the hill and into the village.

# CHAPTER ELEVEN

 ER TEETH NEARLY rattling out of their sockets, Piyali clutched the edge of her seat while Evan took the corner onto the main street on two wheels. There, in front of The White Hare stood a steam cart, puffing as it idled with Mr. Parker at its side. He took one look at their approaching vehicle and flung the valise he held into the cart before climbing behind the wheel.

"Father, no!" Sarah screamed.

Mr. Parker didn't so much as glance over his shoulder. The cart sprung to life, tearing down the muddy, rutted road. Villagers scattered, shaking their fists and cursing.

Evan followed.

Mr. Parker's loaded steam cart rattled and clanged as he fled, its loose contents bouncing above the rim, tossing the occasional paper-wrapped parcel onto the grassy verge of the road. One item jolted loose, but didn't fall free: Mrs. Parker's heavily bandaged arm. It hung limp, swaying and jerking with the motion of the vehicle, a grim reminder that Piyali was in pursuit of a man not deterred by death. Did he seek to hide his crime? Or was the corpse of his wife no more than a sample of an infectious disease to be delivered to his superiors, a gruesome commitment to his orders?

Sarah cried out in distress.

Piyali drew her weapon, but they were too far away. "Closer!" she yelled.

"This wagon doesn't go any faster," Evan yelled back. "But he'll have to slow down to take an upcoming turn. If I leave us at full speed, we can overtake him just before we run off the road. If we pursue him, we'll likely lose the race."

In short, the wagon's fully loaded steam hopper would allow it to outrun a crank cart. She couldn't take the chance. "Don't slow down," she yelled back.

"Get ready!" He gripped the driveshaft with white knuckles.

Ahead the road reversed course in a tight hairpin turn, a turn necessary to descend the steep hillside. The steamstage had slowed considerably with its approach to Aberwyn; Mr. Parker barely engaged the brakes.

Bouncing down the rough road on iron-rimmed wheels, Piyali raised her arm, sighting along the length of her TTX pistol. Three darts were loaded. One to stun. Two to render a man unconscious. A third would kill. Mr. Parker was a large man, and she prayed only a single dart would be required.

"Now!" Evan yelled.

Time seemed to slow as they shot past the steam cart. Careening about the tight turn, Piyali squeezed the trigger. With a whoosh of compressed air, the dart shot forth, striking Mr. Parker directly between the shoulder blades. He howled in anger.

The front wheels of Evan's wagon ran off the road, jolting time back to its proper speed. The vehicle bucked, tossing Piyali free. Hours of training had her tucking into a roll. She hit the ground hard, and her body exploded into pain. Despite the screaming protest of every joint, she forced herself onto her feet and began to run across the muddy grass, back onto the road, pistol firmly in hand.

Mr. Parker's shoulders sagged forward, his hands sliding down the driving wheel as the cart careened down the hillside. Lungs heaving, heart pounding, she chased after him, grateful for her raised hemline. Though the sharp edges of gravel stabbed into the soles of the soft slippers she wore, she could not stop now.

She slid to a halt and gasped for air, trying to steady her arm as she took aim. She fired. The second dart grazed his neck. *Schistosomiasis!* If any of the neurotoxin had entered his system, a third would kill him. Still, better to chance it. To let him escape was unthinkable.

Planting her feet firmly upon the ground, she fired a third and final dart into his arm. Mr. Parker slumped sideways on his seat, then fell, disappearing from view. *Excellent.* Evan ran past her, hauling himself into the cart and yanking on the breaking mechanism. By the time she arrived, he had already dragged Mr. Parker—still breathing—from the cart.

Sarah collapsed at her father's side in a heap. "Will he live?" she asked as Piyali unhooked a pair of manacles from her corset and shackled his wrists.

"Yes." For now. Once Mr. Black took him into custody, she could make no promises.

Face contorted in a mixture of anger and concern, Sarah lifted a shaking hand then laid it upon her father's chest. "And my mother?"

"Dead," Evan answered her simply.

Leaving Sarah to struggle with her grief, Piyali took a deep steadying breath. There was no avoiding it. Mrs. Parker must be examined, the contents of the wagon bed searched. She pulled herself onto the running board. It was impossible to pry her eyes from Mrs. Parker's ghastly remains. The back of her head was caved in, clots of blood matted her hair. Her arm was wrapped in yards of dingy gauze that took Piyali several long minutes to unwind. Exposed to the light of day, Mrs. Parker's arm was not only a scintillating blue, but her hand had swollen to twice its normal size. Untreated, blood poisoning—septicemia—had also taken hold.

Beside her, Evan let out a low whistle. "Murdered, yes, but even so, there's little chance she would have reached Russia alive."

"The frog," she said. They needed to secure the creature.

Evan pried the lid off one of the many crates. Inside, padded with straw, lay several glass jars labeled with his own handwriting. A second crate held dried plant cuttings carefully pressed and wrapped in paper. He dug through a third, then a fourth. All filled with a variety of materials stolen from his greenhouse and laboratory. "Quite the collection they made this past year. To think that I never suspected a thing until the blue frog escaped."

Frantic, Piyali dug through the remaining crates. "It has to be here..." A soft, plopping sound came from a copper teakettle tucked into the straw. Why would anyone pack a teakettle whilst fleeing for Russia? Frowning, she plucked it free. The teakettle was heavier than it ought to be, far heavier than could be accounted for by the addition of a small frog. As she shifted the kettle and reached for its lid, something inside scraped noisily across its base.

"Wait!" Even cried. He dug into the straw and then emptied a glass jar of its contents. "Slowly and carefully." He held the jar close as Piyali pried free the kettle's lid and peered inside.

At first glance all she saw was a thin film of water and shards of the white ceramic pot she'd handed to Sarah, the container of *khu-neh-ari* ointment. But then the light glinted off two small, beady eyes. A dazed and confused frog. She tipped it gently into the glass jar. It looked exactly like the one they had trapped at Seren's Well.

Except it wasn't blue.

"It's green," Evan said, eyebrows knitting in confusion.

"Cured?" And then all the tension melted away as she began to laugh. Gallows humor, perhaps, but the two Russian spies had managed to steal so much, yet botched it in the end. "So close to success, but…" She examined the kettle, then held it up. "A copper teakettle to provide a damp habitat for the frog—not the worst plan. But add in a jar of your ointment and a rough wagon ride through the Welsh countryside…"

"And the frog itself is cured," Evan finished.

Had the Parker's plans not been disrupted—with more time to pack and pad the stolen goods—they might have reached the port of Cardiff with intact specimens. With a ship ready and waiting, there was a small chance the spies and a blue frog would have reached Russia. And then…

No. It didn't bear thinking about.

EVAN BRACED as Piyali straightened and dragged in a deep breath. "The Parker family must be delivered into Mr. Black's custody along with any documents found in their private apartments." Her voice held an edge that informed him she would tolerate no further objections.

"Agreed."

Surprise lifted her eyebrows. "But concerning the blue frog and my report…" She set down the teakettle and brushed a piece of straw from her tunic. "I propose a compromise."

"Go on," he prompted. He wanted to reach out and gather her into his arms, but knew he could not. Terms were being set. There was no avoiding Mr. Black or his men now. A lump of coal burned in his stomach. What kind of future could they have together if they could not find common ground?

"Before the Queen's agents arrive, I propose we soak Mrs. Parker's arm in the copper-liana solution. We treat both Tegan and the water in Seren's Well. If this works, if we can elimi-nate all traces of the parasite, I will petition Mr. Black to allow me to personally monitor the pool for the next several years. Mr. Black and the Queen's agents would receive nothing more than a report about the parasite itself, excluding its origin. I won't include a single reference to the frog." She cleared her throat. "It will, of course, mean convincing everyone that Tegan fabricated the story concerning a certain blue amphibian."

Dark eyes met his. Was Piyali holding her breath as she waited for his response? Did she envision a future which included him? What an amazing woman, one who could be his if he too made this small concession. The infectious parasite would not be preserved, living or dead, but it would be carefully documented along with its cure, a cure he would quietly share with the shaman of the village that had hosted him in Brazil. The Crown would *not* be provided with the means to create semi-invisible men, but neither would Lister biologists be left with no identification or treatment particulars should the intra-cellular parasite ever resurface.

"Tegan will never speak to me again, but I'll manage." With a light heart, he caught her shaking hand, pressing it between his palms. "If I augment that report with a living specimen of the *khu-neh-ari* liana, will you personally recommend me for the position of Director of Tropical Plants in the Lister Botanical Gardens and Greenhouse? I've a sudden desire to relocate to London."

A wide smile brightened Piyali's face. Her eyes sparkled as she answered, "Absolutely."

"Curing unknown tropical diseases, uncovering entrenched Russian spies, firing poisonous darts with deadly precision." He drew her close. "What other mad skills have you acquired these past years?"

Her smile turned coy as her arms slid around his waist. "I'm afraid you'll need government clearance to find out. Have you ever considered working for the Queen?"

"I believe I could be persuaded," he said, then lowered his lips to hers.

---

THE REST of the evening passed in a blur. Sarah, alternately weeping over the death of her mother and railing at her father, was returned to her room at The White Hare. Although they took the precaution of locking her door, neither he nor Piyali considered her a flight risk. Mr. Parker, however, was kept securely restrained and administered regular doses of laudanum to ensure he remained subdued.

Tegan was promptly treated. Clutching his hand and pressing it to her heart, she swore her undying love and loyalty. Until he mentioned that he expected to join Dr. Mukherji soon in London and wished her—and her parents—all the best here in Wales. At that unwelcome and unexpected news, her face soured, and she threw his hand back at him with a frustrated howl.

Together, he and Piyali searched the Parkers' living quarters, finding both her original message—still sealed in its tin cylinder —as well as the punch cards stolen from her trunk. Lips pursed in annoyance, Piyali dashed off a brief message informing Mr. Black that she had apprehended a Russian spy and required backup.

The White Hare's skeet pigeon, though rusty, had taken to the sky easily enough, winging its way to London. A strong response arrived the next day in the form of a silver-ballooned dirigible. The entire village turned out in the rain—jaws hanging open—to watch the unprecedented arrival of a hawk-class vessel descend from the sky and settle in the mud before the tavern.

Two men leapt from its compartment; neither were Mr.

Black. With a glance of apology, Piyali left Evan's side, secreting herself behind closed doors to present her report. Disappointment tightened his chest, but he was not an agent. For the moment, he was nothing to the Crown but an importer of a biological hazard. Step one toward their future involved Piyali arguing on his behalf.

Several hours later, they emerged. Precious few words were exchanged as they began the process of loading evidence—including a potted sample of his liana—into a secure storage compartment of the airship's gondola. A few minutes before their scheduled departure, one of the men led Mr. Parker and Sarah in shackles from the tavern to securely bolt them into their seats.

Mr. Parker's lips pressed into a thin line. He stared stoically into the distance, refusing to acknowledge anyone or anything.

"How is it possible?" Sarah asked, her eyes red and swollen. Gone was her usual ebullience, squashed beneath the truth of her parents' lives. "Russian spies!"

"It's a lot to take in." Piyali placed a hand on her arm. "Cooperate. Answer all their questions truthfully and, if—when—you're cleared of all wrongdoing, I shall do my best to help you start a new life in London. I'll see your textbooks delivered to your cell. Focus on your studies to pass the time and improve your future prospects. When this is over, I'll do what I can to arrange for you to take the entrance exams for Girton's College."

As the airship departed, as all faces turned upward to watch its departure, Evan asked, "Is all well?"

"Mr. Black agreed to my proposal," she answered, tugging him by the hand down the main road and away from the crowd. "The pool is now your—our—responsibility."

Together, they slipped away into the woods. Piyali folded her arm through his as they came to a stop before Seren's Well. Its waters glistened a turquoise blue from all the copper sulfate they had poured into the pool, and branches from the *khu-neh-ari* liana floated on its surface.

Traditions transformed and evolved with time, and another step forward needed to begin today. While Piyali spoke with fellow Queen's agents, he'd spoken with Mr. Price, impressing upon him the need to return his supply of steel pins to the manufacturer, to request that only copper pins be sold in the village store. Even better if Evan could convince the villagers that the *gwragedd annwn* desired payment, not bent pins, in the form of copper farthings. The more copper introduced to the pool, the better.

"I've been granted three days leave," Piyali said, breaking the silence. "Three days to convince you that both you and your plants belong in the Botanical Garden of Lister University."

"Done," he said and reached into his coat pocket. Heart pounding, he lowered himself onto one knee and held up his grandmother's opal and diamond ring, a ring that had burned against his chest all day. "That leaves me three days to convince you to say yes. Dr. Piyali Mukherji, I cannot envision my future without you in it. These years without you nearly killed me. Will you do me the great honor of becoming my wife?"

A tear slid down her cheek as she slipped the ring on her finger. "Yes."

Her answer dispelled the gloom that had descended upon his life some three months past. Intensity of color rushed back into his life, leaving him breathless. Evan leapt to his feet and scooped her into his arms, turning toward his cottage. "How shall we spend the next three days? Planning a wedding? Packing the laboratory and the contents of my greenhouse..."

She tugged on his arm. "Anticipating wedding vows."

# IN PURSUIT OF DRAGONS

CHAPTER ONE

*Scotland*
*March 1885*

Ｎ ATALIA ZAKHAROVA KINROSS, Lady of Kinlarig, knelt on the flagstone hearth seeing to the task of shoveling out the cold, dead ashes of last night's fire. In the far corner of the chamber—part study, part laboratory—a rusty steam maid stood immobile, gathering cobwebs and dust. Coal was too scarce to waste on extravagances such as steambots when one lived in a cold, damp Scottish castle. Particularly when one's husband had preferred to direct all funds to his lavish townhome in Edinburgh.

*The rotten, inbred popinjay.*

Upon his death, a list of outstanding bills had been forwarded to her. A headache—beginning at the back of her neck and spreading upward to encompass her entire skull—had grown as she'd flipped through sheaves of paper detailing his extensive purchases. Unlike her, her husband—Stuart Kinross, Laird of Kinlarig—had been accustomed to living in luxury. Oolong tea from China. Blood oranges from Spain. Embroidered textiles from India. All indulgences he enjoyed because the Department of Cryptozoology had awarded *her* a generous stipend to conduct research into the therapeutic properties of dragon venom. But the funds were deposited in her husband's accounts, affording him complete and total control; the paltry amount he had allocated to his wife barely covered basic research and household expenses.

*Never mind she'd swallowed her pride and begged for more.*

Not once in three years had her absent husband deigned to visit his family's ancestral castle, not until the Department of Cryptozoology declined to continue funding her research. With his lifestyle threatened, he'd returned with a sole purpose in mind. Frowning, Natalia sat back on her heels and studied the treasure trove heaped within the fireplace. A dragon that spent her days pillaging the countryside for items he could pawn—golden goblets, strands of lustrous pearls, or gemstone-studded tiaras—might have pleased him. Alas, the dragon collected nothing so grand. Quite simply, he had decided her dragon was worth more dead than alive.

But to knowingly sell his wife's beloved pet to a lowlife like Rathail, a man who would butcher a rare and precious creature, selling the dragon's parts and pieces on the black market to the highest bidder? Comparing her dead husband to a spineless worm was too kind.

A flash of silver caught her eye. That was new. She plucked the coin out of her dragon's treasure trove, leaving Zia's other prized possessions within the fireplace untouched. Scattered throughout a heap of smooth stones fetched from alongside the nearby River Teith were several items of questionable value: silver spoons, shards of a broken mirror, a pewter tankard, twisted fragments of metal, buttons, a pearl earring, a brass shoe buckle, a key, a handful of iron nails. Natalia's dead husband's pocket watch.

A faint—and entirely inappropriate—smile tugged at her

lips. She couldn't begrudge Zia her trophy, not after what Kinross tried to do.

*Greedy bastard.* What had he expected to happen? She shook her head. Trying to cage a dragon with sharp claws and teeth, never mind the poison glands. Served him right for merely pretending to listen when she'd spoken about her research.

Castle Kinlarig was now legally hers, but without funds, continuing to reside within its walls would soon become untenable. But her options were poor. A fugitive from the Russian government, she'd arrived on British shores with nothing to her name save the possession of a very real, mythological creature. Keen to have a dragon on British soil, the Department of Cryptozoology had offered her asylum in the form of a Scottish husband.

Despite the silver threads in his hair, Kinross was no more than a decade or two older than her and still handsome. In the space of a heartbeat, she'd agreed. Marriage altered her citizenship, provided her a residence outside a quiet, Stirlingshire village, and—via a subsidy—funded her research into the properties of dragon venom.

Still mourning her father, she'd not thought to ask why a Scottish laird would agree to marry a foreign woman, sight unseen. Stupid of her. Her own childhood had been so very lonely that twice now she'd placed her trust in the hands of unworthy men, all in pursuit of safety, security, and hopes of starting a family.

Children, however, were not on Kinross's list of interests. After a perfunctory wedding night, he'd taken his leave, appropriated the vast majority of her money—legally his—and returned to the arms of his mistresses. She'd not seen her husband again. Not until he returned a month past, bringing with him most unwelcome news: he'd sold the dragon. To Rathail, a man who sold exotic animals, piece by piece. Dragon blood. Dragon scales. Teeth. Skin. Bones.

Tucking the coin inside a pocket sewn onto her corset for safekeeping, she bent back to her chore. Her housekeeper, Aileen, would welcome the addition of the half-crown into the household funds. Of late, the cabbage soup they'd been subsisting upon was growing rather thin, a poor substitute for a hot, buttered scone. Her stomach growled. She glanced at the empty bowl resting upon her workbench. They needed money. And the only way to convince the Department of Cryptozoology to renew her grant was to produce results. She was so very close, but how could she continue to collect Zia's venom, depleting her reserves when—

Zia—who had been guarding the door—darted into the great hall. A low, warning hiss skittered over the worn stone floors.

"Come here," a man's voice cajoled, his hands making soft patting sounds. Rathail's hired hunter. A nasty little man who had arrived mere days after Kinross's death, asserting his right to collect one Russian Mountain Dragon. "Come here, girl."

Natalia closed her eyes and muttered under her breath, then leapt to her feet. McKay, her elderly butler, had forgotten again. A lifetime's habit of unlocking the castle's door at dawn was proving impossible to break. It might crush his pride, but she would have to take away his key.

"Do you have a death wish?" she called to Rathail's hunter. She snatched up her crossbow and quiver. "It's unwise to enter without my leave. Again. This behavior is becoming intolerable."

She peered around the edge of the doorframe to the far end of the great hall, marking his position. Tail thrashing, Zia's leathery, vestigial wings unfolded as she rose up onto her hindquarters, unsheathing her claws. Yet still Rathail's man approached, dangling a dead rat by its tail, as if it were a dainty treat when there were hundreds of live rodents in the castle cellars. Teeth bared, Zia lunged, spitting poison. Pungent venom droplets blistered the exposed skin of his hands, and he let loose a string of curses, but the halfwit didn't back away.

*Fool.*

Saving men from dragons wasn't on her list of tasks for the day, but neither did she wish to have the town judge knocking upon her door. Explaining her husband's gruesome remains had been troublesome enough. Her jaw clenched. The judge had grudgingly accepted her explanation, but a second such death might well land her in prison.

"No good?" Rathail's hunter asked Zia, then threw the rat to the floor in frustration. "Perhaps this will make you more obedient." Crouched low to the ground, he pointed a long metal rod in Zia's direction, backing the dragon into a corner.

Outrage shot through Natalia's nerves. Whatever Rathail's hunter had been paid to collect Zia, he was a stupid man to think any price was worth the risk. But what did she expect? This hunter was a mercenary, motivated by money and unencumbered by ethics. Much like her husband.

Taking a deep, steadying breath, Natalia notched an arrow and began to crank the tension spring. An arrow to his shoulder would send a strong message. The simple cloth of the trousers encasing her legs made no sound as she stepped through the door, braced the crossbow against her shoulder, and took aim.

A second too late.

She fired at the very moment the hunter lunged. *Thwack.* She swore. Her arrow had gone wide, skewering the portrait of an ancient Kinross ancestor instead. Distracted, the man blinked, and Zia lunged, slashing him across the torso, ripping four long gashes through his waistcoat and the shirt beneath. He growled his annoyance from between clenched teeth as blood welled on his chest.

Zia looked up, her golden eyes glinting with pride.

Natalia nodded her approval as she drew another arrow from

her quiver, reloading. Rathail's hunter was proving hard to deter. She lifted her weapon. "Go now, and I'll let you live."

Instead of fleeing, the fool looked over his shoulder—a bad plan to break eye contact with a dragon—and unhooked a leather muzzle from his belt. "The creature is bought and paid for, Lady Kinlarig. Rathail is running out of patience. The dragon needs to come with me. Today. Help me crate it, and I'll split the collection fee."

*It.* He didn't know he was dealing with a female *Laudakia alpino* from the crimson of her dorsal crest scales. Rathail was playing his cards close to his chest, not daring—yet—to send a proper cryptozoologist. Which meant his minion wasn't aware that the venom eating through his skin would keep those claw wounds from healing properly. Another swipe from Zia or an arrow through his chest, and he might well bleed out at her feet.

Natalia spit on the ground. Such an offer wasn't worthy of any other answer.

He narrowed his eyes. "Have it your way."

Without warning the man touched the end of his long, metal rod—a voltaic prod—to Zia's scaly skin. A loud, electric crackle sounded, and Zia jerked, her yellow eyes flashing wide before her knees gave out and she crashed to the floor. With a roar, Natalia pulled the trigger and half a second later her arrow pierced his shoulder.

The man screamed—both in pain and in shock. Had he thought her threat empty?

Her focus narrowed to Zia. Though she was unconscious, her chest rose and fell. The metal rod was intended to stun, not kill. Natalia growled. Not so her crossbow. But she'd missed. Again. Too much time in the laboratory and not enough on target practice.

*Enough.* Throwing aside her bow and arrows, she drew her blade from its scabbard. Pointing the rapier at him, she ran down the hall with every intention of skewering him to the wall.

The man's eyes flashed wide the second before he turned tail and ran.

Natalia dropped to her knee beside the injured dragon, skimming a hand over the charred patch of scales. Zia's slitted eyes opened, and she let out a pitiful mewl.

This needed to end. Instead of following the hunter into the courtyard, Natalia tore up the curving staircase to the castle's curtain wall. Her boots pounded across stone as she ran to a mounted arrow gun. She slid an arrow into its notch and took aim at a waiting clockwork horse. She didn't have to wait long.

Rathail's hunter leapt onto his mechanical beast and threw the lever, but before the contraption could take four steps, Natalia pulled the trigger. *Whoosh!* A second arrow pierced his upper arm. The man screamed as the contraption cantered away down the rough and pitted road. Too far now for her to put an arrow through his neck.

Between his injuries and the venom coursing through his blood vessels, he would need to seek out medical care to survive. In a feverish haze, he might babble about a dragon in a castle. But if the villagers didn't come for her, Rathail's hunter—or another man—would be sent to try again. A knot of worry twisted in her stomach.

She and Zia needed to leave Castle Kinlarig. And soon. But where could they run? All their options were poor. Live rough in the nearby hills of the Trossachs? Without assistance, they wouldn't survive long. Move to her husband's townhome in Edinburgh and sell the castle? A city was no place for a dragon. Flee to yet another country? Zia might end in chains. Or worse.

She couldn't allow the dragon to come to harm. Not after Zia's birth had saved Natalia's life. She rubbed a hand over the back of her neck, across the cluster of dragon scales beneath her scarf. After three years, the evidence of her father's act of treason was still embedded in her very skin. A flash of pain ripped through her. But for the discovery of dragons, she would still be in Russia, still have a father. She might even be married and surrounded by children.

Annoyed at herself for allowing her mind to stray down such pathways, she shook her head and began to lower the weapon. A movement caught her eye. Another man. Walking toward her castle. *Walking!* The audacity!

Had Rathail—tiring of his hunter's inability to complete his assigned task—already sent a new man to collect her dragon?

She notched another arrow.

---

ONLY A HANDFUL of sheep dotted the fields on either side of the deserted road that led to Castle Kinlarig. They grazed unaware or unconcerned—impossible to tell with sheep—as a pteryform circled lazily overhead in the dull, gray sky. Late for such a nocturnal creature to still fly, though the sun was notice-ably absent. Rumors had reached his ears that the Russians had managed to train—even saddle—a few such creatures. At the unnerving thought, a whisper of worry brushed over his skin, but Luke Dryden saw no rider upon its back.

Unlike the clockwork horse bolting in his direction.

Its rider slumped forward hanging on to the contraption's neck, an arrow—no, two arrows—protruding from his shoulder.

"Turn back!" Eyes wild, the man yanked at the control lever, slowing the horse, but not stopping. His shirt was torn and bloody. Oozing, pitted ulcers spotted the exposed skin of his face and hands. Not a man in any condition to issue orders, yet he tried. "The creature is bought and paid for. The collection contract is mine alone."

"Creature?" Luke hedged, feigning ignorance and noncha-lance. But inside his stomach, worry twisted itself into a knot. "Insofar as I am aware, men shoot arrows, not beasts."

No one was supposed to know about Zia. That was the

entire reason the Department of Cryptozoology had tucked the dragon away in such a remote location. Hell, he'd even bypassed reporting to his supervisor in Edinburgh—as per protocol—to prevent anyone from following him to this castle, a decision that would likely cost him his job. Yet here was a man ostensibly claiming authority over the Russian Mountain Dragon.

Organic chemistry was Natalia's passion. Fencing followed as a close second, and they'd spent long hours in the great hall, in the castle courtyard, sparing with the antique armor a distant Kinross ancestor had pinned to various walls. A married woman, thus forbidden to him, it was the only physical activity in which they could honorably engage to melt away the tension that stretched between them.

But archery? Not once had he seen her lift the crossbow from the wall, yet—he eyed the man's injuries—her aim was excellent. Still, the dragon's existence was known, and she was taking deadly aim at living men. His stomach twisted. Perseverance and grit had brought him back to Scotland, urging him onward as he traversed mile upon mile. He only hoped he'd arrived in time to extract her from whatever circumstances brought this man to her door.

"A crazy witch defends the dragon," the man spat, his eyes narrow. "Job's barely worth the coin if I have to pay for a suit of armor first." He took in Luke's ragtag appearance, his lack of weaponry, and decided he wasn't competition. "Best turn back, lest she run you through. I'll not be burying your corpse when I return." He shoved the clockwork horse's lever forward and rode away.

Natalia had clearly kept her skills sharp, along with the edge of her blade and the tips of her arrows. For the first time in a short forever, Luke smiled. Hitching his pack higher on his back, he trudged forward, impatient to deliver his news to the woman who held his heart.

He was ten feet from the castle door when an arrow whistled

through the air, embedding its tip in the dirt not three inches from his foot. Perhaps his newfound optimism was misplaced. It had been—

"Two years!" Natalia yelled from above.

He glanced up in time to catch a glimpse of her head disappearing behind the parapet.

*Shit.*

A door at the castle's gate stood open. A pair of rheumy eyes surmounted by white, wiry eyebrows peered at him around its edge, then threw a careful glance over Luke's shoulder. They blinked, and the entirety of old Willie McKay's welcome face appeared.

"Sir." Kinross's ancient butler beckoned him inward. "Your return is fortuitous. Lady Kinlarig is in desperate need of protection. You must take her to Edinburgh immediately and place her under your department's safekeeping." McKay began a slow shuffle down the passageway into the courtyard. "I shall instruct Aileen to pack the lady's trunk."

*Flee.* Luke agreed with the sentiment, though given that last arrow, she was unlikely to concur. He followed the old man. "Will her husband not object?"

McKay made a most interesting noise in the back of his throat. "The laird passed a month ago."

Hope shot through him. *Not* an acceptable response to such news, but if she was widowed, then she was free to remarry. His stomach sank. Impossible. He wasn't a fit husband for *any* woman. "What happened?"

Clearing his throat, McKay stepped into the courtyard and waved at a large, iron-barred cage that sat atop a steam wagon. "A most unfortunate event—"

Thundering feet sounded. A galloping accompanied by the unmistakable scrape of claws over wood and stone. Forked tongue flicking, Zia half-flew, half-slid down the stairs, scampering across the ground to throw herself against Luke's legs, nearly knocking him to the ground. She looked up at him, her golden eyes shining.

He stroked the smooth scales of her head. "How's my girl doing?" he crooned. Slipping a hand into his pocket, he pulled out a lump of sulfur, both a treat *and* good for a dragon's skin. "Did you miss me?" He held it out on his palm.

Zia nuzzled his hand with her drool-laden lips, swallowing the yellow rock whole, and Luke quickly wiped his hands on his trousers, removing any residual toxin.

A Russian Mountain Dragon, they'd told him at the Department of Cryptozoology three years ago. He'd gaped at them in shock, hardly daring to believe his good luck. By virtue of time served, a number of other employees ranked higher than him, and by rights the assignment should have been theirs. But this undertaking came with a complication that most were unwilling to shoulder. A Russian fugitive married to a notorious, loud-mouthed, skirt-chasing Scottish laird. As tensions between Britain and Russia increased concerning the Afghan border, it was imperative the gentleman be placated and the woman well-settled so her presence in Scotland would not be revealed.

He'd seen to that before he left, extracting promises and assurances from his colleagues that they would monitor her situation while he was away. However, the arrows in the man's shoulder and his words indicated their efforts had been insufficient. Good that he arrived with a plan.

He crouched beside the dragon, frowning as he ran his palm over a charred patch of scales just behind her shoulder. If that man had put this mark upon Zia—

"Luke Dryden." Natalia's voice sliced through the air.

With a final pat to the dragon's head, he straightened and met her ice-blue gaze. *Aether*, he'd missed her. Though, judging from the grip she had on the swept hilt of a sixteenth century Italian rapier, she didn't feel the same. Guilt tightened his chest. He'd been wrong not to say a proper farewell.

Her soft-soled, leather-laced boots didn't make a sound as she descended the stairs into the courtyard, her dark scowl brightened only by golden hair that was swept back from her face, braided and tightly secured in a crowning circlet. About her neck, the ever-present scarf. A corset, cut and boned for ease of movement. Gone were her skirts, replaced by trousers that hugged her lean curves… in a manner that was going to see him killed.

He lifted his gaze and nodded, careful not to smile. "Lady Kinlarig." The moment called for diplomacy. He was, after all, long overdue. "I'm sorry for your loss."

She snorted. "Kinross's death, though unanticipated, was not the least bit objectionable." From the look on her face, his death would also be welcome. "I refuse to mourn."

"Many apologies," Luke began. "I did not intend to be away for so many months."

"Months?" Her eyebrows rose. There was a sharp edge to her voice. "Two *years* have passed without so much as a skeet pigeon. After the actions of your department this past year, or lack thereof, I'm surprised you dare return." She tested the weight of the blade in her hand, as if considering which body part of his to remove first.

Clearly he'd made a mistake, not consulting with his colleagues before returning to Castle Kinlarig. "What—"

She stepped her right foot forward, lifting her blade and widening her stance. "I agreed to marry a degenerate laird on the condition that the Department of Cryptozoology provide me with a yearly stipend. *Me.* Instead, the funds were sent to my thieving husband while I worked tirelessly in the service of the Crown." She pulled a parrying dagger from a sheath on her hip and tossed it at his feet. "It's been months since I last heard from your supervisor. Longer still since any funds were sent."

Tail lashing, Zia backed away, looking from Natalia to Luke, confused. McKay tottered out of range.

Though teaching her to wield a sword had begun in jest, Natalia was a quick study and had soon sought to arm herself against discovery, plucking a variety of different weapons from the castle's largely decorative armory. *Largely.* For—despite its age—this rapier's steel blade gleamed in the dim lamplight. She'd sharpened it. He swallowed. Impossible not to imagine her dragging its long length—over and over—across a whetstone, waiting.

He refused to engage. "I don't want to fight with you," Luke said. "Natalia, we need to *speak.*"

"We will do both." She pointed her chin at the ground. "Pick it up."

A mere courtesy, that dagger. He could not hope to stave off her attack with such a blade. Not for long. And certainly not in his travel-fatigued condition.

She lunged, slicing the tip of her sword through the strap of his pack and dropping it to the ground. "Defend yourself."

With a sigh he picked up the blade. "I can take you and Zia someplace safe."

"I'm not going anywhere with you. Nor is Zia."

She attacked, forcing him to parry with the forte—the thickest part—of his blade. Metal clanged against metal. He rocked into a defensive stance, attempting to throw her blade high using the cross-guard of the dagger's hilt, to execute a croisé. Though the muscles of his arm struggled to execute his brain's demands, he was exhausted and out of practice. She barely stepped backward.

"Pfft. Have you not held a blade in two years?" She advanced, slashing at his stomach, forcing him to leap aside to avoid its tip.

"Not in swordplay." Any knives he'd held had been short, sharp and used with great stealth. Escaping a Russian prison involved no duels of honor.

"Play?" Her eyebrows rose. She attacked again.

He parried and bound down with his dagger, pushing her blade away.

"Better," she snapped, advancing upon him with increased speed. Blades clanged and scraped against each other as they circled about the courtyard. She was toying with him, else she'd have already drawn blood. If this was what she needed to release her anger so they could speak rationally, he would oblige.

But his heavy, thick-soled boots weren't made for agility. They were better suited to hiking through mountains. His heel caught upon the edge of a stone, and he tripped. As his arse landed on hard-packed dirt, his dagger slipped, and the tip of Natalia's rapier sliced through the skin of his forearm. He hissed in pain.

No sympathy was forthcoming. Instead, the sole of her shoe planted itself in the middle of his chest, forcing him to lie flat upon the ground. Lips pressed into a flat line, she leaned over his sprawled form, both triumphant and disgusted. "Never have you been so weak, moving like a slug."

Insults. But such a relief to finally hear her voice again. He grunted. "It's been a rough few years."

Confusion twisted her face, and she bent closer. "Why are your eyes yellow?"

CHAPTER TWO

ITHDRAWING HER FOOT from Luke's chest, Natalia held out her hand. They clasped forearms, and she hauled him to his feet. Already the blood dried upon his other arm; her cut merely superficial. Though she was barely breathing deeply, his breaths came fast and shallow. Only now, with most of her irritation burned away, did she see the hollows beneath his cheekbones. His lean, spare frame. His pale skin. Lines bracketed his eyes and mouth, ones that shouldn't be there. If one were to judge solely from his face, ten years had passed, not two.

But most telling, the whites of his eyes were so yellow they fairly glowed. One needn't be a physician to recognize the many features of chronic hepatitis, rapidly progressing to cirrhosis. A chill ran over her. What had happened to him while he was away?

Still, an apology refused to pass her lips. Was it too much to ask for a brief note explaining his return was delayed due to illness? She thought of him as a friend. More than a friend, if she were being honest with herself.

"McKay," she began. "Ensure the front door and the gate are

141

securely locked before resuming your vigil. No one is expected until William's lesson this afternoon."

McKay brightened at the prospect of the young man's arrival. "I've some crates for him to shift in the cellars, afterwards. Those Venetian goblets are packed away down there somewhere. They should fetch a few pounds." He shuffled back to the castle's gate.

Luke's calloused hand slipped free of hers and, as his arm fell away, she turned a stiff back upon him and mounted the stairs that led into the foyer while sliding her rapier into its sheath. Zia flutter-hopped up the stairs in front of her, disappearing into the castle. He followed.

"William?" he asked.

"A student," Natalia answered. "To keep my blade skills well-honed, I took on a boy I caught sneaking about the castle's grounds." Without a partner, her opponents had been limited to immobile steambots and bales of hay. She waited for him to object, to lecture her as to the faulty wisdom of her decision. He was, after all, the one who had taught her much about swordplay. A touch of heat rose to her cheeks.

Soon after her disappointing wedding, Luke had arrived at Castle Kinlarig, tasked with composing a lengthy report detailing the requirements for establishing a dragon refuge in Scotland. Alas, a dragon confined to a castle did precious little, save shift in tiny increments to follow a rectangular box of sunlight as it moved across the floor.

Bored, he'd dogged her steps, watching her in the laboratory as she painstakingly studied dragon venom—carefully suctioning a few microliters at a time from Zia's poison glands —in an attempt to analyze its many protein components.

Isolating the individual peptides, she hoped to determine which were responsible for the massive drops in blood pressure and increased bleeding in the dragon's victims. The difference between poison and pharmaceutical was often a matter of dose.

Potential applications included a treatment for elevated blood pressure and congestive heart failure.

But research was categorized by bursts of activity followed by long periods of *in*activity. And instead of paying attention to her notes, she'd fallen into deep conversations with Luke... and in love with the wrong man.

She'd needed a distraction, something to diffuse the heat building between them. Teasing him about how the Department of Cryptozoology required its employees to pass a basic qualification test in sword skills, she had pried a rapier off the wall of the great hall and begun wildly swinging it about.

Laughing, he'd quickly disarmed her, then offered lessons. She'd accepted. Day after day, hour after hour, he ran her through a variety of exercises—attack and parry, advance and retreat—until her legs threatened to buckle beneath her. All their physical frustration channeled into intense training sessions—swords clanging as Aileen frowned with disapproval —still hadn't defused desires. Particularly as her skills began to match his.

Impossible not to recall the approval upon his lips, the slow brush of his gaze as it fell to her waist, her hips, tracing the outline of her curves the day she'd first presented herself wearing loose trousers. With the twisting, tripping folds of her skirts eliminated, she'd soon discovered a new talent... and won her first bout.

"Natalia." Beneath the dark shadow of the entryway, Luke caught her arm. She turned, the words on the tip of her tongue dying as she stared into his brown eyes. "I've much to tell you. Contacting you was impossible, but know you were always on my mind." He stepped closer, brushing his knuckles over her cheek. "I can't tell you how many times my mind replayed our last moment together."

When he'd stolen a forbidden, yet chaste, kiss. Time fell away. Her heart began to pound. Anger ebbed as she considered apologizing for her hasty judgment. But it had been years. Could she still trust him?

All those hours they'd spent together, talking. She *knew* him. Knew that as a child he'd purchased a hyena fish from a traveling salesman, that he'd snuck into a circus tent to beg a ride on the back of a camel, that London's kraken infestation had inspired him to study cryptozoology. In turn, she'd told him what it was like to grow up in Russia without a mother and within a community of scientists who single-mindedly served the nearby research facility, a village where textbooks were prized and novels were scorned. No one knew her better.

Now he was back and, though her mind counseled restraint, her heart begged for a chance. She angled her face upward. "I'm free now."

"So you are," he whispered, offering a weak smile. "I'm sorry for any difficulties you face due to his death, but I'm not at all sorry to find you widowed. And despite your welcome at the point of a sword, I'm beginning to believe you missed me."

Zia scampered in circles about their feet, her hide banging against Natalia's leg and throwing her off balance. She stumbled closer to Luke. She should admit nothing, keep her thoughts close. But she wanted him to know how deeply his desertion had hurt her.

"Dreadfully," she confessed. "With every fiber of my being. Every day, every hour, every minute. You went to Russia, didn't you?"

"I—" He clearly thought better of making excuses. "Yes. How could I not?"

"Even though I warned you not to go. Even though you didn't do me the simple courtesy of telling me you intended to go despite my wishes." She jabbed a finger into his chest. "When your absence passed its sixth month, when winter swept into Russia, I was certain you'd either been burnt to a crisp by dragon's breath, or frozen inside a snowdrift."

"I never stopped thinking of you." Hunger flared in his eyes. "And I'm very much alive."

"Are you?" She closed her eyes and lifted her chin, a clear invitation. "Prove it."

His mouth descended upon hers. Soft, warm, and oh so welcome. His kiss was tentative at first, as if he expected she might push him away. And well she ought.

Instead, she grabbed his shirt and yanked him against her chest, releasing all the suppressed attraction that had crackled and flashed between them long ago. His visits to study Zia, to record details about a dragon's biology and behavior, had been the highlight of her time in Scotland. And a miserable torment of aching desire. Finally, they were both free to fan that spark.

He dropped his bag and caught her face in his rough hands, deepening their kiss. She welcomed the invasion of his tongue as proof that their desire for each other had not dimmed. If anything, it had grown more desperate with each passing day. He tore his lips away, and they stared at each other, both uncertain.

"Lady Kinlarig." Aileen's strident voice flung them apart. Only four years separated them in age, but McKay's granddaughter had taken an instant dislike to Natalia, a foreigner of no consequence married to the laird without warning or ceremony. Any number of village girls had turned up their noses at Natalia for having swept away their dreams of becoming lady of the castle.

Heat flooded Natalia's cheeks, not from shame, but from allowing her housekeeper to discover her locked in Luke's embrace in what ought to have been a private moment. She forced out the first polite words that rose to mind. "Mr. Dryden has made an unexpected return."

"I see." In her hands, Aileen held a tray. Every morning, she delivered a simple repast to the high table that stretched across the dais at the far end of the great hall, for she refused to enter the laboratory. Once, the task had fallen to the multitude of steambots Kinross had purchased, before household finances became strained and he abandoned the idea of modernizing the castle. Coal was too dear to waste on such luxuries now. Instead, the metal servants now stood to the side of the great hall in a row, blending in with the occasional suit of armor. Though a chill always hung in the vast room, eating in a laboratory was always ill-advised.

"Welcome back, Mr. Dryden." Aileen's face was pinched as she gave the dragon a wide berth. She detested Zia and was happiest when the creature remained inside Natalia's laboratory. "Would you care for some breakfast? It's rather simple, I'm afraid, given our circumstances."

Hoisting his bag, Luke trailed behind the lure of hot tea and cabbage soup, engaging Aileen in chatter. Natalia hung back, lifting fingertips to her lips.

At last. She was free to pursue Luke, to lure him to her bed. A smiled curved her lips upward. From his passionate kiss, she suspected only a minimum of effort would be needed. His attentions—she was certain of it—would not be a disappointment. Though there was the not-so-insignificant question of what ailed him. And the possibility he would recoil at the sight of her bare neck.

Her smile fell away as she recalled her wedding night. After a simple ceremony here in the great hall, Kinross had swept her off her feet, carrying her up the curving stairs to toss her upon a mattress.

His enthusiasm had raised her hopes. After all, a gentleman who had spent the better part of his life in the city surrounded by elegant ladies ought to know his way around female anatomy. Alas, his focus was less upon her as a woman and more upon consummating the marriage with all due speed. After the initial shock, she'd warmed to the act only to be abandoned upon his bed before she could reach—

She frowned.

"Wedded and bedded," her new husband had declared, mere minutes later as he rolled from the mattress. He'd buckled his trousers, bidding her to readjust her clothing, to button her bodice to her chin, to wrap her scarf about her neck. "Hide those beastly scales, and keep them hidden, lest you wish the villagers to turn on you." He'd thrown a punch card upon the bedside table. "I'm off. If this time didn't take, we'll worry about heirs once you've adjusted. Maintain the old family pile of stones as best you can. Send a skeet pigeon if you must."

By the time she'd reached the window, Kinross's steam carriage was rattling down the road. It was the last she'd seen of her husband.

Until he returned for her dragon.

At her feet, Zia let out a soft whimper.

She strode across the hall. That horrid man's past actions continued to plague her. The best she could say about Kinross was that he hadn't mentioned the scattering of dragon scales at the base of her neck to a single soul. A dragon was a fascinating creature, one any number of men would pay dearly to possess. Should her own secret be discovered, she herself might end up under the microscope. Had her dragon not dispatched her husband, would he have sold his wife as well?

Zia dashed across the great hall to Luke's side.

"A year of mourning is traditional," Aileen muttered as she passed Natalia on her way back to the kitchen.

"Yet I must take actions now," Natalia snapped, dropping the silver coin from Zia's treasure hoard upon the empty tray. "Without coin, food and coal cannot be purchased. Eventually, we will run out of luxuries to barter. I intend to depart for Edinburgh soon." Perhaps Luke could argue her case before the director of the Department of Cryptozoology. She would ask. What other choice was left to her? "If you and your grandfather do not wish to accompany me, perhaps your fiancé ought to have the banns called?"

"Perhaps." Aileen agreed, but she bit her lip. Had the romance gone sour? "I'll speak with him." Her leather soles struck the flagstone with more force than necessary as she exited.

Natalia had not yet met this mysterious fiancé. Nor had Aileen offered to introduce them. She suspected she would not be invited to attend the wedding.

She sat beside Luke at the high table, and he pushed a cup of steaming tea in her direction, all while rubbing Zia's head. The dragon sat, leaning against a friend she must have thought long lost. "Thank you." Cradling the warm teacup in her hands and watching him drain his bowl of the much-detested cabbage soup, she cut to the quick. "You're ill."

"A filterable virus." A shadow crept across his face. "Forcibly acquired while in captivity at a secret Russian biotechnology laboratory—Ural Zavód—in the Ural Mountains. They were in need of infected human subjects upon which they might trial an experimental medication. It failed. All subsequent formulations also failed to effect a cure. Long-term ramifications persist." He tugged a paper packet from his pocket and poured a brown, powdered substance—an herb—into his teacup. "Milk thistle," he offered by way of explanation. "An attempt to alleviate some of the damage done to my liver." An earthy scent wafted up as he poured his tea over the ground seeds.

"Ural Zavód," she repeated as her mind spun back the clock. Papa had worked there and, when her aptitude for chemistry became apparent, she too had been recruited. She'd even thought to marry a colleague, though she counted herself lucky to have escaped the callous, malevolent man's grasp. Was it Dimitri who had experimented upon Luke, who had tortured him in the name of science? She couldn't bring herself to ask. But it certainly explained why he'd been unable to contact her. A weight in her chest lifted, even as her stomach twisted at the thought of what Luke must have endured. "I warned you against the attempt. Collecting dragon eggs was a dangerous endeavor, even before scientists—accompanied by armed guards—began to actively hunt them."

"We've had this argument." He met her gaze with a set jaw, unapologetic. "Zia—to my knowledge—is the sole female dragon on the British Isles. Her kind is rare, even in the Urals. Given how prized they are, well, without a male, the species might well face extinction."

Luke shared her father's dream, to establish a refuge in the hills of Scotland where the dragons might live free. He'd fought for the right to launch an expedition into the Ural Mountains of Russia for an entire year. But the Department of Cryptozoology cited increasing tensions with Russia. Expedition denied.

Still, he'd gone. *Insane, driven man.*

"Yet you return empty-handed." Both men had risked so much for so little. One had lost his life; one had lost his health. At least Luke wasn't here to take Zia from her. She pressed a palm to the surface of the worn, wooden trestle table as a new fear raised its head. "Were you followed?"

"Not to my knowledge."

*Wonderful.* Yet another worry took its place in the queue, clamoring for attention. As if the trouble Lord Kinross had drawn down upon her wasn't enough. If this kept up, she would soon run out of arrows. Or be forced to start aiming for men's throats. An unsettling possibility. She cursed under her breath.

The Department of Cryptozoology's failure to provide a stipend this past year was the root cause of her current predicament. Not, it appeared, that Luke was to blame. He'd been abroad, imprisoned, suffering horrific torment. They would need to speak of that. Soon. Not just yet, but where to start?

"But it appears trouble preceded me." Brow furrowed, Luke placed his hand over hers. "The cage in the courtyard, has it anything to do with the laird's death? With the injured man I met claiming rights to seize a dragon?"

"Everything." Her mind flashed back to her husband's last words.

"We've a meeting," he'd informed her. "With a man who will solve our financial woes and remove the creature to his care."

"What!" she'd cried. "How dare you? Zia is mine!" Inasmuch as one could *own* a Russian Mountain Dragon.

"No," he'd replied with entirely too much calm. "We married *before* the most recent Married Women's Property Act was passed. All you possess—livestock included—belongs to me."

*Livestock!*

All her moveable property had become her husband's upon the consummation of their marriage. Never had she been so grateful she'd kept her father's research notes a secret. Yet, with Kinross's death, everything that was his—including this castle— was now hers.

Save the one thing she held most dear.

Luke squeezed her hand, dragging her back to the present. "Natalia?"

She blinked. Focused on his worried expression. "Zia ate him."

His jaw dropped.

"Most of him." Natalia swallowed. It had been a horrible, horrible moment. Not at all an end she would have wished upon anyone. Yet once Kinross had enraged the dragon, instinct had overcome training, and the beast inside Zia ripped free... and into the man who would see her caged, quartered, and sold in pieces for profit.

She pulled her hand away, dropping it to stroke the scales upon Zia's head. The dragon sat between their chairs, eyes closed, her small wings folded tightly against her back, thrilled that her two most favorite people were once again in the same room. Natalia elaborated. "She's but a small dragon, unable to eat a full-grown man in one meal. Enough remained that the village doctor was able to conclusively identify him."

"Zia ate him," he repeated, still gaping.

"I'm to blame for the current hysteria surrounding the rumor of a man-eating pteryform." Natalia glanced down. "A mistake. Some of the locals are terrified. Others are mounting expeditions to bring down the creature. I'm not proud of the misdirection, but pointing out that there's been a dragon in their midst for three years seemed unwise."

Luke barked a laugh. "I see." He stabbed his fingers into his hair and dragged his hand to the back of his neck. "I'm struggling with the concept of Zia attacking someone. She's always been a gentle dragon. She never showed any aversion for Kinross before." He closed his eyes briefly. "The cage. He tried to force her inside?"

She nodded. "Exactly. He sold her, as livestock, for an impressive sum to a man named Rathail. But Zia is no farm animal; she is a rare and protected species. I instructed my husband's solicitor to return the funds, but he claims the money was used to address the deep debt Kinross had accrued, and Rathail continues to insist the dragon is his rightful property."

# CHAPTER THREE

"Rathail," Luke repeated.

*Shit. Shit. Shit.*

After all the pains he'd taken to elude the Russians as he exited their frigid wasteland of a country, Rathail's involvement had already exposed Zia to those unscrupulous men who specialized in selling the parts and pieces of rare and emerging animals. Kraken claws. Pteryform wings. Dragon's blood.

Not that the man or his clients would stop at blood. A vial of poison milked from Zia's jaw would sell for thousands. She also possessed wings, claws, teeth and scales. And those were merely surface features. It pained him to consider what a dragon's liver might be worth on the black market.

"You know him?" Her eyes narrowed.

"Of him." Had Luke or any of his colleagues met him, the man would be behind bars. But the name "Rathail" was an alias. "An unscrupulous trader of exotic animals, he has a price on his head."

"How much?" A mercenary light ignited in her eyes.

"Absolutely not." He shook his head vehemently. A mistake.

He hadn't had a decent night's rest in… years. Their earlier skirmish had awakened the dull headache that had plagued him for months. "Are the castle's finances so awful?"

"Worse." She stood, crossing her arms and frowning. "Hence my husband's attempts to sell Zia. I own a castle and a townhome in Edinburgh and have no funds with which to maintain them. I've sold what I can, exchanging candlesticks and crystal for coal and food. But the villagers haven't much coin, and what use do they have for dark and dingy portraits of Kinross ancestors?" She waved her hand at the great hall.

His eyes caught upon one in particular. An arrow pierced its canvas, protruding from the chest of a dignified and bewigged gentleman. But she was correct. Two long, wooden tables and their chairs stretched the length of the room, their surfaces bare. The mantle too lacked adornment. Gone were any and all decorative ornaments.

He smiled at the mental image of Natalia arriving in the small, Scottish village with a sword strapped to her hip and her arms full of antiques, bartering them away for tea and biscuits.

"It's not funny," she huffed. "Kinross was never generous with funds. But now I've not a farthing left to pay Aileen or McKay. Zia is subsisting on the occasional sheep and whatever fish she manages to catch in the river." She began to pace. "I contacted the Department of Cryptozoology regarding my situation and was sent nothing but a note conveying 'their deepest condolences'. Without results, they've no interest in funding me or my research. I intend to take up residence in the Edinburgh townhome. From there I'll either need to sell the castle or remarry."

He frowned at the thought of Natalia remarrying. He selfishly wanted her for himself, but he had precious little to offer her beyond helping to extract her from this current situation. "Rathail will not cease his attempts to capture Zia, not even if you kill this current hunter. Appealing to the legal department to contest Rathail's claims will do no good. The man is a ghost. Besides, if my department has ceased to provide funds…" During his absence someone had badly mishandled her case.

"Exactly." She threw her hands in the air. "Traveling to the city, however, is proving an impossibility. The steam wagon is broken, Zia is deeply averse to being caged and, even were we to manage all that, setting out upon the road makes us an easy target for Rathail's hunter. To say nothing of managing a dragon in a city."

"All true. Regardless, neither of you are safe here. Zia will not fare well in a smaller home. She needs more space, not less." At the sound of her name, the dragon shifted her weight, nudging his leg in a clear ploy for attention. He swallowed the rest of his tea—its bitter, weedy taste a necessary evil to assist his damaged liver's functions—then obliged Zia. "Best to evacuate the premises quickly while the hunter is recovering."

"And where, pray tell, would you have us go? Into the highland moors?" She narrowed her eyes. "That's exactly what you have planned. *What* are you not telling me?"

It was time. He hoped she wouldn't skewer him. "Upon docking in Edinburgh, I didn't report in to my department. Nor did I come directly here. My brother met me before I even stepped from the ship."

"He's still the gamekeeper for Castle Edinample?"

"He is. A qualified—if unpracticed—assistant. My two years in the Ural Mountains of Russia were not wasted. I did not come home emptyhanded." A grin stretched his face. "I passed him a very important bundle. A male dragonet. My brother waits for us in the Trossachs."

"How?" Natalia gasped, her eyes wide and dancing.

Luke sat a bit taller in his chair as his chest swelled with pride. He had, after all, accomplished the near impossible. "The facility was compromised. Something about the capture and interrogation of a Russian agent in Germany. Equipment and research subjects—prisoners—were being transported to a new location. Mistakes were made, doors were left unlocked. In the chaos, a few other men and I took advantage to break free." No need to tell her about the man he'd killed for the clothes on his back, the keys at his hip. "There was a new dragonet in a cage— a month or two old—I took him with me." Along with a few other items he'd pawned in Riga. "I managed to gather enough rubles to buy a steamer ticket and send a single skeet pigeon."

"Not to me," she huffed.

"No. Absolutely not. The dragon's trail needed to go cold, in case..." His smile faltered. "In case my path had been traced. The timing of the dragon's escape linked to mine. Or my connection to you somehow discovered." He looked away. "During the acute stage of hepatitis, during their horrible 'treatments', I was often delirious with fever. I can't be certain what— if anything—I revealed."

She took his hand, her eyes conciliatory. "You made the right choice, passing the dragonet to him. Not that I'm happy you ignored my warnings. Or didn't tell me about your expedition before you left."

"I thought I'd be gone a few months at most," he confessed. Zia nudged his hand with her snout, insisting he resume his attentions.

"What did you name him, the dragonet?"

"Sasha, after your father."

"He'd have liked that." She blinked back the tears that welled in her blue eyes. "A companion for Zia at last, even if he is merely a dragonet."

Luke stood, gathered Natalia against his chest and kissed the top of her head. When she'd run from Russia, two dragonets had been under her care. Yuri, a young male dragonet, hadn't survived the journey.

Though he offered sympathy, it was impossible to ignore the sweet scent of her soap or the soft warmth of her curves. When she melted against him and her arms wrapped about his waist, his mind strayed to their earlier, interrupted kiss. He let his hand drift up her spine to cup the base of her skull. A widow, she was no longer forbidden. His honor and her virtue would not suffer if—

At his feet, Zia nudged his leg again, harder. Enough to upset his balance. There would be no ignoring her. "What is it, girl?"

The dragon stared at him for a moment with unblinking golden eyes, then turned and left the room. Flapping her wings, she half-flew, half-hopped though the door leading into the adjacent room. Once styled the Earl's Presence Chamber—a title long-since extinct—the room now served as Natalia's laboratory, and its fireplace held Zia's treasure trove.

Zia's head appeared in the doorway to see if they followed.

With a sigh, Natalia released him. "If we're to leave, I've a single request." Her face flushed pink, and his heart ceased to beat while he waited for her next words, hoping. "Share my bed tonight?"

He stopped breathing. "You're certain?" He'd hardly dared hope for her forgiveness, let alone such an invitation. His groin stirred. If only he could sweep her off her feet, he would carry her to her bedchamber this very second. "I'm not at my best." And never would be again. But if she still wanted him...

"Was our earlier kiss not demonstration enough? I'm tired of regrets, and we've waited long enough. Don't make me ask again." Even her ears were now red.

"Oh, I won't." He tucked a stand of golden hair behind her ear, then leaned close to whisper, "The moment I first laid eyes on you, I was lost." She shivered as he pressed his lips to the edge of her jaw, working his way back to her sweet lips. "And there's no need to wait for nightfall."

Zia hissed her impatience, and Natalia sighed. "The interruptions won't cease until we see what Zia is about." Her palm ran over the rough surface of his beard, and a teasing light flickered in her eyes. "But then…"

It took every last effort to step away from her, but the sooner Zia was allowed to show him her latest treasure, the sooner she would settle.

Luke scanned the room as he entered. Alongside one wall stretched a length of tables and cabinets placed end-to-end, their surfaces covered with all manner of chemistry equipment. Beakers and burets. Crucibles and clamps. Filters and flasks. The same cluttered chaos he recalled.

Only now weapons were everywhere. A staggering array of sharp, steel edges gleamed. Propped against the wall, hung from hooks, piled in corners were swords, crossbows, bows and arrows. Even a pike. "It's a wonder there are any weapons left in the great hall."

"We found more stored in the cellars." She lifted a shoulder. "I can't spend every hour at the workbench." She picked up a crossbow and slid a palm over the wooden surface of its tiller as he hoped she might soon run her hand over his— "Swordplay, target practice, knife throwing, all diversions that have proved useful. Save the rifles. I've not the powder or the bullets."

*Thank aether.*

Clamping his jaw shut and ignoring the curved stairs in the corner that led to her bedchamber above, he turned his attention to Zia, kneeling beside her on the thick carpet that stretched before the hearth. The dragon was shoving aside rocks, bits of metal and such, hunting for a particular item she wished to display. He waited patiently.

No fire burned in its grate, but hearth tools lay scattered upon the ground. "You were interrupted."

"By that scoundrel who bore away two perfectly good arrows." She frowned and shifted on her feet. "Ever since… since Zia ate Kinross, she's almost refused to leave her fireside treasures. It's been a cold winter. I've been rationing coal, but —" Natalia gasped and clamped a hand over her mouth.

Zia stepped backward, raising up on her forelegs to lift her gaze to them both. Pride rippled over her reptilian features. Protruding from her pile of treasures were five eggs. Five *dragon* eggs. Light brown, each had red-gold streaks branching across its surface, streaks of lightning that glinted in the faint light.

Speechless, Luke ripped his gaze away from her clutch to stare at the proud mother. His expedition into the Urals had been aimed at this very outcome, yet she'd managed to handle this all on her own.

The dragon nudged his hand, pushing it toward her nest.

Permission granted, Luke reached out and scooped a leathery egg from the hoard with both hands. The smooth egg was warm to the touch.

"Impossible!" Natalia cried, pressing a hand to her heart. "Isn't it?"

Zia flicked her tongue and tipped her head. As he stared—stunned—the dragon opened her mouth and—very carefully—retrieved the egg from his hands. She deposited it back atop her treasure alongside the other eggs, then buried them once again beneath the stones. Once more the dragon nudged at his hands, pushing them toward a pile of cold ashes, urging him to light a fire beside her nest.

"Nest," he said aloud, finding his voice at last. Smiling, he caught Natalia's wide-eyed gaze. "It's not a treasure hoard, it's a nest. And she wants us to keep the fire burning to incubate her eggs. Without the fire, there's no chance the eggs will hatch." In their natural habitat, a male—usually of a mated pair—would spit fire upon the rocks, heating them. But therein lay the problem. Only a *male* Russian Mountain Dragon could breathe fire. As his quest had failed, Zia had no choice but to turn to humans for help. Excitement rippled over him. They needed to shoulder the responsibility of keeping the stones warm.

He shoveled away the cinders and lifted the coal scuttle. Barely any lumps lay within. He set them all upon the grate. "We'll need more coal. Or peat. Anything that will burn." Hell, he'd reduce the castle's furniture to sticks if necessary. If these eggs were viable, it was nothing short of a miracle.

CHAPTER FOUR

"BUT... HOW?" Natalia handed Luke a box of matches. There was precious little coal remaining in the household. Sufficient to last a few more weeks if they were careful. "How could she have produced eggs without the male of her species?"

"Parthenogenesis." The excitement of discovery filled his voice. His eyes sparkled and gleamed.

A shower of sparks fell upon the coal. One caught, and Luke gently blew the tiny flame to life, momentarily distracting her with the sight of his well-formed posterior. How many times had she admired it in times past? Was it as firm as it looked? Blue flames of lust blazed across her skin. She'd know soon enough. He sank back onto his heels, and the flames licking at the coal threw a flickering light across the planes and angles of his face where his experiences these past years had carved the features of his face into hard relief. Dark eyebrows slashed across his face in deep concentration, and there was a slight crookedness to the bridge of his nose as if it had been broken. A faint, white scar cut through the lower edge of his lip. How was it possible he was yet more breathtakingly handsome?

161

"Parthenogenesis," she repeated, forcing her mind to focus on the miracle before them.

The odd term stirred a distant and faint memory. With precious little known about the natural history of dragons, her father had been nothing short of obsessed by the reproductive biology of monitor lizards, thought to be the dragon's closest living relative. Speculation often turned to reproductive behavior.

"Virgin birth," she said softly. How her father would have loved to witness this moment. "A hotly-debated topic among herpetologists, if I recall correctly." She stared down at the pile of metal and stone covering Zia's eggs. All this time she'd been oblivious of their presence. She frowned. Why hadn't Zia tried to alert her? Only now, with the arrival of her favorite, indulgent human did she proudly display her clutch. Had Zia assumed Natalia already knew, given her human had tirelessly stoked the dragon's fire these past six weeks?

"Exactly." Luke's eyes danced. "It's an extremely rare event. An egg formed without fertilization by the male of the species. First observed by Charles Bonnet in 1740. A reproductive strategy mostly confined to invertebrates but known to occur upon rare occasions in amphibians and reptiles."

Luke's exhilaration failed to ignite her own. She was happy for Zia, of course, but this complicated everything immeasurably. Yet another variable, yet another worry to weigh upon her mind. One dragon in Edinburgh would be difficult, but a dragon with five dragonets? She shook her head.

Zia, whose gaze had not left the growing fire, let out a heavy sigh and lowered herself onto the hearthrug. A moment of peace, though the charred mark upon her scales was a stark reminder of the dangers they faced. The eggs must remain a secret. Aether forbid Rathail or his hunter learned of them. Their value on the open market would be incalculable. Attacks to secure Zia and her clutch would be relentless. Natalia could deter the occasional hunter, but holding her ground in an all-out siege upon the castle was another thing altogether. Her chest tightened at the memory of Yuri's tiny body tucked inside her coat, of the scratch of his claws on the skin of her throat, of his eyes closing never to open again. The cold and wet of the Baltic Sea had been too much for the tiny dragonet. Traveling into the hills and mountains of the Trossachs… There was no choice but to delay their travel plans.

"How long must the eggs incubate?" she asked, wrapping her arms across her chest. The presence of these eggs ought to bring her joy. Instead, memories kept knocking at a door she'd locked shut long ago.

"No one is certain," he said. "A seven to eight-week incubation is the estimate recorded in the archives by Sir Ridley Sutton, but he was only recording mythology and hearsay, not fact."

"Zia started begging for fires six weeks past." Shortly after eating Kinross. Aether, she hoped human consumption wasn't a prerequisite for dragon reproduction. "If that's when she laid the eggs, they'll require heat for another week. Possibly two." Her voice was clipped. "I don't suppose he made mention of an exact temperature?"

Luke snorted. "No. But given the males spit fire to heat the rocks, we can conclude it's well above human body temperature."

That fit with her recollection of the dragon egg hunt. The soldiers had tended fires in anticipation of a find while she and the others scaled the rocky cliffs, searching for dragon eggs. She spun away and began to pace, rubbing the scales at the back of her neck beneath her scarf. A successful hunt, but one that had ended tragically for her when she'd slipped and fallen. "We can't leave. Not until they've hatched."

"I disagree." His voice was hard, determined. "Staying here is not an option. This complicates our preparations—we'll need a brazier—but it does not render travel unfeasible." Luke frowned, his tone softening. "Natalia, what is it? What aren't you telling me?"

Secrets from her past boiled to the surface. Nothing she wasn't prepared to share with him, after all, intimacy would lay them bare. Forcing the words from her lips, however, was proving difficult. She'd never divulged her memories of her accident, of those days she'd clung tenuously to life, not with anyone. Like a spark landing upon dry tinder, emotions threatened to overcome her. One moment she'd clung to those rocks with stands of her hair whipping about her face, tossing a smile at Dimitri as they neared the cave's edge. The next moment, all her plans, all her love and hope for the future had been dashed upon the sharp rocks below.

"Natalia?" Luke's voice called as if from far away.

But from that pit of despair, hope had emerged. Her father had saved her, restored her ability to walk. She glanced at her workbench. She had Papa's notebook, a collection of scientific equipment and reagents. Certainly she was no cell biologist, but she could follow a protocol. Luke might live for years, but his health would steadily decline. It already had. Gone was the robust vitality she remembered, though the grit and determination she'd always admired still blazed. She wanted him.

But these dragon eggs presented her—him—with a unique opportunity. One she'd never spoken of. A possibility that hadn't existed in over three years. Her husband, the blackguard, had glimpsed the results of her secret and recoiled. Would Luke? No. But neither did she wish to be placed under the microscope. Yet she could not withhold the possibility of a cure. How—where—to begin?

She forced her feet to stop, her fingers to unlatch from her arms, and lifted her gaze to his questioning eyes. She needed to tell him everything. He deserved to know. "When the eggs hatch, I might be able to..."

"We can't stay here, waiting for the dragonets to hatch. Easier to transport them now." Luke unbent from his position on the floor and stood. He swayed and caught himself on the mantle as all the blood drained at once from his face.

She rushed to his side, offering a steadying hand. "What's wrong?" She regretted their earlier skirmish. He was too drained.

"I'm fine," he insisted.

"You're not." Even Zia looked up in alarm. Did he not trust her enough to let down his own guard?

His shoulders sagged in admission. "My condition flares from time to time, when I'm ill or overtired. I might have pushed myself a bit too hard during that last leg of my journey home."

*Home.* To her, not his family. Her heart squeezed. "It's more than that," she said.

This wasn't something rest could cure. The ultimate outcome of his captivity in Russia would be a prolonged and painful death. She refused to dismiss his condition. He *needed* more than milk thistle tea. "Did they treat you with dragon's blood?"

She'd asked Papa about such treatments once, the day he'd pressed her to develop a sulfated purine derivative in her laboratory, an immune-suppressing drug he hoped might enable him to transplant dragon tissues into humans. Even then, she'd questioned the wisdom of such experiments. Glancing at Zia, bedded down before the fire, she recalled his words.

"*Da.* Dragon's blood treats. It does not cure. Not even the entirety of the creature's blood at once can cure." Papa had lifted a finger, wagging it back and forth. "Caging an animal for such purposes, to drain its blood regularly, this I cannot condone."

He had argued against the use of such treatments, putting forth his own proposal: dragon stem cells. If a medication could be found—or synthesized—to suppress the innate immune system, there was a chance that permanent cures could be effected.

But his colleagues had brushed aside her father's hypothesis as nonsensical ramblings.

"They did," Luke said, snapping her back to the present. His knuckles were white as they gripped the mantle. "Once it was determined their medication had no effect on the virus, the scientists undertook a new approach, using rubber tubing to run blood straight from the creature's veins into my own."

"What!" Her jaw dropped in horror. "They ought to know better. Dragon's blood is far more acidic than ours. It must be neutralized—with the simple addition of sodium bicarbonate—before an infusion can be safely performed. Such a process could have killed you."

"They often came close." He pinched the bridge of his nose. "It was hellish. I swear I could feel the dragon's blood burn a path through my veins and arteries. My heart would race and I would struggle to breathe. All while a monstrous headache engulfed my skull with its vice-like grip. Sometimes seizures." He dragged in a deep breath. "That said, when the worst had passed, I felt better. Almost normal." He looked rueful.

"For how long?" His answer would be telling. The more ill a patient, the shorter the duration of relief.

"A week. Sometimes two."

Not long, then. But if he refused to stay, was it enough time to reach his brother? Regardless, a transfusion would temporarily stabilize his condition until the dragon eggs hatched. It would provide her with time to review Papa's notes, to consider if a cure was even possible. Her laboratory was equipped for chemical analysis, not cell biology.

He shook his head. "No. I see what you're thinking, Natalia. It's not right to ask that of Zia."

"One treatment." The possibility hung in the air between them. "With *neutralized* dragon's blood." She held up a hand when he began to object again. "You struggled to resist my sword attack on the flat ground of the castle courtyard. Yet you propose to climb into the highland mountains carrying a lit brazier and five dragon eggs? And when Rathail's hunter follows?" She shook her head. "I can't manage it alone. You need to be in fighting form. For Zia's sake—for the brood of dragonets on the way—let us help you."

HIS SHOULDERS SLUMPED under the weight of inescapable fact. Natalia was right. He wasn't physically fit enough to offer much help on their journey or even during a fight if they remained at Castle Kinlarig. Without time to rest and recover, he might drag them down. He only need undergo this treatment one more time. He was willing to endure the pain—for he doubted she could eliminate all the symptoms—if it meant seeing her, Zia and the dragon eggs safe.

And he'd be liar if he didn't admit that he was thinking of a night or two spent in her bed. At last. Their affair would—by necessity—be brief. He wouldn't saddle her with an ailing husband. But he wanted their time together to be memorable. And for the right reasons.

Except Natalia was an organic chemist, not a physician or even a biologist. He frowned, wondering if he was about to play pin cushion to her attempts. "You've done this before, trans-fused dragon's blood into a human?"

She darted a glance at her laboratory workbench. "It's more an infusion, the slow injection of a substance into a vein." Her voice was detached yet determined. He wasn't escaping this treatment.

"Not an answer, Natalia."

"No," she admitted on a sigh. "But I once helped my father do so by neutralizing dragon's blood. You're a cryptozoologist with anatomical knowledge. You've taken samples of her blood in the past, so if you direct the needle…"

He closed his eyes a brief moment, resigned. It *would* help. "Very well. Let's do it."

With a sharp nod, she spun on her heel.

While Natalia located a syringe, he lowered himself once more onto the rug beside Zia, a process that was more difficult than it ought to be. The dragon dropped her chin on his knee, staring up into his eyes with what he hoped was sympathy. "A brief prick of pain." He rubbed her head in apology. "I'll be as quick as I can."

As children, he and his brother had dreamed of working with large, dangerous animals, staging mock battles in which they saved all of Edinburgh from such terrors as giant spiders, vampire bats and feathered serpents. They'd upset their mother and disgruntled their father who wished them both to become staid, upstanding members of society. Bankers like him.

But John had become a gamekeeper for a wealthy gentleman, and Luke had taken a government position in hopes that the Crown held close secrets about far more exotic creatures than might be found on a wealthy gentleman's estate. He hadn't been disappointed.

With no living species existing on the British Isles, there was debate among the cryptozoology community as to the very existence of dragons. Nonetheless, news of sightings from far-flung corners of the globe generated much excitement and speculation as to their origins. Were they an emerging species—like the kraken—or merely rare, a breed hunted to the brink of extinction, surviving only by retreating into distant and harsh environments where humans rarely wandered? Regardless, most considered dragons mythological. He himself had first-hand knowledge of only one species, but if all were hunted with the tenacity of those in the Ural Mountains, they might well remain so. He couldn't protect them all, but he would do anything he could to ensure the continuation of this particular species.

"You've grown so beautiful in my absence, Zia." He skimmed a hand over her scarlet dorsal crest scales. Their sheen had intensified since he left. An indication of sexual maturity? He considered the eggs nestled in their heap of smooth river rocks and assorted treasures. Or perhaps motherhood? He'd missed the opportunity to observe the changes, though perhaps he was better off for not having witnessed Kinross's death. Luke suspected the enormous intake of protein and nutrients was responsible for triggering parthenogenesis. A curious thought to tuck away for future contemplation. "I'll do my best to make this quick and as painless as possible." He lifted her tail, tapping his fingers along its underside, accustoming her to his touch. Zia closed her eyes, enjoying the attention.

Natalia sat beside him and pressed a bottle of ethyl alcohol into his hand along with a ball of cotton. Her forehead wrinkled. "The tail?"

"The ventral coccygeal vein," he answered, swabbing scales with the disinfectant as his heart rate jumped. "Easiest place to draw blood. She didn't object the last time I drew blood to check her sulfur levels, but if you'll hold her snout—a precaution in the event she decides to snap at us for such an insult?"

"A tiny prick, *lapochka*," Natalia crooned to the dragon, carefully wrapping her hands around the dragon's snout. She met his eyes briefly, nodding her encouragement. "For Luke."

Zia jerked—but didn't fight—as he slid the sharp, steel needle between two scales. A second later, blood rushed into the syringe as he pulled back the plunger, collecting ten milliliters of red dragon's blood. More than enough. He pressed another ball of cotton to the injection site as Zia flicked her tongue, largely unperturbed. Handing the sample to Natalia, he reminded himself why this needed to happen. That vial alone would sell for thousands on the black market. The least of the cruelties that Zia would endure should Rathail manage to take possession of their dragon.

Spinning in a circle upon her carpet, Zia turned, dropping her head into his lap, demanding attention in reparation for injury. He obliged, happy to soothe his own regrets.

At her workbench, Natalia carefully measured a white powder out onto a creased square of paper, weighing it upon a microscale. Satisfied, she mixed the chemical with the dragon's blood in a crucible, then proceeded to remove tiny samples, using litmus paper to test the acidity of the solution. Twisting her lips, she repeated the procedure. When the color of the sample finally turned a deep green—rather than a yellow-green—she drew the neutralized blood into a new syringe.

She knelt beside him. "Ready?"

"Resigned is perhaps the better term." He rolled the cuff of his sleeve above his elbow and tied a tourniquet. A blue vein stood in relief against his skin.

Swallowing, she set her jaw and took aim with the needle. He loved that, her determined persistence, her refusal to ever surrender. But her hand shook ever so slightly and the angle of her approach ensured a miss. His heart swelled and the corner of his mouth hitched upward. Earlier she'd pointed the tip of a sword at him, now she struggled to jab him with a tiny needle. He wrapped his fingers about hers and adjusted her aim. "Have you ever done this before?"

"No." She swallowed.

"I'll guide the needle; you inject the blood." With his help, the sharp tip pierced the skin of his forearm and slid at an angle into his vein. "Good. Now press the plunger down."

She squeezed slowly, sending dragon's blood rushing into his blood vessels, then withdrew the needle. "Done." She exhaled, releasing the breath she was holding. "Do you feel anything?"

Not once in the Ural Zavód had a single scientist inquired about his comfort. If anything, Dimitri Kravchuk had taken a certain glee from Luke's pain as the foreign fluid coursed into his body, burning a path through his arteries to perfuse his tissues. Sadistic, when a few moments with a simple chemical could have alleviated all the pain.

Needing her close, he wrapped his hand about her neck, over the soft wool of her scarf, and drew her forehead against his, breathing in her sweet, spicy scent. Then, closing his eyes, he considered her question. No pain rushed through his blood vessels. His heart rate was stable, his respiration unaffected. "Nothing yet. Save the slight strengthening of a headache." An understatement. As they sat, an otherwise peaceful scene upon the hearth, his headache—one that never quite left him anymore —crept up the back of his head and sank its claws into his temples. "But I haven't slept much in the past few days." Another understatement. He'd been in a hurry to reach her side, sleeping only when exhaustion forced him to seek out a pile of hay in a nearby barn.

Setting aside the syringe, she stood and held out a hand. "Come. We'll discuss your plans for Zia and Sasha later, after you've rested."

"I'm fine here. On the hearthrug." The room he'd once occupied was at the other side of the castle over the kitchens. Too far.

"Nonsense. We'll begin as we mean to go on." A slight blush tinged her cheeks. "You'll take my bed. Alone this time."

He took her hand and rose, unable to remember the last time he'd slept upon a mattress that wasn't infested with one biting insect or another. "I'm filthy." The castle hadn't been modernized. In the past, he'd made use of the nearby river, but inside Castle Kinlarig, his only options were a wet cloth or a hip bath in cold water—water she would have to carry from the courtyard's well.

A half shrug. "There's an ewer and pitcher, but you might as well topple directly into bed. I've not yet sold all the extra sheets." Natalia pulled him toward the curving stairs that led to her bedchamber.

He followed, unwilling to resist, and when she yanked back the bedcovers and gave him a gentle shove, he fell onto her soft, feather-filled mattress with a weary sigh and closed his eyes. Much as he wished to tug her to his side, waves of exhaustion dragged him down. Later, after he'd rested.

She drew a blanket over him. "Luke?" Her words were a soft, warm whisper at his ear.

"Yes?" He struggled to crack an eyelid.

"I must ask." Her face was suffused with pain. "At the Ural Zavód, did you ever encounter one Dimitri Kravchuk?"

Luke cursed and his head pounded. So much for drifting into a peaceful slumber. "He's the bastard responsible for my suffering. He's dead now." Probably. He had planted a knife in the man's thigh and left him bleeding out on the floor. Far too quick and kind an end for such a monster. But even if Luke had been inclined to repay the man for all the pain he had inflicted, only a narrow window of time had been open to him. Luke had snatched the man's keys, unfettered his fellow prisoners and uncaged the dragon.

"Good."

Luke didn't care for the distant tone of her voice or the way she averted her eyes. "You knew him." A statement, not a question.

"Yes." Still as a statue, Natalia's face hardened. Her voice grew cold and ice crept into her eyes. "He was my father's protégé and would have been the logical choice to succeed him, to carry on my father's work."

"Your father's work," he repeated. Had Kravchuk turned unwanted attentions upon his mentor's daughter? "Did he hurt you? What aren't you telling me?"

"I've a lesson." She spun away, lifting a sword propped against the wall. "William. He acts as my eyes in the village and will have news of Rathail's man. Any sign of recovery, and he'll send warning. You can rest without worry." With a zing, she slid the sword into a scabbard, strapping both to the belt at her waist. She could defend herself should trouble return but, damn it, he wished himself fit to fight by her side.

"Kravchuk, who was he to you?" he asked, ignoring the vise that clamped about his skull. Though he was certain he wouldn't like the answer, he had to know.

Natalia slid a knife into her boot, then lifted fierce eyes to meet his. "A man I once thought to marry."

CHAPTER FIVE

Natalia rubbed her hand absently over the base of her neck beneath her scarf as she flipped through the pages of Papa's notebook, scanning his detailed records. Even now, three years later, evidence of her father's act of treason was still embedded in her very skin. Evidence of the unauthorized and reckless experiment that had restored her ability to walk, but sent her into permanent exile. His supervisors had been furious when he refused to explain what he had done with the dragon's eggshell after the hatchling crawled free.

*Can I do this?* No need to offer Luke false hope if she couldn't.

She was an organic chemist. Any and all biological knowledge she possessed had been absorbed at home, when Papa had rambled on about the propagation of "stem cells", a term first used by the German scientist Ernst Haeckel. Not her field, but a fascinating concept nonetheless.

Dragon's blood contained a scattering of rare hematopoietic cells. Those her father had been able to isolate only hinted at the potential of those stem cells he had cultivated from the extraembryonic tissues of Zia's newly-hatched egg. Cells he had used to cure his only child, Natalia.

True, the implantation of dragon stem cells came with unexpected—and not always welcome—side effects, but they also held out the possibility of curing the man she loved. *Loved.* Luke, the only man to ever capture her heart.

Out of tradition and convenience, she'd agreed to marry Dimitri Kravchuk, hoping they might one day grow to care for each other. Marrying the Laird of Kinlarig had been a desperate grab at a brighter future. Both had been a mistake. She'd not truly known either man, but Luke? Attraction had been instantaneous, but the friendship—and eventually love—had grown over the space of many months. For him, she would do her best to replicate Papa's work.

She possessed a fuge. The glassware, the pipettes and test tubes were ready and waiting. The reagents she could mix. She could even cobble together a makeshift incubator. But the growth media—a liquid that would approximate body fluids— was an impossibility. There was no choice but to skip the growth phase of Papa's instructions, using only the primary stem cells she could collect.

Movement caught her eye. William, out in the courtyard, had begun his warmup drills. Son of a local mill-worker, he'd stumbled upon one of her training sessions while delivering coal. The boy—young man, really—had begged for lessons. She'd agreed. With Luke gone, she'd needed a sparring partner, someone to keep her skills sharp in the event that her whereabouts would one day be discovered.

They had. But not until her own husband betrayed her. Her jaw tensed. It was proving impossible to set aside her anger at him, at Dimitri Kravchuk, as their sins continued to haunt her.

Natalia closed the notebook and tucked it back in a drawer. Once Luke was rested, they would need to discuss the possibilities and risks of such a treatment. Was she a fool to invite him to her bed—*push* him into it—when he'd yet to lay eyes on her concealed deformity? He loved Zia so very much, but perhaps he wouldn't want a woman who was part dragon—if only the tiniest fraction—in his arms. In his life. For that was what she wanted, wasn't it? To not just share a bed, but a life?

Regardless, she needed to show him, and soon. It would be irresponsible of her not to reveal the possible long-term and unpredictable side effects of dragon stem cell therapy. And if he turned away from her in disgust, well, that was his prerogative. His choice to reject the possibility of a complete recovery—at least physically—from his time in the Ural Zavód.

For now, she had a lesson to teach. She snatched up two swords, dull and blunted ones intended only for practice, then grabbed a third, sharpened rapier. William had earned it.

Striding through the great hall, her mind circled back to Dimitri Kravchuk. May his corpse rot in hell. To think she'd thought to marry him. When she'd fallen from the cliffs—moments after discovering the dragon's cave, a nest filled with eggs within—had he climbed down to her aid? No. Instead, he'd climbed up the last few feet to the cave and disappeared inside. While *others* attended to her on the ground, bracing her neck, carrying her home. Her fists tightened on the blades she held.

Not only had he not come to his mentor's defense when Papa broke protocol to save her—performing a procedure forever marking her as different—Dimitri Kravchuk had taken it as a personal affront that *anyone* dared touch any part of the dragon eggs which he himself had collected from the nest. He'd made her father's life a living hell.

Fearing they were to be sent to a *katorga* labor camp in Siberia for his actions, her father had bid her to pack. They were leaving, fleeing Russia, stealing away with Zia and Yuri—two tiny hatchlings—in hopes of establishing a breeding colony as well as his research on foreign soil. But Papa had never reached the train. Shot by their pursuers—guards who intended the same end for Natalia—he'd fallen, dead before his body hit the ground. Weeping, she had snatched up his notebook and run, leaping onto the already-moving train, determined to reach Scotland and carry out his wishes. But Yuri was sickly and—despite her every effort to keep the dragonets warm and properly fed—Zia alone survived the journey.

Without a male, there was no hope of a breeding colony. And so Natalia kept her secret—and Papa's notebook—carefully concealed. But now, with Dimitri Kravchuk the likely villain responsible for Luke's condition, it was time to dust off old, unhappy memories and turn them out into the light so that she could right the wrong done to him. To unwind her scarf and share with Luke the one story she'd never told.

Much had changed in the past few hours. She could at last see a path forward if only he would agree to her plans. Yet she needed to rein in her expectations. One step at a time, for there were numerous obstacles yet to hurdle.

"Lady Kinlarig?" Aileen's voice managed to be both subservient and disapproving at the same time. It wore on her nerves. "A moment of your time?"

Natalia stopped in the foyer. As it was connected to the kitchens, it was all but impossible to enter or exit the castle without Aileen taking note. "Yes, Aileen?" She pressed her lips together and braced herself.

With only four years between them, they ought to have been friends. As it was, they barely managed to occupy the same room. Resentment permeated their every interaction. Natalia—a foreigner of no consequence—had married the town's most eligible bachelor, simultaneously achieving the dream of every young woman in town and snatching away the very possibility that they might one day become the lady of the castle. No matter Kinross had been a miserable prize. Aileen disliked Zia even more, blaming the arrival of the dragon for ruining her life. The enforced secrecy of all activities within the castle made her existence a rather lonely one. Not once had Natalia seen her pet Zia, though of late the woman had made a few tentative overtures toward befriending the dragon. Perhaps out of fear of becoming her next victim?

"Shall I air out Mr. Dryden's former bedchamber?" Eyebrows raised, Aileen leaned to the side, looking behind Natalia as if expecting Luke to appear.

The rooms above the kitchen—the warmest in the castle— were currently occupied by McKay and his granddaughter. An unusual privilege, but given a mere three individuals lived within the castle walls and that her butler, McKay, was ancient and not in particularly good health, enforcing traditional servant quarters would be cruel. The bedchamber above theirs belonged to Luke. Or it had.

"Thank you, but that will be unnecessary." For years Natalia had confined her rebellions to wearing trousers and pressing ancient weapons back into service. If she wished to take a lover, why hide it? It wasn't as if Aileen took pains to hide her unchaperoned jaunts—not even from her grandfather—to the river's edge to meet her lover, now fiancé. "We do need to take more care with castle security. The gate was left unlocked allowing an intruder to reach the great hall. Given the recent attacks on the castle—"

"Attacks might be overstating it a bit, wouldn't you say?" Aileen interrupted on a sigh. "Was it really necessary to put an arrow through that man's shoulder? If you'd let Zia go, we could all move on to new lives." So much for Aileen warming to Zia's presence. "The Laird of Kinlarig sold the dragon. He was within his rights and given the creature ate him…"

A thought flashed to mind. How much had she shared with her lover? "You haven't told—"

"Michael?" Aileen crossed her arms. "Of course not. I swore to keep your not-so-mythical beast a secret, and I have. What he knows is that I've no interest in shouldering the role of old retainer tied to the estate by the tradition of generations. I'm to meet him soon, to discuss our wedding. You'll have to find someone else to manage the Edinburgh townhome. The financial situation here worsens by the day, and there's little hope of stretching supplies into the summer. I'm done."

"I'm sorry for that." Natalia felt an inexplicable upwelling of sympathy. The McKays had stood by her side through a rough winter without pay. "The bed hangings in Mr. Dryden's room are of exceptional quality, are they not?"

"They are."

"Take them." She waved her hand. "Take them all. The hangings, the sheets, the feather mattress and pillows."

Aileen's eyes grew wide. "Truly?"

There was no reason for them to be at odds, and Aileen *had* sacrificed much attending to both her grandfather and a strange, foreign woman with a dangerous creature in tow. She deserved a chance to build a life of her own, one not so solitary and lonely. "Consider them a wedding gift. I wish you all the best." Natalia didn't wait for a response. She had extended an olive branch. Aileen would either take advantage of the opportunity, or she would not. Her emotions were tattered and raw. Perhaps a bout with her student in the fresh air and sunlight would lift her spirits.

---

CONSCIOUSNESS SWAM TO THE SURFACE, and Luke forced open his eyes. He pushed himself up onto his elbows before he could sink back into the warm, soft embrace of Natalia's mattress. He'd not slept so deeply in ages, nor felt so... normal. Despite that, the sun still hung high in the sky. He'd slept no more than a few hours. Amazing, the effects of a few milliliters of *neutralized* dragon's blood.

Telling that his Russian captor had deliberately chosen to torment Luke by skipping such a small—yet critical—step. He hadn't the slightest regret about killing Dimitri Kravchuk, not after all the tortures the man had inflicted upon him in the name of science.

Two years ago, deep lines of disapproval had carved themselves into the face of Luke's supervisor when he pointed out that British-Russian tensions were unlikely to resolve anytime soon and proposed to make the journey on his own, without any reliance upon or support from the department. Nonetheless, he'd been granted six months' leave, a small stack of untraceable bank notes, and a stern warning that the department would disavow any involvement.

Traveling up the Kama river to Perm, climbing into the Ural Mountains, Luke had entertained dreams of greatness. Of praise and accolades for his accomplishments in the field of cryptozoology by safeguarding the future of a rare species of Mountain Dragon. While he'd found numerous caves displaying evidence of prior habitation, locating an active lair had taken far, far longer than he'd hoped. And he hadn't been the only one looking.

All hope of a bright future had died the day the Russians captured him. Turned into a laboratory rat, the damage done to his liver by that vicious pathogen was irreparable. Whatever resurrection of good health this final treatment of dragon's blood had brought him, it wouldn't last. But he'd make the best of it while he could.

Both in and out of Natalia's bed. An opportunity for which he'd never dared hope.

Smiling, Luke threw back the covers and swung his stocking-clad feet over the edge of the bed. He pulled on his boots. A glance in a mirror revealed that the whites of his eyes were a most disturbing yellow. And he smelled. *That* he could fix. He rubbed a hand across the rough stubble of his beard. The judicious application of a razor wouldn't be amiss either.

Ignoring the ewer of water on a nearby table, he grabbed his rucksack, snagged a sword for himself and made his way to his old bedchamber above the kitchens. All was as he'd left it. He pulled a skeet pigeon from his trunk, dashed off a brief note explaining the situation and requesting immediate assistance from the department. After winding the mechanism, he tossed the mechanical bird from the window, praying it would reach Edinburgh and his supervisor without delay.

Luke grabbed clean clothes, a linen towel and located his razor. Passing through the kitchens, he snagged the extra key to the postern door and headed out. In the courtyard, Natalia trained a young man, making the adolescent work for every touch he won. He hesitated. Perhaps he shouldn't leave them here alone? No. He shook his head. There wasn't the slightest chance the hunter had recovered yet from his venom-laced claw wounds. He'd be lucky if those medieval arrows didn't cause sepsis. Regardless, Luke would wash quickly.

He slipped out the postern door, locking it behind him, and made his way down a path to the river's edge. Assuring himself there was no audience, he set down his rucksack and stripped bare. He tossed his clothes across the hull of an overturned boat that sat on the riverbank, half-consumed by weeds, then waded in, quickly applying soap and razor before making his way onto the shore to dress.

As Luke climbed back toward the castle rubbing the towel over his hair, the unmistakable sound of lovemaking met his ears. He must have veered down a different fork of the path.

There was a gasp of horror, and he yanked away the cloth, turning, attempting to cast his gaze down—anywhere but at the two lovers. Alas, he failed.

Aileen half-sat upon a moss-covered wall of a rubble-strewn ruin with her skirts hiked up about her waist. A man, his arms wrapped about her, his trousers undone and shoved low about his hips, lifted his mouth from her neck. Both faces flushed with interrupted lust and embarrassment.

"Sorry. So, so sorry." And he was, very much so. Not once

had he ever wished to gaze upon Aileen's bare bosom. Jaw slack, he began to turn away—except the man's face was familiar.

A scene flashed to mind. Luke upon his knees while guards surrounded him, each pointing a loaded musket at his chest. Their captain striding over the cave's rocky ledge, barking questions in Russian that he hadn't understood. A strike to the side of his head that had split his lip and dropped him to the ground. Rough manacles biting into his wrists as he was dragged away. A key turning in a lock, imprisoning him in the Ural Zavód. *This* was the man who had stolen his freedom.

"You!" Luke tossed aside his rucksack and drew the sword slung upon his hip, retreating as fast as the uneven and root-tangled ground allowed. But a single infusion of dragon's blood could not undo all the damage of those endless months locked inside the Ural Zavód. He was at a decided disadvantage.

Misha Ivanov—Aileen's lover—also drew a blade. A shorter, curved knife. He lashed out. Only the man's need to pull up his trousers kept his knife from slicing through Luke's throat.

"Michael!" Aileen called, yanking her bodice back into place and flapping at her rucked skirts. "Stop! He's... a friend."

Ivanov ignored her, crouching low as he circled around Luke, looking for an opportunity to strike. And found it. He lunged, slashing his blade at Luke's stomach.

Luke deflected the attack with his sword. *Clang.* Reverberations jolted up his arm, jarring his shoulder and nearly making him lose his grip. This would end badly. Ivanov's skills might not be on par with Natalia's, but this former soldier was also stronger, murderous, and completely devoid of empathy.

Again, Ivanov rushed toward him. This time, luck wasn't on Luke's side. He blocked the worst of the strike, but the tip of the curved blade sliced through his shirt, through the skin of his left bicep. A sharp tear of pain. Blood, warm and sticky, soaked his sleeve.

He stumbled. The next slash came hard upon the last. There

was no chance he could win this fight. No chance he'd survive to warn Natalia that Rathail's hunter wasn't the only threat. The Russians had ferreted out their location.

His face an emotionless mask, Ivanov swung his blade down toward Luke's shoulder. A teeth-rattling screech rent the air as their blades slid past each other and caught at the hilts. Arm shaking, Luke struggled to hold off the Russian. With every last ounce of his strength, he shoved the man backward.

A fleeting victory. Ivanov's lip curled, and he lunged forward. Luke leapt backward, but his foot caught upon a tree root and he fell. Exposed.

"Michael!" Aileen ran forward, stumbling to a halt before her lover, her arms spread wide. "Please. Luke won't," she blushed a furious crimson, "say anything about... about what we were doing. Not to my grandfather or anyone else." She glanced over her shoulder. "Will you?"

Sad, that he'd been reduced to hiding behind a woman's skirts, grateful for her defense. He and Ivanov had crossed blades but three times and his chest heaved with the effort. Had he refused the dragon's blood, he'd already be a corpse upon the path. He clapped a palm over the gash in his arm. The cut was deep enough to require stitches.

"Of course not." Luke himself would do his best to wipe the vision of the Russian mixing work with pleasure from his memory. His concerns lay elsewhere. If Ivanov had been in the village long enough to seduce Aileen, then he wanted more from Natalia than her dragon.

*Shit.*

Ivanov lowered his arm. "You are certain?" *Almost a convincing Scottish accent.* A man who could blend into his environment so well was more than a mere guard.

"Go," Aileen said. She stepped closer and kissed her beau on the cheek.

His free hand fell upon her hip, and he pulled her close,

whispering into her ear, all while keeping a close eye on Luke. Her face paled, but she nodded. Ivanov slid something from his pocket and pressed it into her hand. She swallowed, then tucked the item into a small pouch tied at her waist.

Releasing her, Ivanov slid his knife back into its sheath and stalked over to Luke's rucksack. He opened it and proceeded to examine each item within as if it might be a direct threat to his lady love. But there was only one item inside that held any value to Luke. And, damn him, Ivanov found it. With a nasty grin stretching across his face, the Russian pulled out the paper packet of milk thistle seed, flicked open its paper flap, and dumped the contents onto the ground.

Luke cursed, but dared not raise further objection.

"Nothing." Dropping the rucksack to the ground, Ivanov looked to Aileen—his inside woman—and nodded. "You will let me know if he causes you any trouble?"

"Immediately."

With a brief kiss to her lips, the Russian took his leave, disappearing around the bend. He stalked off into the forest, headed who knew where. Worry twisted Luke's stomach. Two men in this corner of Scotland with an interest in dragons was two men too many. Without assistance, escaping the castle unnoticed would be difficult if not impossible.

Aileen stooped to stuff Luke's possessions back into his bag. "I'm sorry. My fiancé is fiercely protective. You rather took us by surprise." Her face was bright red, and she didn't meet his eyes.

He stood, slowly and painfully sheathing his sword. Imagining Ivanov as protective of anyone but himself made him shake his head. "Fiancé?" he repeated. He tore a strip of cloth from the hem of his shirt, cringing as he bound the bleeding gash. A makeshift bandage until he could locate a needle and thread.

"Grandfather will warm to him," she said, catching Luke by his elbow and leading him along the path. "Soon, when Michael concludes his negotiations to invest in the textile mill upriver, we will marry."

Luke glanced at Aileen. Her chin was lifted and her shoulders pulled back. Proud and working hard to convince herself such an event would come to pass. Determined enough that she'd let Ivanov—*er*—lift her skirts in the woods, an unwise risk. He should warn her—would warn her—*after* he'd spoken with Natalia. For now, he would watch his words around the young woman.

---

"HOLD IT HIGHER," Natalia instructed William, expecting she might regret teaching him this maneuver. Though she'd given their practice session her all, he'd bested her twice today already. Not only had he grown three inches this past winter, his body had begun to take on the hard, angular planes of manhood. "Turn your wrist a touch to the right. Yes, like that. Now thrust the blade toward your enemy's bowels."

"Like this?" William lunged at the straw figure set up inside the courtyard.

"Exactly like that." There wasn't much more she could teach him. Regret tinged her smile. She was proud of her student but needed to terminate their lessons. Not only did Luke's arrival mean she needed to plan for their departure, it had drastically altered her plans for today's laboratory work.

Her last set of experiments had indicated that she was close to synthesizing a modified version of dragon's venom, but something about the structure was wrong, possibly the isomerism. But she'd come closer to unlocking its exact composition than she'd ever managed in Russia when her supervisors had rolled their eyes at her efforts—heart disease, why work to treat the useless elderly?—but tolerated her because of her father, whose brilliance was much prized.

Luke's health came first, and he had no need of a drug to lower his blood pressure. So instead of refining dragon's venom—a purification process useful both for her research and for coating the tips of arrows—she needed to assess, then rearrange and adapt her equipment to suit a cell biology project.

"That's enough for today," she said.

Would her father be proud of her, or horrified that she'd held back his breakthrough from the scientific world? She tugged at her scarf, wishing she could unwind it and toss it away. Too long she'd been hiding, protecting secrets inside thick stone walls. Her life in Castle Kinlarig was a lonely one. Luke's renewed presence had served to underscore that fact. And though she did not wish to return to Russia, she missed interacting with like-minded scientists. Here—in a quiet corner of Scotland—she was cut off from all news of innovations in her field, from all academic conversations that might inform her own work.

Not that she wished to abandon Zia, but with assistance, with someone else to oversee the dragon, she would be free to travel to Edinburgh, to rejoin the research world and learn what advancements had been made while she was hidden away. She longed to take on another project—one not tied to dragons—so she might discuss her work and publish her findings.

Shoulders slumping, William held the rapier out—hilt first—to her.

Reflexively, Natalia reached for it. Then stopped. "Keep it."

"Truly?"

"Truly." With a nod, she continued. "You're ready. That fencing studio you wish to open in Edinburgh? If your uncle was serious about allowing you to work for him, to set up a studio in the back of his warehouse, it's time. You've my permission to take a selection of weapons and armor from the great hall."

William's grin nearly split his face in two, but his excitement was quickly followed by suspicion. "Why?" His eyes narrowed. "Are you leaving? Did something happen to your dragon?"

A few villagers had guessed the truth. Mostly children as they were the ones able to set aside disbelief. She'd caught a few prowling the castle grounds, hoping for a glimpse, but William had taken it one step further. He'd pestered McKay—a great uncle of sorts—to allow him to work within the castle walls from time to time, assisting with all the odd jobs that required more strength than the butler had left to him.

Natalia wagged a finger back and forth. "You know nothing about such a creature. Hush." Only a promise of lessons in swordsmanship had convinced William to stop pestering her with questions about dragons... and to discourage other young visitors. "There's a man in the village who wishes to capture her. I cannot let that happen, and so I must leave to take her elsewhere."

"But you promised I could meet her someday." His voice held a hint of a boyish whine. "And if you're leaving..."

So she had. "Let me see what I can arrange."

As per her agreement with the Department of Cryptozoology, she kept Zia carefully hidden away in the laboratory whenever William—a non-resident—was inside the castle's walls. But they'd terminated her funding, so perhaps such strict secrecy was no longer binding. After all, William had made himself as essential as McKay and Aileen.

"About that man," William began, his voice eager. "The one you shot an arrow through, he might have an assistant now. There's a new hunter in town. I can follow him to the pub tonight, find out why he's here."

*An assistant?* The tiny hairs on the back of her neck rose. "No. Stay away. Far away."

"I'll only listen..."

"I'd rather you not become tangled in whatever—" The postern door opened and Luke and Aileen entered. She'd seen them both leave, but individually. Her eyebrows drew together. Both looked rumpled and— Luke was bleeding. Her heart leapt into her throat, and she had to choke back a cry of distress as she rushed in their direction. William followed behind her. "What happened?"

Luke glanced at the young man and frowned. "A small disagreement with Aileen's fiancé." He pressed his lips together and gave a small shake of his head.

Aileen's mouth flattened. "He was defending my honor."

"William," Natalia said. "Time to go. Be certain McKay locks the castle gate behind you."

"Aww," William objected, but he turned and did as his fencing master bid him, proudly carrying away his weapon.

Wrinkling her nose against the noxious odor of the thin, watery soup—cabbage with parsnips this time—simmering upon the surface of the stove, Natalia set a tea kettle to boil. "Have we any whisky?"

"Some." Aileen placed a sewing kit upon the table, dropped a rag beside it, then—twisting her lips in disapproval—fetched the bottle. "But from the look of his eyes, Mr. Dryden's liver is pickled enough." She crossed her arms and frowned. "What is it with all the swords? Have none of you ever fired a pistol?"

"The antique weapons in Castle Kinlarig were collected for display," Natalia answered. "No one thought to stock gunpowder or the appropriate bullets. Items hard to justify on a restricted budget. Not to mention the alarming possibility of a misfire. Such old weapons are unreliable."

"Swords still function when they're wet, and one needn't stop to reload," Luke added, grimacing as he rolled his sleeve above his wound. "And mine was taken from me..." He lifted his gaze to Natalia's.

*In the Ural Mountains.* She didn't need him to say it aloud.

Pouring the last of the whisky into a glass, she dropped the needle and thread into the alcohol before blotting Luke's arm. The wound wasn't too deep and, despite the mud on his trousers, he smelled clean and fresh, like clear river water. A vast improvement. She slid her gaze sideways. Aileen, other the other hand... "Care to explain what happened?"

Aileen's bodice gaped and strands of hair floated loose from her coiffure. Color rose high upon her cheeks. "Michael was taken by surprise and overreacted. Nothing to fret about. Mr. Dryden will be fine."

A gross understatement, given he required stitches. Luke's immune system was already compromised. An infected wound was the last thing he needed. But she bit back the comment. "Did Michael at least agree to call the banns?"

Shifting on her feet, Aileen looked away. "We were about to discuss that when—" She shoved a handful of cloth strips into Natalia's palm. "You have this under control. I need to..." Hand flapping, she fled the kitchens. Natalia laughed. "Did you catch them—"

"I did." Luke pulled a face. "Horrifying enough, but we have another problem." He craned his neck to be certain Aileen was out of earshot. "Her fiancé's name isn't Michael, it's Misha. Misha Ivanov."

# CHAPTER SIX

SHE GLANCED UP SHARPLY. "Misha Ivanov. A Russian." Her heart began to pound. *They'd found her.*

Two years ago she would have questioned the presence of any man who wandered so freely about the edges of her property. But when Aileen mentioned he was in the wool industry and negotiating to purchase cloth produced at the mill upstream, Natalia had dismissed him without another thought. Stupid of her.

"You're being watched," Luke said. "Closely. Do you know him?"

Natalia shook her head. "No. We've not met. Nor is the name familiar." Though her insides had turned to jelly, the cut in his arm required her immediate attention. She took a deep breath and pinched the two halves together. "How—exactly—do *you* know him?" She braced herself for the answer.

"He was the man who caught me, a guard from the Ural Zavód." Luke hissed as the sharp steel bit through his skin, but he didn't move. "No, more than a guard, though I'm not certain what to call him. Agent? Spy?"

"No mention of me or Zia?" She slid the needle through his

skin. A second stitch. It steadied her nerves to count them.

"None." His teeth gritted against the pain, and he fell silent.

Luke had taken pains to cover his tracks and would worry he'd led the man to her gate. On that count she could reassure him. "Michael—Misha Ivanov—arrived in town a few months ago, perhaps a week or two before Lord Kinross's death. He can't have learned about my presence from you."

"Thank aether."

Three. Four. It was done. She tied a knot. Blotted the wound once more, then wrapped a strip of cloth about his bare arm. Only then did she allow her mind to churn. Rathail's hunter and now a Russian spy. First one, then the other. She voiced her suspicion aloud. "If Rathail made it known that he would soon come into possession of a Russian Mountain Dragon…"

"Word might have reached Russian ears." Luke swore. She agreed with every profane word that fell from his lips. "Easy enough to send an agent to investigate," he continued, "to dally with the castle's pretty, young housekeeper."

With the recent financial difficulties and Lord Kinross's death, Natalia could well understand Aileen's hopes for marriage. Who wouldn't want to flee? "She was an easy target."

"Ivanov's Scottish brogue is very convincing," Luke agreed.

She frowned. In two months' time, Ivanov had made no move against Zia. Or her. Or even Rathail's man. Had Luke not stumbled across him in the woods, his presence would have remained undiscovered. What could he possibly—

"Come." She turned on her heel and strode though the great hall to her laboratory. Zia's head lifted, her golden eyes tracking her movement as Natalia rushed across the room to yank open a drawer. Safe. Papa's notes were safe. Only then did she realize she was shaking. She'd not bothered to secure them. No one here knew about the experiment, and they were written in Cyrillic. But a Russian now lurked outside her castle, quietly insinuating himself into Aileen's life. A dragon and a person might not be easily transported, but a handful of research notes? Easily pilfered by a lovestruck housekeeper.

That explained Aileen's tremulous overtures. She was terrified of Zia, especially after Lord Kinross's grisly death, and for the past six weeks, the dragon had rarely left the laboratory. Ivanov had convinced Aileen—against every instinct—to befriend the dragon that guarded the secrets he wished to steal. Or perhaps just to copy. Why go through the effort of dragging home two fugitives if the science was unsound? She wasn't safe, not even inside her own home, not when Aileen could be so easily seduced.

"Natalia?" Luke's voice was soft, concerned. "Is something wrong?"

"No, but I—" She turned, about to share her revelation, but lost her voice. Luke had closed the door to the laboratory and unbuttoned the collar of his shirt. She stared at the hollow of his bare throat. How much time did they have left to them? Alone? With a bedchamber only a flight of stairs away? "It's nothing."

It wasn't. But it could wait a little bit longer. A few inches deeper, and his wound would have been far, far more serious. She watched, her mouth dry, as the two halves of his shirt fell apart, while he peeled the ruined garment from his torso and tossed it upon the flames of the fire burning steadily in the grate.

Kinross, for all his superior breeding, hadn't been a gentleman at all. While not cruel, he'd cared not a whit for her pleasure, only his, and what it bought him. Her first time with a man had been a disappointment.

It had, however, been enlightening. Luke—she was absolutely certain—wouldn't leave her bed before she was well and truly satisfied.

"Natalia?" Heat crept into his voice.

"Mmm." She licked her lips, unable to tear her gaze away

from his bare chest where, despite his illness, muscles still rippled as he prowled across the room to stand before her. His trousers hung low upon his hips, a sheathed sword still strapped to his belt.

"You're staring as if you've never seen a man's chest before." A corner of his mouth twitched upward, and his dark eyes flashed.

She hadn't. Not really. Removal of clothing wasn't necessary to consummate a marriage. But this was about pleasure, about their mutual desire, and she wanted to *see* him.

"An entire year, fencing a hot, sweaty man, and not once did he ever remove his shirt." She ran an experimental fingertip over the curve of his clavicle, and he stepped closer.

"You were married." He brushed his lips across hers.

A shiver of longing ran across her skin, humming as it dove deeper and sparked every nerve ending to life. Her breath came quicker. "No longer an obstacle. But your wounded arm might be."

"It's fine." Another kiss, this time to the corner of her mouth, then to the edge of her jaw. Soft and teasing. "Besides, I've waited years to touch you." Broad hands landed upon her hips, pulling her snug against his obvious desire. "There's no reason we need wait for darkness to fall, not when I want to explore every inch of your skin. Slowly."

*Every inch.* She swallowed and pushed at his chest. Something fluttered low in her stomach. It was time, time to uncover her secret. "Wait."

He tensed. But he stepped back, his eyes questioning. "I thought—"

"Correctly." Rising onto her toes, she pressed a kiss to his lips. "But there's something you need to see first. Come." She lifted her father's notebook from the drawer then, without meeting his gaze, climbed the stairs to her bedchamber and dropped the yellowed pages upon the table. She closed her eyes for a brief moment and took a deep breath, praying he wouldn't recoil in horror.

She turned about to find Luke waiting patiently, despite his frown and the questions written across his face. He lifted an eyebrow as she untied the knot of her scarf.

"I don't wear it to honor tradition." Taking a deep breath, she pulled it from her neck and turned away, exposing her nape, allowing him to gaze upon the strange scales that grew from her skin. Shaking, she awaited judgment. This was a moment of truth. Would he be repulsed?

"Aether," he breathed. "How? Why?"

She glanced over her shoulder but saw nothing except curiosity and awe. "The real reason I had to flee Russia." How to sum up such a defining moment in a few succinct words? "I fell from the cliffs—dragon egg hunting—and broke my neck."

"Broke?"

"I never would have walked again, save my father refused to let me die. When one of the eggs hatched, he broke every rule and took an enormous risk, collecting and transplanting cells he isolated from the extraembryonic membranes that remained behind inside the dragon's eggshell. Stem cells, he called them, undifferentiated cells capable of becoming, repairing... anything."

"And it worked." Luke let out a low whistle as he moved closer. "Impressive. May I touch?"

She nodded, relieved he didn't consider them an aberration of nature.

The rough pad of his finger skimmed across a scale, sending a shiver down her spine. "You can feel that?"

"Yes. They're a part of my skin, a part of me." She held her breath, waiting. "Most of them are clustered about the lower cervical vertebrae—where the grafting took place—but dragon stem cells possess a migratory inclination..."

"There are more?" His warm lips pressed against the scattering of scales at her nape, sending a rush of heat through her entire body. "Might I resume explorations?"

Still worried, she half-turned in his arms, studying his face. "If you're certain you wish to continue."

A low laugh escaped him, his breath hot on her neck. "Never doubt it, Natalia." His fingers released one of the clasps that held her corset closed. "I'll have questions later." Another fell open. And another. "Many." The leather parted, hanging from its narrow straps at her shoulders. "But for now, my only goal is to make you pant my name while you—"

"Luke," she whispered as he flicked open the button of her waistband and tugged her chemise free. His palm skimmed upward over the soft curve of her stomach, her ribs, until he cupped the weight of her breast.

"It's a start," he murmured against her neck, then nipped at her skin. "But I'm aiming for a much louder cry." He raised both arms at once, pulling off her chemise and corset vest in one smooth motion. His fingers trailed down her vertebrae, one by one, following the path of the dragon scales. "So beautiful, my dragon lady."

*Beautiful?*

With a soft laugh, she turned to face him and began to toy with the buttons that held the fall of his trousers closed. "You find them… attractive?"

"Incredibly." His voice was low and rough. "They're a part of you."

She loved him so much, had missed him so much. "When you didn't return—"

"You were in my thoughts every single day." He caught her lips for a long, slow kiss. "Never daring to hope you would ever be free." His fingers stabbed into her hair, into the braided twist wrapped about her crown. "That you could ever be mine."

"Not free, perhaps," she whispered. "But yours ever since you first lifted a blade against me."

With a low rumble of a laugh, he brought his mouth down. Their next kiss was hard, possessive, a tangle of tongues as they claimed each other.

Slowly, step by step, he walked backward. Until he bumped into the base of her bed. Large, soft and canopied. But there would be no drawing the curtains closed.

He moved away, pulling off boots, stockings, trousers while she did the same. She stared, taking in the magnificent length of his member as it sprang free, dark curls at its root. Reaching, she cupped the sac that hung beneath. With a low growl, his arms were around her, tumbling her onto the mattress, naked, as they gave themselves over to hunger and need. The peaked tips of her breasts brushed the crisp hairs of his chest as she shoved her fingers into this thick hair and kissed him with all the passion she'd locked away for over three years. The press of his hard length against her soft thigh left her breathless and wanting oh so much more.

She slid her hands down his back, admiring the tight muscles that flexed beneath his firm skin—until she grasped his buttocks. Spreading her legs, she dug her nails into their flesh and yanked him closer.

The low groan from the back of his throat let her know he approved of her touch. And yet he pulled away, trailing kisses down her body, his lips sucking at the tips of her breasts, teeth nipping at their tips before nibbling lower, ever closer to that pulsing, aching center between her thighs. He spread her legs wider.

"Luke!" she cried, when he parted her folds, taking her in his mouth, his tongue stroking her small sensitive nub as his hands slid up and down her thighs.

So close. So close, and yet she wanted—needed—more. She pushed at his shoulders, tugging at his hair until he lifted his face, his eyes glassy. "Luke, please. I want you in me. Now."

He crawled up her body, his eyes hungry, and braced his

heavy weight on his elbows. She wound her arms around him and pulled him to her, closing her eyes to commit the feel of his body to memory. He notched his cock against her wet opening and she slid her legs upward about him, wrapping them about his hips. A hot, thick pressure pushed into her. Slowly, easing into her channel, deeper and deeper still. Stretching her.

She looked up into his eyes and saw tightly wound control, self-restraint balanced on a knife's edge. He was giving her body time to adjust, treating her as if she were fragile. But it only made the need build, made her want more. She flexed her hips, and he moved deeper inside of her. Such exquisite fullness.

Then he cupped her face, took her lips with his and began to move inside her. Gently at first, then thrusting harder, faster. Spirals of pleasure circled around and through her body, their coils tightening. Gasping, she tore her mouth away to focus on the need gathering where they joined, where friction built to glorious heights as he drove into her again and again.

With a sudden flash, fire ignited, racing across her skin, sending her entire body into an exquisite convulsion. "Luke!" Spasms tore through her as she ground her core against him, dragging forth every last ounce of pleasure of her climax.

Poised above her, the muscles of Luke's neck and arms strained as he drove into her chasing his own release. Beautiful and all hers. With a roar, he thrust deeply, once, twice, then pulled free, spending himself—hot and wet—upon her belly.

---

SATED, relaxed and happy, Luke lay beside her, relieved he'd had the presence of mind to withdraw. Taking her to bed had been everything he'd ever dared hope for. But still he wanted more, wanted her for himself, this amazing woman. He never wanted to let her go. But his would be a short forever. She deserved a chance to change her mind, to leave—unencumbered

—should his condition become too much to bear. Already, the cut to his arm ached more than it ought, a reminder that this lifespan would be short.

He'd followed Natalia up the curving stairs, distracted by the alluring sway of her hips, without the vaguest notion of what she was about to reveal. Dragon scales. A side effect of a miraculous treatment. She'd broken her neck, but lived, even walked again, her health completely restored. Already he'd been breathless with anticipation, but to find she hid yet more wonders had stolen away his last breath.

"Twenty-one months and twenty-three days," Natalia whispered.

No accusation surfaced in her voice, rather a wistfulness, reminding them of all the time they'd lost. He pulled her against his side and pressed a kiss to her hair. "I should have told you, even though you would have threatened to run me through." He'd been so naïve, so confident as he left on his quest. "I wanted to take advantage of the summer months. To fetch a dragon, then return with my prize for the lady of the castle." For the woman he loved but could never have, not completely.

"But the Department of Cryptozoology turned you down." Natalia frowned. "As they should have."

"They did." He cringed at the memory. "Repeatedly. But I kept pleading the case for establishing a dragon sanctuary on British soil and, eventually, my supervisor agreed to let me go. An unofficial and deniable one-man expedition into Russia." He'd left immediately. A boat to St. Petersburg. A train—via Moscow—to Perm. From there hiking into the mountains.

His mind drifted back to the raw beauty of the pine-covered mountains, to the quaint villages tucked in their valleys. Carrying his gear upon his back, he'd slept in the wilderness, enjoying the solitude, the freedom, traveling by foot into the peaks of the Urals.

"I found a cave. A mother with two dragonets scampering about her feet. Young, but too old to easily transport to Scotland." Quietly, carefully, he'd backed away from the cave. "Armed men swooped in. Too many to fight." He closed his eyes. "They killed the mother, penned the dragonets. Perhaps I should be grateful I was not killed as well."

He opened his eyes to find her above him, her blue eyes bright with passion. "I, for one, am grateful that you were not."

During his captivity, he'd often lost hope and simply wished for it all to end. "But for thoughts of you, I might have given up. I was no better than a laboratory rat." He brushed a hand over the surface of her braid. She claimed it kept her hair up and out of the way, but Luke thought of it as her golden, shimmering crown. He'd not yet had the pleasure of uncoiling, unbraiding its twists. Imagining the glory of such hair spread across her shoulders as she rode atop him made his groin stir with approval.

"Go on." Captivated by his story, she searched his eyes for more.

Doing his best to ignore the soft press of her bare breasts against his chest, he continued. "After they decided I knew nothing of interest, I was injected with an unknown pathogen, thrown in solitary confinement, and left to endure the fevers that followed. From time to time, they would drag me into the infirmary and I would catch glimpses of the two dragonets in cages, miserable and defeated, their blood used for a scattering of 'treatments' that did little to improve my condition. I lost track of time."

A tear ran down her cheek. "Finish," she whispered.

"There's not much more to tell." He offered her a faint smile. Delirious with fevers half the time, much of the time had been a painful blur. "My Russian improved. A little. Enough to understand that this past winter a spy was captured in Germany. Secrets had been spilled, and an entire research facility north of

Moscow had to be shut down. As a precaution, all biotechnological research was being relocated." Her eyes widened for she had worked within the extensive network of corridors and rooms that comprised the Ural Zavód. "In the chaos an opportunity presented itself. I left a man for dead. And escaped with a dragon."

"Dimitri Kravchuk," she said, her voice flat. "Good."

"You were to marry him." Luke seethed at the thought. What had the man done?

"I was young and foolish." Her face contorted as she rolled away to sit upon the edge of the mattress. "Not once did he visit me after the… accident. Not so much as to hold my hand while the village doctor informed my father there was nothing to do but measure his daughter for a coffin."

Letting out a low hiss from between his teeth, Luke pushed himself upright and wrapped his arms about her, glad he'd ended the man's life.

She turned her teary-eyed face toward him. "Any love he professed was a lie. Or secondary to his desire for advancement. My father broke the rules to save me, and Dimitri reported him. The treatment had worked, and we had to flee. Lest he end in prison, and me under a microscope."

Much as Luke had. "Dimitri, did you love him?"

"No." She shook her head. "My father wished for me to marry his protégé. There was no one who had captured my heart, so I agreed." A tear slid down her cheek. "But for his actions, my father would still be alive."

They sat—silent—for a long moment, taking comfort in each other's arms. Luke silently vowed that neither of them would ever fall into Russian hands. Not them, not Zia or her eggs, and certainly not her father's notations.

"Notations," he said aloud, his gaze lifting to the table across the room. "The laboratory notebook."

She swallowed and nodded. "And dragon eggs about to

hatch. If I follow his protocol, collect the stem cells from the membranes inside their shells, there's a chance I can cure you. Permanently. There are certain risks, but..." Her eyes pled with him to let her try.

"A cure?" He all but forgot to breathe. He'd accept almost any risk for a permanent cure.

"It means we can't leave the castle, can't head for the Trossachs." She pressed a hand to his chest. "Not yet. Everything I need is here."

She slid from the bed and pulled her chemise over her head to guard against the cold of the bedchamber where no fire burned. But its neckline gaped, revealing the sexy scattering of scales at her nape, and its hem skimmed the back of her thighs, below the curve of her arse. One glimpse of her backside, and the wanting—the need—began again.

Already half-hard, he climbed from the bed and dragged on his trousers before crossing the room to peer over her shoulder at the old notebook—thin for such an important treatise—filled with brittle, yellowed pages and words inked in Cyrillic. Luke knew only a smattering of Russian, picked up by listening to what little conversation filtered down the hallway. He couldn't read a single word.

"All of Papa's work, everything he accomplished in that one-week time span beginning the night Zia emerged from her egg, is here." She tapped on the notebook. "I've kept Papa's secret— my secret—because I cannot be certain it will not end up in the wrong hands."

"And cause an extinction by sending an army of unscrupulous men into the Ural Mountains hunting for dragon eggs." And it would, if this miracle she promised was truly possible. "A week." He shoved his fingers into his wild hair. "Maybe two. That's a lot of time to wait." He'd hoped to leave Castle Kinlarig much, much sooner. "Waiting, with Ivanov and Rathail's hunter circling, seems unwise."

"But we should stay." She dropped the notebook and began to pace, her face flushed with excitement. "With you restored to health, we can travel at will. An opportunity like this might never happen again. When Zia's eggs hatch, I will have an abundance of material. But I can only collect the stem cells, I can't culture them. I've not the proper equipment—an incubator—or growth media to allow them time to replicate. I'll collect those I can. Inject them all."

"Into my liver." He lifted his eyebrows, curious. "To divide and grow inside me?" He'd endured worse. If this was the path to a cure, he'd follow it.

"It's the only way." She ran her fingers over the back of her neck, tracing a fingertip over the edge of a scale. "There will be side effects as they engraft." She looked at him. "Unpredictable side effects. And you'll need to take a few doses of a horrid drug to prevent xenograft rejection. But dragon cells divide quickly and integrate thoroughly. They'll replace damaged tissue, restore connective tissue, and commingle with existing cells. You will be healed."

"Healed." Was it possible? He hardly dared hope.

"Dragon stem cells defy explanation. Did you notice how quickly Zia recovered from the Voltaic prod burn?"

True. As they'd passed the dragon while she guarded her clutch, there'd been no sign of the charred scales. Instead, the spot bore new scales, ones that were a slightly lighter shade than those that surrounded them. He whistled. "A matter of hours." His skin tingled. Would he grow his own scales? He rather hoped he would.

"It's why I've not handed over Papa's notes to the Department of Cryptozoology. He knew the British would be unable to turn him away, not with such knowledge—and two dragons—in his possession. But..." Her voice trailed off as a distant look passed across her face.

"He was killed..."

A quick nod. "I decided to withhold such knowledge until I'd thoroughly evaluated my new employer. When they handed me a useless husband, paltry funds, and a cold, damp castle, I decided I did not wish to place the power of dragon stem cells in the hands of a government, any government." She shrugged. "Besides, without a male, without dragon eggs, the entire project was an impossibility."

"And now?"

"I find myself breaking my own rules to save a man." She pressed a soft kiss to his lips. "This will, of course, go to your head."

It rather did.

He wanted this. He did. So badly it hurt. "Safer to leave," he said, meeting her gaze. For her, he was willing to delay—even forgo—the treatment. "For you, Zia and her brood. If we can reach the Trossachs, there will be future opportunities." *If.* He wasn't at all certain he was capable of helping her fend off an attack, especially on the move.

"Healed!" Natalia poked a finger into his chest to emphasize her point. "Permanently. No more need of milk thistle tea or dragon's blood. *That* is worth the risk. It's worth every risk." She wrapped her arms about his waist and tipped her face upward. "If not for yourself, consider my own selfish wishes to keep you with me, in my life and in my bed, for years to come."

Warmth spread over his heart. "If that is what you want."

"It is."

A low, soft hiss slithered up the stairways. A yelp and a thud. Then a sharp cry.

Natalia snatched up her sword and took off down the curving, stone stairs.

"Wait!" Luke called, following. Too late. He caught a glimpse of her white cotton chemise as she leapt into her laboratory, sword at the ready.

"LADY KINLARIG," Aileen cried, terrified. "Call her off."

Luke rounded the last of the stairs to find the dragon hissing, her teeth bared and her tongue flicking as she took slow steps toward the woman. Her leathery wings extended, readying for an attack.

"Zia, no," Natalia ordered, her voice firm, but she still gripped her weapon. "Come."

With great reluctance, the dragon stilled, then folded her wings and turned away, stalking back to stand beside the fireplace, her body tense and on alert. Defending her brood.

He prayed Aileen knew nothing about the dragon eggs. Luke moved to stand beside Natalia. Silent, but holding his own blade.

"What brings you to my laboratory, Aileen?" Suspicion threaded its way through Natalia's voice, and with good reason. It was a well-known fact that Aileen disliked Zia and avoided her at all costs. Except, now there was the question of her Russian lover.

"Might it have anything to do with this?" Luke bent,

scooping a yellow lump from the floor and holding it aloft. "Sulfur. A bribe for the dragon. Is this what your fiancé handed you when he whispered in your ear? What, exactly, does he want you to locate?"

Aileen lifted her chin. "I've no idea where that came from." She flapped her hand at a tray upon the laboratory workbench, shifting toward the door. "You left the tea kettle boiling, so I…" Her gaze flicked between Natalia and Luke, only just realizing how very little they wore. A furious red blush stained her cheeks. And then her gaze fell upon Natalia's bare neck.

Natalia slapped her palm over the few scales that crept from the edge of her neck onto her shoulder.

"I'll go now." Aileen bolted from the room.

Luke stalked behind Aileen, shoving the heavy wooden door closed. Turning, he leaned against it. The throbbing in his arm wasn't lessening. "That rather confirms it. Ivanov is after your father's notes."

"And finally convinced her to ferret them out. I'll keep them close from now on." Natalia pushed shut a drawer that was cracked open, then turned her attention to the tea set that rested upon her workbench. "Not once has Aileen ever brought me tea. How could she possibly think we wouldn't find her behavior suspicious? Yet we've barely eaten today." She poured a cup of tea, sniffed it, then took a sip. "It's fine. No point in poisoning us before she's found what she's after."

He closed the distance between them, taking a warm potato scone folded in a napkin from her hands, his mind on anything but food. The cotton of her chemise hung loosely over the peaked tips of her breasts, a seductive reminder of recent activities. He shifted, half-aroused, tempted to ignore their situation a few more hours, to lead her back to bed, to bury himself deep inside her once more.

With a smile that invited him to do exactly that, she rose up onto her toes and pressed a soft kiss to his lips, leaving him breathless with desire.

*Thunk.*

The sound came from the direction of the fireplace. Both of them turned to stare at Zia, who had plucked an egg from her nest and dropped it upon the floor. The dragon lifted her head, blinked her golden eyes once, then turned her attention back to her brood, nudging aside rocks and other treasure pieces, gently taking each egg in her mouth before rotating it into a new position. Satisfied, she lowered herself onto her belly beside them, then cocked her head slightly as if daring them to comment on her actions.

*Dammit.* So much for sex.

Frowning, Natalia set aside her tea cup to lift the solitary, gold-streaked egg from the cold, flagstone floor. "It's still warm. And the shell is intact." She crouched beside Zia, then pushed aside stones and treasures to tuck the rejected egg deep into the dragon's hoard beside the others. "Why would she do that?"

A frisson of worry skittered down his spine. "It's thought dragons will push non-viable eggs from their nests."

Natalia added more coal to the fire burning in the grate, as if more heat might convince Zia to keep all her eggs. "You think something is wrong with that particular egg?" She stroked Zia's head. Instead of relaxing into the attention, the dragon remained alert.

"Possibly. Time will tell." He could hear the strain in his voice. Too quickly he'd latched on to the hope of a cure that dragon stem cells might offer. If something was wrong with the eggs, that hope could be snatched away in the blink of an eye. He forced himself to explain. "Parthenogenesis is not a common way for a vertebrate species to reproduce. All five eggs might well be non-viable."

And he did wish to live, to fight off the disease that now all but defined his life. His cirrhotic liver, yellow-orange and riddled with disease plagued him daily. He snorted. An unappealing organ, that one gave no thought until it ceased to function properly. Only then could one arrive at a true appreciation for its many duties.

Remaining at Castle Kinlarig was a risk, but his tangle with Misha had underscored the sad fact that not even dragon's blood had restored his strength enough to successfully help Natalia defend against an attack while transporting Zia and her eggs.

Still, logic argued that Natalia's treatment and recovery might have been a fluke, a one-time miracle enacted by a renowned, experienced cell biologist, a remedy they were incapable of reproducing with limited resources and experience. Especially if the eggs were non-viable. Had Zia—much like chickens without a rooster—laid a clutch of unfertilized eggs? Was it nothing but instinct for her to stand guard? So little was known about the reproductive habits of the rare Russian Mountain Dragon species.

"Is there no way to know?" Natalia's eyebrows drew together. "If none of the eggs will ever hatch..."

Then hope for a cure must be abandoned and alternate plans made. "We could try candling."

"Candling?"

"A way to look inside developing eggs. Hold the egg against a bright and concentrated source of light—not necessarily a candle —and it's possible to see blood vessels and a shadow of the embryo within."

"So an unfertilized or infertile egg—" She crossed her arms which pulled her chemise tight across her glorious breasts. Aether, he wanted nothing more than to take her back to bed and finish exploring every last inch of her skin. She caught the direction of his gaze and plumped her breasts up further, throwing him a sultry look.

His lips started to twitch. But he needed to focus on science, not sex.

He coughed, cleared his throat, then choked out a response. "Will appear mostly clear, perhaps with some spots beneath the shell. But first," he pushed a firm note into his voice, "we need to dress. Not only is it impossible to concentrate with such beauty before me, it's cold, and I'm beginning to worry yet more visitors might arrive."

She sighed. "A regrettable possibility."

A few minutes later, wrapped once again in cotton, wool and leather, they stepped back into the laboratory. While Natalia hunted for a working decilamp, Luke crouched beside the fireplace, crooning sweet nothings to the dragon as he held out the lump of sulfur, hoping to coax Zia away from her nest. Unsettling to think how well Ivanov knew his way about dragons.

Zia pushed onto her feet. She took a hesitant step toward him, then paused, turning back toward her treasure hoard. *Shit.* Again the dragon began to shift the stones. Tongue flicking, she touched—tasted—each egg. Then with the tip of her snout, she rolled an egg back onto the stone floor. Then another.

His heart sank.

"Still in working order," Natalia called, giving the small device in her hand a final forceful shake to fully excite the bioluminescent bacteria within. "Faint, but it brightened after I injected a little substrate into the gel chamber." Her gaze followed his to the floor and her face fell. "Not promising."

Not at all, but hope twisted in his chest, begging for a chance. "Let's have a look before we make a pronouncement?"

While Zia watched, he lifted the first rejected egg, its gold streaks glimmering in the lamplight. Natalia brought the light to the tip of the dragon egg, and the interior illuminated. One end glowed a deep red, the other a golden yellow. A network of blood vessels threaded beneath the surface.

Luke exhaled, letting out a breath he'd not known he was holding. "Blood vessels indicate it is—or was—viable." He pointed at the dark red end. "The embryo is here. The light space at the other end is the air sac."

"So it's viable?" Hope flared in her bright eyes.

He was about to say "fertilized" but stopped himself. Parthenogenesis. "It might be, but it's awfully small for a six-week-old egg. Unless the dragonet within moves as we watch, we can't be certain." But they couldn't return the egg to Zia's nest. "We'll keep this egg separate but warm, then watch to see if it continues to develop."

For now, he placed the rejected egg on the hearth on the far side of the coal fire—close enough to keep it warm, but far from Zia's nest—and stacked a number of warm river rocks about it.

The movement sent a shooting pain through his arm, one that radiated out from the cut Ivanov had dealt him. Infected? Already? They'd taken care to sterilize the needle and thread. And less than two hours had passed since he'd returned from the river. Far too soon for an infection to flare. Something wasn't right.

When he straightened, Natalia already held the decilamp against the shell of the second rejected egg. "Mostly clear and golden, but there's a small, darker section." She looked up with sad eyes. "The embryo died?"

Drawn in, he nodded. "This," he pointed at a circlet of red beneath the shell, "is called a blood ring. It forms when the embryo dies and the blood vessels detach from the interior of the shell. From the small size of the fetus, I'd say this one died some time ago."

Zia pawed at his leg, dragging claws down the leg of his trousers. Her tongue flicked in and out and her tail thrashed.

"I think she wants it back," Natalia said. "But whatever for?"

He shrugged and set the second, non-viable egg down before her. The dragon lifted the egg in her mouth, flutter-hopped a few feet away, then dropped it to the floor. She lifted her forefoot and brought it down swiftly and decisively upon the egg. *Splat!* The contents oozed from beneath her feet. Soundly rejected.

"Zia!" Natalia scolded.

"No." He snatched up a rag and bent to mop up the mess, cringing at the pain in his shoulder the movement caused. "It's good instinct. A rotten egg—one incubating harmful bacteria—can destroy the whole brood." Luke wondered if she would seek out the second egg, but the dragon returned to her nest, settling down once again into sentry position.

"What of the remaining three?" She lowered herself onto the rug beside Zia, absently stroking her head. "Should we candle them as well? I never considered parthenogenic eggs a possibility. After Kinross's death, I thought her refusal to leave her treasure hoard, her constant pestering for me to light a fire, was shock. I should have investigated further. Had I known, I would have kept the fire burning, helped keep a closer watch over her eggs."

Likely the large *meal* Zia had made of the laird—with unusually high concentrations of nutrients and calories—was the environmental trigger that stimulated the atypical reproductive strategy. No need to enlighten Natalia with that grim thought. He sat upon the floor beside her and took her free hand in his. Though small and elegant, it was also skillful and strong. And demanding. Whether it gripped a test tube, a sword or—his heart gave a great thud—him, she was a rare find of a woman. Decisive, leaving no one in doubt of her intentions. And yet so fragile underneath.

An accident had broken her spine, and the treatment forced her to flee Russia, bringing about her father's death. And now his own country had failed her, relying too heavily upon a so-called gentleman who thought only of himself and refused to answer her repeated requests for help. Yet still she blamed herself for the outcome of a rare reproductive event that might have been compromised by improper incubation?

He frowned, unwilling to let guilt define her memory of this moment. "How could you possibly have known? Zia hid her eggs well. Besides, who in their right mind would dig into a dragon's treasure pile without good reason or permission? You're not responsible for this situation."

Her laugh was bitter. "Am I not? But for me, my father might be alive, we might be in Russia, and you would not be ill."

"Stop." He squeezed her hand. "I count it a rare privilege to have met you, to have worked with a dragon I consider a friend." All he wanted was to see her, Zia and her brood safe.

*Lie.*

With one foot in the grave, he'd somehow managed to convince himself that would be enough. But the moment she'd dangled the possibility of a cure before him, everything had shifted. He wanted to be with her. As her lover, as her husband, as the father of her children. But though he might feel relatively well at the moment, his health would eventually begin to fail. He would become a burden. Unless...

He stared at the eggs nestled inside the dragon hoard. If they weren't viable, he and Natalia ought to make plans to leave immediately. But if they were—he glanced at the sad-eyed beauty beside him—then he was willing to wait, to serve as laboratory rat one last time.

---

It ought to be cozy, sitting before a fire with Luke, holding his hand while, outside, day faded into night. But instead of dreaming of a future together, she was brooding over the past, over things that could not be altered. Too long she'd existed in such a state, tied to a dissolute, opportunist of a husband who had done nothing save foist the care and keeping of his family estate upon her while pilfering from governmental funds earmarked for *her* research.

Free at last, it was time to take decisive action to secure a better future for herself. Luke in her bed was only a beginning. She wanted more. So, so much more. But if there was no cure for his illness, her dreams of spending a lifetime—hers—with him would crumble, slowly but surely. Every hope she had for their future hinged upon a viable egg.

"I can't wait," she said. "The uncertainty will kill me." She reached out to touch the tip of a half-buried egg, then addressed Zia. "May I?"

Zia nudged her hand toward her brood, as if proud to have her offspring admired.

She pushed aside a brass doorknob and a few stones before placing her fingertips upon an egg. She looked to Zia. No objection. Gently, she lifted an egg free, careful to keep it near the flames. Luke handed her the decilamp, and she touched the light to the shell of the egg, illuminating its golden-red interior.

Within a large mass of dark red shifted.

"It's alive!" she gasped.

"And nearly ready to hatch." His voice held a note of excitement, but it was tempered with relief. Or was that apprehension?

One by one, they examined all three eggs. All contained viable embryos. Three dragonets due to hatch in less than two-weeks' time. She looked to Luke with a grin, but her smile fell away as she studied his face. "What's wrong?"

He gave a quick shake of his head. "Nothing."

She frowned. "You doubt my laboratory skills, my ability to culture stem cells? It's true, I have no formal training, and I didn't help Papa with the original experiment." She'd been flat on her back in a bed, wondering when she would die. "It is a risk. My plan might well fail."

Luke shifted, touching his fingers lightly to his injured arm, then dropping them away, clearly uncomfortable. He drew a deep breath. "It bothers me that Ivanov is out there, scheming…" He shook his head. "I want the cure. But I also want you safe. And I'm certain Ivanov—now that his true identity has been discovered—won't wait two weeks before pressing his agenda."

Nor was she. But to step beyond the castle walls was to expose themselves to capture. By Ivanov or Rathail's hunter. Even if they altered their plans, fled for the city and somehow managed to reach Edinburgh, once they arrived, what then? Bone-deep, she knew men in formal attire would swoop in—citing various rules and regulations—snatching away Zia and her clutch. Without a newly-hatched dragon egg or access to a laboratory, all hope of curing Luke would be lost.

And *that* was unacceptable.

"We need to stay." She closed her eyes and forced the truth from deep in her heart. "Three years ago I fell in love with a man I couldn't have. My feelings haven't changed, but my plans have. I want more than a few years. I want a lifetime. I'll do everything—anything—to cure you." Snapping open her eyes, she pinned him with her gaze. "Give me that chance?"

"Natalia, I—" Luke swayed, nearly toppling to the floor.

She caught him about the shoulders and pressed a palm to his brow. Only minutes before he'd seemed fine, but now he was hot. Feverish.

"My arm." He unbuttoned his shirt and shrugged it from his shoulder. "It feels infected."

Already? Her mind raced. How was it possible? They'd been so careful. And the dragon's blood should have helped quell any complications. Eyebrows furrowed, she unwound the bandage and gasped. Red, inflamed streaks radiated from the wound, and pus oozed from beneath the threads that pierced his skin. "Aether, how?" This was no simple infection. Something more was going on.

He cursed. "I might not make it two days, forget about two weeks. It was that damn sword of Misha's. A polluted sword."

"Polluted?"

He grimaced. "Some guards in the Ural Zavód carried them, blades dipped in a brew of noxious bacteria and allowed to dry. A single nick can be deadly."

No. Absolutely not. Her heart flipped over and began to beat irregularly. She would not lose Luke to a bacterial infection. She jumped to her feet and ran to her workbench, snatching up a bottle of ethyl alcohol, a scalpel and a clean cloth. Kneeling at his side a moment later, she said, "Brace yourself. This *will* hurt."

Luke dragged in a deep breath and held it. He gave a short nod.

As the stitches fell away, a thin, yellow-green liquid trickled down his arm. A lump formed in her throat as she pressed at the inflamed tissue, draining it, trying to maintain a calm demeanor when she wanted to cry out in alarm. She needed to clean it, kill as many bacteria as possible so that his immune system had a chance to fight the infection. She poured a measure of ethyl alcohol directly into the open wound, and Luke hissed and spat a long string of colorful curses, some in Russian. Concerned, Zia nudged his thigh.

"A most interesting prison vocabulary." Her voice shook. A feeble attempt to inject a certain lightness into her voice, despite the growing panic that tightened like an iron band about her chest. The wound was angry and septic, a ticking bomb. She set the bottle aside—an easy arm's length away—before loosely wrapping a clean cloth about his upper arm. "We'll try that again in an hour's time."

Luke slumped, pale. "We need a new plan." He looked at her with tired eyes. The hollows beneath his cheekbones seemed more pronounced. "I sent a skeet pigeon to Edinburgh, to the Department of Cryptozoology. There's a faint possibility they might send help."

He was making plans for her, plans that wouldn't include

him. She opened her mouth to object. Closed it. If this infection proceeded apace, he would be unfit for travel in a matter of hours. Her heart jumped. With fear for him, with fear for herself. She'd not traveled anywhere, not since fleeing Russia three years past.

"It's possible," he began. "If you exit through the postern door and—"

"Lady Kinlarig!" Aileen pushed the thick wood of the door open, stumbling into the room. "Two pteryformes!" She pointed at the window set into the stone wall and flapped her hand. "With men upon their backs!"

Natalia ran to the window, and her jaw fell open. Silhouetted by the setting sun, two human forms—mounted upon the creatures' backs and holding reins—swooped low above the castle.

One such beast had been circling the town for some time now, but that was not uncommon in this part of Scotland. Zia would often peer out the window at it, hissing, perhaps envious of another reptile whose wings were strong enough, wide enough to lift their entire body into the sky. But they were *wild* beasts. Natalia had never seen one with a rider. Until now. *Aether!* Had Misha Ivanov *flown* into Scotland? And who rode by his side? She'd thought herself safe behind stone walls and bolted iron gates, but if a man could saddle and ride such a creature such barriers wouldn't stop him. She tried to swallow her mounting panic.

"It can't be!" Aileen grabbed her arm. "*Michael?*" Shock and denial were at war in her voice.

"Misha," Luke corrected as he made his way across the room, slowly, and with great effort.

"Your sword-wielding, *Russian* fiancé, Misha Ivanov." Ice dripped from Natalia's voice.

Stupid of her not to insist upon meeting the man, but Aileen hadn't offered. Of late, Natalia had put special effort into avoiding her more than usual. The humming and the slight skip in her step as the housekeeper worked had been irritating, exacerbated by the smug and pitying smiles Aileen had bestowed upon her—the poor Lady of Kinlarig, young widow.

"He's only following orders!" Aileen backed away, and though she defended her intended, a certain stricken look stole across her face. Did she just now realize a man such as Misha might not return her loyalty? "*You* stole the dragon. The papers…"

The pteryform riders circled back, lower this time. Clawed feet extended, they landed with grace *inside* the castle courtyard. Dismounting, their two riders shoved flight goggles upward upon foreheads and waited.

Ice crystalized in Natalia's veins as she recognized one of the riders. Mouth open, she gaped at Luke. *How was it possible?*

Luke cursed. Not just because their unwelcome visitors arrived fully armed and garbed in leather, but because Ivanov was accompanied by one Dimitri Kravchuk. "How is he not dead?"

Natalia grabbed a sword. She added another blade to the belt at her waist and slid one into her boot, one that she could throw.

Tiresome, this constant state of alert. The lairds of yore had armies. All she had was an ill—if determined—man and a dragon. Not only did Zia not breathe fire, her scales weren't impenetrable, and she couldn't fly, not really. Though her poison glands, sharp teeth and claws were quite effective at close range.

"You can't mean to confront them," Luke objected. He stabbed his fingers into his hair, fisting them as he shook his head in disbelief.

"What else am I to do?" She met his gaze with her eyebrows raised. "If they knock from *inside* the castle walls, McKay will open the door to them. Do you think the haughty disdain of a seventy-year-old butler will deter them from their plans?" She snatched up her scarf and wound it around her neck, concealing the dragon scales. Her mistake to have thought the cloth no longer necessary. "Perhaps I can buy us time." She pinned Aileen with a look. "Stay with Mr. Dryden. Be quiet. Do *not* alarm Zia." Stiffening her spine, she marched off to battle.

## CHAPTER EIGHT

$O$UTSIDE TWILIGHT HAD fallen and the moon rose over the hills. In the distance, a bell rang. A gentle breeze brought in the crisp, cool air of the nearby river and ruffled a carpet of snowdrops. A peaceful night.

*Elsewhere.*

The main keep of Castle Kinlarig rose six stories, its curtain wall forty feet. It boasted walls that were six feet thick and a surround of defensive earthworks. But when the enemy could fly above it all to land within the courtyard, withstanding a siege became an impossibility. What point in hiding? Better to fully understand the situation she faced. Natalia pushed open the door and descended the stairs to stand before her enemies.

The air vibrated with tense hostility.

She detested both men. With his sword, Misha Ivanov had wounded Luke, perhaps fatally. But Dimitri Kravchuk? His presence made her blood boil. To turn on his mentor, to not lift a finger when armed guards hunted her and her father with loaded weapons. To stoop so low as to forcibly inject an unknown virus into a healthy man so that he might *endeavor* to cure him with untreated dragon's blood. To think she'd once thought to marry the blackguard.

Ivanov—well-muscled and gripping a curved sword—stood a step behind Kravchuk, his face carefully blank as he awaited command. Not a man she could imagine bending on one knee to propose to a love-struck Scottish lass.

Dimitri, dressed in a leather flight jacket and trousers with a sword strapped to his side, looked no less lethal. His handsome face was familiar, but his eyes were cool and appraising. Her last glimpse of him had been from a distance, as she lay immobile upon a makeshift litter while men carried her away from the rocky base of the dragon cliffs. Did he now marvel at her ability to stand, to walk, to lift a sword?

Behind him, the two enormous beasts dug claws into the gravel and stretched out their long necks, huffing clouds of sulfurous breath into the wind as they spread their leathery wings wide. The keratinous skin covering their chests was thick, dark and... burnt? The rumors had been true, then, that her Russian colleagues in Kadskoye had succeeded in bioengineering a military-grade beast. A worrisome development.

"Control your beasts," Natalia demanded, refusing to cower before them, no matter a simple command could end her with one snap of their sharp beaks.

With a quick motion of his hands, Dimitri signaled to the two creatures behind him. With a final flap, they folded their wings against their sides and settled onto the ground, reluctantly obedient.

"What do you want?" Natalia planted fists on hips. Aggressive posturing that was completely unenforceable. Should they choose to force the situation, to attack, she would not emerge the victor. But, *by blade's edge*, she would make them regret the effort.

At Natalia's brave—and perhaps foolish—challenge, Dimitri smiled. "You need to ask?" It was a grin that had once charmed her and convinced her father to serve as his mentor. Until he'd abandoned her broken body, then betrayed the man who wished only to cure his daughter. "My betrothed, there was no need for you to run." His accent a reminder of her homeland, yet so very unwelcome falling from his lips. "Your father alone broke the rules. We've searched for years, but the British government hid you well. Until Rathail made it known that his catalogue of goods would soon include a certain rare species of dragon."

Silently, she cursed her husband's name.

Dimitri took a step forward, and she lifted her sword. "I am not your betrothed, you cold-hearted, opportunistic bastard. Not so much as a word of sympathy reached my ears as I lay dying." She spit on the ground. "No, you were too busy exploiting the opportunity, crowing over *our* find, over the dragon eggs we located *together*. Carrying them back to the Ural Zavód, watching over them, celebrating the hatchlings. What did my father do, save to use the scraps you tossed away to attempt a cure?"

"One that worked." He took another step forward, one with a slight hitch. Light spilling from the castle's interior glinted off ice chips deeply embedded in his frozen eyes as he assessed her form. "One that ought to be shared."

Her fingers twitched with a need to claw the arrogant expression from his face. "With you? A man who betrayed the woman he professed to love, all so that he might crown himself director of dragon research?" Natalia shook her head. Her heart had been right to save itself for Luke, the polar opposite of the man who stood before her. "Go. When you ordered my father killed, you destroyed the only man who could give you the knowledge you pursue. Go. Leave me in peace. There's nothing here for you."

"There's a dragon." Dimitri's eyes narrowed. "A Russian dragon. One that a man named Rathail seeks to sell, piece by piece upon the black market, an unacceptable end."

*Agreed.* Though she refused to voice the shared sentiment.

Dimitri flicked a hand, and Ivanov strode to his pteryform's side to unknot a rope fastened about the neck of a large, canvas sack. The body of Rathail's hunter slid free and slumped onto the ground with a soft *thud*. A dark, clotted gash gaped at this throat.

Ice shot through her body and, for a moment, she forgot to breathe.

"It proved impossible to convince him my claim to the dragon was stronger." Dimitri's eyes warned her she faced a similar end if she refused to cooperate. "Agree to hand over your father's notations and assist the dragon into its cage," he waved a hand toward the corner of the courtyard where Kinross had met his untimely end attempting to force a hungry dragon behind bars, "and I will leave you—and your lover—to enjoy the damp and cold of this indefensible pile of rocks. The walking dead are of no concern to me."

A cold sweat broke out over her skin. He knew of Luke's wound and approved. Another inconvenient man who thought to block him from acquiring something he desired, easily swatted away. How many bodies littered his path? "I have no notes, no record of my father's work." But she couldn't deny Zia's presence. Her hand tightened on the hilt of her sword. There was little hope of a peaceful resolution.

"Please." Dimitri cocked his head, ignoring her implied threat. "You don't truly expect me to believe that, do you? Ivanov attempted to extract them from you peacefully, to cultivate a friendship with Rathail's hunter. Alas," his grin grew sharp, "my intended had developed a certain amount of bite. He was right to send me word, if only that I might look upon you and fully recognize your father's brilliance."

"Michael!" Aileen ran down the stairs and into the castle courtyard, heedless of the tension, sparing not the slightest glance for Natalia, Dimitri, the pteryformes or the dead body that lay at their feet.

As she rushed past, the sleeve of her dress caught at the scarf loosely wrapped about Natalia's neck. As it fell open, Natalia clutched at it with white knuckles. Too late. She held her breath, suppressing a scream. Luke was right; meeting with them face to face had been a mistake.

Dimitri's visage brightened. "No record of your father's work?" He leaned forward, eyebrows raised. "Not written, perhaps, upon paper, but upon your skin. I must amend my original offer. Both you and the dragon will be returning to Russia."

"I married the Laird of Kinlarig. I'm Scottish now." She'd be damned if she would be dragged back to the Ural Zavód where scientists would tie her to a gurney and biopsy her spine, uncaring of her pain and agony as they sought to unravel the process by which Papa had restored his daughter's ability to walk.

"What is this about you working for the Russians?" Aileen cried, falling against her lover's chest, clutching at the cloth of his shirt and searching his face.

Dimitri rolled his eyes skyward. Amusement and disdain twisted together as he addressed Ivanov in Russian. "Swept up in a bit of local skirt?"

"You know as well as I the value of pillow talk," he answered, still in Russian, ignoring the woman who clung to him.

Aileen's mouth fell open, gaping at the foreign words that dropped from his lips. "It's true, you're Russian?"

"Any long-term interest?" Dimitri asked Ivanov.

He shook his head, his next words the only hint that a cold lump of clay hadn't replaced his heart. "She's harmless. Grant her and her grandfather safe passage."

"Done."

"Speak to *me*." Aileen pressed her hands to either side of

Ivanov's face, forcing his gaze to her. "Don't do this. We have plans. I'm carrying your child! We *must* marry."

"He *has* a wife," Dimitri stated bluntly, switching back to English and addressing Aileen directly. "You see the impossibility."

"A wife?" Aileen dropped her arms, backing away and pressing a hand to her chest as if the truth sliced through her heart with a rusty, burred edge.

"It's true." Jaw set, Ivanov unhooked a pouch from his belt and held it out. "For the baby."

"No." Aileen sobbed as tears ran down her cheeks. "No, we have *plans*. Don't do this to me."

Much as she disliked the woman, Natalia's heart wept. She snatched the purse—heavy with coins—from Ivanov, then gently took Aileen's elbow, drawing her away. "I'm so sorry. Come back inside. We'll figure out what to do."

"All this emotion is exhausting and pointless." Contempt tugged at Dimitri's features. "Do we have an understanding, Natalia? Will you agree not to resist repatriation for the chance to save your lover?"

Luke's life for hers? The choice was easy. But for her, Luke wouldn't be ill, wouldn't be dying. If she cooperated, dosed him with enough dragon's blood, he could smuggle the dragon eggs to Edinburgh. Someone there must speak—*read*—Russian. With Papa's notebook in hand, a scientist might be able to undo the damage done to Luke's liver. Cured, he could later take the young dragonets to his brother, to the refuge in the highlands.

But only if she sacrificed herself. And Zia.

Luke would never agree to such a plan.

Nor would she. Not until all other options were exhausted. She pushed Aileen toward the castle, then lied through her teeth. "We do."

"Wise decision." Dimitri snapped his fingers at the ptery-formes, and they rose, stretching their wings and tossing their heads. "Enjoy your final night together, but pack your bags. It's time to return home."

***

LUKE UTTERED a soft curse as the pteryformes and their riders disappeared into dark clouds that blotted out the moonlight. They'd be back, but for now, a brief reprieve had been granted. He'd half expected Ivanov and Kravchuk to force their way past Natalia and storm the castle, swords drawn. Especially once Aileen rushed out into the courtyard, exposing Natalia's secret. Kravchuk had been far too interested in her neckline. A bad omen.

His mistake for stabbing Dimitri in the leg. He should have driven that knife into the man's heart and given it a violent twist.

"Aether!" exclaimed William. Natalia's young student had *not* gone home. He'd snuck back into the castle and now stood beside Luke, gaping, his hand wrapped about the hilt of a sword. Of late, a rather standard pose here, even within the castle. "That dead man is the one Lady Kinlarig shot full of arrows this morning! Who, exactly, are the men *riding* pteryformes?"

Luke wasn't certain if the young man was shocked or impressed.

Rathail's hunter had fallen from a canvas bag and lay motionless upon the ground, a bloody gash at his neck. He was still there, a dark lump in the middle of the courtyard. Natalia had been right to drag Aileen away.

"No one you wish to meet," Luke said, sagging against the wall. In the short time Natalia had been gone, not only had his body temperature soared, but William had entered the laboratory claiming McKay had ordered him to deliver coal, a task that would take him conveniently close to the fireplace and a certain not-so-mythological dragon.

But Luke was too feverish, too worried to protest. He hadn't even been able to stop Aileen from rushing from the room, intent upon confronting her lover. Every last ounce of his attention had since been fixed upon events unfolding in the courtyard. Now, with the danger aloft and out of sight, William was full of questions.

"It *is* real," the young man whispered, halting a respectable distance away from Zia, awestruck. "From what I heard in the pub, I thought it would be bigger." Question after question poured from the boy's mouth. The dragon, it seemed, was not at all a well-kept secret. Not after Rathail's hunter had arrived and begun asking questions. "And its wings are puny. Not a chance it can fly. Can it at least breathe fire?" He stepped closer, peering at the fireplace. "Are those eggs buried in a treasure hoard?"

No point in denying what William could see with his own eyes. Besides, he wielded a sword with skill, and his loyalty to Natalia might yet be useful. If Luke could no longer assist her, perhaps William could. Though the thought of setting such a young man against the likes of Ivanov and Kravchuk troubled him. "It's female," Luke answered, blinking. "She can't fly, not really. Only males—which are twice the size—spit fire. They've a kind of thermite in their crop." He pressed a hand to his forehead. His arm throbbed, and he was burning up. "Eggs, yes."

William glanced about. "Where's the other dragon then?"

"There isn't one. Not here."

He tugged an ear. "But she laid eggs."

"It's complicated."

The door cracked and William—clutching a sword—dropped into the *en garde* position. With a glance toward Luke, he lifted his blade. "Who goes there?"

"William?" Natalia stepped into the laboratory, frowning. "I thought I told you to go home. It's not safe here."

"I came back to help you save the dragon." William lowered the sword. "To warn you that the man you shot an arrow into had gone missing." He glanced at the window. "He's dead now, but he spent most of the day in the pub convincing the villagers that you don't deserve to be Lady Kinlarig, that they ought to help him chase you and the beast from the castle."

*Wonderful.* First Rathail's hunter. A pair of Russians. And next a mob of villagers carrying torches and pitchforks? The room tipped, and Luke eased himself down onto a bench, focusing his gaze on the floor in the event it decided to rush up at him.

Natalia crossed the room and knelt beside him to press a palm to his forehead. The level of worry in her eyes rose to a new level. "They want me to surrender Zia and my father's notes." She swallowed. "And myself."

"Not happening." Luke caught her wrist and pinned her with his gaze. "Don't even think to try it."

"Er." William shifted from foot to foot. "Can I... pet the dragon?"

"Yes. Carefully." Luke dug the lump of sulfur from his pocket. "Approach her slowly, let her taste your hand, then offer her this treat. If she hisses, back away quickly. If she spits venom, it will hurt. Badly."

"Venom? Fearsome!" William took the sulfur, then set about winning the friendship of the dragon. A few minutes later, they were fast friends. He knelt upon the carpet, stroking Zia's head while the dragon basked in his worship, eyes closed, a low, rumbly sound vibrating deep in her throat. The dragon shifted forward, resting her chin on his knees. William flashed them a grin.

"I gather there won't be a wedding for Aileen and Ivanov?"

Natalia followed his gaze to the pouch of coins tied to her belt. "A poor substitute for promises. Aileen's intended has left her in," she cleared her throat, "a difficult situation."

"A bairn on the way?" William asked bluntly, all ears.

Natalia winced, but nodded. "She's a bit distraught at the moment. When her senses return, I'll give the money to her." She glanced at Luke. "These developments complicate our situation."

*Understatement of the year.* "We need to send her and McKay away. Far away. In a manner that will not link them to our... quest."

"I could take them with me to Edinburgh, drop them off at your townhouse," William offered.

"With you?" Luke asked.

"Fencing and ancient swordplay techniques are all the rage." William puffed his chest. "Lady Kinlarig is allowing me to take a collection of weapons to the city. I've plans to open a fencing studio."

"Perfect." Luke straightened on his bench, trying to ignore the dull, vague pain that was settling in beneath the right side of his ribs. The infection must be triggering a relapse. He dragged in a steadying breath. "Pack a crate full of weapons, load it into the steam wagon. As pteryformes are nocturnal, you'll leave at dawn. When they catch up to you—and they will—you answer any questions they ask. Cooperate without a fight. Do I make myself clear?"

Though he nodded, William asked the obvious question. "But what of *you?* You can't stay here, alone to fight those men and their beasts. You're ill. Lady Kinlarig wields a sword, and the dragon is amazing, but she's not... well, she's too small to put up much of a fight. I mean, if you were caught off guard, like the laird, but..." The young man trailed off, realizing that he'd said too much.

"We have plans," Natalia said. Pain rippled across her face, and she glanced at the dragon eggs. An egg cracked open would provide the membranes she sought, but likely at the expense of the dragonet within.

"No," Luke said. "There will be no sacrificing." Nothing beyond another dose of dragon's blood. But one thing at a time. He turned his attention to William. "Better for you not to know too many details. There are crates in the cellar."

The boy nodded and gently pushed at Zia's head until—with a sigh—she pulled away. He stood.

"Take whatever you want from the great hall," Natalia dropped her hands onto William's shoulders and steered him toward the door. "But remember to focus on that which you'll need to open a studio." She ruffled his hair. "No stealing any crossbows."

"Aww." The young man flashed her an unrepentant grin.

"Off with you. Don't worry about Aileen. I'll speak with her and ensure she agrees to our plan. Soon." She closed the door behind William, turned about and fell backward against it. Exhaustion pulled at her features. "Care to share your brilliant plan?"

"There's an abandoned boat in the weeds. A simple motor with a propeller. A bit rusty, but—"

"You want to head up the river, toward the Trossachs?" She pushed off the door, frowning. Crossed the room to sit beside him upon the bench. "They'll follow us, attack us en route. Even if Zia donates more of her blood, not only are you sick— and looking worse by the moment—this plan of yours will carry us far beyond any laboratories." She lifted his hand, brushing her thumb over his knuckles. "Any hope for a cure..."

*Gone.*

Zia let out a low chirr, then stood and stretched her wings, pacing in circles about the room. Something was wrong. His eyes darted to the windows, searching the dark night outside. Nothing. He listened, but could hear nothing. William would be deep in the cellars, gathering packing materials. Was that what the dragon sensed?

"How long since she last ate?" Hunger, another possibility. "She's not left that nest unguarded since I've arrived."

"And rarely before that." Natalia stood and headed back toward the door. "Perhaps she simply needs to go out. Zia?"

But the dragon ignored her, continuing to pace the flagstones, lifting her nose and flicking her tongue. Sampling the environment as if searching out something amiss. Then Zia stopped, motionless but for the flicking of her forked-tongue. Sensing something, she darted forward, stopping before Luke's makeshift nest.

"Zia, no!" Natalia dove for the rejected egg at the same time Luke leapt to his feet, trying to ignore the slight tilting of the room as he too lunged forward.

But they were both too late. Zia already gripped it between her jaws. With the flick of her head, she threw it aside.

*Crunch.*

With an anguished cry, Natalia scooped the broken egg from the floor into her hands. Within the fragments of shell curled a tiny dragonet, a significant yolk sac still attached. She lay still, unmoving. There was no first breath of atmospheric air. No rise and fall of the ribcage. Not so much as a twitch of her toe. Far too young, far too small to have had any hope of survival.

"I'm sorry." Luke lifted the tiny creature free from the shell, checking and rechecking to be certain there was nothing to be done.

Natalia looked up at him, tears brimming in her eyes. "Is she—"

He shook his head. "Dead." But only recently. "Zia sensed something. Remember, this dragonet wasn't developing at the same pace as the others, as the viable ones."

"Insufficient heat?" Guilt threaded through her voice.

Tempting to lie by way of comfort, but Natalia wouldn't appreciate such an instinct. "Possibly," he admitted. "But there could have been any number of causes. Things go wrong in development all the time."

Silent, they stood for a long moment, watching as Zia resumed her sentinel position, guarding her three remaining eggs.

Then Natalia gasped.

"Luke." He looked up to see her staring down at egg remnants—fluids, blood vessels and membranes—in her hands. Not in horror, but in wonder. "Stem cells. If the dragonet died recently—and not due to disease or congenital defect, then I'm holding stem cells. This is a chance to turn misfortune and death into something good. This means we don't need to wait for the other dragonets to hatch. If there are viable stem cells here, I can collect them." She spun on her heel and strode to her workbench.

Quietly, he followed her, laying the tiny dragonet upon a stretch of cotton batting. Perhaps they could spare a few moments for a quiet burial before they departed. He touched her arm. "The others leave at dawn. If we're to have any hope of evading Ivanov and Kravchuk, we need to depart at the same hour. That's less than twelve hours to arrange our escape. That can't possibly be long enough." All laboratory procedures seemed to require long, drawn out protocols with carefully timed steps. "If I've any hope of accompanying you, wouldn't dragon's blood be the better approach?"

"There's time," she insisted, fetching a beaker from a shelf filled with glassware. Natalia carefully placed the egg remnants inside, then turned to the shelves, lifting down bottles of various reagents. An intense fire lit her eyes. "And if this works, it will work fast. Your fever, your liver... any minor complaint will be remedied before the sun rises."

"That fast?" His heart leapt beneath his ribs. Unbelievable. Yet he couldn't help but hope...

"I need three hours." Keeping her eyes on her task, she

pipetted a clear liquid into the beaker, rinsing the inside surface of the shells, collecting any and all tissues from their surfaces. "To collect all the cells, then to isolate the amniotic stem cells." She swirled the contents of the beaker. "These cells—according to Papa's notes—are highly mitotic, undifferentiated and immunoprivileged. Chances are the stem cells will colonize and proliferate not just inside your liver, but within additional tissue, in locations we are not specifically targeting. Because there will only be a tiny number of them, I suggest you take the anti-rejection medication to guard against any xenogenic immune response."

Wonder at her brilliant mind filled him, overflowing. But he didn't follow. "Perhaps in simpler words?"

She glanced up at him. "I'm going to collect the cells and inject them into your liver. They might all die, but with luck, they'll grow and spread inside of you. The medication will help keep your body from rejecting them, even though the temporary suppression of your immune system is likely to spike your fever even further. As to the stem cells, I can't predict the side effects, but they're likely to be… interesting." Her wobbly smile wasn't reassuring. "I doubt you'll acquire the ability to breathe fire, but…"

He was to become a human Petri dish. Wonderful.

But this might be his only chance to attempt such a stem cell treatment. If his liver managed to repair itself, he could live with a few patches of scales upon his skin so long as it meant he could spend his life with her.

"Here." Natalia paused, rummaged in a drawer, tossing one item after another aside—a broken pocket watch, a small radial clamp and a snap tinder lighter—before she pulled out a packet of pills and shook one free. "Take this. It's a sulfated purine derivative, a bit hard on the liver and, given the infection festering inside your wound, I don't want to risk more than one dose to suppress the immune system while the stem cells colonize the tissue."

*Risk.* Everything was happening so fast. He had two choices. Decline and pray his body fought off the bacteria infecting his arm. Or accept the risk, take a leap of faith, and hope for a miracle. What real choice was there? He took the pill from her and washed it down with a gulp of cold tea.

He had little to lose and everything to gain.

## CHAPTER NINE

Rubbing her aching neck and rolling her shoulders, Natalia straightened, triumphant. She let the lightness in her chest bubble upward into a broad smile. Papa would be so proud. The isolated, pluripotent dragon stem cells now floated in a swirl of specially-formulated liquid media —one containing vitamins, inorganic salts, amino acids and glucose—recovering from several rounds of fractionation, digestive enzyme assaults, and differential density spins in the fuge. The cells needed a few minutes to rest—according to her father's notations—but time ran short. A glance at her timepiece informed her that if they were to abandon Castle Kinlarig at dawn, they would need to attempt this most basic of stem cell transplants within the next hour.

Particularly as Luke's infected wound grew more worrisome. Neither the application of more ethyl alcohol nor an additional treatment of dragon's blood—both performed hastily while cells spun—had done much to reduce the putrid-smelling pus that oozed from the cut or slow the spread of the red streaks.

The excitement of realizing the dragon eggs could hold the cure for Luke's illness had all but vaporized when Ivanov and

Dimitri had landed in her courtyard with their demands. Not enough time was left to slowly work her way through her father's instructions, checking and double-checking each step. Instead she was rushed, harried and increasingly distressed by thoughts of what might happen should this impromptu treatment fail.

Her smile faltered. What if her best wasn't good enough? If this attempt failed, there would be no second chance. There wasn't time, not even if she were willing to sacrifice a dragonet. Luke might well die. She and Zia would be hauled back to Russia along with the dragon eggs where all would suffer untold torments. Worry gnawed at the inside of her stomach and began to crawl its way upward to lodge beneath her heart. She didn't want to ever be parted from Luke again. Not for *any* reason.

Zia was back to guarding her remaining three eggs and barely shifted as Natalia set about gathering supplies. After placing the vial containing the precious cells upon a metal tray alongside a syringe and needle of intimidating size, she made her way into the great hall where, as she'd worked, spates of crashing and banging had echoed. She stepped into the room, taking in the scene before her.

Luke—feverish—sat upon a chair, ignoring pain and discomfort to keep an eye on castle activity when he ought to be in bed, resting. He gave her a faint smile, tipping his head toward William's industriousness. Hay was strewn across the floor as the young man worked to pack swords and armor into crates. At her approach, he paused at his task.

"Impressive progress," she said. An entire wall was bare.

"This is the last crate," William said. "The steam wagon is fixed and loaded, and I've filled the coal hopper. Mr. Dryden and I," he cleared his throat, "took care of the body."

"He means," Luke interjected, "that we dragged Rathail's hunter to the river and gave him the send-off he deserved."

"So we did." A corner of William's mouth twitched, but he

shifted on his feet. "If you can convince Aileen to depart, we could leave at first light. I poked my head into the kitchens to let them know of our plans, but she was weeping still, and I'm not certain she heard my words through her tears. McKay is at an utter loss."

"I'll speak with them." Internally, she cringed. Coping with an emotional Aileen would be trying. She would want to shake sense into her—but would need to fight the urge. Possibly Aileen's teeth would rattle loose first. "It's late. Mr. Dryden is ill. Head home, gather your things and snatch a few hours rest." Surely Aileen could be made to see reason by dawn?

William hammered a few more nails, then heaved a crate onto his shoulder, calling a brief, "Good night."

Alone, she sank onto a chair beside Luke, tipping her weary head onto his shoulder, drawing strength from his presence even as her hand sought out his wrist, taking measure of his pulse. Weak and thready. It grew more worrisome every time she checked. The only way to save him now was to charge bravely ahead.

"Is it time?" he asked. "Shall we adjourn to your laboratory?" Impossible to tell if that was anticipation or worry in his voice. Probably both.

How many times had they sat here together at the high table of the great hall, deeply engrossed in conversation, or battled each other in the expanse of this space when the weather did not permit them to spar in the courtyard? Always careful to keep any physical contact fleeting, constantly aware of the forbidden attraction that simmered between them.

She'd been a married woman, her continued presence in this country dependent upon the goodwill of her absent husband and the funds provided to her by the very institution that employed Luke. *Lady* Kinlarig could not afford to tarnish her reputation. It didn't matter that the lord of the castle traipsed about with an actress upon each of his arms, entertaining his women with funds meant to delve into the organic chemistry of dragon venom in search of medical applications. Her appeals to the Department of Cryptozoology fell on deaf ears. She was to rise above it. To work without complaint while she waited for her laird to return home, to declare his intent to sire an heir.

And that was exactly what she would have done, had they not sent one Mr. Luke Dryden. He was back. They were both free. To be able to lean against Luke without a guilty conscious was a priceless luxury. But one she wouldn't be able to enjoy for long if his arm did not heal, his liver failed or—a more immediately relevant possibility—if Dimitri and Ivanov ran him through with a blade. A decided possibility should they attempt to run. Outside the relative safety of the castle, the Russians held the air advantage and, as sick as he was, Luke would be easy prey. Even at full strength, the odds would be against them. She could fret all she wished, but if they did not risk the stem cell treatment, a dark cloud hung over their future. Time to chase after everything she'd dreamed of: a loving husband and children. Zia free and happy surrounded by her own brood.

"Soon. We've a moment. The cells are resting. Recovering from the shock they've been put through." Threading her fingers between his, she squeezed his rough, calloused and all-too warm hand. "With all that's happened, do you not regret the day you learned dragons are real?"

"Not in the slightest." Luke dropped a kiss on top of her hair, and she smiled. It had been far too long since she'd felt cherished. "Father tried for years to discourage my dreams of working with extraordinary creatures. Banking, he insisted, was the path to happiness and security. But his plans for his son were a lost cause from the first moment I watched a pteryform soar overhead and announced I would become a—"

"Zookeeper." She'd heard the story long ago. Smiling, she tipped her face upward and basked in the warmth of his passion.

"Dragonkeeper has an even better ring to it." He tucked a

loose strand of her hair behind her ear and trailed the backs of his fingers over the edge of her jaw. A shiver ran across her skin. "I fell in love with you the day we met." His voice was a whispered confession, but as she leaned forward and closed her eyes, his hand fell away. Disappointed, her eyes fluttered open. "When this is over, Natalia, you could attend a Season in London. Dissolute gentlemen are in the habit of stalking young heiresses. Perhaps you might turn the game on its head and snag yourself a wealthy industrialist, one who could maintain this castle and support your research."

Her lips flattened into a hard line. A declaration of love followed by a suggestion she wed another? "Absolutely not." She stood and crossed her arms, tucking her balled fists beneath her arms. Slapping a sick man wasn't an option. But perhaps after she cured him...

"Relying on government funds is always an uncertain existence."

"As is relying on a man." She threw him a sideways glare. Particularly ones who took themselves off to hunt dragon eggs in the Ural Mountains. She kept those words to herself. He'd made no promises to her. How could he, married as she was?

*Was.* Widows had certain freedoms in this country. Perhaps she was a fool to dream of marrying again? She drew in a steadying breath.

"This corner of Scotland is lovely," she continued. "But I've no intention of continuing to molder away within the walls of this damp castle. I've begun negotiations with a distant Kinross cousin. If he cannot or will not offer a fair price, I intend to sell it to the highest bidder. The townhouse in Edinburgh should be more than sufficient for my needs." How she would manage Zia and her dragonets if there was no safe haven for them in the Trossachs was beyond her, but she'd cope with that problem later.

"I'm sorry." Luke winced. "But it needed to be said."

She disagreed. But she was done contemplating any future until their immediate obstacles were behind them. Uncurling her fingers, she held out a hand to Luke. From the bilious look upon his face, the anti-rejection medication was working at full strength. "Come. If you're still willing, it's time to perform the transplant."

"I've everything to gain, and nothing to lose." He looked up, the pale shade of his face highlighting the dark shadows beneath his cheekbones, but he grasped her hand. "However awful the cure, it can't be worse than the disease."

"Careful." Lips twisting, she pulled him upright. "You might yet regret your words. I'm a chemist, not a cell biologist, and attempting to follow a recipe for the first time. This might not work. But if it does, dragon stem cells are extremely aggressive. The effects, if they occur, are rapid and potent." She swallowed hard—willing her voice not to tremble—and finished. "We'll know in a matter of hours if I've succeeded in isolating them—if there's hope for a cure."

She wished she were as confident of success as she pretended to be, but any direct experience with dragon stem cells was limited to being the patient, not the physician. A memory of misery. Lying motionless in a bed. Tears flowing from the corners of her eyes. Every breath a struggle as death circled in the dark shadows overhead, waiting for an opportunity to sink its claws deep.

Luke's situation was not so dire, but the regenerative effects were likely to be unpleasant. No, that was putting it too mildly. Painful? Pure agony? Save for a necessary conversation with Aileen, she would stay by his side and attempt to ease his torment.

"Aggressive?" A look of worry crossed Luke's face. "Tell me, what was it like for you?"

Natalia was the first—and to her knowledge, only—human to ever undergo a dragon stem cell transplant and had never shared her story. Not a single living soul had any idea what she'd undergone.

While Dimitri had gloated and basked in the limelight of retrieving dragon eggs from the surrounding mountains in time for all to witness the hatchlings emerge, Papa had quietly collected the egg shell fragments. Busy shaking hands and rubbing shoulders with his superiors in a quest to elevate his position within the Ural Zavód, Dimitri hadn't noticed his mentor silently cultivating a cell type never before documented. Only when her father's absence from the laboratory was noted, did Dimitri think to wonder what had become of his betrothed.

Not that he took the trouble to visit, bastard that he was.

She swallowed. "I was hazy and nauseous—an effect of the anti-rejection medication—when my father arrived at my beside."

Luke nodded, urging her on with hope in his eyes. Hope she was about to pierce with a sharp lance.

"Numb from the neck down, I felt nothing as he injected small colonies of stem cells alongside the fractured vertebrae of my neck. Not a single twinge, not even when the needle punctured the membranes protecting my spinal cord as he inserted a number of stem cells directly into my cerebral spinal fluid." Closing her eyes, she forced the memory past her lips. Her body started to shake at the effort of voicing the memory. "An hour, maybe two, passed. Then there was a sudden burning sensation, a jolt as if an electric current raced down my back. Pain and pressure enveloped me as the stem cells invaded and repaired every bit of damaged tissue." They'd ripped down her spine, crawled over her nerve cord, dividing with unrelenting purpose. Locked in a nightmare, she'd felt every single cell as it crept about, ripping out damaged tissue to assemble something new. "I thought I was going to die."

He squeezed her hand. "But..."

"By morning scales were breaking through the skin of my

back and neck." Building their keratin scaffolds with shocking speed. "The itch at the base of my neck, along the length of my spine, was almost unbearable. Papa nearly fell off his chair when I suddenly sat up and reached behind to scratch at a cluster of scales." No one had expected the transplant to work at all, let alone so quickly. "In less than twenty-four hours, I could walk again. All pain had vanished."

Undiluted awe lit Luke's eyes from within. "Amazing."

"It was." But with success came anguish. Bitterness surfaced. "It was also the end of my time in Russia. Dimitri turned in my father, his own mentor."

While her father sat by her bedside, Dimitri had searched the laboratory, collecting the few random scribbles Papa had left behind upon forgotten scraps of paper. The evidence was thin, but accusations and demands were made. Thinly veiled threats. Papa was to share the details of his experiment with his superiors—of which Dimitri now numbered—immediately, else he would be arrested, his daughter remanded into custody for observation.

Unthinkable. Dragon stem cells were a potent remedy and—in the wrong hands—too easily abused. Yet today—if all went well—she would set wrongs to right and give them all a chance at a brighter future.

"That bastard," Luke hissed. He reached for her, wrapping his arms about her.

With her recovered ability to walk, there really was no other choice but to flee. In a final act of treason, Papa had stolen the dragonets—Zia and Yuri—from the laboratory and... "We ran. The train was pulling away from the station. But Papa, he wasn't fast enough." *Go!* he'd yelled, pushing her in front of him, out of the way. Blocking her body with his own. "The guards caught sight of him." Her voice faltered. "Shot him where he stood." She brushed away a tear that ran down her cheek. The bullet had dropped him to the cinders beside the track. He'd sacrificed himself to save her.

Weeping, she'd clutched Zia and Yuri to her chest. Numb, she'd followed the plan. West to Scotland. To Edinburgh. To the Department of Cryptozoology. Throwing herself on their mercy.

"I'm so sorry." Luke kissed her forehead and, for a moment, she allowed herself to savor the warm, comforting circle of his arms. But only for a moment. She would not allow another man she loved to fall on her behalf. Not while it was within her power to prevent it. The very thought of failure made her heart twist within her chest.

Shoving away memories of the past, she focused upon what must be done in the here and now. She cleared her throat and pulled back. "I'll collect the cells. Make yourself comfortable in my bed." A touch of heat rose to her cheeks. "If this works, you're going to feel much worse before you feel any improvements."

"It will work," he said with a confidence she didn't at all feel, tugging her back against his chest to press a fierce and fevered kiss to her lips, reminding her of other things worth fighting for. "Perhaps even fast enough for us to explore any interesting side effects that might result."

*L*UKE STRIPPED OFF HIS waistcoat and shirt, pulled off his boots and then stretched out upon the bed.

Holding his pocket watch in his hand, he noted the hour. Half past nine o'clock in the evening. Nine hours until sunrise. What if these stem cells didn't work? Or didn't work fast enough? But if they did…

Despite the fever heating his skin, entertaining such thoughts already had him in a state of half-arousal. He wanted nothing more than to free the weight of her breasts from that corset that teased his eyes with every glance he'd dared allow to skim its intimately-contoured leather surface, to slip his hands beneath the loose gathers of her tunic while nibbling at the curve of her neck, to…

He tugged a blanket to his waist, hiding his interest. But if the procedure worked, he had every intention of dragging her back into his arms and into this very bed. He'd thought himself reconciled to a brief affair—until she'd announced her intention to sell the castle, refusing to even consider marrying a wealthy gentleman to save this ancient pile of rocks. Pure relief had swept over him, and he'd begun to wonder if perhaps he could convince her to marry a certain dragonkeeper? Would she be willing to exchange the title of Lady Kinlarig for the simpler one of Mrs. Dryden?

"Ready?" Steel and glass rattled upon a metal tray, yanking him out of his thoughts as Natalia crossed the room to his side.

Sitting up, he swallowed at the sight of the large bore needle screwed into the barrel of a syringe that held a cloudy, pinkish-orange fluid. Beside it rested a bottle of ethyl alcohol and cotton lint. "That's it? A single injection?" But then what had he expected from mere shell fragments?

"I was only able to collect a few thousand or so cells." She set the tray on the bedside table and flashed him a tense smile that did nothing to settle his nerves. Was he worried? Of course. But without risk there was no reward. "Without an incubator or appropriate growth media to culture the cells—to allow them to replicate—we've no choice but to make do."

Tugging a thick textbook from beneath her arm, she placed it between them upon the mattress and began flipping through the pages, stopping at a diagram of the liver. "Our next step is to determine aim. Any and all input as to where I should send these cells is encouraged."

A wave of apprehension rolled over him, collapsing all lingering thoughts of bed sport. A chemist masquerading as a biologist who was in turn playing doctor. Between the two of them, he was the one with more in-depth anatomical knowledge. But of rare and unusual animals. Still, human anatomy couldn't be that different, could it?

Her finger landed on the image. "Here?" She sounded doubtful. "If I angle the needle upward and into the liver from beneath the right side of the rib cage?"

He bent over the text, scanned the image and the words inscribed beside it, then shrugged. "The largest lobe does present a broad target." A more refined target—such as the hepatic portal vein—would require abdominal surgery. *That* wasn't happening.

"Agreed. The largest lobe it is."

Though their words were bold and confident, threading through their voices was the slightest of tremors.

Eyeballing the location of the human liver beneath the rib cage on the textbook's page—and carefully accounting for left-right—he moved a finger alongside the lower edge of his right ribcage to the side of his sternum, attempting to pinpoint the same location to which she pointed. The cure for his condition felt as if it had been reduced to a game of darts played in a public house. Better than a game of chance, but not by much.

He pushed inward, then hissed between clenched teeth as a deep, gnawing ache radiated outward from his fingertip sending tendrils of pain wrapping around his back.

"Luke?" Her face contorted with worry.

"Found a likely spot," he gasped. And fell back onto the pillows, careful to keep his fingertip firmly in place. "Aim here. I'm ready." He'd been sick for so long, he wasn't certain he knew what healthy felt like anymore.

She touched the lint to the lip of the glass bottle, soaking the fibers with alcohol. "If you'll move your finger." He lifted his hand, and there was a flash of wet, then cold as the ethyl alcohol touched his skin and evaporated. "Brace yourself." Lifting the syringe, she smiled, though her body was tense with the effort. "Take a deep breath, hold it, and—whatever you do—don't move."

His heart raced. They'd reached the point of no return. He dragged in a deep breath, gritted his teeth and—though every instinct screamed at him to squeeze his eyes shut—focused upon the bed hangings that stretched above while holding every muscle in his body rigid.

A sharp pain bit into the skin beneath his rib cage and radiated outward into his right shoulder. A dull sensation of pressure followed as she depressed the plunger. Then a moment later—for good or ill—it was done.

He exhaled as Natalia pressed a soft piece of lint against the injection site and held it there. For several long minutes—measured only by the thudding of his heart—in which he hardly dared move, their eyes locked.

Concern wrinkled her brow. "Do you feel anything?"

The continued aching throb of the infected cut on his arm, but otherwise... "Nothing—" His eyebrows drew together, and he pressed his palm beneath his ribcage, where an odd, subtle pressure built. "It feels... warm?"

"A good sign." She lifted away the lint. A tiny pinprick was the only outward indication that anything unusual had transpired. Pulling the blanket over his bare chest, Natalia stood. "Rest. Sleep if you can. I hate to leave you, but I need to speak with Aileen. Before she takes it into her mind to act rashly. Again."

"Go. She shouldn't stay here." Men—for more would follow —seeking a dragon wouldn't hesitate to stoop to low tactics. A rush of heat flooded his heart. Were the stem cells already on the move? The textbook had shown a direct connection between the liver and the heart. Possible then. He'd wonder about it more. Later. When his mind wasn't drifting. He felt so very tired...

"Luke?" Concern colored her voice.

"I'm fine. Just sleepy." He forced himself to finish. "Find out everything she told Ivanov. If he sent reports to anyone but Kravchuk."

"Of course." She smoothed his brow. "Now sleep. I'll be right back."

He caught her hand and pressed a kiss to her palm, then let her go. The sooner she spoke with Aileen, the sooner she would return. As his eyelids grew heavy, he caught a final flash of color.

His love wrapping a scarf about her neck, concealing her secret. From everyone but him.

A heavy weight pressed down upon him, sinking him ever deeper into the feather mattress. He listened to the faint foot-falls of Natalia's exit as sleep caught at him, pulling him into blessed oblivion.

A moment later, an odd crawling sensation overtook his innards.

His eyes snapped open. *So soon?* Anxiety pressed down on his chest. "Natalia?"

THE KITCHENS—WITH its massive fireplace, enormous cast iron range, and line of steam servants all standing at attention and collecting cobwebs—was meant to be a busy, bustling and warm room. The heart of the castle. Instead, it was reduced to a drafty, cold space. Its only occupants sat, hunched and motionless, at the long, scarred worktable while the ever-present cabbage soup simmered over a small coal fire burning in the range.

Aileen lifted her head from her hands to glance at Natalia with a tear-stained face, before turning her back.

"Lady Kinlarig!" McKay lurched to his feet when Natalia stepped into the room. "I'm so sorry. My granddaughter's actions are shameful. A betrayal of your trust—"

She held up a hand. "I'll speak with her directly in a moment." McKay's face collapsed, but he held his tongue. "You've heard the noise, seen William dashing about the castle?"

"Indeed." McKay cleared his throat. "My deepest apologies for allowing the lad into our household. He harbors the misconception that he has been granted permission to run off with a large portion of the weapons collection. I attempted to bring the situation to your attention, but Mr. Dryden prevented me from speaking to you, claiming pressing concerns in the laboratory."

"Is that so?" Luke, her very own guard. Natalia suppressed a smile. It had been a long time since anyone had looked out for her.

"It is." McKay scowled as he worked to straighten his spine. "Over my objections, William has been hard at work all evening loading the steam wagon. Would you believe he had the temerity to *order* us to pack our bags, to *inform* us that we are to evacuate to the Edinburgh townhouse?" He sniffed. "A Kinross has never abandoned his lands, and a McKay has always stood by his side."

*His.*

Any plans the last laird might have had for an heir had been cut short before he'd attempted to resume relations with his long-abandoned wife. Had he treated Zia with respect and not as an investment to be sold in times of need, Natalia might well have cooperated with his desire to sire a child. After all, divorce had not been an option—not when Zia was legally recognized as his property, and Natalia had always longed for a family.

Instead, the fool had baited a dragon. Without such basic common sense, it was fortunate, perhaps, that he had sired no children.

As it stood *she* was the last Kinross, a tenuous and nominal designation only. But to ensure his cooperation and move McKay and his granddaughter out of harm's way, she would embrace her status as Lady Kinlarig. For the sake of the youngest McKay who now found herself in a fraught situation.

Not to mention the state of household funds, a pressing concern. Selling the castle and its contents would—at the very least—staunch the rate at which their finances deteriorated. It would buy all of them time to make alternative plans for their futures.

"The Laird of Kinlarig's death has led to a dispute over the legal definition of moveable property, in particular, livestock," Natalia began. "The men who besiege our castle will not cease their attempts to exert their presumed authority. Until certain matters are settled, we will be more comfortable adjourning to the townhome." Where her husband had kept mistresses, whisky and aether knew what else. She hoped his paramours hadn't carried off everything saleable, but odds were faint. "I'm counting on your wisdom and experience to help restore the family's good name. That task begins in Edinburgh."

*That* brought McKay's chin up. "If we must."

"We must." She injected as much authority as she could manage into her voice. "The townhome will no doubt require a firm hand and extensive reorganization. William has loaded the steam wagon and filled its fire box. He leaves at dawn. Will you please accompany him?"

McKay's eyes glittered, perhaps at the thought of once again having an extensive staff to do his every bidding. "I will, but..." His gaze drifted to Aileen who sat quietly at the table, refusing to look in their direction.

There was one more McKay to convince, and for that Natalia required a few private moments.

"Today's... excitement has overtired Mr. Dryden and dragged him to bed, but I hope his condition will soon turn a corner." She tapped the iron shoulder of the motionless steam cook. "Given we are to leave Castle Kinlarig, perhaps we might indulge, use our remaining supplies—coal, flour, sugar—to prepare a substantial breakfast? This steambot, I seem to recall, was most excellent at baking."

"I'll see to it, my lady," McKay said, then busied himself with the task of firing up the steam cook.

Exhausted by the events of the day, she dropped onto the bench beside Aileen. Perhaps, for the first time in over three years of forced coexistence, they might manage to see eye to eye.

"Michael—Misha Ivanov—is a bastard and not worth your

tears." Natalia unhooked the sack of coins from her belt and held it out. "Refusing his money accomplishes nothing save to make you poorer."

Aileen caught up the heavy pouch, then turned red-rimmed eyes to meet Natalia's gaze. "You can't possibly wish me to work in your city townhome, not with me in," Aileen flapped a hand at her waistline, "in such a situation."

McKay sucked in a shocked breath of air. He turned, trundling to the far side of the kitchen to riffle through an assortment of recipe punch cards.

Three years of accumulated resentments towered between her and Aileen and was not an easy wall to scale. Yet, for the sake of the child's future and McKay's pride, she'd see it surmounted. "There's no need for us to work at cross purposes. Nor must we be friends to form an alliance. Shall we set aside all personal differences and speak plainly?"

For a long moment Aileen said nothing, and Natalia's hope began to flag. Perhaps bitterness ran too deep?

"How do you propose I remedy my situation?" Aileen asked, her eyes narrow.

"Take a new name," Natalia said. "Attach the title missus before it. As our families dwindle, so too do those who can prove that you are not, in fact, a young widow. Particularly in the city."

Aileen looked doubtful. Such was not a traditional stance here in Britain where housekeepers were generally unmarried and childless. "You would let me continue as a housekeeper, after…"

"If you wish to keep the child? Yes." She dropped her voice. "Perhaps I ought to abandon you, but I feel a certain responsibility, given my presence at Castle Kinlarig precipitated our current situation." She smoothed her hand over the scarf at her neck. "Dragons. Unwelcome men misrepresenting themselves while stalking our grounds before dropping into our courtyard astride pteryformes."

Aileen's face twisted. "Mr. Dryden called him Misha?"

"Misha Ivanov. His Russian name. Michael is an anglicized form. He was sent here to collect information about the dragon, about my work."

"And found seduction the path of least resistance." Aileen slumped under the weight of the inescapable truth. Her lover was a married man. A hard-hearted mercenary. A foreigner not welcome on British soil. They had no future.

The time for difficult questions had arrived. "I need to know how much and exactly what you told him."

"Michael—*Misha*—wished to know about the town rumors that the castle housed a flying reptile. I told him you had a pet lizard. Whatever you call that creature's method of flapping about the halls, it's certainly not *flying*."

True.

"It wasn't until after we..." Aileen cleared her throat. "He asked if I was your laboratory assistant and was disappointed when I told him I wanted nothing to do with chemistry or poisons. But he started pressing for more information. That's when I knew he had no interest in textile mills. I confronted him. He told me it was a matter of British security." She lowered her eyes, her voice petulant. "I didn't want to go anywhere near that awful beast, or step into that foul-smelling laboratory of yours, but by then I had begun to suspect..." Her hand fell upon her abdomen. "I'm sorry. I couldn't risk him leaving me."

"That's why you've been trying to befriend Zia." Irritation zinged through her, tempered by sympathy for the situation Aileen had found herself in.

Aileen nodded. "He gave me a yellow rock earlier, promised no dragon could resist such a treat. He told me as soon as he could confirm you weren't a threat, we could marry and move to

Edinburgh." A fresh tear trickled down her cheek, and she slapped it away. "I was a fool. He's a spy, but not one of ours."

If only she and Aileen had been on speaking terms, if only Natalia had insisted upon meeting her suitor, they might have nipped their situation in the bud. But there was nothing to do save keep a keen eye so that they might avoid such a situation in the future should Russia ever show interest in her again. Assuming they survived *this* encounter.

"So will you go?" Natalia asked. "To the Edinburgh townhome?"

"I don't see how," Aileen stated. "Michael and that other man will never let *you* pass. We won't reach Stirling, let alone Edinburgh. Not so long as they have," she flapped a hand, "those beasts to fly upon. They will swoop down, confiscate your dragon and lead you away in chains." She slanted a questioning glance at Natalia, at the scarf about her neck. "What about your *skin disease* interests them so?"

*Everything.* "I have no idea." She needed to return to Luke's bedside. If the transplant had been successful, the dragon stem cells would begin their work soon, and he ought not be left alone. "I won't be traveling to Edinburgh. Not yet. Mr. Dryden and I have other arrangements for Zia."

Aileen's lips twisted. "More details I shouldn't know?"

"For your own safety. For mine." And because Natalia didn't quite trust her. "You can't share what you don't know." She would ask once more. A final attempt to save Aileen from herself. "Will you go?"

"I'll go," she said, but grudgingly. "I can't promise I'll stay, not forever, but I'll help my grandfather set the house to rights."

"Good enough." Standing, Natalia raised her voice, inviting McKay—who now had the steam cook huffing and puffing—back into the conversation. "Pteryformes are nocturnal, that is why you must leave at dawn. The steam wagon will travel the most obvious route to Edinburgh, your destination and intentions not at all a mystery. Expect Ivanov and Kravchuk to track you as dusk falls, perhaps sooner. Hide nothing. Do what you must to keep yourselves safe. With luck, Mr. Dryden, Zia and I will be well away."

McKay, realizing that the two women had finally come to terms, unbent, turned and stopped feigning deafness. He held up a punch card. "I've a likely recipe for cream cakes."

In an unprecedented move, Aileen threw her arms about Natalia, giving her a brief, but fierce hug before hopping away, color high upon her cheeks. "Thank you. I'll bring a tea tray up?"

Her housekeeper—no matter their newly reconciled state—couldn't be allowed to learn of the dragon eggs. If questioned—and she would be—news of them would be sent home to Russia, redoubling efforts to track them. A lost dragon was one thing. Rumors of an improbable cure would fade to myth. But whispers about a clutch of eggs would invite speculation about a breeding colony of dragons in the mountains of Scotland, and her former countrymen would never cease their hunt.

"What, brave the dragon who nips at your ankles?" She shook her head, a smile tugging at her lips as she filled a large pitcher with cool water for Luke. "No need. Leave it outside the laboratory door." A door which would be locked. "Mr. Dryden and I have our own preparations to make."

A touch of mischief crossed Aileen's face, and she winked. "Ones I'm better off not knowing about?"

*She certainly hoped so.* It was Natalia's turn to blush.

*L*UKE CLUTCHED AT THE BEDDING. A thousand clawed kraken tentacles gripped his intestines. Spiders with needle-like legs crawled through his veins and arteries. Fire ants ran beneath his skin turning every square inch of his flesh to ash.

*Thud.* A heavy weight landed on his chest, forcing all but his last breath from his lungs. *Flick.* A lash of a damp tongue. *Swish.* A rough tail skittering across bed sheets.

He pried open scalded eyelids and found himself staring into Zia's golden eyes. The dragon had somehow managed to flutter-hop onto the bed, onto his chest. Concerned enough to leave her eggs in order to investigate disturbing sounds from the above bedchamber. She flicked her tongue out to touch his nose, then she nudged her smooth snout beneath one hand and tossed it in the air, slipping beneath to ensure his palm fell upon her head. *Pet me.*

"Natalia?" he rasped.

Silence.

His legs were tangled in twists of bedclothes and every pillow had been tossed to the floor. He pushed at the dragon, panting at the effort of shifting her bulk. But Zia's weight was significant, and he couldn't breathe. Disappointed or disturbed, Zia moved to the bottom of the bed, pinning his feet beneath her stomach as he gasped for air.

*Tap, tap, tap.* The sound of boots on the stairs.

He turned his aching head. "Natalia?"

"Zia!" Natalia scolded as she stepped into the room. "Down."

With an irritated flapping of wings, the dragon departed, stomping noisily across the floor, before slinking back down the stairs, no doubt to oversee her unhatched eggs. But not before pausing to stare for a long moment at her mistress, as if to accuse her of abandoning her favorite man.

Luke was in complete agreement. "Need water," he whispered.

In a heartbeat, Natalia was by his side, holding a cool glass to his dry, cracked lips as he took in great gulps of water. "Aether, you're burning up."

"Thank you," he said as she set aside the cup to tuck pillows beneath his head. "These cells, I swear they've invaded the entirety of my body." He described the disturbing sensations coursing throughout him.

"We did inject them directly into a most highly perfused organ." She mopped his forehead with a damp cloth, though her presence alone was calming. "But these stem cells do seem most potent and intent."

"*Something* is happening," he said. "It feels as if I'm being turned inside out."

"I'm so sorry." She clasped his hand to her chest, staring down at him with worry etched into every feature. "I've spoken with Aileen. Everything is settled, and I'll not leave you again until this is over. Can you sleep?"

"Perhaps." The corner of his mouth hitched upward. "If a beautiful woman were to lay by my side and run her fingers soothingly through my hair."

Though she rolled her eyes, her fingers were already unbuckling the sword belt from her waist. With a clatter, the various items clipped to it fell to the ground. She dropped her sweet arse onto the mattress beside him and began to unlace her knee-high boots. *Thunk. Thunk.* She peeled away stockings, her scarf. And then she was climbing in beside him, though regrettably still dressed in trousers, tunic and corset.

When her soft curves finally rested against his side, and her arm draped over his waist, the various creatures that held his body in their grip were pacified, slowing—if not ceasing—their mad scramble to alter all they found amiss within him.

He closed his eyes, submitting to their repairs.

LUKE'S heated skin smoldered through the layers of clothing she wore, but whenever she moved away, he would begin to groan and writhe in his sleep, a slumber so deep she could not rouse him. And so she stayed, committed to keeping her arms wrapped about a veritable furnace, unwilling to disturb—however slightly—his healing process.

Time passed in a haze as she drifted in and out of a light sleep, waking to blot Luke's forehead, to hold yet another glass of water to his lips. He imbibed an impressive quantity of water as enzymatic cascades worked overtime, shredding away damaged tissues within his body before setting about the process of repairing and restructuring.

Eventually, exhaustion claimed her, and she fell into her own fevered dreams.

Dreams which became increasingly erotic until her eyes fluttered open. *Not a dream.*

Luke's hard body was pressed against her backside, and

though his erection made his interest evident, it was his fingers that moved, working magic wherever they touched.

Already, he'd tugged loose the drawstring of her chemise and managed to unbuckle the top two fasteners of her leather corset. Not that she minded. Not at all. The slow slide of his rough skin over her puckered nipple sent a rush of warmth between her legs.

"Mmm," she hummed. She tipped her head backward against his shoulder and her braid tumbled free. *Someone* had been stealing hairpins while she slept. "Feeling better?"

"Much." He nipped her earlobe, his hot breath brushing across the curve of her neck. "The wound to my arm, healed. All pain, gone. But I still feel as if a fire is burning inside. Whatever transformations your cells have wrought, they've left me ravenous." He rolled her nipple between his fingers. "Any objection if I proceed to devour you?" His rough voice woke every last nerve.

"None," she gasped out, feeling wanton. "Though I'd rather be claimed." She twitched her hips backward to emphasize her point. "Fully. Completely."

A growl of approval tore from his throat, and his hand tightened on her breast, his fingers pinching her nipple and ripping a cry of pleasure from her throat.

Buckle by buckle, her corset fell open beneath his fingers. Gathering the material of her chemise in his fist, he yanked it upward, then spread the surface of his palm across the expanse of her bare stomach. The heat of his touch and the cool rush of air sent shivers running over her skin.

All the while, his lips kissed, bit, and then soothed the skin of her neck just below her ear, fanning the flames of desire yet higher. She squirmed in his embrace—her hands falling upon forearms that seemed to have muscles of braided wire— desperate to pull away, if only to rip the clothing from her body. But he held her tight against his stiff cock, all while slowly slipping his hand beneath the waistband of her trousers.

His fingertips spread her slick folds, resuming their earlier exploration of all that brought her pleasure. His hand slid deeper, pushing a finger into her tight channel, working her gently, until her hips began to jerk against his hand and a delicious pressure threatened to crest.

"No." She grabbed his wrist and pulled his hand away. "Not this way. I want you inside me." Buried deep while she reached for her pleasure.

Twisting, she stabbed her fingers into his thick hair, dragging his mouth to hers. Their tongues tangled, and she tasted the salt of his sweat and the heat of his desire. Fire licked over her skin.

He reared back. "Clothes. Off."

Her braid tumbled loose as she rose up on her knees, shrugging off her corset and pulling her chemise over her head. Luke growled in appreciation, his hands yanking the soft wool of her trousers down her hips. Then he lifted his gaze to hers.

"Your eyes." She clasped his face—rough with stubble— between her palms, staring. "They're not brown anymore—not entirely. There are flecks of gold streaking through them. They all but glow." *Glorious.*

Toppling her backward, he stripped away the last of her clothing, then loomed over her. "Has anything else changed?" He grinned as her gaze traveled over his naked glory.

"I hardly had the chance to look earlier," she protested. But, *aether*, he was magnificent. Impossible not to run her hands over the hard planes and angles of his chest, his strong shoulders, his bulging arms. Strong. Healthy. Vibrant. "Before that, no matter how badly I wished to touch you so, I was a married woman."

"Was." He flipped onto his back, ridding himself of his own clothing.

She gasped. At the magnificent view, of course, but also at

the scattering of scales beneath the edge of his rib cage where the needle had pierced his flesh. She dropped a fingertip to them, brushing their surface. "Can you feel that?"

"I can." He glanced down, flexing the muscles of his abdomen. A delighted grin stretched his mouth. "What of my arm?"

Natalia unwound the bandage. Another clustering of scales traced an alluring path across his biceps. She leaned close, pressing soft kisses to them. *Thank aether.* The treatment had worked. Blinking back the tears that welled in her eyes, she lifted her gaze and stared into his blazing eyes. "Fully healed." And more evenly matched for the fight that was to come. She pushed the thought aside. First, a celebration.

"An amazing recovery." She sat up, her eyes drawn across the room to a lamp glowing upon the hearthside table. "Are you not the least bit—?" *Hungry.* But that word died on her lips. A tray rested there—one that must have been left outside the laboratory door—and it was empty, its contents devoured. "You ate everything?" It was clear she'd slept deeply, but how long?

Luke pulled her down on top of him. A rumbling laugh resonated in his chest. "Not everything."

---

SOFT BREASTS and hard nipples slid over his chest as Natalia shifted away, reaching for her pocket watch. Her thigh grazed his rampant erection as she landed on her stomach, sending his mind into a blazing swirl of need. He rolled onto his side and smoothed a hand over the rise of her arse, a desperate attempt to rein himself in while she noted the time. With a fingertip, he traced a path across the scales clustered at the base of her spine. Green, with a flash of red fire.

"Four o'clock!" She dropped the pocket watch and glanced

over her shoulder. Light danced in her eyes. A coy smile tipped the corner of her lips upward. "Like what you see?"

*Aether*, was that an invitation? He'd planned to hold back, to bring her to a climax before sinking into her sweet, wet sex. But this... Yes, *this* was what he wanted. To drive into her until she screamed his name.

Never before had he felt so alive, so strong. So filled with lust. But she was inexperienced... he shouldn't...

And yet...

He rose up and pulled her onto her knees, bent her forward until she fell upon her hands. He caught at her loose braid, giving it a sharp tug before dragging his hand down her back, across the scattering of scales that glinted in the moonlight. He stilled. "Do you want it like this? From behind?" *Rutting like animals?* He held his breath. Did the beasts inside them both pant for this, for a primitive coupling, an explosive release? His cock throbbed.

But he waited.

She dropped to her elbows. "Yes." Her voice was husky, her desire echoing his.

Still he held back. Nudging her knees apart, he slid a finger over her slick folds until she cried out, her voice a mixture of desperation and desire. His breath hitched with need. "Please."

Steadying her hips with one hand, he guided the broad head of his cock to her damp entrance. And sank into her tight channel a single inch. Easing out, he pushed forward again.

"Oh, Luke," she rasped. "Yes. More." She edged her knees farther apart, and he sank deeper, his hips pressing flush to hers.

His fingers dug into the soft, pliant flesh of her hips as his body blazed with lust. Impossible not to move. He drew back, and with one thrust, drove into her completely, into her tight, squeezing channel. "Natalia!" His breath was ragged.

Squirming, she arched her back and cried out, panting, groaning feverish words of encouragement that raced across his skin and burned in his ears as he plunged into her again and again, claiming her body with long, hard strokes.

His climax gathered at the base of his spine, drawing ever tighter. Buried deep, he paused. "No," he rasped, then slid free. He wanted to see her face, watch her eyes as they blazed with heat. For him.

"Luke!" A cry of frustration.

He pulled at her legs, dropping her onto her stomach, rolling her onto her back. Catching her mouth with his, he kissed her deeply.

She bit his lip, then wrenched her mouth away. "I need…"

Spreading her legs, she yanked him against her swollen center, and he slid inside. Her legs lifted, her ankles wrapped about his hips pulling him closer. Nails dug into the skin of his arse, and her pelvis tipped upward, encouraging his powerful, pistoning strokes.

He levered up onto his arms, shifting to thrust higher against her center. "Come!" he ordered.

Her sex clenched, clamping down on him. "Luke!" Her blue eyes blazed as she screamed his name.

Primitive satisfaction rushed through him, and he strained against her, grinding as he chased his own climax. With a roar, he drove into her with a final stroke and the world about him exploded. Lights flashed. Blood pounded. Air rushed from his chest. And his body collapsed. Just enough sense remained for him to tilt to the side, twisting as his shoulders hit the mattress. But he didn't let go. She came with him—hot, sweaty and limp —and landed upon his chest.

"Aether," he breathed, finally dragging enough oxygen into his lungs. He wrapped his arms tight about her.

"Magnificent." She dropped a tired head to his shoulder—her blonde braid a ragged tangle—and slipped a weary arm about his waist. "And still a few hours until dawn."

"Again?" A laugh rumbled in his chest, but already his cock

twitched with interest.

With a fading voice, she whispered, "Soon." And drifted to sleep, snoring softly.

Luke stared at the bed canopy that arched above him. Health restored. Wrapped in the arms of the woman he loved. Safe. Everything he wanted within reach.

If he could but remove the one last remaining threat. Running would buy them time, but it wouldn't solve their problems, not permanently.

Ivanov and Kravchuk would have to be eliminated.

---

A MURMUR of muffled voices woke her. "Luke," she said, reaching out an arm. "We need to dress." But no one was there. The mattress beside her was cool.

Natalia snapped her eyes open and sat upright, clutching the sheet to her bare breasts as Luke—fully dressed—strolled back into the bedchamber, carrying a new tray laden with a teapot, cups and an abundance of baked treats. He moved with ease, without a hint of exhaustion or pain.

*Not a dream.* They'd done it. He was cured. Possibilities stretched before them, if only they could outrun, out-fight Ivanov and Kravchuk and their winged mounts. Excitement faded as a heaviness settled in her stomach. Another battle loomed, and she was so very tired of fighting. Of running. She wanted more time with Luke alone—here and now—but their best chance of surviving a confrontation with Dimitri and Ivanov was to draw them out unexpectedly, in daylight, when their pteryformes' vision was—at the very least—compromised.

Zia trundled along behind Luke, her tail swishing. Routine had been disrupted—on many levels—and she was keeping the newest human to enter the equation carefully in her line of sight.

Slivers of brilliant gold flashed in his eyes. "I wondered when you'd wake." He set down the tray and nodded at the window. A faint glimmer of light spilled through its thick glass. "The steam wagon is loaded. William, Aileen and McKay are shuttering windows and making last minute preparations. Our boat awaits, ready, save for its passengers. I took the liberty of coating a quiver's worth of arrows with your laboratory-refined venom to pair with your deadly aim and crossbow." He stopped beside the bed, his gaze caressing her exposed skin. Every nerve stood at attention, begging for more time. "About last night…"

She dropped the sheet. Grabbing his waistcoat with both hands, she pulled him down on top of her and kissed him, deeply, regretting every moment lost to slumber. The sword fastened to his hip pressed against her thigh as his hands fell upon her waist, sliding upward over her rib cage to cup the weight of her breasts.

But they were out of time.

Though he pulled away, a suggestive smile teased his lips, and an appreciative gaze slid over her nakedness, their thoughts both straying in the same carnal direction.

"Last night was amazing," she whispered, though words alone failed to convey how her world had tilted off axis, redefining and expanding the concept of bedroom sport. She needed *this* man in her life. Always and forever. No other would do.

Luke's expression sobered. "About last night, we forgot to…" He swallowed. "If there are consequences—"

Her lips parted in shock. Not horror. Any children of Luke's would be welcome, but she'd not wish to forcibly bind him to her that way. "We were careless."

"Swept up in the moment as we were, the fault lies with us both." He tipped up her chin. "If you conceive, we'll marry?"

Not at all the impassioned proposal a woman desired, but would she turn him away? Not a chance. She loved him. Tired of living a life apart, she had no use for an empty title or a drafty castle. But after her first cold, practical marriage, she wanted more than an offer of marriage that followed on the heels of a "mistake".

"This isn't the time for such a discussion." Natalia slid from the bed, pulling on her clothes, shoving her feet into her boots and lacing them tightly. She buckled her belt about her waist and slid daggers into place. "No." She held up a hand when he would press the matter. "We must focus, lest we not survive the day or, worse, find ourselves transported back to Russia."

His hand fell on the hilt of his rapier, and determination hardened his face. "Not a chance I'll allow that to happen."

She had no doubt he would do his best to prevent such an occurrence. But there was another weakness. "My father's notes." How she wished he could have met Luke, witnessed this triumph, recognized the potency of uncultured dragon stem cells. Lifting them from the table, she caught Luke's gaze, then turned to the fireplace. The yellowed pages were her last physical connection to her father. Her chest ached at the thought of destroying them, but she couldn't risk them falling into the wrong hands.

"Natalia, are you certain?" Worry filled his eyes. "This cure has been nothing short of miraculous."

"But in the wrong hands, the outcome could be monstrous. Cells harvested from a dragon's egg, from the developing embryo itself, might be even more potent. Conservation of a species will not even land on their list of priorities." She swallowed. "The process is fresh in my mind. Perhaps, when this is over, I'll put pen to paper." *Perhaps.*

She brushed aside a stray tear. Decision reached, she tossed the folded sheets of paper onto the smoldering coals, and watched as their edges sparked, caught fire, and disintegrated into ash.

## CHAPTER TWELVE

WHITE-FACED BUT RESOLUTE, Aileen climbed into the steam wagon beside her grandfather. The vehicle chuffed and puffed as pistons churned inside their cylinders, ready to propel them down the rutted road. William held the steering pole, his face bright with excitement, no doubt relishing the potential for danger, for a sword fight, for a new life in the city.

"Do not," Natalia warned for what must be the twenty-third time, "under any circumstances, skirmish with Ivanov or Kravchuk. Keep your charges well in mind. You must reach Edinburgh *safely*."

"I've already given you my word." William pulled his wiry shoulders back and puffed out his narrow chest. "Repeatedly. We'll reach your Edinburgh townhouse. The Russians have no interest in me, and," he glanced at Aileen, "nothing but disdain for that which they ought to value." He squinted at the horizon where the bright sun crept into a cloudless sky. A rare, spring event in Scotland. "Best take advantage of the light."

Pteryformes were, by nature, nocturnal. Not that they couldn't be roused and coaxed—with the promise of fresh meat

—to fly during daylight. A highly likely and unfortunate possibility. With a final nod and a sharp tug at the steering pole, William set the steam wagon in motion.

"We need to hurry." Luke caught at her hand, yanking her thoughts back to their most-pressing situation.

Together they dashed back through the castle's gate—locking it behind them—and into the kitchens where Zia paced, unsettled, beside the brazier and her three eggs, well aware that today's activities were anything but routine. Her tongue flicked as she rushed toward them with unusual speed and reared back to drop her clawed front feet on Luke's thighs.

"It's okay." He stroked a hand over her head. "You'll love the mountains, the rocks. So much more interesting than a boring castle. A new home. A new friend." He grinned. "With luck and a handful of years, perhaps grand-dragonets."

Natalia snorted. It was a few hours travel up the River Teith to Callander, their gateway into the highlands and, from there, the Trossachs. Not that either of them expected to reach it before their hasty departure was discovered. Odds were trouble would arrive long before they reached the small village.

She lifted the heavy coal scuttle—lined as it was with river stones heated for the first leg of their journey—that held Zia's clutch and turned toward the stairway that led downward to the postern door in the curtain wall. Slinging their rucksack across his shoulder, Luke hefted the brazier and its carefully banked fire and followed.

A quick turn of the iron key in the door, and they stepped outside the relative safety of the castle's walls and struck out upon the path that led to the river's edge. Low-hanging branches caught at her hair, at the braid she'd carefully plaited and re-pinned about the crown of her head. Though she hurried, she was careful not to trip upon rocks and roots that jutted from the uneven ground at her feet. Dropping her precious cargo was not an option.

A few minutes later she stopped at the river's edge, searching for the boat Luke swore he'd examined last night while she slept. He slipped past and began tossing aside a layer of cut branches and underbrush to reveal their escape vessel: a small dinghy—its wood so old and rough they were certain to end with splinters. An odd—and equally old—motor was bolted to its stern. Everything would fit, but without much room to spare. He tossed their rucksack into the boat, beside a reassuring cache of assorted weapons, then shoved the boat halfway into the shallow water that rushed past.

Holding her hand, Luke steadied her while she stepped into the boat as it wobbled on its keel. *It would be fine*, her mind insisted, once they were out on the water. Providing it didn't leak. Or the motor didn't seize.

Luke caught her curious glance. "A modified Trouvé outboard. A bit rusty, but I was able to coax it back to life." He lifted Zia into the dinghy, then very carefully placed the brazier and the coal scuttle into the hull. "Hang on."

He gave the boat a great shove, and then leapt onto it as the current caught it, turning the vessel downstream toward Stirling. *Away* from the Trossachs. Natalia caught up the oars, straightening them, doing what she could to keep them from drifting too far while Luke cranked the flywheel. A moment later, the engine roared to life, and he dropped onto a seat, gripped the tiller, and steered them upstream. She tucked away the oars and turned her attention to their weapons cache.

Clipping her quiver to her belt, she caught up her crossbow. When they were discovered—for it was inevitable, especially given the din of the outboard motor—arrows would be their first and best line of defense. She notched one in place, careful to avoid its metal-tipped point as she cranked the tension spring.

Only then did she look up. The rising sun illuminated the

flowing river with a brilliant, golden light. A beautiful dawn in a cloudless sky. Excellent for spotting an approaching enemy.

Still, despite her intended vigilance, Natalia's gaze drifted downward to Luke. His thick, dark hair blew in the wind, while the rising sun threw the planes of his face into both light and shadow. She marveled at the ripple of muscle beneath fabric. At the complete and total restoration of his strength.

His eyes danced when he caught hers, and he grinned. Desire sparked inside of her as she returned his smile. There was no denying the exhilaration that accompanied an infusion of dragon stem cells. She'd certainly enjoyed the sexual potency they'd bestowed upon him.

A screech tore through the air, and a dark silhouette appeared in the sky. Pteryformes. Zia opened her mouth, echoing the call with her own primal cry before draping herself over the scuttle that held her clutch, wings outstretched.

*Dammit*, she'd hoped for more time. Ivanov and Dimitri must have set a watch to have discovered William's departure so quickly, to have questioned him, to have already redirected their attention back to Castle Kinlarig and its surrounds.

Tempting as it was to turn toward the shore in anticipation of a fight, open water was their best hope of gaining an advantage; when the pteryformes swooped toward them, she could take better aim without trees to block her sight. Luke's shoulders tensed. Wrapping rope about the tiller, he lashed the outboard motor in place and pointed the boat directly up the river, buying them a few minutes of hands-free navigation before they reached the first bend.

He dragged forth a long rifle and proceeded to breech-load a bullet into the weapon.

Her jaw dropped. "How did you find bullets?" she called. She'd hunted throughout the castle, hoping to find a stash. Even offering a silver tea set to the townspeople in trade for a handful of bullets. But they were nowhere to be found.

"In the pockets of Rathail's hunter," he called back over the noise of the engine.

*Of course.* She should have thought to look.

Regardless, the crossbow was her weapon. Hours upon hours spent in the castle courtyard at target practice. She'd skewered one man, why not a flying reptile?

As the shadow of its great wings passed overhead, she squinted and took aim. "On the right!" she yelled, claiming her mark. Though she had little chance of hitting Dimitri from this angle, nothing would please her more than to drop his ride from underneath him.

Luke too had a score to settle, but he pointed his rifle toward the beast on the left, aiming for Ivanov and leaving Dimitri to her. Pride swelled in her chest. In this fight they were well-matched, each counting on the other's skills to elude capture.

Bullets splashed into the water beside them; the report of gunfire followed.

*Thwack.* Her arrow flashed through the sky and tore a hole through the Dimitri's mount's leathery wing. She cursed. Not enough damage to slow the flying reptile. There was nothing to do but pray the tip of the arrow had sent enough venom burning through its wing to discourage cooperation with its handler.

*Bang.* Ivanov screamed as Luke's bullet hit its mark.

Round one fell to them.

Luke reloaded.

She notched another arrow as the pteryformes banked and turned, swooping lower this time. Again, she aimed for the only spot that might prove vulnerable on the oversized, featherless bird: where wing met body.

Bullets slammed into the wood of their boat, shattered slivers erupted into the air. The boat rocked, and Zia bellowed her displeasure at the threat to her clutch.

*Thwack. Bang.* They both fired at once. A bullet struck Dimitri, but he held fast as his beast circled higher into the sky.

The arrow, however, tore through the second creature's forearm, and Ivanov's pteryform screamed, rearing away and crashing into the trees along the bank, ripping its rider from its back. Ivanov fell, striking the riverbank with a thud, his neck bent at an unnatural angle. A dark glee rushed through her at the fitting death of a vile man who had so casually and coldly thought to put a convenient end to Luke's life.

"A brilliantly placed arrow," Luke said, flashing her an approving smile that made her heart swell with pride. "One down."

But there was no time to enjoy their victory; the first bend of the river approached. Luke tossed his rifle aside, then cut the engine. They would not crash headlong into the riverbank, but they now lost the advantage of speed, of controlling—to some degree—their direction. Silence descended as the boat began to drift slowly downstream.

Luke lifted a finely-honed rapier and slid a dagger from his belt. "Only three bullets remained in the dead hunter's pocket." The gold flecks in his eyes glinted. "Worth hauling that rifle along, however, if only to injure that bastard, Kravchuk."

The final pteryform aloft turned, circling back toward them.

Momentary elation quickly faded and was replaced by renewed fear. The danger was not at all past. "Be careful," she begged. "Dimitri might want to capture me alive, but he won't spare a second thought for your life."

"He needs to be killed," Luke stated flatly. "He can't be allowed to escape, to return to Russia with news of anything, including our location."

"Agreed." With a glance at Zia, at the eggs, Natalia reassured herself of their relative safety, then braced her legs and lifted her crossbow once more. Icy resolve steeled her spine as she prepared to take down her former fiancé before his mount flew close enough that Luke would find a use for his sword.

With a blood-curdling cry, the winged reptile folded its wings, obscuring Dimitri—her would-be target—and dove.

Luke swore and lifted his blade. "Does he mean to sink us?"

"Possibly."

Correcting for speed, distance, drift and wind, Natalia took her best shot. And missed. Before she could reload, a flash of light glinted off silver metal, and Dimitri dropped onto their boat with a crash, blade in hand. "I've come for what is rightfully mine," he snarled.

"I belong to no one save myself," Natalia replied, chin lifted. "And a dragon should never be subjected to your oversight."

"We'll see about that."

The boat rocked violently, scattering hot coals from the brazier as Dimitri stomped over the cache of weapons, intent on slicing Luke's neck. Natalia dropped her crossbow and bent to draw a knife from her boot—one she could throw—all while reaching with her free hand to splash river water into the boat. A hiss of steam rose into the air. Fire averted, she waited, watching for an opening to enter the fray, but Luke and Zia stood between her and the Russian. Heart in her throat, she reached for the coal scuttle, helping Zia to drag the precious eggs away from the fight.

Luke deflected the first attack with relative ease, and shock rippled across Dimitri's face. "What is this?" he asked, brow furrowed. Assured of easy prey by Ivanov's poisoned blade, the Russian had dropped onto their boat unprepared to struggle for a victory. She hoped it was a fatal mistake.

With a roar, Luke attacked.

Blades clanged and slashed through the air, with Luke's newfound strength lending him the upper hand as the boat drifted ever closer to the shore. *Slash!* Blood bloomed on Dimitri's shirt. *Rip!* The Russian retaliated, slicing though the cloth covering Luke's thigh. Blood seeped forth.

The battle raged on.

Zia lunged, sinking her venom-laced teeth into Dimitri's ankle. The Russian yelled, striking out at the beast latched to his boot as Luke took aim at Dimitri's side. The boat rocked, nearly tipping them all into the river.

*An opening.* But as Natalia adjusted her grip on the hilt of her knife, preparing to throw, a dark shadow swooped low. With a rush of cool air, Dimitri's pteryform stretched out a clawed leg. But not to save its master or to carry away the man battling against him. Instead, it snatched the handle of the coal scuttle, lifting the dragon eggs into the sky.

"No!" But her scream was futile. Somehow that cursed beast had recognized the precious cargo they carried.

With a blood-curdling howl, Zia launched herself from the boat and into the river. *Splash.* Her short legs churned furiously and her small wings flapped as she swam the short distance to the shore in desperate pursuit of her young.

Dread clawed at Natalia's throat. If the beast dropped its plunder, there was no chance the tiny dragonets—still within their leathery shells—would survive. Rage blazed as she narrowed her gaze back upon the man who had—with cold-hearted intent—set in motion the events that brought them to this desperate day.

Rage pounded in her ears, but with the pteryform in the sky, there was nothing to be done. Save end the man who had initiated this attack.

*Thud.* The dingy bumped, then scraped along the edge of the river. Catching on unseen rocks and debris beneath the water's surface, it began to tip onto its side.

"Go!" Luke yelled.

She leapt from the boat and into mud. Luke vaulted to land beside her. Together they ran up the riverbank, over the rocks and weeds, seeking solid footing.

Dimitri followed.

The sword fight resumed, and the clang of blades rang

through the woods as the two men attacked and parried, occasionally grappling in close quarters or drawing blood. Neither managed to land a serious wound, though she could see Dimitri weakening from the dragon venom.

Crouching, blade in hand, Natalia waited. She threw occasional glances at the sky, watching with her heart in her throat, to track where the pteryform might land. It was circling the field just beyond the copse of trees beside them. Should it land, there might still be hope that they could rescue the eggs.

Luke shifted his approach and attacked, forcing Dimitri to dodge sideways and driving him backward. *Toward her.* For a heartbeat, their gazes met. He was offering her the chance to extract her revenge. For her injury, her father's death, her exile. And for hurting the man she loved.

*Now.*

With ice in her veins she lunged, slicing deeply through the muscles of Dimitri's back. He screamed as blood welled, then stumbled. As he struggled for balance, realization washed over his face. He could no longer hope to fend them both off. Not with dragon venom pumping through his veins. All but dead, yet still on his feet, he *turned his back* on Luke and locked his heated gaze on her.

"Why so much hate? Why couldn't you just let us go?" she yelled. Her muscles shook with emotion, with a need to understand.

"If only you'd had the decency to die when you fell from that cave, I wouldn't have had to spend the last three years living under your father's shadow." A sneer pulled at his lips. "You and your father's foolish altruism held us all back, when so much power easily lay within our grasp. He should have shared the potential of his work. With *me.*"

Dimitri charged.

She lifted her blade and stood her ground.

*Ffffftt!* Luke's blade pierced Dimitri's torso—from back to front.

Eyes wide, the Russian staggered, wrapping his hands about the blade that protruded from his chest, as if he might manage to pry it free and resume the fight. But blood welled in his mouth and trickled from its corners. He stumbled. *Snap!* The thin blade broke in two. With a look of shock, he collapsed to the ground.

Natalia stood, shaking. The man who had betrayed her father, who had tortured the man she loved, was dead. A man she'd once thought to marry. Ought she feel something other than the cold pleasure of justice?

---

It was over. Luke stared at the dead man lying on the ground waiting to feel something. Relief? Remorse? Elation? All he could summon was disgust. For the wasted opportunities and resources that Kravchuk had thrown away like a child who could never be satisfied, no matter the bounty laid at his feet.

"Zia's eggs!" Natalia yelled, tipping her face upward to search the trees above her. She stepped backward, tripping over Kravchuk's body.

Luke caught her, wrapped his arms about her waist and pressed a quick kiss to her lips. *Aether*, his heart nearly burst with love. She'd fought so bravely. "Eggs?"

Finding her balance, she pointed behind him at the winged creature the Russian had ridden. "When Dimitri dropped onto the boat, the pteryform snatched away the coal scuttle!"

*Shit.* Not over. His arms loosened their hold even as his muscles tensed, readying themselves for another battle.

"The creature was circling, coming in for a landing nearby, over there in the field. But—" Natalia's hand fell upon his arm. "You seem fine, but you're wounded."

"Mostly superficial cuts. We'll see to them later." He looked over her shoulder, searching through the undergrowth for the missing dragon. "That explains why Zia leapt from the boat."

There was a roar, followed by an ear-piercing shriek. An unmistakable sound of two enraged reptiles.

"Zia!" Natalia cried.

He and Natalia took off at a run. Just beyond the trees, a field opened before them where Zia snarled and gnashed her teeth, facing down a wounded pteryform some five times her size. The pteryform hissed and clawed the ground. Snapping, it lunged. But Zia darted out of reach, turning her head to spit venom onto the beast's broadside. As the toxin frothed and bubbled atop its thick hide, a faint odor of sulfur—as if someone had struck a match—rose into the air.

Zia was holding her own. He bit back his praise, lest he distract her.

With a roar, the pteryform threw its head backward and let loose a furious cry.

"There!" Natalia pointed.

Behind the pteryform, the coal scuttle lay tipped upon its side. One egg was still nestled midst the warm stones. Two others had rolled free, their gold streaks glimmering in the sunlight.

She grabbed at his hand, yanking him along as she crouched low to run behind the distracted pteryform, all but diving head-long into the undergrowth. Together, they half-walked, half-crawled along the edge of the field, skulking past the dueling creatures until they were only a few yards away from the dragon eggs.

Without warning, Natalia dashed out from their sketchy cover and snatched up the handle of the coal scuttle, pulling it back into relative safety. One egg saved. But pteryformes had excellent hearing, and it turned on its hind legs with a roar, searching the underbrush to find another foe at its back. Stretching its neck, the creature took a step forward.

Luke dragged Natalia behind the thick trunk of a tree. Staying was foolish—they ought to turn tail and run—but leaving the two eggs, leaving Zia to fend for herself wasn't an option.

Zia let loose an enraged squeal, then flutter-hopped behind the pteryform, snapping and biting at its ankles. Venom dripped from Zia's jaws as her teeth sank into the tough hide, and the rotten smell of hydrogen sulfide grew stronger.

Distracted, the pteryform turned again to hiss at this not-insignificant annoyance.

Though bloody and battered, energy still coursed through Luke's veins. He credited the stem cells. Crouching low, he braced his feet against the ground and prepared to run. "I'll grab the eggs. Can you cover me?"

Pushing the coal scuttle behind the trunk of a tree, Natalia drew a throwing knife from her boot. She tested the weight of the blade in her hand. "There's little chance I can do more than cause it a moment's annoyance."

He pointed at a farmhouse in the distance; they needed walls if they were to stand a chance against the pteryform's sharp beak and massive claws. "Then we run. We reach its door, then draw the creature's attention, give Zia a chance to find cover."

She nodded. "Ready?"

"Ready." He tensed.

Natalia stepped into the open and took a deep breath, focusing on her target. Waiting. She gave a sharp whistle and the great winged reptile turned, surveilling her with a single enormous eye. As the blade left her hand, Luke darted forward, gathering up a dragon egg in each arm, tucking them close to his chest before veering into the thin cover of the underbrush toward the coal scuttle.

From the corner of his eye, he saw the enormous creature

rear back, a knife embedded in the side of its torso just beneath the front edge of its wing. Zia darted forward, ripping a chunk of flesh from the beast's hindquarters.

Skidding through forest detritus to the coal scuttle, Luke dropped the two eggs inside and closed his hand about the handle, every muscle tensed for escape.

"Wait," Natalia said, pointing.

Above the field, a shadow passed. He looked up with dread. The other pteryform had returned and now circled, calling to its companion below. The grounded—and wounded—creature replied with a ground-shaking roar, then began to flap its enormous wings, rising into the air.

At his side, Natalia called to Zia, urging the dragon into the copse of trees at the river's edge, all while taking steps in the direction of the farmhouse. Should the two pteryformes decide to attack, amidst the tree trunks, they would find it difficult—though not impossible—to maneuver.

But though the cries of the two beasts rent the air and shattered the morning peace for miles, they no longer had masters to command them and their forms circled ever higher into the sky. Perhaps, seeing no reason to continue to tangle with sharp and biting adversaries without good reason, they sought a lair to lick their wounds and hide from the bright morning sun. Not that Luke cared. Their silhouettes disappeared into the distance.

The dragon bumped against his leg, tipping her head sideways to inspect the contents of the scuttle he held. He set it upon the ground and ran a hand over her head. "There you go, Zia. Safe and sound."

He turned and Natalia threw herself into his arms, wrapping hers about his neck, triumph flashing in her eyes. "We did it!"

He pulled her against his chest. "Accomplished the impossible at least three times since dawn." Desire flared, and he spun her around, pressing her back to the bark of the tree, spreading his fingers wide to grip the flare of her hips.

Her eyes darkened. "Only a kiss." Her voice was husky. "We're about to have company."

In the distance, William's voice called. With only a few minutes until they were discovered, Luke reined in every instinct. Save one. Dragons. A sword fight. And the battle won. Claiming the lips of a lady—his love—felt as necessary as drawing his next breath.

NATALIA STOOD BESIDE Luke atop a rocky promontory overlooking Loch Lubnaig as Zia and Sasha acquainted themselves with each other. Over rough grasses and scattered scree, they walked side by side, tongues flicking as they explored the many cracks and crevices, searching for a space to serve as a home.

"Took you long enough," Luke's brother said, then muttered under his breath about fire-spitting dragons and sparks and the inconvenience of an entire wardrobe of now-charred clothing. John Dryden—waiting impatiently for over a week in the Trossachs—had happily turned over care of the young male dragon to them. He slapped his brother on the shoulder. "Looks like Scotland agrees with you."

Luke snorted, but didn't elaborate.

With little more than a sideways glance and a twist of his lips, he'd taken in Luke's restored health and dropped the keys to a small cottage—where the dragon eggs rested, warm and safe beside the hearth—into his hands. Soon, their tiny egg teeth would pierce through the shells and they would have their hands full. "I'm needed back at the estate. Send a skeet pigeon when you pick a date." With a grin, he departed.

William had caught the empty, flat-bottomed boat as it drifted past them on the road to Stirling, then turned back for Castle Kinlarig to look for its missing occupants. Relieved to find them safe, if bruised and battered, he'd happily reported that Aileen and McKay were unharmed. After discovering the bed of the wagon held not much but crated swords and armor, the Russians had spotted the ploy and wasted little time with questions before taking to the air.

Adjourning briefly to the castle for bandages and fresh supplies, Natalia had given William a fierce hug and promised to visit the city soon. Then she and Luke had set out once again upon the River Teith, reaching the small town of Callandar—unmolested—by late afternoon. Inquiries directed them to his brother, some distance further north alongside Loch Lubnaig. Unwilling and unable to stop, lest they reveal the reality of drag-ons, they pressed onward. Sleeping—for the most part—beneath the stars, they'd reached his brother's temporary residence the following day.

Alone at last, Luke cleared his throat. "I retract my earlier suggestion. That you marry a wealthy gentleman. Let the castle crumble. So long as we're together—"

"I refuse to be your kept woman." His gaze snapped to hers, but she softened her harsh words with flashing eyes and laughter that rose to ride upon the wind. "I insist we marry." She pressed a palm to her heart. "I love you. I have ever since you first taught me the proper way to wield a sword." Waving a hand, she continued. "I don't wish to own a castle, Luke. I've had enough of its dark, dank stone walls. A distant relative of some consequence wishes to purchase the rock pile and its lands. No doubt keen to style himself the next laird."

He grinned. "Is this a proposal, Lady Kinlarig?"

"It is." She swatted his arm. "Don't be difficult. Will you marry me, Luke Dryden?"

"You wish to live with a dragonkeeper in a cottage beside a loch?" He tipped up her chin.

"For now. Provided we spend a portion of each year in the city so that I might consult with colleagues. We'll need to install a small laboratory, of course. And eventually, we'll need more room for the children."

"Children?" His eyes lit up.

"Several." Leaning into his touch, she lifted her hands to his shoulders, drawing him closer still. Brushing her lips over his. "Say yes."

"Yes," he whispered, then nipped her earlobe sending a tremor of need through her entire body.

Her next words came on a gasp. "The cottage bed looked sturdy. Shall we investigate?"

"Immediately." He scooped her into his arms and strode down the hillside.

Laughing, she wrapped her arms about his neck, planning all the different ways they might make use of a—relatively—empty cottage.

# A REFLECTION OF SHADOWS

CHAPTER ONE

*London*
*February 1885*

*L*OOPS OF FINE CHAIN coiled as Colleen returned Lady
Sophia's golden locket to its velvet pouch. *Done.* She
closed the safe, gave the dial a spin and rehung the
heavy oil painting to hide the strongbox from view. Odd, that a
man of Lord Aldridge's means would choose to stare at blurry
haystacks in a field. Years of creeping into the libraries and
studies of wealthy gentlemen had taught her that most preferred
to gaze upon portraits of themselves. Or of a distinguished
ancestor. A favorite dog. Occasionally a beautiful wife.

All, however, kept at least one bottle of single malt scotch
whisky on hand. Liquid sunshine in a bottle. Drifting across the
dark room to the lord's liquor cabinet, she considered the array
of choices before her, tracing the zigs and zags of the pattern cut
into a crystal decanter with a leather-clad fingertip.

The household was quiet. All servants had retired. Lord
Aldridge himself would be careful to be elsewhere this evening.
Still, she shouldn't. Not once in four years had she helped

herself to the smallest of nips. But tonight's task had gone smoothly, without the slightest hitch. And she was officially off the job.

Retired.

With a blemish free record.

A smile stole across her face. Already her bags were packed. Soon her cat, Sorcha, would return from her city prowl, and London would be nothing but a sooty memory.

She ought to celebrate. Lord Aldridge wouldn't begrudge her a drink for saving his daughter—and her dowry—from a marriage to a good-for-nothing scoundrel with significant gambling debts, would he? She pulled the stopper from the decanter and poured herself a splash.

Generous dowries made for wonderful bait, but sometimes they hooked a bottom feeder.

Livid, the earl had turned to *Witherspoon and Associates: Private matters handled with discretion.* His daughter had been compromised—a polite way of saying she'd allowed herself to be seduced by a treasure hunter without regard for the consequences. Pressing for an engagement announcement, the reprobate had threatened to display her engraved locket while sharing detailed stories of his conquest. Shameful behavior. And all mere days before the naïve girl was to be presented to society. The very kind of situation which Witherspoon and Associates was often employed to handle. Colleen had retrieved the locket while Mr. Witherspoon himself arranged for the offending gentleman's debt to be called in, casting any nasty rumors that oozed from his mouth into doubt.

Glass in hand, Colleen sank into the large chair behind Lord Aldridge's desk, tipping backward to rest her booted feet on its surface. Swirling the whisky, she took a sip. Dignified, with a seamless blend of rich fruit, spice and just a hint of peat. Aether, she missed Scotland. Missed the quiet countryside surrounding Craigieburn and the nearby village, where none of its populace ever glanced at her askance for, though golden eyes might be rare, there wasn't a single family who couldn't name a relative whose eyes glimmered in the dark.

Everything had changed the night the bridge carrying her parents' train across the River Tay collapsed, killing all aboard. Her chest still ached at the memory of burying empty coffins, of standing in the graveyard surrounded by well-meaning villagers but without a single family member beside her. She'd felt so very alone.

With her father's death, she'd become a laird in her own right, but tied up as her inheritance was in legal verbiage, her title was nominal until she reached her twenty-fifth birthday. Life in London under the thumb of her uncle—her mother's disapproving brother—had become her new reality.

Only three more days to go.

Once she ripped control of the property from her uncle's hands, she could finally tackle the ever-lengthening list of repairs on her family's home and surrounding properties. Five long years had passed since she'd last crossed its borders.

The door creaked.

Abandoning her drink, she dropped her feet to the ground and slipped into the shadows mere moments before another individual slipped into the room. She'd not expected Lord Aldridge's study to be such a popular destination this evening. Was his daughter's dowry so grand that men would have her by whatever means necessary?

Her hand slid to her boot, hovering above the dirk sheathed there. She was a sneak thief, working silently and alone. Unaccustomed to any interference. The blade was for self-defense, not for drawing blood over a silly girl's locket. Not once had she ever needed to resort to violence. Neither, however, did she wish to fail at her last task.

*Please, not here. Not tonight.*

The man shifted. Heredity, unnatural or otherwise, had

provided her with the advantage of keen nighttime vision. The faint light cast by the thin sliver of a waning moon was enough to fully illuminate Mr. Torrington's familiar form. Dark hair. A straight nose. The honed planes and angles of a handsome face. A set to his jaw that spoke of single-minded purpose and a razor-sharp mind.

*Friend not foe.* Her heart started beating again. With new purpose.

She'd always enjoyed watching the Queen's agent work. Reveled in stepping out of the shadows to materialize beside him. Colleen grinned. The first time she'd tapped his shoulder in the dark, he'd jumped so far and so high that she'd expected his own eyes to reflect the light of his lamp. But not only was Mr. Nicholas Torrington's lineage noble, his family tree contained no inexplicable branches.

Still, they both lived dual lives. One kept hidden from the *ton*, the other highly visible. For years, they'd flirted as their paths crossed. On rooftops, inside locked rooms, down dark alleyways. In ballrooms, at garden parties, in the hallways of the theater. Neither betraying the other's secrets with so much as a stray comment or shared glance at an inopportune moment.

Time passed and small conversations grew longer. An inexplicable bond formed. One that had snapped some months past.

With the coming of fall, gentry retreated to their country estates, and London society thinned. Still, small gatherings were held. On All Hallows' Eve, Mr. Torrington—eyes glittering—had lured her out onto a balcony where torches affixed to the balustrade burned. In the flickering light, he'd pressed a soft kiss to her mouth, and the ground beneath her feet shifted all while dragonflies took wing in her stomach. Would he propose they merge their assorted lives? If so, how would she answer? Forming an attachment to a London gentleman was not at all compatible with her plans.

But a giggling couple had wandered out behind them, and

whatever he'd been about to say had died on his lips. The evening ended in disappointment, and no flowers had arrived for her the next day, no note. Not a single indication that he wished to discuss the possibility of joining their two lives. She'd not seen or heard from him since.

Irritation had faded into a dull, empty ache, and she'd thrown herself into work and another flirtation. One that had been decidedly misguided on her part. Her fault for allowing emotion to direct her behavior. Had her dowry not been perceived as worthless, her life might have taken a turn not unlike that of her client's daughter for Mr. Glover was becoming an unavoidable and increasing irritation.

There was a faint click, and a dull, red light flickered to life. A shade with a long wavelength, one barely visible to most human eyes. Curious. Decilamps usually glowed a greenish-blue. A recent advance placed in the hands of the Queen's agents? Mr. Torrington's eye caught upon the unfinished drink as he crossed to the desk, popped open its locked drawers with ease and rifled through its contents.

Was it coincidence that led him to this very study on this particular night?

Possibly. Lord Aldridge sat on the board of the Lister Institute, a group with close ties to the Queen's agents. Still, she needed to be certain.

Frowning, Mr. Torrington prowled about the edges of the room, peering behind paintings. Colleen's heart stopped and she forgot to breathe as he lifted the blurry haystacks, setting the painting aside to contemplate the numbers etched into the dial upon the safe. She couldn't allow anything to leave the lockbox tonight lest she stand accused. Frozen, she watched as he pressed his ear to the door and spun the dial with deft and capable fingers. Left four spins, right for three, left for two, then a twist to the right. *Pop.* The door fell open. She cursed silently as he inspected each box. Gold and silver. Emeralds, rubies and diamonds. But he took nothing. With a soft huff, he closed the door and rehung the painting.

Once again, she breathed.

She ought to stay silent, wait for him to leave, then slide down the drainpipe and disappear. After all, curiosity always killed the cat. But something about him still tugged at her heart, and soon she would quit London, never to see him again. With the necklace—and all of the contents of the safe—secure, she could afford to indulge a whim. "Can't find what you're looking for?" Mr. Torrington whipped about, lifting his decilamp as he reached for his weapon. The light seared her eyes, and she averted her gaze. "Do you mind?"

"Lady Stewart?" Incredulity laced his voice. "What are you doing here?" The beam of light lowered, and he dropped his hand from his hip, away from the TTX pistol hidden beneath his coat.

Adrenaline buzzed through her veins as the inevitable attraction flared. Impossible to leave now without playing their old game of cat and mouse. This time, however, if he let himself be caught, she had no intention of allowing him to slip away with a mere kiss.

Curving her lips into a smile, she sauntered back to the desk to lift her glass. "Enjoying a glass of whisky, neat. I'd offer you one, but you appear frustrated." Smoothing a gloved hand over the curve of her hip, over her close-fitting trousers, she invited his interest. "As if satisfaction is just beyond your reach..." She let the suggestion hang between them.

"Are you offering to help bring my evening to an exciting finish?" His broad shoulders relaxed, and his eyes—a narrow rim of brilliant blue surrounding dark pupils—flashed. To his credit, only then did his gaze drop. "Or merely offering a professional consultation?"

HER ANSWERING LAUGH was low and throaty. Despite the gravity of his mission, Nick found it impossible not to respond to her teasing. Like him, Lady Stewart was garbed entirely in black. A hooded cape about her shoulders. A shirt beneath a buckled corset. Pouches hung from a low-slung belt. Leather gloves stretched to her elbows. Trousers hugged her hips and thighs. But the boots... As always, those held his gaze with the tenacity of a pteryform trap. Leather and laced, they rose from her trim ankles, sheathing her long and shapely legs before releasing their grasp a few inches above her knees. Those brain cells that had not entirely abandoned work noted the stitching at her calf. Since they'd last crossed paths, she'd added a long—and likely sharp—blade to her attire.

His heart gave a great thud, then took off racing while the room grew warmer by several degrees.

Aether, he'd missed her. Missed the bustled and skirted woman who wore tinted spectacles and hugged the walls at society events. Missed the leather-clad seductress whose amber eyes flashed as they glinted back at him across the dark room, daring him to—

What, exactly?

His eyes lifted to her full lips, and he found himself stepping closer, not at all certain that she wouldn't bite. After disappearing from her life—from London—these past three months, she'd likely draw blood. But, like cream rising to the top, finding out the answer had become an immediate priority.

So much for a formal call that landed them both upon a settee in a parlor while her aunt supervised awkward courtship conversation. Better, perhaps, that they'd met here, where he could speak freely about the possibility of merging their realities.

As soon as he'd claimed a kiss.

He chanced another step closer.

"That would depend, Mr. Torrington, upon your goal." She

set down her glass and propped a hip against the desk. "I certainly can't assist you if we're working at cross purposes."

Ah, she did indeed hold a grudge. He couldn't blame her. But the lead he'd chased into Scotland this winter—one involving a snowy owl—had required he depart immediately and under an assumed name. When Nick had finally located the cryptid hunter, the slitty-eyed purveyor of rare and unusual creatures had denied selling any animals, let alone owls, to men involved in medical experimentation. Was he trustworthy? No. But the man swore up and down that he wanted nothing to do with any of "that shape-shifting nonsense." Nick had stopped by the Department of Cryptozoology in Edinburgh, but found it a tangled, bureaucratic mess. Abandoning hope of their assistance, he'd left the north and returned to London to find himself once again an uncle, but his sister's health worsening.

He pushed aside all grim thoughts. There would be plenty of time for them later.

At the moment, the woman he wished to make his bride required his full attention. New leads concerning the shadow committee operating in London had emerged in his absence and, should *those* prove valid, Nick would at last have means to infiltrate the group—which would once again mean abandoning Lady Stewart. This time, however, he vowed he would not leave her wondering at his intentions.

His mouth twitched, fighting a smile. "You want *me* to divulge secrets to an employee of a private agency?" He kept his voice light and teasing.

Nick could, however, do exactly that. Tonight, he wasn't acting as a Queen's agent. Instead he was chasing a rumor, one that promised hope for his ailing sister. For years, he'd worked to develop a treatment, but none of the cardiac medications he'd worked upon improved her condition. If anything, they worsened it. Then, recently, he'd heard a whisper about a medical device used to stimulate a paralyzed heart to beat once more. Quietly, he'd begun asking questions.

A board member involved in the oversight of Lister Laboratories, Lord Aldridge had denied the technology's existence. "I've yet to lay eyes on a convincing blueprint," he'd scoffed. "The theory is in place, but for now it remains nothing but a future possibility." Yet a nagging feeling in Nick's gut insisted that the earl knew something more. If there was a treatment under development that might help his sister, he would find it, and searching the earl's private residence was a first and obvious step. Alas, it fell outside the bounds of the task assigned to him by the duke and, therefore, he could not request direct assistance from the agency.

Tipping his head, he considered the woman before him. Lady Stewart would make a most excellent silent, stealthy partner.

She narrowed her eyes as she pushed off the desk. "If your task this evening does not involve the contents of that safe, we might be able to find common ground." Lean, lithe, and light on her feet, Lady Stewart circled about him, inching closer. But Nick didn't reach for her. He had the distinct feeling that should he make the slightest move in her direction, she might leap out the window.

*The open window.*

He'd watched her do exactly that too many times to count.

"Was that why you watched from the corners?" he asked, turning to keep her in his sights. "Was there something in the safe *you* wanted?"

"What I want is for all its contents to remain securely locked within."

Nick had found nothing of interest in the safe, nor the entirety of the study. Save a certain lady who had interrupted his search.

"Done." Perhaps Lady Stewart *could* help. He'd never before considered partnering with her—heat swelled in his chest—

leastways not in terms of working a job together. His eyes slid once again over her form-fitting trousers. Yet they'd passed each other in the dark for years, prowling about London in the small hours of the night. So many untapped skills paced before him. "Any chance you—and your cat—would consider working with a new partner?" He glanced behind her, searching the shadows. "Where *is* your familiar?" Lady Stewart rarely prowled London at night without the overlarge, black cat who shadowed her every step.

"Sorcha often wanders off on her own. Cat business." She shrugged. "She's always returned. No need to worry."

But she did. Nick could see it in her eyes.

Lady Stewart lifted her eyebrows. "Why would a Queen's agent consider hiring a common sneak thief?"

"Please, you're anything but common," he scoffed. Society might look askance at her unusual eyes, but they conferred upon her amazing nighttime vision. Her other senses were heightened as well, not to mention her physical prowess. "Four years living this dual life and not once caught."

"Five," she corrected, stopping in front of him. Close enough so that he could see the fine locks of hair that had wrestled free from a twisted knot at her nape. "A lady without plans to marry needs to look after herself." The faint, familiar scent of wild-flowers drifted past—now mixed with a hint of whisky—and his breath caught, trapping the scent within his lungs.

"Without plans, or without offers?" Yes, he was fishing. And hoping for a glimmer of encouragement. He knew a few agents who mixed business with pleasure. A few ended up married, the exact state to which he aspired. Would a brief alliance with a competent—his gaze skimmed over the curve of her neck—and beautiful thief help or hurt his cause?

Her eyes narrowed. "Does it matter?"

"Only if you're about to inform me I've competition for your attention." Her face froze, and a crack shot through his hopes, threatening to shatter his plans. He prayed she wouldn't mention another man's name. "Work called me away before I had a chance to speak."

"Is that an apology?"

"It is." He stared into her amber eyes. "I've missed you."

"Marriage," she huffed. "I've no interest in agreeing to terms that would force me to curtail any of my activities."

"Nor should you." The crack retreated, and he found himself able to breathe deeply once more.

A single step brought her body mere inches away from his. "Most of the *ton*—most men—would disagree."

"Not this man." He struggled to hold on to the thread of their conversation. "A woman should not be forced to waste her talents."

Her eyes flashed. "Yet, more often than not, we must hide them."

*As she had hers.* "But not from me."

"Trust that I place in your word as a gentleman and a Queen's agent... and our mutual ability to reveal the other's predilection for nighttime prowling..."

"From which you've announced your retirement. I do hope you'll reconsider, but in the meantime, do you propose to resume your celebration?"

"Possibly." She tipped her head. "Provided you've no conditions, no assumptions that what we share here, tonight, will lead any further?"

"None. Hopes, yes. But I'll not force them upon you." His gaze fixed upon her soft, wide mouth. "Does that qualify me to join the festivities?"

Her fingers wrapped about the black, silk cravat at his throat, and she tugged him closer. "It does."

Dropping his hands lightly upon the warm leather encasing her narrow waist, he lowered his mouth to hers, intending to gently explore the shape of her lips, to tease forth her arousal.

But as her lips parted, her fingers slid about his neck urging him closer and shattering the last of his preconceptions about her experience. There was no hesitation, no awkwardness to her response that might encourage him to slow down. Instead, her soft moan was pure carnality.

Desire surged, and his tongue slipped inside her mouth to tangle with her own, to drink in her taste. Whisky, rich and seductive with a hint of spice. Warm and intoxicating, like the scent of her skin.

With a throaty growl, he slid his hands down her back, past her bottom to catch at her thighs. Lifting her firmly against his hard length, he spun about to drop her onto the edge of the desk.

Without breaking their kiss, he circled his fingers about her ankles, then dragged his palms upward over leather and lacing until they reached her knees. With a mewl of approval, she spread her legs, inviting him yet closer. A roar rushed through his veins.

*Aether, she was a perfect fit.*

He nudged against her, and her body shuddered. Kissing her, holding her, touching her was all consuming. His heart raced as fantasies of taking her on the desk swirled through his mind. No, not fantasies, for even now her fingers tugged at the clasps that held his trousers closed. Not in ages had such wild anticipation driven him senseless. He flexed his hips, and she groaned her encouragement.

But one moment his fingers were dipping beneath the rise of her corset, and the next she'd shoved him away. "Did you hear that?" she hissed. "Someone is coming."

Nick heard nothing but the pounding of blood in his ears.

"Go!" She pushed at his shoulder as she dropped onto her feet. "The window!"

He heard the footsteps now—growing closer—and turned to

follow. She was already halfway out and reaching for a drainpipe.

"Hurry!" Her eyes flashed green-gold.

He followed quickly, but by the time his feet hit the ground, she was gone.

CHAPTER TWO

"I CAN'T BELIEVE Lady Sophia would do such a thing." Isabella shuddered. "She's so quiet and demure... and with her debut tomorrow night!"

Eyebrows arched, Colleen looked over her shoulder to where her aunt—in name only, for Isabella was but two years older—leaned against the bedpost. Her hand smoothed across her lower abdomen where a gentle roundness had begun to announce the eventual arrival of her uncle's heir. For after five years of barrenness, Isabella insisted the child would not dare be anything but male, refusing to discuss any other possibility.

Including the near certainty that the growing babe was *not* her husband's.

Colleen wasn't the only one sneaking in and out of the town-house windows during the night. Isabella had taken a lover. A nimble one, given the paucity of vegetation surrounding her aunt's window. Though they'd been careful to be quiet, Colleen's ears had heard far more than she wished.

Worried, she'd forced the topic a few nights past. "You're certain my uncle doesn't suspect?" She'd spoken gently. "He has a vindictive streak."

"It was his idea," Isabella had stammered. "I didn't wish to be unfaithful, but he insisted there must be a child. What I didn't expect was to..."

"Fall in love?" Colleen had finished. There was, after all, no longer a need for her paramour's continued attention. Though she wished her aunt every happiness, her uncle's conceit would not tolerate any societal doubt. "Be careful. Of late Mr. Vanderburn has begun conducting nighttime patrols of the grounds. Now that the deed is done, your husband won't chance any rumors clouding the infant's birth." So ended their conversation. Soon after, such visits had ceased, and Isabella had folded into herself, growing quiet and pensive.

Not that it terminated Mr. Vanderburn's steely-eyed vigil. For years, her uncle's thick-necked henchman carried out his errands via the service entrance, rarely lingering longer than it took to steal a treat from the kitchens. Of late, however, he'd begun turning up in the most unlikely places at the most inconvenient of times, hampering her ease of movement. Something she considered suspicious, given it was the dead of winter.

It was a most excellent time to retire.

The steam maid huffed, waiting impatiently for her charge to face forward once more. Steam Adelle—a fancy, new model imported from France—had little patience for her Scottish charge. They were always in conflict, for Colleen refused to bend to the steambot's notions of fashion.

"It's *always* the quiet ones." She ignored the puffs of steam escaping the steambot's collar. "Have you learned nothing from my stories?"

Isabella—her uncle's bride of six months when Colleen arrived—had quickly grown wise to her plea of a headache to absent herself from various social events. Isabella had taken to arriving at her door—curative cup of tea in hand—at inconvenient moments asking questions Colleen did not care to answer.

She'd dodged them all... until she'd been caught with one leg out her window.

Ever since, Isabella had become her partner-in-crime. In exchange for scandalous—yet professionally filtered—gossip, her aunt helped conceal Colleen's odd comings and goings, prattling on about her niece's delicate health.

"Enough to deftly navigate the tangles of society. The occasional well-placed comment has kept the sharp-tongued matrons at bay." Isabella threw her a satisfied smile. "No worries, I've not once even hinted at my source."

"Nor have I intentionally applied my skills to interfere with your... diversion." For they kept each other's secrets close. "I've no idea who he is, but if there's ever trouble, you need only ask for my assistance."

Isabella gave a nod, but her gaze fell away. "He's said much the same." She crossed to the window—always cracked open, even in the dead of winter—and peered down at the saucer of milk that balanced on a ledge outside. Legend insisted that such offerings would dispose the cat sìth to offer good blessings in return. "Sorcha's been away for nearly two weeks now. Longer than usual."

An undisguised appeal for another topic of conversation.

Aside from Colleen, Isabella was the only other human whose touch the cat permitted. The cat sìth was more wildcat than house cat and belonged in northern Scotland where several of her kind freely roamed the woods upon Stewart lands and beyond. Such cats were considered by many to be fairy creatures and featured prominently in the myths and legends of Scotland, including farfetched stories explaining her family's origins. Rarely did any condescend to live inside four walls.

Sorcha was an exception. Colleen's steadfast companion since before her parents' death, the cat sìth had refused to stay behind when her favorite human was forced from her home, leaping onto the steam carriage as it carried Colleen away to London.

Though her uncle took a narrow-eyed view of his niece's pet, he'd allowed the cat to stay, provided the creature remained above stairs or outside. The household at large took a dim view of her pet for most found Sorcha's steady, golden stare unnerving and had a tendency to mutter with suspicion—and the atavistic fear that encompassed centuries of superstition—about the similarity of the cat's eyes to Colleen's.

Here in the city, her cat was less revered and more feared. She'd heard the word "familiar" muttered more than once. Only Mr. Torrington used the term in lighthearted jest.

"She'll be back," Colleen insisted, though her assurance sounded false even to her own ears. Three weeks was the longest the cat had ever vanished. Of late, she had begun to visit Sorcha's London haunts, hoping to catch a glimpse of the feline.

"Are you certain you truly wish to retire, to leave town? I'll miss you." Isabella's lips curved upward and a hint of cunning lit her eyes. "And the gossip. Perhaps when things grow dull or difficult, I'll follow you north and fling myself upon your hospitality."

"I will, of course, return for the child's birth." Colleen wouldn't miss it. Assuming her uncle did not object. Steam Adelle let out a prolonged spout of steam, and Colleen turned back toward the dressing table to let the steam maid continue the work she found so necessary. "Though you—and your baby —will always be welcome at my home in Scotland. The air is fresh, and the landscape is stunning," she sighed at the memory, "but you might grow weary of the quiet and the cold."

*Would she, rattling around the tower house all alone?*

Years spent slinking about the gritty streets of London in the wee hours had honed her skills in a way that rural life could not. Houses here in the city were close enough that one might leap from roof to roof, feet never touching the ground. Gargoyled drainpipes and corniced ledges provided quick and convenient vertical ascents, with the ever-present crank hacks and steam carriages useful obstacles to dart between when one needed to evade a pursuer.

And a certain Queen's agent might turn up at any moment. She'd miss their flirtations most of all.

The steam maid stabbed a final hairpin into Colleen's hair, then rolled back, crossed her arms and huffed. A puff of acrid smoke escaped before she clamped her metal mouth shut. It was always the same silent argument with Steam Adelle. On the dressing table before Colleen was spread an assortment of punch cards, all programs for elaborate and popular upsweeps. All of which she'd rejected in favor of her usual, a simple chignon.

"As I've explained too many times to count, Steam Adelle," Colleen grumbled, "plain is a necessity for afternoon tea."

It was especially hard to hide in the small, brightly-lit parlor. But with no cosmetics and her spectacles—tinted a smoky gray with cerium to hide her amber eyes and block the glare of over-bright lights—no gentleman caller dared compliment her beauty lest he risk sounding like a fool. She smiled at her reflection in the mirror. Her walking dress—a muted blue and green tartan set with red—was but one more layer of camouflage. It over-emphasized her heritage and gave would-be suitors pause. The precise reason Colleen loved it. Fading into the background was an underappreciated talent.

"Are you certain you've told me *everything* about last night?" Isabella squinted at Colleen with suspicion. "Mr. Glover has returned from his journey and is certain to call, yet the usual irritation isn't etched into your face." She tapped her chin. "In fact, you look rather... high-spirited, considering your eyes have a touch of exhaustion about them."

She cringed. With no plans to marry, Colleen had discreetly taken an occasional lover over the past few years, ones who assured her they had no designs upon matrimony. Women, after all, had the same urges as men, whether they wished to admit to it or not. Alas, her most recent affair had gone… badly.

Curiosity—and perhaps a touch of bored irritation—had convinced her to permit one Mr. Travis Glover—tall, blond, and handsome—to coax her down a hallway and into a locked room while others still whirled upon the dance floor. A regrettable decision. Without preamble, he'd tossed her onto a divan and lifted her skirts. The experience had been a stunning disappointment. One she had no desire to repeat with him. Ever. Which had made his impassioned proposal the following day mystifying. She'd declined, of course. Yet ever since, he'd made a pest of himself.

He called at tea time and peppered her with endless questions about her Scottish estate, insisted upon a dance at every ball, and established an ill-defined partnership with her uncle. Of late, every time she turned about, he was present, staring at her with possessive eyes before making yet another attempt to worm his way into her life. It was exasperating.

This morning, flowers had arrived—an enormous bouquet of roses—and she'd allowed herself to hope. Were they from a certain man whose recent absence had stolen away the joy from her work, from her life? Whose unexpected return had flooded her heart with warmth?

Alas, they weren't from Mr. Torrington. And they ought to be. For after years of turning her nose up at what the marriage mart had to offer, there was at last one particular eligible London gentleman whose suit she would consider. *Consider*. For though his words had hinted at a full partnership, both as his wife and as a business partner, she needed to be certain.

He knew about her lands in the north—and her unusual eyes

bothered him not one bit. If he proposed, ought she accept? Scotland called to her, and she needed to go. Still, she clung to the possibility that could have the best of both worlds, spending time at Craigieburn in the north as well as in London.

Unless Mr. Torrington had reconsidered in the bright light of day? For there was no indication that he intended to make his romantic interest in her common knowledge. No note. No flowers. No meeting arranged to speak with her uncle, formality though it would be.

A forlorn ache settled beneath her ribs. The uncertainty would drive her mad.

"What *is* wrong with Mr. Glover?" her uncle had snarled at her across the breakfast table, fingers crumpling the edges of his neatly pressed newspaper. "He's asked for your hand, and I've given my consent."

*Where to begin?* But her uncle wanted her agreement, not her objections. Nothing good ever came from crossing him, so Colleen had kept her thoughts close and her gaze demurely lowered. "I don't believe we suit," she'd answered vaguely. As always, she had fixed her eyes upon a faint char mark, where a spark from a steambot had vaulted from its firebox onto the polished wood of the table.

"How many gentlemen have declared themselves willing to overlook your paltry dowry and low-bred background?"

"None." Circumstances she'd actively encouraged. But her tone was respectful, as expected.

"Precisely." He'd muttered about his sister abandoning her heritage to elope with an aberrant Scotsman. "Mr. Glover is a second son and holds a satisfactory position in society. Your stubborn refusal to consider his bid for your hand is unacceptable. There will be no more playing the invalid under my roof. You will attend any and all social events to which you have been invited—including the Aldridge girl's debutant ball—wherein I expect you to entertain Mr. Glover's attentions while you reconsider your stance." His nostrils flared. "Am I clear?

"Yes, sir." It was the expected reply, but gone were the days when a guardian could force a marriage. Had her father not seen fit to leave his estate in her uncle's care until she was twenty-five, Colleen would have left this household the moment she reached her majority some four years past. Why her uncle had taken a sudden interest in seeing her married after so many years of virtual neglect, she could not begin to imagine, but she could certainly endure another three days of Mr. Glover's stiff—if overly saccharine—courtship.

Particularly if Mr. Torrington also saw fit to reappear at *ton* gatherings. He could provide her with a public excuse to turn her back on Mr. Glover. Her heart gave a great thud.

Lying awake last night, Colleen's mind had replayed their encounter over and over. A single kiss had tilted her world upon its axis, and a second had sent it spinning. Had they not been interrupted, where might the moment have led?

She'd barely slept at all.

"So? Is there a new gentleman in your life?" Isabella was still awaiting an answer. But Colleen wouldn't be detailing how very exciting it had been to be dropped upon a solid desk and kissed by a man as if only she could quench the fire that burned within him.

"It's nothing. Merely a close encounter with the competition." Mr. Torrington's intentions were not yet clear. Until he made them so, she would keep his words to herself. She pressed her fingertips against her flushed cheeks. This wouldn't do. Much as she would welcome Mr. Torrington's presence were he to call, she had difficulty imagining him perched on the overstuffed divan in the parlor. Mr. Glover, however, would certainly be in attendance, and she did not wish to give him the slightest encouragement.

"Nothing?" Isabella tugged a folded letter from her bodice.

Pinched between thumb and forefinger, she dangled it just out of Colleen's reach. "Then you weren't expecting a missive from..."

With a single swipe, she snagged the missive. Her pulse leapt. A renewed offer from Mr. Torrington? As Isabella laughed, she tore open the envelope and unfolded the paper within.

> *Lady Stewart,*
>
> *It is with great regret that I write to inform you that there has been a most unfortunate accident. A contingent of boys from the Gordon Academy were en route to Inverness when they experienced a small fire aboard the school dirigible. Though ignition of hydrogen was averted when all hands rushed to extinguish the flames, the helm was abandoned and the airship crashed into the south-west corner. The boys were rescued and sustained only a few minor injuries, but the roof has suffered considerable damage.*
>
> *Your servant,*
>
> *Watts*

Her estate manager had attached a quote for the roof's repair. Stonework, wooden beams, slate shingles... the supplies required were lengthy. And that was before they accounted for wages to pay the workmen. Her stomach slid to her toes, and her heart dropped to the floor beside it. All the extra funds she'd saved for an emergency? Gone.

Isabella, who had been reading over her shoulder, sighed, "Oh, Colleen. I'm so sorry."

She nodded absently, her mind already leaping ahead to the only logical solution: she needed speak with Mr. Witherspoon. The safer, smaller—and ethically principled—jobs she usually insisted upon would keep her in London for months—and under her uncle's thumb. Taking a room at a hotel would increase costs and extend her stay in the city indefinitely. But if she asked her employer for riskier tasks, ones with generous compensation, she need only complete a handful of jobs.

Her uncle would be furious if—when—he learned she'd failed to present herself at tea. But there was no time to waste. She lifted her gaze and met Isabella's knowing grin. "Will you cover for me one more time?"

CHAPTER THREE


OLD TO WATCH FOR a blonde woman with a distracted air who favored pink, Nick strolled past the entrance to the Rankine Institute for what felt like the hundredth time. Though the Queen's agents had ties to the engineering school, he preferred to keep his unofficial inquiries carefully away from any eavesdropping bureaucratic ears. Hence his reluctance to enter the building.

He had, however, attracted unwanted attention. A particularly burly guard—who had taken up his post an hour ago—now tracked his every step. Eyes narrowed and arms crossed, his scowl suggested he would like to grab Nick by the scruff of his neck and drag him into a dark alley. Only his gentlemanly attire —the cut of his coat's lapels and the fall of his trousers—kept him safe.

Though he'd failed to find any incriminating evidence, Nick could not dismiss his suspicions of Lord Aldridge. While the man's desk had revealed nothing—save the woman he wished to marry was more adventurous than he'd dared hope—there might yet be more information hidden in less obvious locations within the house. Or at the Lister Institute but, much as Nick longed to search the gentleman's office, security was extremely high. That would be his last resort.

A polished steam carriage pulled to the side of the street and stopped, waiting. More and more crank hacks rattled and clicked past on the street as the well-to-do working middle class hired transport home. Foot traffic also increased, forcing him to step to the side of the pavement. The sun hung low in the sky as he tugged his pocket watch from his waistcoat to confirm the time. Mr. Jackson had suggested that the engineer he sought—a newlywed keen to bask in the afterglow of a honeymoon—made a habit of leaving promptly at five. Except when she didn't. A Queen's agent in training, unexpected assignments were guaranteed.

It was now five past.

He'd contemplated paying a call at Lady Stewart's residence, but wanted to present her with a lead, not merely a ring. *Gah*, his mother had been far too excited when he'd asked her for the heirloom, flapping her hands and darting from her chair to hug him tight. The anticipation of more grandchildren always set her face alight.

"I've yet to propose," he'd cautioned her. "She might decline."

"I've seen how she looks at you." His mother had pinched his cheek. "She won't."

Nick wasn't nearly as confident. Lady Stewart had an independent streak a mile long. Not that he wished to cage or leash her. No, he wanted a wife that was his equal. What better way to show her exactly that, than by taking her out on the town while most of the city slept? Which is why he paced the street in the growing dark hoping to latch on to another lead. Not solely motivated by saving his sister, but also by a growing emotion that he struggled to name. It was more than desire, but was it love?

The attraction had been instantaneous that first night

they'd met eye to eye on a dark rooftop. A shock of awareness had rippled through him and set his pulse racing like a runaway steam train careening down a mountainside. He'd teased. She'd laughed… and responded with a flirtatious comment of her own. Encounter had followed encounter—both while running free across the cityscape or whirling across the confines of a dance floor—and their conversations deepened. The death of her parents, her unusual eyes, and her desire to leave London. His frustration with laboratory work, the irritations of being a second spare, his sister's heart condition.

The birth of his precious niece had exacerbated his sister's heart condition. Blue fingernails and fainting spells—otherwise known as Adams-Stokes syncope and seizures—were now commonplace rather than occasional events, and Anna's pulse rarely exceeded forty beats per minute, a severe bradycardia that even atropine injections could not accelerate.

At any moment, her heart could simply… stop.

Her husband—a Naval officer on assignment in the South China Sea—had been sent for, though at the rate his sister continued to deteriorate, he wasn't at all certain an airship could carry the lieutenant home fast enough.

Nick unclenched his jaw and rolled his shoulders. Strolling, he reminded himself, not stalking.

"There's nothing you—or anyone—can do, Nicholas," Anna had murmured, cradling her infant daughter and smiling down upon the sleeping child with wonder. Marriage and the wished for pregnancy had been a risk she'd taken despite all medical advice. "I've accepted my fate and regret nothing. My daughter is a miracle, nothing less."

It was a miracle that Anna had survived the delivery. But he'd bit his tongue. Anna might be resigned to an invalid's life and an early death, but he wanted nothing but health and happiness for his sister. He wanted his niece to know her mother, but without a method to restart Anna's heart when it ceased beating...

He'd glanced at the collection of contraptions gathering dust in the corner of her room. All generated low levels of harmless electricity, designed to stimulate the nervous system and prod her heart to greater effort.

"None of the... less invasive medical devices worked?"

"None."

Which explained the newest contraption—P.C. Hutchinson's Magneto-Shock Machine—and the full-time nurse. Covered in knobs and dials, it hummed at a low level, ready to generate a burst of electricity. All well and good until one took note that it sported a metal probe designed to be inserted through the chest wall and directly into the ventricles of the heart. *That* was just as likely to be deadly as curative.

He'd quizzed the nurse directly and reached the horrified conclusion that there was merit in such a device, if also a high risk of infection. The machine would only be used if Anna's heart refused to beat after three minutes, before which a less invasive approach—percussive pacing and chest compressions— would be attempted. It hadn't made him feel any better, but at the four-minute time point, brain death would threaten. Such an action would be a last-ditch effort.

"But know that I've not given up hope." He never had. Never would. "I'm still looking for a solution."

Anna had squeezed his hand. "I know."

For three years he'd served as co-investigator of a cardio-physiology laboratory in the basement of Lister Laboratories. They'd isolated and studied a number of cardiac glycosides, chemicals with structures similar to that of digitalis—a drug extracted from the foxglove plant that strengthened the force of a heartbeat—but though many had proven to be alternative treatments for those suffering from congestive heart failure, for Anna, each had proved toxic. Only atropine—a derivative of deadly nightshade—had increased her heart rate. Until, with the worsening of her condition, it didn't.

This past year, work as a Queen's agent had placed increasing demands on Nick's time, and he'd spent less and less time in the laboratory. Instead, he'd found himself chasing reports about a small group in London who believed in such nonsense as selkies, werewolves and witches, in creatures who could alter their physical form. Believing was one thing, but attempting to force it was another. Rumors midst the cryptid hunter community were rife, but when confronted directly none —like his lead in Scotland—could provide any proof or name names. Locating—forget infiltrating—this shadow committee suspected of such unethical behavior was proving difficult.

When he wasn't chasing down men suspected of animal cruelty, Nick had turned his attention to chasing another whisper he'd heard uttered in the hallowed halls of Lister Labo- ratories. He'd taken that rumor directly to one particular board member. Lord Aldridge. The man had hesitated—for the briefest of moments—before denying that he knew of any such researcher.

"I've caught word of an independent scientist working upon a novel method to restart the heart once it has stopped beating. Not," he waved his hand at the monstrous, invasive machine beside them, "this. But a small, miniaturized, cardio-pacing device that can be implanted into the chest wall, one that will monitor the heartbeat and deliver a tiny, well-timed electrical burst to the cardiac tissue when it detects no beats."

"I'd rather," Anna hadn't met his gaze, "that you spend your time courting Lady Stewart, for I'd very much like to see you married before I…" The baby had begun to cry in her cradle, and his sister had scooped up Clara, jiggling and cooing as she rocked the infant back to sleep.

He'd taken that as his cue to depart.

Marriage. Device hunting. Stop a ring of gentlemen from

turning their interests in shape-shifting creatures upon humans. While he waited for new information on the last, he thought he might combine the pursuit of the first two activities and take Lady Stewart prowling about London in an attempt to win her heart.

The sun hung low in the sky by the time a young woman wearing a rose walking dress stepped forth from the building and paused beneath the portico, pinning a straw hat to tousled and crimped blonde hair.

"Mrs. Leighton?" Nick inquired.

Her hand slipped into the folds of her skirts and into a conveniently located pocket. No doubt her fingers wrapped about the hilt of a knife or the handle of a small firearm. Her eyebrows lifted. "Have we met?"

"Allow me to introduce myself." Careful to maintain a respectful distance between them, Nick doffed his top hat and bowed. "Mr. Torrington, begging a few moments of your time. I'm sorry if my approach caused you concern." He straightened and drew back the edge of his coat, providing her with a glimpse of his TTX pistol. The burly man stepped into the doorframe, his fingers curling into a fist, but the weapon gave him pause. Nick shot him a smug glance. "We have a mutual colleague. Mr. Jackson suggested you might be able to provide insight into a particular conundrum I've encountered."

Mrs. Leighton held up a hand. "It's fine, Cyrus." She led Nick a few steps away to stand beside a lamppost. Foot traffic flowed about them, and the street noise of passing clockwork horses, crank hacks and steam carriages provided a certain measure of privacy. But her hand didn't leave her pocket; not all the suspicion had left her eyes. "What information is it you seek?"

Nick ducked to avoid losing an eye to the prong of a parasol. "Mr. Jackson informed me your work encompasses the miniaturization of portable energy sources, a Markoid battery was mentioned."

Her eyes slid sideways and she frowned. "Mr. Jackson should not have spoken so freely, but go on."

"There is rumor of a new medical device, one that proposes to stimulate the heart should it cease to beat by delivering an electrical impulse."

Concern—and maybe a touch of horror—furrowed her brow. "I make it a point never to associate with galvanists."

*That* drew him up short. "I wasn't..." Or was he? If his search for information had exhausted reputable sources, ought he look elsewhere? Most galvanists were charlatans, preying upon a family's desperation to bring a relative back to life, but... "I'm not looking for a confidence man who has constructed a grand device, one that fills a room with wires and spinning gears to produce impressive arcs of electricity that would cause a corpse to twitch and jerk, but rather someone with a more furtive bent. A scientist who works toward his own ends quietly, out of the public eye, focusing primarily upon the heart. One disinclined to publish his or her findings and who may have escaped the notice of the larger scientific community."

"And you came to me because...?" She shifted on her feet. Uncomfortable with the concept or did she know something?

"Because the device I'm searching for would be intended for the living. To keep their heart beating, jolting it back into motion mere seconds after it ceased to beat." His effort was aimed at keeping Anna's heart beating steadily and fast enough to sustain life. "The power source would need to be small, compact and safe. Mr. Jackson insinuated that your research into alternate power sources for automatons occasionally brings you into contact with some of the more unsavory characters who occupy the fringes of your field of study."

"He would," she quipped, "after a particularly unfortunate incident on the train." But her shoulders relaxed. "This past summer an unscrupulous foreign investor attempted to steal my prototype. He was caught and interrogated. A list of people interested in purchasing my battery was compiled, but most sought to power automatons. But as to biological uses..." She tapped two gloved fingers upon her lips. "One woman, a spiritualist, was convinced that regular stimuli to the occipital lobe of the brain might allow an individual to detect—to see—the presence of spirits."

"No." Nick shook his head.

"Another," Mrs. Leighton's voice dropped, "hoped to revive flagging male virility."

Heat crept into his cheeks. "Certainly not."

A tiny smile crept onto her face. "The heart is a muscle, is it not?"

"It is."

"Then you might want to speak with the third scientist. Classically trained at the University of Edinburgh, Dr. Gregory Farquhar's thesis presented a study of how the electrical stimulation of nerves causes muscle fibers to contract." A certain gleam entered her eyes and Nick realized she'd been toying with him, tweaking his nose with the nonsensical possibilities of her battery before finally handing over the information he sought. "He's quite mad, however. His intended use of my battery? To power a portable device to jolt the bodies of dead animals in the hopes that they might reanimate in an altered form."

In short, transmutation. The transformation of one species into another. Not over the course of generations, but via a process best described as sorcery. And by a mere battery. Was such a thing even possible?

Nick fought to keep his jaw off the pavement. Had his hunt for a remedy for Anna's heart condition uncovered new information pointing directly to a key member of the shadow committee he sought?

"Thank you, Mrs. Leighton." He bowed. "You've provided me with much to consider."

"You're quite welcome, Mr. Torrington." She lifted a hand and the driver of the steam carriage hopped down to hold open a door. "Please keep all information about my research under tight wraps."

"Of course." He handed her into the waiting steam carriage.

With a solid lead in his pocket, he'd intended to hasten to Lady Stewart's side to present her with the promise of an adventure. He was certain she would prefer such a gift to hothouse flowers. But if this information fell under the umbrella of Queen's agents' business, could he justify the risk of sharing such a promising detail?

## CHAPTER FOUR

REFLEXIVELY, COLLEEN glanced over her uncle's shoulder to assess the light levels in Lord Aldridge's ballroom. In a nod to tradition, the crystal drops of the central chandelier glittered in the flickering light of wax candles. Along the walls, gas jets burned within milky-white globes to cast a steadier light. Not a single Lucifer lamp was in evidence as its harsher blue-white light was considered unflattering to a lady's complexion.

Bright enough that any odd reflections from Colleen's eyes would likely go unnoticed were she to tuck her tinted lenses away. Yet given the antics she planned this evening, it was best if she left her spectacles perched upon her nose. It would not be her eccentricities she wished commented upon when tongues wagged about tonight's events.

In the receiving line, Lady Aldridge stood beside her daughter, Lady Sophia, whose gown—what with its profusion of pale blue ruffles and lace—threatened to swallow her whole. Though her deportment was demure and polite, there were faint shadows beneath her eyes and a certain tightness to her shoulders. She had the look of a cat subjected to a leash. Or a cage.

Lady Sophia glanced up, their eyes locked, and Colleen could swear she saw a flash of fire deep inside those pale, silver eyes.

Had the young woman *deliberately* left her distinctive necklace in a forbidden man's bed? She fought the upward curve of her lips. Colleen counted it as a distinct possibility. If Lady Sophia also possessed claws, there would be more trouble before her parents managed to shove her down the aisle. *If* they succeeded in forcing her to wed at all.

"Come along." Isabella hooked her arm about Colleen's, leaning close as they stepped into the ballroom. "This had best work. My husband made an unanticipated appearance in my dressing room in which I was *instructed* to begin planning your wedding to Mr. Glover."

Colleen sucked a breath of air past her teeth. "Do not overexert yourself."

Out of the coal scuttle and into the grate. Anger and annoyance clasped hands and began to whirl deep inside her chest. Of all the nights! The moment Mr. Glover had her in his sights, he would stick to her like taffy on teeth.

Isabella snorted. "If there's another gentleman in your life, now would be a good time for him to present himself as an alternative."

Anger ran down her spine like molten steel, then cooled, stiffening her resolve. "I'll rescue *myself* from Mr. Glover." Though Mr. Torrington might offer for her hand, she was still contemplating the merits of such a union. First, she needed to complete her new assignment. The task was simple, but she *needed* the money.

She scanned the ballroom. In one corner, a steam orchestra hidden behind a wall of potted rhododendrons played a waltz as guests whirled and swirled about the floor. Mr. Glover was not among them, but a refreshment room opened off the ballroom and bustled with activity. What with his sweet tooth, they were almost certain to find him within.

"Do you remember the plan?" Colleen steered them in the direction of the refreshment room.

"I do."

It was a touch risky. She'd never caused a public scene before, but Mr. Glover's persistent advances must be terminated *and* the package must be placed. Guests were still arriving, making their way up the grand staircase to the ballroom which meant *now* was the best time to put her plan into action. To the right of the entryway was Lord Aldridge's library. If all went well, both tasks would be accomplished in quick succession. Her heart began to pound. Her uncle might well turn her out on the doorstep tomorrow morning, but if she accomplished her aim, there would be more than enough in her bank account to pay for a room at Claridge's.

He was already irritated at his wife and niece's impromptu "shopping trip," one that had left the steam butler turning guests—and one Mr. Glover—away from the townhome during regularly scheduled calling hours. Though they'd later purchased silk stockings, their first stop had been at her employer's door.

"Back so soon?" Mr. Witherspoon had looked up from his desk, amused, as she stepped into his office. Dark and wood-paneled, its walls were lined with hefty legal tomes. One might hire him to draft a will, but more often than not, gentlemen arrived with difficulties that required a more unofficial and delicate solution. "Only yesterday you informed me of your retirement."

"An unanticipated situation arose." Embarrassment heated her cheeks. She'd made much of returning to Scotland. "Fixing it requires—"

"Funds." He set aside his fountain pen. "How much?"

The sum she named widened his eyes, and Mr. Witherspoon leaned back in his chair and steepled his fingers. "How quickly, Lady Stewart, do you wish to amass your rewards?"

"Within five days." She swallowed, hoping it wasn't an impossibility. Fixing the roof of Craigieburn Castle before heavy rains could do yet more damage was a pressing matter. "I know I ask the impossible, but—"

"There is an assignment I intended for another associate, but given your exemplary performance over the past few years, I'm happy to place it in your hands. It involves an obfuscation chain that will require you to return to Lord Aldridge's home this very evening. Might you be attending Lady Sophia's debut ball?"

Excitement and relief filled her lungs, restoring her ability to breathe deeply. Was it possible she would not need to alter her plans? "I am."

"There is only one small obstacle you need to overcome." He'd pursed his lips. "Three years ago you declined to work on the more… gray cases."

"Needs must."

"Very well. Listen closely."

The task involved an obfuscation chain. She would be but one link of many and wouldn't know what she was passing along—or why. There was little to no risk involved, beyond being caught with the item in hand. In which case, no one would step forward to protect her. That the compensation for this single job was enough to cover the cost of roof repairs was telling. Someone was skirting the law, and she would need to bend her morals.

She ignored the queasy flutter in her stomach. "I'll take it."

Though she'd not asked, it was unlikely Lord Aldridge knew his home was the platform for yet another operation carried out by Witherspoon and Associates. Not that he'd be surprised. Ballrooms were always filled with undercurrents of activity.

"Ready?" Her aunt snapped her attention back to the task at hand.

She nodded. "Ready." Better to finish this soon, before there was any chance of Mr. Torrington's arrival. She did not wish for him to intervene.

"Mrs. Wilson!" Isabella hailed an acquaintance, abandoning Colleen's side as she began to make her way across the polished floor.

"Miss Stewart," a gentleman whose name she could not recall greeted her. Always "miss" never "lady". How the English hated to acknowledge that an unmarried woman might hold a title, even one that was little more than a courtesy. "Fine, dry weather we've had these past few days."

"Quite lovely," she answered, not meeting his eyes. Indeed, it made the rooftops far less treacherous.

Isabella disappeared into the refreshment room.

A few more acquaintances nodded, some making a weak effort to engage her in polite conversation. Long minutes passed, but her dull answers failed to inspire further comment, and awareness of her existence begin to fade until her silent presence was no more than decorative, much like the wallpaper.

Her pale, yellow ballgown was unremarkable. Its neckline did not plunge. Its sleeves did not bare her shoulders. And the swags that fell from her hips to gather in a generous bustle upon her backside did nothing to accentuate her figure. The only adornment was an overabundance of fabric flowers clustered at one shoulder and upon her opposite hip. When the moment arrived, her sudden change in behavior would draw sharp attention.

It was time. Isabella hadn't reappeared, which meant Mr. Glover was within.

Touching her fingers to the red, tartan rosette she'd tucked in among the other blooms, Colleen stepped into the crush of guests, wending her way toward the refreshment room.

The box suspended beneath her bustle and within its wire cage resumed its soft bumping against the backside of her knees. It was a simple rosewood box inlaid with Mother of

Pearl, hinged, and fitted with an ornate lock to which she had not been given a key. Despite its small size, the carriage ride here had been most uncomfortable, and she longed to be rid of her package. Not to mention Mr. Glover's unflagging courtship.

The refreshment table groaned beneath all manner of delicacies. A tall centerpiece lifted a much-embellished pineapple aloft. Towering artistic cakes that rose at intervals were surrounded by lower arrangements of ices, biscuits and iced cakes. Champagne and lemonade were among the many offerings.

Isabella stood beside Mr. Glover, who was collecting an assortment of treats upon a plate. Powdered sugar dusted his mustache. A gentle touch to his sleeve and a murmured word from her aunt shifted his attention toward the door. His gaze caught hers. An ingratiating smile stretched across his face, and he quickly abandoned his plate to snatch up two glasses of champagne.

As she'd suspected. Unable to wring assent from her in private, he would now attempt a more public venue.

The chase was on.

Pivoting on her heel, she exited the room and threaded her way through guests—jostling elbows and knocking dance cards from the hands of more than one gentleman. Irritated young ladies hissed their displeasure as she passed.

"Miss Stewart!" Irritation twisted through Mr. Glover's voice as she exited the ballroom. Gleeful at his consternation, Colleen bit down on her lip, fighting an entirely unprofessional urge to laugh as she grabbed at the doorframe and rounded the corner into the upper hall. Clutching at her skirts, she rushed down the stairs past the new arrivals—whose eyes widened to stare—and into the empty library.

Thrusting a hand beneath her bustle, her fingers found the clasps that held the package within. *Click. Click.* The rosewood box fell free. Drawing it from beneath the silk swags, Colleen placed it on the table beside the globe—as instructed—then hurried across the room to stand before a window overlooking the street. Across the street stretched Hyde Park, cultivated and clipped for the pleasures of London's populace. Nature, tamed and domesticated. But at least outside a cool breeze could ruffle the leaves upon branches and moonlight reached the ground unfiltered by thick panes of wavy glass.

"Colleen!" Mr. Glover boomed as he strode into the library, his hands—now empty of celebratory champagne—spread wide. Annoyance and confusion twisted his face. Had he even noticed that he had addressed her in a most improper and informal manner?

Arms crossed, she drew herself up straight as she turned to face him, peering down her nose through her gray lenses. "Lady Stewart."

A few guests appeared at the doorway with unabashed curiosity written across their faces. She fought back any hint of satisfaction from her face. The perfect audience.

Mr. Glover came to a halt before her and swept a bow. "My apologies, The Much Honored Lady Stewart of Craigieburn." Though his movements and words gave every impression of a courtly greeting, his voice was tight. "I spoke with your uncle and explained that we *must* marry. He's given us his blessing and has begun the paperwork."

*How dare they?* The impudence! "I don't wish to—" A thought struck her like a blow to the stomach. "You..." She couldn't force the words past her lips. If he'd detailed their—incredibly brief and disappointing—affair, that would explain her uncle's sudden insistence that she marry. Fire ignited inside her chest. If Mr. Glover had indeed besmirched her honor, she would see him suffer.

He took a step forward. "I've been to Scotland."

"To Craigieburn Castle?" Was that where he had disappeared to these last few weeks? A cold trickle of fear ran through her body at such an excessive act of devotion. She took a small step sideways, shifting away.

He nodded, his eyes feverish. "Your dowry is beautiful. It's a tall and stately tower house, a castle in its own right. We'll make it our home."

"No, Mr. Glover, we will not." Keeping her voice civil was a struggle. In three days Craigieburn and its lands would be under *her* control, and she wouldn't be signing it over to anyone. Ever. "I've declined your offer and asked you to cease pressing your attentions upon me."

"This ridiculousness must end." His eyes narrowed, and he blew out an exasperated huff. "We've been intimate. We must marry."

"I disagree." Why was he so insistent? Why her? She wasn't an heiress. She brought him no social connections. And this certainly wasn't a love match. Save a brief fumble in the dark, they shared nothing. *Nothing.* "There were no consequences," she informed him in a soft voice. Her precautions had been effective, thank goodness.

"Miss Stewart?" Her voice trembling with the effort to oppose ingrained instincts that private conversations were not to be interrupted, a young woman stepped into the library. "Do you require assistance?"

Mr. Glover called over his shoulder, "Miss Stewart has made me the happiest of men by agreeing to become my fiancée."

"I've done no such thing!" Colleen cried, raising her voice for the benefit of their audience. Her anger was tempered by the thought that no one would link her presence in the library with anything save this argument. The obfuscation chain—her part in it—had been executed perfectly. "I've given you my answer, and it's my consent, not my uncle's, that you require. Do stop. You're making a scene."

"Stop being so difficult," he hissed. From his pocket, he withdrew a ring. "Now slip this on, and let us return to the ball.

We'll share the next waltz." He reached for her, and she jumped back.

"How dare you take such liberties!" She raised a hand to slap his face, but he caught her wrist midair.

The audience gasped. A gentleman broke free from the gaping crowd at the doorway. One Mr. Nicholas Torrington. "Sir, this is unseemly."

Colleen's stomach sank. Not only had she wished to rescue herself, she didn't want him to see her playing the role of a woman teetering on the edge of hysteria. But, alas, he was present. And if they were to work as partners, she might as well test his mettle. Would he see through her charade? Step onstage and carve himself a role in this dramatic production?

Mr. Glover ignored him and spoke through clenched teeth. "Come now, be reasonable. You permitted my attentions. I did not drag you into that room. It was you who misled *me*. Such behavior comes with an implicit agreement."

"I agreed to a brief liaison," she said. "Not a lifetime!"

"I believe Lady Stewart has made her position clear." Mr. Torrington's hand landed on Mr. Glover's shoulder, wheeling him about so that *he* stood face to face with Mr. Glover, his broad back and wide shoulders blocking her humiliation from onlookers.

*Aether! He'd been close enough to overhear their last exchange.* Blood rushed to her face, and she closed her eyes for a moment, reminding herself that she'd *wanted* a public scene. If not this particular one. Not one in which Mr. Glover refused to concede defeat. Her last days in London would be a misery. And if he followed her to Scotland, what then?

Colleen forced her eyes open, bracing herself for more ugliness. Mr. Torrington's right hand had moved to the small of his back. Pinched between his thumb and forefinger was a silver filigree ring set with an amber stone.

"Your behavior is presumptuous, sir," Mr. Torrington chided. "I too have been courting Lady Stewart." He waggled the ring.

He'd planned to propose tonight? Her stomach twisted. She still wasn't certain marriage was something she wanted. Did he truly expect her to place his ring on her finger?

While accepting an offer of marriage was not at all the end to the public commotion she had planned, it would serve nicely. And, with her latest task complete, she was free to take on new employment. She drew in a deep breath. A betrothal *would* allow them to spend time together without inviting too much censure. Perhaps if she viewed it as a trial engagement while she assisted him with his endeavors? Might they also find time to trial their... physical compatibility?

"Moreover," he continued, waggling the ring again, insistently. She plucked the silver band from his fingers and slid it over her glove and onto her finger. It wasn't as if she'd be required to follow through with an actual wedding. A young lady was entitled to change her mind, though the gratification that swelled his next words hinted that his actions might not at all be a performance. "She has accepted me and wears *my* ring."

## CHAPTER FIVE

CLASPING HIS FIANCÉE'S hand, Nick drew her forward, displaying the ring upon her finger to the audience before them. Hushed whispers erupted as speculation spread through the crowd. For years, he'd managed to steer clear of the marriage mart. It helped that two brothers stood between him and the eventual inheritance of a viscount's title. Still, irritation would curdle the features of a number of mothers and daughters once the news reached the guests upstairs.

Though he forced a pleasant smile onto his face, inwardly he cringed. What should have been a shared private moment following an impassioned proposal involving actual words had been turned into a spectacle played out before a roomful of gossip-inclined *ton*. Not ideal. He never would have dared attempt such a stunt had he not known how adverse she was to societal attention.

"I'm sorry, Mr. Glover." Lady Stewart lifted her voice, and he had the decided impression she carefully chose the words that would appear on tomorrow's scandal sheets. A niggling suspicion that she'd staged this altercation warned him that there was more at play here than a lover's spat. "My heart belongs to another."

"Impossible," Glover barked. Fury set his mustache quivering like a hairy caterpillar having heart palpitations. "I would have been informed. Your uncle—"

"Perhaps you'd best take that up with him." Nick's tone would have warned off a normal man, but Lady Stewart's admirer had a fervent look about his eyes that suggested—no, promised—he would be trouble.

"You may count on it."

Glaring, Glover turned on his heel and stormed from the room, off to lodge a loud and vociferous complaint to her uncle. Trouble would come next from that direction. Her guardian, Lord Maynard, was known for his uncharitable business ventures. Whatever arrangements he and Glover had arrived at, Nick's sudden intervention wouldn't be welcome. Not that he cared.

Would that he could toss Lady Stewart in a waiting steam carriage and take to the streets to settle things between them privately. Alas, that would only inflame the situation. As their time together here could now be measured in mere minutes, he cupped her elbow and drew her toward a service door fitted into the room's paneling. "Come," he said, "let's find you a quiet corner to regain your composure."

She sniffed, but held her tongue and allowed him to lead her down the hall, past a servant's staircase—sidestepping a clockwork hoist that carried stacks of empty plates and fingerprint smudged crystal along a downward track toward the kitchens—and into the conservatory.

He drew her into an alcove behind a potted plant where they could face each other and speak in relative privacy.

"Regain my composure?" His fiancée lifted an eyebrow. "How very patronizing." Indignant amber eyes flashed behind her grey lenses, and Nick was struck by a desire to pluck them from her face that he might bask in the full heat of their brilliance, in the golden glow that was almost an exact match to the color of the amber ring that now adorned her finger.

Nick cleared his throat. "Apologies, but what kind of agent would I be, shattering the carefully crafted illusion you present to the *ton*? Though Mr. Glover's bleating tonight has drawn unprecedented attention in your direction, you might still aspire to slip quietly from the role of wallflower into that of stately matron."

"A wallflower potted and rooted and content to remain upon the shelf." Her chin lifted.

"Is that so?" he countered. "Then you should not have encouraged the attentions of Mr. Glover, a man with a tendency to boast within the confines of his club."

"He did not!" Her eyes grew tight as she muttered a curse. "Of course he did. What did you hear?"

"You won't like it."

"Nonetheless, I prefer to know, lest I be taken by surprise. What nasty rumors has he spread? Leave nothing out."

With the name Dr. Gregory Farquhar in hand, Nick had headed to a club favored by second and third sons who eschewed the tradition of military or church service to pursue alternative paths. Among them were a number of physicians who might know something of this cardiologist's past, of his present.

And so one had. "Stay far, far away from him," he was cautioned. "Whatever promise he once showed, he's descended into madness and no longer even pretends to see patients. His wife grows ever more bitter as her husband toils away in that basement laboratory of his doing aether knows what." With some reluctance and repeated warnings, he'd been given Dr. Farquhar's direction.

Though the hour grew late, Nick had decided a brief visit was in order. Perhaps if he approached Dr. Farquhar as one scientist to another, offering flattery and a willing ear, the man might invite him into his laboratory. Unlikely, but worth a try.

Fortifying himself, Nick had tossed back his drink and rose. En route to the door, he'd passed a rowdy bunch of gentlemen, tormenting one of their own about his supposed "conquest".

"Are you insane? She has no dowry. Leastways, not one worth mentioning."

"You don't have to marry the first woman you bed, Glover. Not even if you leave a bun in the oven."

"She's hardly the first," he'd snapped. "And it's not her that I value, but what she will bring to our marriage."

Sniggers erupted. "She's a freak," a second man said. "Hiding those strange eyes of hers behind smoky glass, slipping in and out of rooms when no one's looking."

Nick had slowed his steps, wondering.

"Save yourself," a third advised. "She turned down your offer. Consider yourself fortunate. We'll take you to Mrs. Fowler's house…"

A brothel. He'd heard enough.

Dr. Farquhar lived in a relatively new townhome—terraced— on a respectable street not far from The British Museum. The man's steam butler had taken Nick's card, but declared the good doctor not at home and unable to say when he would return. The usual lies, for Nick had not missed the twitch of a curtain that covered an upper window. For a brief moment, he'd stared into the wild eyes of a white-haired man. The physician himself?

With a normal, civilized conversation ruled out, Nick had returned home to dress for the ball and arrived at Lord Aldridge's front door to find chaos and turmoil surrounding the very woman that drew him to tonight's societal event.

"Mr. Torrington, tell me." Lady Stewart scowled, correctly anticipating what he had to share.

"Much what you'd expect." He cleared his throat. She deserved to know. "Bets were being taken. Odds were rather in favor of you declining his offer, despite… well… his boasts of sexual conquest that would force you to accept his suit."

"I will claw his eyes out." Her face flushed, but she did not turn away from Nick's gaze. "But I won't pretend I've been chaste all these years in London. Are you certain you don't wish to retract your unspoken offer?" She lifted her hand and began to slide the ring from her finger.

He caught her hand with his. "No." Were there certain primitive instincts fixed in his brainstem that objected? Yes. But the higher centers of his brain admired her refusal to conceal the truth. "I'll admit to a selfish urge to guard your reputation and an inclination to defend your honor by resurrecting the tradition of pistols at dawn, but it's not your maidenly virtue that draws me." The corner of his mouth kicked up. The words he'd practiced in his mind fell away. Instead he spoke the raw truth. "Not only do I like you, Lady Colleen Stewart, I admire you. Your quick mind, your skills as a sneak thief, your refusal to conform to society's will. And," he trailed a finger down the side of her face, "your kisses send fire racing through my veins. You're the only woman I wish to make my bride. But if *I* don't suit *you*, then by all means, return my ring."

The pulse at her throat fluttered. The attraction between them was palpable. No, combustible. Yet her hesitation spoke volumes and her words, when they finally came, were soft. "Might we… consider this a trial engagement?"

"A trial engagement." He lifted an eyebrow.

"We've known each other for years now, but only in fleeting snatches." She took a deep breath. "I'd not thought to marry anyone. Not before you. But—"

"You wish to know me better first."

She nodded. "And you ought to know me better as well. There are freedoms I do not wish to relinquish."

"You wish to discuss terms." Fair enough, especially given

her uncle certainly wouldn't be inclined to negotiate a favorable marriage contract on her behalf. "Contracts and finances."

"Of course. Much as I loved my father, he tied me—legally—to an awful man he himself did not respect—and all due to a misplaced view of a woman's abilities. I'll not willingly or blindly speak vows without securing my future rights."

"The last thing I want is a reluctant or apprehensive bride."

"Additionally, you might not appreciate the attention an engagement to me brings. Your own reputation will suffer."

"Not nearly as much as yours." Gentlemen were permitted their wild oats, but the slightest hint of indiscretion forever stained an unmarried woman's reputation.

"And," her voice dropped as her lips curved upward, "we ought to see if we… suit."

Heat crept up beneath his collar and cravat. Nick stepped closer. "Are you suggesting—"

She flicked her fingers against his waistcoat, directly over his concealed TTX pistol. "I wish to see how you conduct yourself in the field."

"You want me to lead you into excitement and danger upon the dark streets of nighttime London?" Never had he thought to woo a woman in such a manner, but he found himself warming to the many possibilities that long hours of prolonged surveillance might provide.

"I do." She laughed, then became all business. "Now, tell me what you have in mind for our first outing together, and what is it you seek."

A tiny, irritating voice counseled him that he ought not include her on tonight's undertaking, reminding him that the scientist might well be employed by the Committee for the Exploration of Anthropomorphic Peculiarities, or CEAP as it was sometimes referred to among the Queen's agents. Nick could do this alone. He could sneak into Dr. Farquhar's laboratory without assistance. A partner to watch one's back was valuable, but not imperative. So asserted his mind. Other parts of his anatomy continued to insist that the presence of this particular woman was, in fact, very necessary. But those parts—ones that were upright and alert—had no business running a mission.

Still, when put to a vote, his gray matter lost.

"A medical device. One merely rumored to exist, so finding it is not a certainty. To begin, I've a basement laboratory I wish to search. Quietly and discreetly." For her, he tried to separate the task at hand from any future they might or might not share. "Regardless of the outcome of our trial engagement, you will be paid." He named a sum. "For each evening you assist my endeavors. A bonus of twice that if—when—we find the device."

A titter of laughter met their ears and though the other couple that wandered past was lost in each other's eyes, he stepped yet closer to Lady Stewart, dropping a hand lightly upon her waist to discourage any interruption of their conversation.

"A generous offer." She leaned forward, breathing her next question into his ear. "And what of our trial engagement?" Her fingertips smoothed the lapel upon his jacket.

"Formal and chaste." He swallowed, fixing his gaze upon the unremarkable cluster of fabric flowers pinned to her shoulder.

"Is that so." She bit her lower lip, toying with the top button of his waistcoat. "How... disappointing."

He laughed, then pulled her into his arms so that she might feel his stiffness against the soft swell of her stomach. "Unless you wish otherwise. Though it is by no means a condition of either our engagement or your employment."

"Well, then, let's see what opportunities present themselves." She dropped her hand, then slid her arms beneath his coat and about his waist. "Shall we begin tonight?"

"Yes." His cock twitched, but he ignored its enthusiasm. This was not the place for anything but a kiss. People—some of them irate—would soon come looking for her. For them. Not only would her uncle take offense, but their scene in the library might well have overshadowed Lady Sophia's debut. "When will your household be asleep?"

She rolled her eyes. "After Mr. Glover's uncalled for furor? My uncle will rant, but my aunt will silently applaud my actions. By three in the morning, I will have been sent to my room. Any further outrage will be set aside for breakfast pleasantries."

He snorted. "Taken to task over tea and toast?"

"It does tend to put off one's appetite."

"Colleen?" a voice called in the distance. Their time was up.

"My aunt," she said, but didn't pull away. "Now that we're engaged, you may call me by my given name."

"As a fiancé ought. Might he also be permitted a liberty?"

"If I may call you by yours?"

"Of course."

"Well, then. But only a small one for the moment." Her fingers slipped beneath the edge of his waistcoat and ran over the linen of his shirt, tracing the muscle that ran down his back. "Appearances must be maintained, Nicholas."

He brushed his lips along the edge of her jaw and whispered, "Not Nicholas. Nick." Then he captured her mouth with his own, tasting honey and soft sighs as he explored its sweet shape. A perfect fit. He was about to deepen their embrace when the leaves beside him rustled.

"Colleen!" her aunt exclaimed, staring openly through the foliage. "What is this I hear of an engagement?"

He took a step back, releasing his fiancée. "Soon," he whispered. If there was time to seek out a private corner of London after they searched the laboratory...

Behind her spectacles, Colleen's eyes flashed as if her mind charted a similar course. "The mews," she whispered, then dropped her hands from his waist and—at an impatient huff—turned toward the interruption. "Mr. Torrington, you've met Lady Maynard."

"Many times." He turned and bowed. "Always a pleasure."

Colleen's aunt was a classic beauty—and older than her niece by a scant few years. He'd heard speculation about the manner of Lord Maynard's first wife's death. None of them pleasant, all of them centered around her inability to provide an heir.

"So *this* is the gentleman that kept you up at night and has set the ball abuzz." Lady Maynard threw him a saucy glance.

Nick slid his questioning gaze back to Colleen.

"She knows only about *my* occupation."

In other words, Nick's employment with the Queen's agents had not been discussed.

"And the cat's," Lady Maynard added. "Your timing leaves much to be desired, but better late than never. Not that my irate husband agrees. I'll do what I can to smooth your path, but you had best pay a visit tomorrow. My advice? Bring a competent solicitor."

"A solicitor?" Nick asked.

Lady Maynard's eyes widened as she glanced from him to Colleen. "Does it not strike you as odd that your uncle is—after years of ignoring your presence—suddenly so very interested in finding you a husband? One of *his* choosing? It's rare his temper flares. He's up to something."

"So noted," Nick replied.

A commotion broke out in the hallway.

Lady Maynard caught up Colleen's hand, grinned at the amber ring, then tugged. "Come. Mr. Glover is grousing about breach of promise, and I've sent for the steam carriage. We have minutes to fabricate a story involving a lengthy courtship and a secret engagement." She winked. "Clearly, the truth won't do."

CHAPTER SIX

BY HALF-PAST TWO, the house was perfectly silent, and Colleen slid from her bed. No cat stretched upon the covers or performed brief ablutions before leaping to the ground to twine about her ankles. Instead, the tin of tuna sat untouched upon the windowsill. Each day Colleen's concern grew.

Despite the white patch upon Sorcha's chest, her otherwise black fur always set superstitious individuals on edge, leaving Colleen forever worried that the cat might become a target. But how did one hunt—especially in London—for a wildcat that did not wish to be found? Not that it would stop her. If she wasn't back by morning, Colleen would try.

Stretching, she turned her mind to tonight's activities. The only specifics she'd been given were device, basement and laboratory. Never had she taken on a job so woefully under informed, with little to no control as to its execution. Still, with the funds to repair her roof secured, she could afford this slight indulgence. For once, pay was not a pivotal factor. Adventure—and a handsome, exciting man—called. For the first time, she would roam London's streets for the thrill, rather than the necessity.

A current of excitement shot through her as she lifted the lid of her trunk and contemplated her wardrobe with a smile. What *did* one wear to both explore the laboratory of a—presumably— mad scientist *and* seduce one's partner?

French silk. Blood-red silk bloomers and a matching silk camisole. But that was all the indulgence she could spare. Priorities, as always, involved avoiding discovery and the ability to affect a quick escape. To that end she chose a lightly boned corset, a high-necked blouse and linen breeches that tucked into boots that laced to the knees. All black.

She wound her dark hair into a tight knot, fastening it in place with pins sharp enough to draw blood. A belt followed, one adorned with loops from which she suspended a number of useful items such as lock picks, a coiled Rapunzel rope, and a purse filled with smoke bombs—a useful distraction when one needed to make a hasty exit. She slid a long, thin blade into the sheathe within her boot and swung a hooded cape about her shoulders. While warm, its fabric provided the added advantage of hiding her features and her eyes from anyone who might later recall a flash of unusual brilliance.

And to that end, the amber ring upon her finger must remain behind. A perfect fit and the exact color of her eyes, it was evidence that Nick's proposal, albeit unconventional, was far more than a passing whim. Though she remained wary at the thought of a lifetime commitment, a certain warmth spread through her at the idea of calling him her husband. Placing the ring upon her dressing table, Colleen stepped to her window and searched the misty shadows. Confident her uncle's minion was not about, she climbed out and leapt free, sliding down the drainpipe and into the murky gloom as she made her way to the mews.

At exactly five minutes to three, her ride appeared.

Beneath a lamppost that struggled to cast a dim pool of light through the fog, Nick sat upon a tarnished brass clockwork horse that had seen better days. Soot darkened its leather mane, muck crusted its hooves, and its eyes stared in two different directions, suggesting its winding springs might be wild and unmanageable. Much like its rider's appearance.

He wore brown-striped trousers tucked into tall boots and a long leather coat, one that bore a number of disturbing stains—all unidentifiable in origin—and was fastened closed by a row of brass buckles that marched down his chest. A highwayman of old. Rough and tumble to her sleek and sophisticated. A thrill coursed through her.

With two steps and a leap, she landed behind him on the saddle and wrapped her arms about his waist. He threw an amused glance over his shoulder, then flipped a lever, setting them off at a sedate, non-attention-gathering pace. She pressed her face against his shoulder, inhaling the pleasant scent of gear oil and saddle soap. A far cry from the earlier over-perfumed and sweaty ballroom crowd. "Whom do we hope to rob?"

He huffed a laugh. "Dr. Gregory Farquhar of 28 Bloomsbury Street. He's avoiding me. Our visit will be more exploratory in nature than acquisitive. I've no idea if the device even exists."

They had a bit of a ride ahead of them. Time, then, to admire the taut stomach beneath her arms, the broad back crushed against her chest, and the way her hips slid forward on the poorly sprung saddle with each awkward step the clockwork creature took until they were pressed against his firm rear, their thighs tightly aligned. She had the sneaking suspicion that Nick had chosen this beast for more reasons than its off-putting appearance.

"Why the device?" It was easy to forget that her arms encircled more than a Queen's agent. Mr. Nicholas Torrington was also a scientist. His entire career was spurred by a hunt for a cure—or a treatment—for his sister, Anna, whose heart struggled to beat. On the rare occasions his sister ventured into society, she always appeared vaguely blue. "Have the drugs failed?"

"For Anna, yes." The clockwork horse clopped forward a few steps before he continued. "For years, I've attempted to strengthen her heart, hunting for novel drugs, but finding few. Atropine. Digitalis. Hawthorn. None have the desired effects. Her only hope now is locating a rumored device that will restart a stalled heart."

Her breath caught as images of cadavers jolted with bolts of electricity sprang to mind. "Is this Dr. Farquhar a galvanist?" Such quacks were little better than the spiritualists a few decades past who had hinted at the possibility of life after death. Under the guise of medicine, some slightly less insane men sold elaborate devices while expounding upon the benefits of electricity to restore health and vigor. She'd seen men with paste-pots and handbills gluing advertisements for electrotherapy clinics to walls.

"He once trained as a cardiac electrophysiologist," Nick said, focusing her mental ramblings. "Today? The exact direction of his work is unclear, but he might well be a galvanist focusing upon cardiac tissue. I should warn you that there's a strong likelihood he's experimenting upon animals."

Animals. Most likely stray ones. But not necessarily. A hired man with a catch pole would snag any convenient animal that had the misfortune to wander past. One such as a roaming cat sìth. Worry twisted her stomach even though her mind insisted Sorcha was far too wild and resourceful to ever find herself trapped. Besides, Dr. Farquhar's house was near The British Museum, far outside her established territory. Still…

"What do you know of heart anatomy and physiology?" Nick asked. His voice broke the grip of her concerns.

"Next to nothing." Save he always made hers beat faster. "What—exactly—is wrong?"

"Are you aware that the heart is composed of a unique kind of muscle tissue that will spontaneously contract?"

"I am now."

"A heartbeat initiates at the top of the heart. First two chambers known as the atria contract, then a signal spreads downward via a net of connecting fibers. When the stimulus reaches the lower two chambers, the ventricles, they contract, pumping blood into the lungs and throughout the body."

She slid her palm upward, until she could feel the beat of his heart. "Thump-thump, thump-thump." At her words, it leapt beneath her hand. Warmed by gratification, she smiled against his back.

"Exactly. Normally, such an electrical impulse travels through the heart at a rate of sixty to seventy times per minute."

Nick tugged on the reins, turning the clockwork horse onto Oxford Street. The street lamps did their best, but the night was moonless and thick with fog. Those out and about moved as if anonymity was assured, as if they were no more than flitting shadows. For them it might be dark, but for Colleen's eyes the gaslight was enough to cast everything in a faint gray light. On their left, a passing figure in leather and wool flicked a cigar stump into the street. A ruffian wearing ragged trousers slept in a doorway beside a mangy dog. A crank hack passed on their right carrying home a man wearing a top hat.

She tugged her hood forward. Better safe than sorry. "And Anna?"

"As low as forty beats per minute." Nick paid no mind to the skulking shapes in the streets. "When we were children, it wasn't as bad. Her heart's rhythm was slow—only fifty beats per minute—and occasionally skipped a beat. From time to time, she might grow lightheaded or a touch dizzy but, for the most part, she was fine. After much fussing, the doctors concluded that her heart was damaged, that something blocked the rhythm from propagating to the lower chambers. But there was nothing to be done." He took a deep breath. "Of late, it has grown much worse."

Sympathy tugged at her chest. "How so?"

"Shortness of breath. Heart palpitations. Her hands are always cold, her fingernails blue. From time to time, she collapses without warning, twitching. To the touch, her slow pulse is seemingly absent. There's nothing to be done save limit her exertions."

"That's awful! What changed?"

For a long moment, Nick fell silent, seeming to struggle with her question. "Anna was advised never to marry."

"But she did." Colleen remembered the announcement. And what often followed some nine months later? Love might pain the heart, though it would do no direct damage. But… "There's a child." One did not require a medical degree to know that childbearing—childbirth—could place a strain on the heart.

"Yes. Though the infant is fine, Anna's condition grew worse following delivery, and she began having fainting attacks." He blew out a sudden breath. "There's a fifty percent chance of mortality within a year of such a seizure."

Meaning each time she collapsed, her family could do nothing but watch and hope that *this* time her heart would restart. And, when it did, brace themselves for the next episode. She tightened her arms about Nick's waist. "If we locate this device, you propose to…?" She trailed off, praying there was hope.

"Evaluate its potential," he finished. "It's time I set aside medications to pay more attention to the work of the electro-physiologists. Anna lives on the sharp edge of fear, preparing daily for the eventuality that the next seizure might well take her life. Imagine if there's a way to guard against that possibility?"

Colleen attempted to digest the enormity of the situation facing his sister. She opened her mouth to ask another question, but a glow of light clouded by dense smoke caught her eye. In the distance, a rattle grew nearer and nearer. And louder and louder.

The dreadful cry of "Fire!" reached her ears at the same moment a great steam pumper fire engine roared onto the street, taking the corner on two wheels and followed closely by a fire wagon carrying coils of hose. People poured from buildings, half-dressed—some in their nightclothes—all shouting and clamoring as they thronged through the streets following the engine like a pack of hounds.

"Hold tight!" Nick shoved the lever forward, sending their clockwork horse into a gallop, weaving expertly through the swelling mob—then reining back to a sudden stop at Blooms-bury Street. In the face of the dull roar of the fire, the fire brigade worked quickly, sending arcs of water onto a blazing townhome while pickpockets threaded through the crowd taking full advantage of the commotion.

Though quiet shadows were preferable, a burning house would be a convenient distraction while they searched the laboratory. She slid from the clockwork horse, but Nick made no move to dismount. Instead, a curse fell from his lips.

No. Could it be— "Is that... 28 Bloomsbury Street?"

"It is." Nick's jaw tightened.

The timing *was* curiously suspicious. Yet they hunted a life-saving medical device, not some secret government technology pursued by biotechnological spies. *Or so she'd been led to believe.* Her gaze slid sideways. "Then *you* should interview its mistress." She pointed to a woman who stood beside the fire wagon—conspicuously alone—with a blanket wrapped about her nightdress. No neighbors rushed to her side to offer comfort. No tears streaked down her soot-blackened face. Odd.

Lips pressed into a grim line, Nick dismounted and paid a boy to watch the clockwork horse, promising far more if they were both still present when he returned. He elbowed his way to the woman's side. "Mrs. Farquhar?"

"Yes?" Suspicion tinged her voice, and she clutched the blanket tighter.

Columns of smoke and steam rose from the burning heap as the firemen doused the fire. Colleen stood to the side, keeping her face well-hidden in the shadows—a challenge beside this blaze—yet with her ear finely tuned to the nuances of their every word.

"I need to speak with your husband," Nick said. "Now. Is he nearby?"

"No," Mrs. Farquhar's eyes sidled away. "So if you're here to collect his findings…"

Nick stiffened. Colleen's ears pricked.

"Don't deny it," the woman grumbled. "That outlandish dress of yours doesn't fool me. You work for *him*. I warned the likes of you that Gregory was a bad gamble. The bastard did a runner."

"And took his invention with him?"

The fire was nearly out, and the crowds began to disperse. The firemen, exhausted, worked quietly to stow their equipment. She squinted. Broken glass. Charred wood. Dripping, soot-blackened water. The house was now uninhabitable, but the gaps in the structure made by flames and collapsing wood made the lowest floor, sunken beneath street level, accessible. Easy enough to pass through the kitchen and reach those rooms behind it where the laboratory would be located.

"Oh, is that what we're calling it?" Mrs. Farquhar groused. "Nasty business, all of this. Why else would he run? Either way, that rosewood box you're after? It's not here."

Ice crystalized in her blood, and a shiver ran across her skin. A rosewood box. She'd bet her entire bank account that she'd had her hands on that very box just a few hours past. Dammit. A sick twist of nausea swirled in her stomach. She had lowered her standards to accept a gray assignment and look where it had led. Anna's life dangled in peril all because—

No. This was not her fault. Colleen took a deep breath and concentrated upon the conversation.

Nick was pressing Mrs. Farquhar for more information. "Did he give you any details about the men he worked for?"

"No." She backed away, shaking her head, all but snarling at Nick. "I'll not fall for any tricks. This is a test, and I'll not fail. You'll not get anything more from me. Go away."

It didn't matter. She knew that the buyer—whomever he was—had arranged for one of Mr. Witherspoon's other associates to meet with Dr. Farquhar, initiating the process by which his invention had been passed along an obfuscation chain. Which meant, quite simply, that it was—or would be—in the hands of another unscrupulous soul. Why, then, this burning of his house? Something felt wrong. Either it was part of the cover up, or someone had secrets to hide. The obvious choice, to question Mr. Witherspoon, was pointless. He would tell her nothing.

That meant they had a laboratory to investigate. Then a scientist to locate.

# CHAPTER SEVEN

THE FIREMEN'S BACKS were turned, presenting Colleen with opportunity. A few long strides and a quick vault over an iron railing dropped her into the front service well of the house. Though it was dark, her eyes needed no more than the tiniest pinpoint of light to see clearly.

As she passed down the charred, acrid remains of the hallway, glancing into various workrooms, numerous damp, brownish-green frogs hopped about her feet, and a dozen rats with soot-streaked and matted fur scurried along the baseboard frantically seeking a way out. More than once, she'd been grateful for her knee-high boots, but never so thankful as she was now.

A heavy, half-closed iron door barred entry to a side room. There was only one reason for such security here in the basement. *This* must be the laboratory. She shoved at the door, forcing it to flex upon its hinges, and a panicked, lightly-singed weasel loped past her ankles seeking a path to freedom.

In the laboratory, the vile smell of chemicals and charred flesh assaulted her nose and sent her stomach roiling. Broken glass crunched beneath her feet, and something squishy shifted and slid. A mistake, looking down at the toes of her boots, for she found herself in the middle of a shallow puddle where thin, white threads twisted and curled as they died a slow death. Worms?

She grimaced and forced herself to survey the room.

Not every experimental subject had escaped. Not even close. Wire cages held blackened lumps of flesh, and glass tanks were occupied by frogs floating belly up. Bile rose to her throat, and she averted her eyes from the lifeless captives, only to find herself face to face with charred shelving and the rows of skulls it held. Small mammals, all of them, none of which she could identify, save those that were feline. Larger than that of house cats, smaller than that of a wildcat.

A frisson of dread ran down her spine. There were multiple skulls of cat sìth. Was it possible that cryptid hunters had found a landholder willing to turn a blind eye to poaching? Alarm morphed into anger.

In the center of the room stood a steel work table. Lining the walls were countertops and cabinets and yet more shelves. Or, rather, there had been. Most were charred, their contents destroyed, shattered or otherwise altered beyond recognition— save a partially collapsed, wood-framed box fitted with cracked and smudged glass panes with metal tubing that led to a low-set window. An experiment of some kind had been set up inside a fume hood and interrupted when the fire broke out.

"Colleen?" Nick called as if from a distance, searching for her, but she didn't answer.

A faint mewl emerged from within the fume hood. One that sounded decidedly like an injured cat. *Exactly* as Sorcha had the night she'd returned home injured, limping with a gash across her leg. Feral animals were always a threat in the dark alleys she roamed.

She dashed across the room, swiping at the glass with her forearm, but only managing to smear the sticky residue. She pushed and rattled at the frame, forcing it to roll upward along two metal tracks. Inside were fluid-filled bottles, wires, a bucket of water, a scalpel and forceps. And a wire cage containing an exceptionally large black cat with a torn ear and a pinch of white upon its chest. Two slitted, golden eyes peered up at her.

"Sorcha!" Her voice was both a wail of grief and one of relief. Only then did she take note of the bandages wound about the cat's legs, the shaved patches of bare skin upon her chest and shoulder. "What did that horrid man do to you?"

Crouching, the cat sìth hissed and bared her sharp teeth.

"It's me, sweetie. Come to take you home." First to her uncle's, but then, yes, all the way back to northern Scotland. "You poor thing." She tugged off a glove and reached out, giving the frightened cat sìth a moment to identify her as friend, not enemy. When they located Dr. Farquhar she'd make him answer for his mistreatments. "The moment we're home, I'll find you a saucer of cream." And spoil her rotten, as a fairy cat ought to be.

The cat sniffed her fingers, then twitched, directing her gaze over Colleen's shoulder. A low growl emanated from the cat sìth's throat seconds before Nick pointed his decilamp at the cat's cage.

"He's a friend," she crooned to the cat, comforting her by letting a little Doric slip into her words. "Nae worrie."

"Colleen?" He stood beside her. "Is that—?"

"My familiar?"

"Sorcha."

"Yes. And she's badly hurt." Her worse fears realized.

Nick pulled a second decilamp from a pocket and handed it to her. "I know your vision is excellent, but..."

She took the offered light. "It does improve things." And it did. They'd never spoken directly about her unusual eyes or any of her other catlike skills, something they would need to address were this engagement to progress beyond its trial status. Something she'd worry about later. "I'll need to keep her in the cage for now, until her panic subsides."

Colleen snapped upright, remembering why they were here. She glanced about the laboratory and said, "Perhaps you can make more sense of what remains. I passed a number of fleeing frogs and rats and even a weasel." She flicked the light across the skull-laden shelves, past the caged corpses. "Dr. Farquhar's other victims weren't so lucky."

For now, dawn approached. They needed to comb through the wreckage for clues. What exactly was Dr. Farquhar about and where might he have run? Reluctantly, she turned away from Sorcha and began to poke through the wreckage.

Nick, however, moved to stand before the fume hood, examining its contents. Sorcha, quiet now, stared at him through narrowed eyes. "A bottle of chloroform, for use as an anesthetic." He traced a length of wire from beneath the cracked window to the remnants of a large mechanical contraption, one that was minimally charred yet still unidentifiable to her eyes. "This machine bears a striking resemblance to the one in my own home, used to send a jolt of electricity to the heart."

Colleen cringed. Both for Anna and for the poor animals— dead and alive—that might have endured its use.

"Disappointing. I was hoping to find evidence of something much smaller." Nick tipped the bucket full of water. "And this was likely filled with ice."

"Ice?" She looked up from the pile of soggy papers she'd tried to separate. Alas, not only were they glued together, but the ink had run to the point of illegibility.

"Extreme cold stops the heart."

"He was—" Her mouth fell open in horror.

"Stopping hearts so that he might practice restarting them?" His voice grew distant. "Yes."

Anger marched up her spine, setting her skin alight. Frogs

and rats she could perhaps understand. One had to begin some-where. But cats?

*Wait.*

Something about Nick's voice sounded off. She narrowed her eyes. "What is it you're not telling me?"

He hesitated. "Queen's agent's business."

"That's Sorcha in there. That makes it my business too." The words emerged as a growl. "We can work together on this, or at cross purposes. Your choice."

Nick blew out a long breath. "Fine. Dr. Farquhar's sanity is questionable."

*Obviously.* But she kept her mouth shut, waiting.

"It has been suggested that Dr. Farquhar has an interest in animal transmutation. In short, sorcery."

*Or witchcraft.*

Which might explain his interest in Sorcha. In the cat sìth. Was it possible he believed the stories?

"Tell me," Nick urged. "Even to my weak eyes, it's as clear as day that you know something more. We are both partners and a betrothed couple. Isn't it time to peel away all pretenses?"

She knew quite a bit more, and he was right. They couldn't work effectively as a team if they kept details—however small—from each other. "Sorcha is no house cat." She hesitated, uncer-tain how to explain the feline to an Englishman.

"Not new information, Colleen." His voice was flat. "I've watched the two of you skulking about London for years now. What, exactly, is she?"

"Cat sìth, a kind of hybrid cat—part wild, part domesticated. A number of them live in the woods of my family's estate. Some say they're fairy. Others believe that the cat sìth is the animal form of a witch, one who can transform into a cat nine times. Legend, myth, folk tale. Take your pick. Regardless, Dr. Farquhar —by name—is Scottish. He ought to have respected tradition and not subjected a rare and precious animal to such treatment." She crossed her arms. "I can see from your face that this information holds significance."

"It does," Nick admitted. "But it's a long, complicated story that needs to wait." He waved at the fume hood. "This doesn't fit with Mrs. Farquhar's account of the situation."

"What do you mean?" She dropped the ruined papers and crossed to his side.

"If he planned to set fire to his laboratory and bolt with his device, why would he have set up an experiment involving a rare and precious animal?"

*Why indeed?*

"After you abandoned me," he glanced sideways at her, eyebrow raised, "his wife admitted she'd pressed her husband to demand more money for his work. Denied, she claims he accepted a more lucrative offer." Nick waved his free hand, and Sorcha snarled. "Yet if he was here, working in his laboratory when the fire was set—"

"Then his wife told you a passel of lies."

"Exactly."

"I see no evidence of his body. You?"

"None. Rather, a door open to the rear garden."

So Farquhar had left, run for his life and left the cat sìth to her fate. Were fairies real, the man would have tripped and died on the doorstep while making his exit. Pursing her lips, she threw a final glance about the laboratory. "There's no indication of where he might have gone, and there's nothing else here that's salvageable. Shall we go question her further?"

His expression hardened, turning his face to granite. "Yes."

She hefted Sorcha's cage into her arms.

Ever the gentleman, Nick reached for it, but the cat sìth hissed, and he stepped back. "Something tells me she'll shred my hands and arms through the bars. Should we not simply set her free?" he asked, though from the look on his face, he already knew the answer to that.

"Were she not injured and afraid." Even in Colleen's care, the large cat crouched with narrowed eyes, decidedly displeased and only just managing to tolerate her rescue efforts. "I don't want her to bolt." She wouldn't risk losing Sorcha to the city or men like Dr. Farquhar again.

They tromped back onto the street. Only a few gawkers lingered, staring at the burned-out building, marveling that the firemen had been able to save anything about it. The scent of the fire hung in the air, so thick and pungent Colleen could smell nothing else.

About the still-dark edges of the streets, figures skulked, scampering away like rats when she turned her eyes directly upon them. Though all appeared guilty of something, most were servants, late to their morning posts. Some looked as if they bided their time, hoping for a chance to loot the shell of a building for any valuables that had survived the blaze. One man, in particular, glared at her from across the street, but by the time she turned Nick's attention in his direction, he'd disappeared.

They persisted, but no matter how many people they questioned or the number of dark alleys they stalked, there was no sign of Mrs. Farquhar. Neighbors curled their lips when questioned and denied knowing where she might have sought refuge for the remainder of the night.

As Nick's frustration grew, so too did Colleen's sense of unease. Nick's hunt for a medical device, her participation in an obfuscation chain, and this fire were all tightly linked. And both of them knew more than they were sharing.

As a glimmer of light filled the morning sky, Nick turned to Colleen. "Time to admit defeat. For the moment. You need to return home before your absence is discovered."

Impossible to argue with that statement. Besides, he needed to know about her latest task for Witherspoon and Associates. Sooner rather than later. Once they'd retrieved the clockwork horse, lashed the cage—covered by Nick's coat—to the saddle and were well on their way back to Mayfair, Colleen could no longer suppress her stomach-churning knowledge. She very much doubted her employer would be willing to name names. Not, at least, without first charging Nick an exorbitant fee. "There's something you need to know."

# CHAPTER EIGHT

ESTORED BY A few hours' sleep and dressed once more like a respectable gentleman, Nick pulled his phaeton to the edge of the street and tossed the clockwork horse's reins to a boy before flipping him a coin. His was not the only vehicle present. Was The Much Honored Colleen Stewart of Craigieburn beset with unwelcome guests? He expected so. Glover and his ugliness were certain to be among them, attempting to claim what was not his.

Despite the mounting frustration that had followed Colleen's horseback revelation, Nick smiled. When he'd seen that man backing Colleen into a corner, his blood pressure had spiked and set his blood on fire. Only later—when reason returned—did he realize that she'd had Glover exactly where she'd wanted him: in a position of public humiliation. As she was normally one to avoid the limelight, it was an excellent move. No one would ever guess what she'd been about. With such drama before them, who would notice the addition of an unassuming rose-wood box upon a table beside a globe? He certainly hadn't.

Nick's "rescue" had been entirely unnecessary. Yet she'd accepted his ring. Allowed him to publicly claim her. But convincing her that they belonged together long-term? That would take time and trust, the first tentative bonds of which had been established last night.

As dawn threatened, he'd dropped Colleen in the dark shadow of her choice before returning to the scene of the ball where the house was quiet with exhaustion and oblivious to his reentry.

No surprise. The rosewood box—contents unknown—was gone.

It burned that he'd stood so close.

An obfuscation chain, a rosewood box, a fire, a fairy cat. Not only was it not a coincidence, but Colleen was the common thread running throughout. All those times he'd teased about Sorcha being her "familiar" and not once had she said a word. Upon reflection, he ought to have asked sooner. The creature wasn't a proper house cat. Its legs were a bit too long, its tail a touch too thick. Much like a Scottish wildcat, save it was black, had a white patch of fur upon its chest and was overlarge. And apparently believed by some capable of transforming into a human female. To that end, he needed to bring her into his confidence and inform her of the existence of CEAP and a shadow committee within London itself.

Step one: rid her of Mr. Glover's attentions so that they might progress to step two: a morning drive in the park wherein he might learn her employer's price. Convincing her employer to reveal the name of the ultimate buyer, she'd explained, would cost him dearly—should he agree at all. His family, he'd assured her, could well afford the price. Everything hinged upon learning the buyer's name.

No, not everything. But he expected the task of locating Dr. Farquhar might prove difficult or impossible.

Nick mounted the stairs, took a deep breath and knocked, bracing for objections to his presence.

The door flew open. Lady Maynard herself stood before him,

her eyes red-rimmed and her nose pink and swollen. "Thank aether!" she cried, reaching out to catch him by the sleeve, dragging him inside and slamming the door behind him. "You're late. Please tell me your solicitor is not far behind."

"I'm afraid I didn't—"

"Believe me?" she huffed. "Most gentlemen know of my husband's love for legal entanglements and unorthodox dealings."

Stacks of trunks and boxes lined the entryway. Perched atop, a wicker basket. A pair of golden eyes peered forth, watching his every move. Sorcha. Were Colleen and her cat being sent away? If so, he'd offer them sanctuary.

"This is highly irregular, my lady." A flustered steam butler rolled back and forth, clutching a silver salver while attempting to navigate past his mistress to reach Nick.

"Hurry, Mr. Torrington," Lady Maynard urged, ignoring the steambot and pushing him toward a tightly closed door. From within came muffled cries of outrage. Lady Maynard's voice dropped. "This morning Mr. Glover arrived with a special license and a minister. You must do something!"

That explained the luggage. Lord Maynard intended to ship his niece off with her husband. Immediately.

With a curse, he burst into the parlor to find Colleen and a group of squabbling gentlemen gathered about a large desk. In a far corner, a silent, thick-necked man stood. Nick would save the question as to why a man such as Maynard felt it necessary to employ a bodyguard for later.

For now, he had eyes only for his fiancée who stood, arms crossed and jaw clenched, bristling with indignation. Once again, she was dressed every inch the respectable lady. Neatly knotted hair and tinted round spectacles. A somber blue gown and sensible shoes. All fashioned to hide her true spirit.

How many had ever seen her in her element, free and unencumbered by society's restrictions? The flash of amber eyes, the lithe bend and twist of her form, the grin of a woman who dared to sneak kisses from a man. He could swear he'd seen a flash of red silk beneath her black shirt last night and hoped she'd entertained thoughts of seduction. He'd all but cursed the first rays of sunlight that forced him to abandon the chance to learn the answer.

Never had a woman captured his interest so completely.

He was glad to see his ring upon her finger, proof of the claim he was about to make.

"What is the meaning of this?" His voice thundered.

Lord Maynard turned a pinched face in Nick's direction. Like his starched, stiff collar the man never unbent. "You."

Colleen glanced at Nick, and her shoulders dropped ever so slightly. "As I explained, Uncle. Mr. Nicholas Torrington proposed, and I have accepted. This," she waved a hand at the minister, "is an unseemly spectacle."

Mr. Glover flushed an angry red, pointing the fountain pen at Nick as if he might run his competition through. "I saw you at the club. You've heard the rumors. They're all true. Had she wished to take a different husband, Miss Stewart should not have lifted her petticoats. You can't possibly want a compromised woman."

Sharp indrawn breaths sucked all the oxygen from the room at once.

"Mr. Glover!" her uncle warned.

"Bite your tongue!" Nick couldn't say he was happy that she had a past, but so too did he—and Nick would never utter such words about any woman with the intent to shame her into compliance.

"How dare you!" Colleen's eyes flashed with fire behind her tinted lenses. Her fingers clawed into the folds of the blue gown she wore. Had Glover any idea how close he was to having his eyes gouged out? "Not for an entire dragon's hoard would I marry an unsophisticated boor such as yourself."

"He has a valid claim," her uncle insisted in a calm and controlled voice, though irritation narrowed his eyes. "The settlement is quite fair, and Mr. Glover comes from a good family."

Outrage rolled off Nick's back in waves. *This* was how her family protected her? He couldn't begin to imagine treating his sister in such a manner. He opened his mouth to protest, but Colleen spoke first.

"This is the nineteenth century!" Anger shook her body. Behind gray lenses, her eyes flashed. "You can't bind me to a man of your choosing to force his fealty. Find a way to solidify your business dealings that doesn't require some misguided feudal maneuver." She drew breath. "Enough of this. My twenty-fifth birthday is in two days, and I intend to return to Craigieburn to run the estate *myself*."

She'd mis-stepped. Her uncle's gaze slipped to the amber ring upon her finger, and his lips twisted with suspicion.

Nick crossed the room to stand before Lord Maynard. He dropped his voice to a low growl. "When we wed, *Lady* Stewart will retain all rights to funds and properties in her name. And, yes, I promised she herself will oversee the Craigieburn estate." He held out a hand, beckoning Colleen to his side. As she came, tension fell away from his shoulders. His protection wasn't strictly necessary, but it felt good to offer it, to have her accept it without question. "I care not about her romantic past, only her future with me. If family connections matter, may I remind you that my father is a viscount. But more importantly, Lady Stewart has *accepted* my suit."

Her uncle's eyes narrowed. Clearly, the man wished to refuse him.

The clergyman cleared his throat. "I'm afraid the names are already inked. This turn of events will require a new license."

"No!" Mr. Glover cried out. "She is promised to me!"

"It will require no such thing," Nick stated. "We plan to marry in Lady Stewart's own kirk."

Another gasp. But this time it was Lady Maynard, who looked to be suppressing a smile. But it recalled to mind her presence, and her husband's frown etched itself deeper into the granite of his face.

"Unacceptable. Your outrageous behavior caused quite the upset last night, and I want no further disgrace touching my family. You must marry here. As soon as possible." He turned to the clergyman. "How long to obtain a new license?"

Mr. Glover yelled a protest, while the clergyman answered, "A few hours?"

Nick's mind frantically sought a way to delay the actual event. He'd have her as his bride willingly. Or not at all. A special license was too fast, but a wedding in Scotland required twenty-one days of residency. That would provide them with at least three weeks to alter course. He must hold fast to his insistence of a Scottish wedding.

Beside him, Colleen stiffened. "Scandal," she spoke slowly and clearly, "will not touch you," she glanced at her aunt, "or yours. Unless you persist with your protests."

Her uncle's face paled.

Touché. Though he could only guess at the particulars, Nick recognized blackmail when he saw it. He fought to keep the amusement from his face.

"I will marry whomever I choose, whenever and wherever I choose," she continued. "You've never cared about my reputation or marital status before, and I've no idea why you should involve yourself now. I will, however, bow to your sensibilities and vacate the premises. I intend to take a room at Claridge's."

"Nonsense." Nick turned to Colleen. "My family will welcome you with open arms. We've rooms aplenty and both my mother and my sister can serve as chaperones. If you'll gather a few of your most important possessions—"

Lord Maynard slapped his hand down upon his desk, his lips pressed into a white line as he glared at his niece. "Think beyond yourself, beyond the next year. Neither you nor Mr. Torrington have family in Scotland. Speculation will run rampant should you, like your unreasonable mother, persist with this plan. Is that how you wish to begin the next stage of your life?"

At the mention of her mother, Colleen's back snapped ramrod straight yet, much to his annoyance, Nick rather agreed with her uncle on this point. Scandal aside, the Duke of Avesbury wanted him here in London working, not haring off to Scotland at a moment's notice to marry. Not when a ceremony in the city would serve much the same purpose. But he kept his opinion to himself.

Colleen turned her face toward Nick, her eyes full of questions she could not voice aloud in present company. She'd brightened at the mention of marrying in Scotland, but recent developments in London demanded their immediate attention. And they'd yet to discuss any aspect of a future together. He played for time.

"The choice is yours." One did not capture the heart of a wild creature by backing her into a corner. "And not one that must be made this very moment. Better to make a reasoned decision." He watched her internal struggle, noting the moment when logic gained the upper hand.

"Very well," she said. "We will remain in the city for the present while we consider my uncle's perspective. But," eyes filled with apology, Colleen's gaze slid toward her aunt even as her shoulders stiffened, "I refuse to remain here under household arrest with *that man*," she lifted her chin at the thick-necked brute who stood silently in the corner of the room, "dogging my every footstep."

"Fine," her uncle bit out, appearing to capitulate, but there was a stubborn set to his jaw. "Your fiancé's house or a hotel, I care not." He turned his attention to Nick. "Rather than feed the flames of last night's upset, I would prefer we meet later." A pointed glance was thrown at Colleen. "Alone. A meeting wherein two gentlemen discuss possibilities for the future of a favorable relationship between our respective families."

Something oily roiled beneath the surface of the lord's words. An unpleasant conversation lay in Nick's immediate future. "Very well. Tomorrow?"

"Tomorrow. Two o'clock in the afternoon."

"Agreed." That left Nick plenty of time to consult with his solicitor.

Glover's mouth fell open as he stared at Lord Maynard. "Tell me you are not actually considering Torrington!"

"And why not?" The lord snarled at the man he'd thought to welcome into the family not a quarter hour past. "I cannot force her hand, and you failed to secure her interest."

"You will regret this! All of you." Eyes blazing, Glover stormed from the room.

Colleen's uncle reached out and pulled a cord behind his desk. "If you'll see yourselves out, there is much to which I must attend." He crooked his finger at the thick-necked man in the corner. "Mr. Vanderburn..."

The steam butler appeared at the door, ushering them outward and away from the lord's presence.

CHAPTER NINE

MINUTES LATER, tears ran down Lady Maynard's face as she and Colleen held each other's hands promising the other that this was not a permanent separation. At their feet, Sorcha crouched inside her wicker cage, ears flat and tail switching while a steam footman loaded a single trunk onto his phaeton, lashing it in place. The process drew the attention of the finely dressed. Curious faces turned in their direction then, eyes wide, their steps hastened as they hurried to be the first to spread the news of Lady Stewart's departure with one Mr. Torrington. Fresh scandal, the life and blood of the *ton*. Even if they married, speculation surrounding the circumstances of their engagement would take some time to die down.

Resigned, Nick sighed and turned to pay the boy looking after his clockwork horse.

"No!" Colleen cried, and he spun back to find a man with a shock of wild, unkempt hair attempting to wrest the wicker basket that held Sorcha from her arms. Inside, the cat sìth hissed and spit. A large paw—claws unsheathed—swiped from between two bars and drew blood moments before Nick delivered a sharp left hook to the man's jaw. Hard enough to discourage him, to send him staggering, but not enough to render him unconscious.

Colleen backed away, clutching the basket to her chest.

Hand pressed to his jaw, the attacker's feral gaze jumped from Colleen to Nick and back again. "I was promised the cat sìth would be mine!" Blood welled from the deep gouges scratched into his arm.

"Who made you such promises?" Nick demanded, wondering why the man's face seemed familiar.

"The committee, of course," he spat.

"What is the meaning of this?" The lord's bodyguard, Mr. Vanderburn, scowled from the top of the stairs.

The attacker glanced at the lord's minion, then scuttled off at a dead sprint. Only then did Nick notice his sooty, singed trousers. *The missing scientist, Dr. Farquhar!*

*Dammit.* Queen's agents were expected to maintain a low public profile. But after six months of failed leads, he wasn't letting this one go. "Stay here," he ordered Colleen, then gave chase.

He wanted answers. "Stop!" he yelled. "Thief!" A lie, perhaps, but one that would draw the attention of the many policemen who patrolled Mayfair. With luck, he might gain assistance and be mistaken for a private citizen trying to regain his stolen purse.

Though the older, spindly-legged scientist was no match for Nick in a foot race, what he lacked in speed, he made up for in lunacy, dashing into the busy street. An ill-advised attempt to weave between clockwork horses and steam carriages sent him bouncing off iron wheels and into a tumble before nearly meeting his end beneath steel hoofs.

Nick cursed. Not a chance he would risk such a death. He waited for an opening, only to see Dr. Farquhar stagger back onto his feet. No. There could be no escape. He needed to end this now. He yanked his TTX pistol free from its holster and took aim.

*Zwing.* Nick's dart found its mark.

A constable skidded to a halt beside him. "You can't—" His eyes widened as they took in the make and model of Nick's weapon, a sidearm issued only to Queen's agents. In a heartbeat, the policeman became his ally, yanking out his whistle and waving at traffic.

Farquhar was getting away. Again, Nick took aim. *Zwing.* A second dart landed neatly between the man's shoulder blades. He slowed. Wavered. And finally fell.

"Well, that's something to see," the policeman commented, his voice ringing with awe and a bit of dark hope. "I hear a third dart kills?"

"I need him alive," Nick said, irritated that he'd been forced to act in such a public location. "And restrained." Answers would have to wait.

On the far side of the street, a small knot of uncertain people gathered about the paralyzed man. One ventured close to pluck the dart from Farquhar's back and hold it up, peering at it while others, too well-bred to draw close, forced their slack jaws closed, pretending nothing was amiss.

"Yes, sir!" The constable blew hard on his whistle. Wading out into traffic arms spread wide, he brought the entire street to a standstill before waving Nick across.

He snatched back the dart. "If it's potent enough to drop a fleeing suspect, should you be handling it?"

"Well I—" Offended, the man stalked off.

The other onlookers drew back, moving away from the presumed thief as Nick searched Farquhar's pockets, turning up nothing but a smooth snail shell and a handful of loose coins. Added to a missing cravat and the lightly singed, rumpled clothing he wore suggested the man had not intended to leave his home last night. And he looked to have spent a rough night on the street, trailing them here, rather than turning to friends or neighbors.

Where was his wife? Was she an accomplice or an adversary? Why had he not run to his employer, pleading his innocence and begging assistance? And what, exactly, did he plan to do with the cat sìth when his laboratory was a lost cause?

Nick wanted answers to each and every question, but it would be hours before the man woke up, and even then Farquhar would be groggy and disoriented. What to do with him in the meantime? Even now, he could see his phaeton approaching with Colleen at the reins, her expression daring anyone to challenge her as she wove her way through the stopped traffic. He couldn't very well toss off her trunk and replace it with Farquhar's limp body.

Or could he?

No. He shook off the thought. Not only would the Duke of Avesbury have his head for such a public display as it already was, Nick did not wish to invite any aspect of his work into his personal living space or that of his family.

Another constable joined them. "You can't just—" But the first elbowed the second in the ribs, lifting his chin to point at Nick's TTX pistol. "Sorry, sir. My apologies, sir."

"Is there a station house nearby, one with a cell?"

"Of course, sir!" the constable rocked onto his toes. "Not more than two blocks away. Shall we assist him to a cell?"

"Yes, please." A compromise. Treated like a common thief, Farquhar would draw less attention and perhaps lessen the paperwork that was certain to land on Nick's desk. "This man's name is Dr. Gregory Farquhar. He stole something extremely rare and valuable. Moreover, he is wanted for questioning with regards to an intentionally set fire that occurred early this morning. Lock him up, but treat him with kid gloves. He'll wake in a few hours. Send word to me here." He handed the policeman a punch card and a few coins. "By *private* skeet pigeon." The card would provide the clockwork bird direction and the coins the funds to do so—the municipal flock was notoriously rusty and unreliable—with an extra bonus added to ensure they were motivated to see the task done.

"Will do, sir!" the constable barked.

"Mr. Torrington?" Colleen inquired, stiff and formal from her perch. "Is that—"

Nick vaulted into his vehicle, landing beside her and the voluminous froth of her skirts. "Dr. Farquhar? Yes." The two police officers slung their arms beneath those of the mad scientist and heaved him upward, dragging him down the pavement. "They'll take him into custody. When he wakes, we'll question him."

"We." A note of doubt hung in her voice. She tugged on the reins, pulling the control lever to a sedate, proper level three, then took the corner, directing them toward his family's townhome. A light rain began to fall, dampening the feather that sprouted from a bonnet carefully pinned in place upon her head.

"Yes, we. Partners, remember?" He let his gaze fall upon the black buttons that marched up the front of her coat. "Easiest for us to enter the station dressed as a lord and his lady, but wear sensible shoes. And a skirt that won't brush the floor. Detainees are often ill, and there's no predicting if a mop has touched the floor in recent years."

Colleen threw him a small smile. "A point in your favor, fiancé, that you escort me to such delightful locations."

The burden on his shoulders lifted ever so slightly. "And in yours, if you can resist the temptation to strangle the man who caged your familiar." Behind them, the cat sìth cried a pitiable displeasure at being stuffed in a cage and hauled about London streets. "How is Sorcha?"

"Physically, the wounds are superficial. Dr. Farquhar appears only to have punctured a vein. The patches of shaved skin must have been preparation for further experimentation. The fire stopped him before he could do any significant damage."

"What is supposed to happen," he began, "when you mistreat a fairy cat?"

"Nothing good," she said. "Show a King Cat kindness—a saucer of milk or a fresh-caught fish—and good fortune follows. Mistreat him, and misfortune descends. All the dairy cows go dry. Or, should you be so unlucky to have a death in the family, the cat sìth might steal the soul of the dead before burial."

"Or a wife, for example, might decide to burn your townhome to the ground and lay the blame at your feet."

She laughed. "Exactly." Snapping the reins, Colleen slowed the horse, expertly weaving through a knot of traffic at the intersection.

"And if your cat sìth happens to be a witch?"

"Ah, the darker myth. She can take the form of a cat nine times."

"And after the ninth?"

"Stuck."

"And left wandering the Scottish countryside, perhaps to be trapped by cryptid hunters and sold on the black market as a curiosity." He glanced at the wicker carrier. "Or they accompany young women with beautiful, flashing eyes to London."

Colleen stared straight ahead. "I'm not a witch."

"I didn't think you were." He reached out and squeezed her arm. "I meant only to note the similarities. It can't be coincidence that Sorcha, in particular, ended up in his laboratory."

"Dr. Farquhar values Sorcha—enough to follow us in an attempt to reclaim her—but not over himself, or he wouldn't have abandoned her to the fire." Colleen fell silent, as carts and carriages rattled past them. She slid a glance in his direction. "You mentioned a long, complicated story. Queen's agent's business. Could this mad scientist really believe Sorcha is a witch in cat form?"

He would tell her all about CEAP, all about the shadow committees that the Queen's agents hunted. Not here on the streets, but soon. Before they interviewed Farquhar.

"Aether, I hope not," Nick sighed. "I need answers. A solution to Anna's condition. Not the mentally disordered ramblings of a thwarted researcher who has abandoned key steps of the scientific process in his quest to prove an obscure folk tale from his childhood." He recalled Mrs. Leighton's words. "Unfortunately, it seems he might. There have been whispers of men exploring the possibilities of animal transmutation, a kind of sorcery where an animal shifts into a human form, then back again."

She sucked in a breath. "Like the witches associated with the cat sìth."

"Exactly like that." And though Colleen possessed a number of catlike skills—excellent night vision, good hearing and astounding agility—she was all woman. One who could help him untangle fact from fiction. "He'll wake in a few hours. We'll question him then."

His family's townhome drew into view.

"About your family—"

"They will be thrilled to have you as their guest." He grinned. "Or, rather, in their clutches. My mother wants nothing more than to see all of her children married. But—" He held up his hand as she drew breath to protest. "If you prefer, I will inform her—and my father—that this is a work arrangement. That our engagement is a façade constructed for the benefit of society while we investigate a situation at the Duke of Avesbury's command."

"Perhaps that's best," she said. He tried not to let his disappointment surface. "I want to accept your offer, but what we know about each other has been gained in such snatches. Spending an extended amount of time in each other's company is the only appealing aspect of the situation in which we find ourselves. Well, that and departing my uncle's household." A long, silent moment passed before she slanted him a glance from beneath long, dark lashes and, when she spoke, her voice held a note of invitation. "And when opportunity permits, perhaps we might explore our..." A patch of bright color bloomed high upon her cheeks. "Physical compatibility?"

Nick's heart leapt to life inside his ribcage and began to pound. Other interested portions of his anatomy also took note. "I'd hoped as much, but a gentleman should never presume. Kisses, no matter how hot they burn, need not progress. If you wish, we can discuss terms."

"I'm no innocent," she said. "As you well know. Without any expectations that I would ever marry, I have taken the occasional lover. Quietly and discreetly." Her lips pressed into a flat line. "At least in the past. None have been so crass as to publicly announce such a fact until now."

Once made public, such a perceived transgression was rarely, if one was female and unmarried, forgiven. "What is it you want from an affair?"

"What do I want?" Her odd glance suggested not a single lover had ever asked. "I want...more. I'm no delicate flower." Her very ears were now pink.

Ah, she wanted excitement. Passion. Tightly controlled in the presence of all other *ton*, she thought he might be willing to unleash the woman who prowled through London beneath the moon, slipping in and out of rooms in the dark of night. Aether, he wanted that too.

He leaned close to her ear and growled, "Large, solid desks can be accommodating. It's a shame we were interrupted. Chairs. Walls. Floors." He paused. "Soft mattresses too have their charms."

"And yet are so very prosaic," she breathed. "I was hoping you might have other ideas." Her hands tightened on the reins.

"In two days, I celebrate my twenty-fifth birthday. Shall we mark that as the day we decide if a future as husband and wife suits?"

"Two days. Will that be long enough?" he asked, stiff with arousal. Her chest rose and fell quickly beneath her buttoned cape. He blinked, forcing himself to stop speculating about layers that clung more closely to her skin. "Two days of close companionship while we uncover whatever Farquhar is about, and investigate if he's made any discoveries that might prove useful."

"I expect it will be all society is willing to afford us. If that. Now, speaking of Dr. Farquhar…" Without taking her eyes from the road, she reached into a small purse that hung from a chain about her waist and drew forth a long, narrow slip of paper. "I launched a skeet pigeon at dawn and have a response. Mr. Witherspoon is not pleased, but in light of Mrs. Farquhar's arsonist tendencies and Anna's pressing need, he will provide a name for three thousand pounds."

Nick nearly choked. "Three thousand pounds?" He snatched it from her fingers, his eyes focusing on the ink-scrawled figure, upon the bank instructions as to where the money was to be deposited. "For a name?"

"Clients would swiftly abandon him," her lips twisted, "if it became known he was willing to sell their information. Therefore, even as a special favor to me, a breach in client confidentiality does not come cheap."

CHAPTER TEN

ESIDE HER, NICK fell silent. Overhead, gathering clouds darkened the skies as a faint mist strengthened into a steady rain. Her gray lenses filtered the remaining light such that when she stole a long glance at his tight face, his features stood out in high relief. All of them tense. Three thousand pounds was a small fortune. Far more than most would be willing to spend on an ill relative—particularly a female—for the *chance* at a cure. No, not even a cure, a treatment. One his sister would be reliant upon her entire life. Should it work. And all that dependent upon finding the current whereabouts of one particular rosewood box and the precious object contained within.

"Ready?" They'd arrived at his family's townhome. Tall, terraced and proud, it stood at attention beside its clones, all of them neatly lined up alongside this side of the square.

He took a deep breath. "My family knows I work for the Queen. Nothing specific, but they hold no illusions that I spend all my time locked within four walls of a laboratory. I'll inform my mother that you have a similar profession, that our engagement is temporary, a societal necessity while we work together.

But…" He caught up her hand, stroking his thumb over the amber stone. "Not only is this my grandmother's ring, it's an exact match to the color of your eyes. My mother and sister will doubt our story."

"As well they should." The longer she was with Nick, the less she wanted to part ways. "We're playing for time. Time alone. Time to interview a mad scientist."

"Time," he repeated. "That my sister might not have."

"And will therefore use as efficiently as possible." She gave him a weak smile. "What with your swift capture of Dr. Farquhar, the price Mr. Witherspoon demands for a mere name might not be worth paying. Not if you can persuade the scientist to share his secrets. Why, we may have answers before nightfall."

"That may be, but I like to know all the players in a game, to roll over every log to see what crawls out. Whoever purchased the device from Mrs. Farquhar went through much effort to conceal his identity, and I want that name. Regardless, we'll find time for a courtship. Even if we must squeeze it in between interrogations." The corner of his mouth curved upward. "Poetry and roses? Sweet nothings whispered in your ear?"

He hadn't released her fingers, had made no move to climb down from the phaeton, but instead stared into her eyes as if answers could be found deep within their depths. Eyes were often said to be "windows to the soul". What, then, did he imagine he might see?

She cared for him very much. Admired him. Enjoyed his company. Ached for his touch. But she wasn't—not yet—in love with him. Though it wouldn't take much for her to tumble hat over boots. Time to lighten the mood, if only briefly.

"Only if they're suggestive." Colleen leaned close and teased the shell of his ear with her lips, quite satisfied when his hand tightened about hers. "And only if you're prepared to act upon them. Tell me, how seriously will your mother and sister take their assigned role of chaperone?"

"We shouldn't need one on a public street, Lady Stewart," he chided, though lights danced once more in his eyes. Good. She didn't want to dwell on what their future may or may not hold. Not when the present demanded their full attention. "Now hand over the reins to the groom. Sorcha may be Scottish, but you'll never convince me *any* cat enjoys the rain."

She gave him a cheeky grin and reached for the wicker carrier. "If you insist, Mr. Torrington."

If her feet hesitated before crossing the threshold, she blamed the sight before her. She'd left the past five years behind her the moment she exited her uncle's house. Even if she wished it, there would be no reversing course.

Inside, a steam butler waited. Her uncle's was old and creaky with neglect. Forever belching clouds of smoke, the hallways were dark and gloomy, a challenge to keep clean. Here, the black and white marble-tiled floor gleamed. A tall hallway mirror sparkled, and the furniture was glossy. Even the steam butler himself bore the most lustrous metallic accessories she'd ever seen. All polished daily, she expected.

"Lady Stewart, this is Hopsworth." Colleen nodded. "Hopsworth, this is my fiancée." At Nick's announcement, the steambot's wire eyebrows slid to the top of his forehead. "Circumstances dictate that she reside here for the next several days. Have a steam footman retrieve her trunk, then send him to collect the remainder of her luggage from Lord Maynard." He gave the address.

"Yes, sir."

"Is my mother home?"

"Not at present. She is out paying calls. Your sister and niece, however, are in the nursery," Hopsworth tipped his head toward a tightly closed door, "your father in the study."

"Excellent. I'll speak with him while Lady Stewart settles in. Please show her to my old room."

Hinges—forced to bend further than their design permitted —protested with a loud creak as the steambot drew himself ramrod straight. The slightest puff of disapproving steam escaped his neatly crimped collar. "Yours, sir?"

"Don't pop a bolt, Hopsworth. It's not as if I currently occupy it." He flipped back the blanket covering Sorcha's carrier, and the cat hissed, swiping her clawed arm at the steam butler who reeled back, hands raised. Was he afraid his metal casing might scratch? "That wildcat in her arms is accustomed to roaming free," Nick continued, "and requires outside access. My room provides a convenient trellis. As the cat has suffered a recent trauma, she must be given time to familiarize herself with new surroundings. Once Lady Stewart's things are placed in my room, no one save myself is to enter. For any reason. Not even the steam staff. They're to leave a saucer of cream and a tin of tuna on the floor outside the door twice daily."

Such thoughtfulness. Far, far better than any bouquet of roses.

"Yes, sir." Hopsworth's jaw snapped shut with an echoing clang. "Lady Stewart, if you'll follow me?" With a final glance at Sorcha, the steam butler hooked himself to a rail lift, punched a button, and a great clattering and turning of gears yanked the steambot up the stairway.

"One of the latest models," Nick said, "but in his chest beats the mechanical heart of an eighty-year-old." He waved toward the stairs. "Go explore. I've a rather sturdy—if prosaic—bed."

"Don't think I won't assess its possibilities." She winked. "But despite your orders, I'm not at all convinced we won't be interrupted. The entire household will be wondering what we're about."

He laughed and dropped a quick kiss upon her lips. "So they will."

She widened her eyes in mock fear. "Don't leave me to face them alone."

"No worries. I won't be long. I'll speak to my father about transferring the funds to Mr. Witherspoon, then I'll take you to my sister."

A few minutes later, Colleen stepped into Nick's room. Though faint, she caught his scent on the air as it swirled with her entry. Spicy, soapy with a hint of musk. The usual shapes of furniture lined the walls, all failing to catch her attention save one. A large, canopied bed dominated the room. Despite her brazen words, her skin heated, threatening to burst into flame. Would she sleep alone tonight? Or would he climb the aforementioned trellis to join her?

She tore her eyes away, scratching Sorcha's chin through the bars as she crossed to the window, cracking it open. Indeed, the structure was convenient—and not just for prowling felines. "Perfect," she told the cat. "Access to both the ground and the roof. Though I'm certain you miss the moors, the forests and the abundance of lively rabbits, it'll do. We'll be home soon enough." For, despite Isabella's presence, her uncle's townhome had only ever been a temporary residence. A necessary stop before returning to her true life.

Last night—or rather, early this morning—she had scrambled through her window, dragging the monstrous metal cage with her. She'd released Sorcha, then snuck to the kitchens alone, returning with a tray. Ravenous, the cat sìth had consumed an entire leg of mutton before lapping up the promised bowl of cream and executing a lengthy bath before the small fire that burned in the grate. Colleen had crawled into bed and, when she awoke the next morning, found the feline curled into a ball beside her, seemingly no worse for her misadventure.

But there'd been little time to rejoice, for a pounding upon her bedroom door had woken her, and last night's drama surrounding her engagement resumed. "I've been sent to help you pack," Isabella had announced, brushing away tears. "You uncle insists that you're to marry Mr. Glover. Today."

"What!" She'd leapt from the bed. "But I accepted Mr. Torrington's offer! Publicly!"

Her uncle was delusional if he thought to force her hand. Finish packing she would, but only because she refused to ever spend another night under his roof. A room at Claridge's it would be. Her every move would be studied and analyzed by hotel staff and the wealthy, outspoken American girls who had traveled overseas to bag and drag a British peer to the altar, but at least she would be free to come and go as she pleased.

The only setback had been getting there, as her uncle had forbidden the steam staff to remove her possessions to a cart until she'd signed a marriage certificate and settlement both binding her to Mr. Glover *and* granting him control of the Craigieburn estate. An event that would never come to pass. She'd been about to leave the townhome with no more than the clothes on her back and a cat sìth in her arms when Nick had arrived.

Midst the chaos that followed, her uncle had abruptly reversed his position, turning against the formerly favored Mr. Glover, and holding out an olive branch to the man *she'd* chosen. Colleen didn't trust it, not for a single second. Nick— or his family—had something her uncle wanted. Badly. But what?

A knock sounded on the bedroom door, and she turned away from the window.

"Your trunk, Lady Stewart." Hopsworth waved in a steam footman, then followed to place a tray upon the floor. "Cream and tuna. All further feline meals will be left outside in the hall as requested. Is there anything else you need?"

"Thank you, no." She promptly locked the door leading to the hallway after the steambots had exited. Placing the carrier before the cream, she unfastened the buckles that held the wicker lid shut. While Sorcha considered her new surroundings, Colleen set about unpacking a few essentials.

In anticipation of Dr. Farquhar's interrogation and the effluvium of a prison cell, subtle adjustments to her attire were in order. There was nothing to do about her corset or the multiple petticoats or the form-fitting bodice until the rest of her luggage arrived. But she could remove impediments to movement. And boots laced to the knee—not the silk slippers she wore—were better suited to tromping through halls that led to—she very much hoped—a dank and rat-infested prison cell.

She slipped her dirk into the sheath sewn into said boots and replaced the thin chain that held her purse with her thick leather belt, one that not only held a number of essential items, but provided D-loops allowing her to hike her heavy skirts.

With nothing left to do save wait, Colleen began to explore the room, avoiding, for now, the bed. Beside a leather armchair, a small side table groaned beneath a lamp and a stack of weighty tomes. She lifted one. *Diseases of the Heart*. Anatomy was not a topic she'd spent much time investigating but, when he wasn't running about on Queen's errands, such was how Nick spent his time. Given she was about to join him on his current quest, it might be wise to educate herself about matters concerning the human heart.

She gave the Lucifer lamp a good shake, plopped down into the chair and cracked open the text.

---

"THE SCOTTISH GIRL IS A SNEAK THIEF?" His father's expression—no, his entire body—was so stiff, his face so tight that the lightest tap might shatter him, sending pieces crashing to the floor.

Much like an unrepentant cat, Nick couldn't help swatting at the delicate bauble. "She works to fund her own future. Much as

I do. And she is properly addressed as Lady Stewart," he corrected his father. "The Much Honored Colleen Stewart of Craigieburn. A landholder in her own right." In two short days, she would control the property in its entirety. "Common knowledge, yet no one—for all their insistence upon propriety—bothers to address her correctly."

"It's the eyes," the viscount snapped. "They're not natural." Anything that fell outside a carefully delineated range of human characteristics was unacceptable to the *ton*. "Impossible not to notice them, even behind those odd spectacles. She has the eyes of her sire, the Laird of Craigieburn." His father huffed. "With so many eligible females parading through the ballrooms, you pick the one with nothing to her name but Scottish soil and a decrepit castle. No, not even a castle. It's an aging tower house that will do nothing but drain your bank account to its last shilling. If modernizing it is even a possibility. Don't look at me like that. I made inquiries about her when your mother informed me you'd laid claim to your grandmother's amber ring. Dare I inquire as to why you have brought her *here*? To our family home *before* the wedding?"

Impulse. Instinct. Need. The bone deep knowledge that they belonged together.

"I told you. She's a piece of the puzzle." And... Fine. The image of her reclining in the dark, feet upon a desk and whisky in hand refused to leave his mind. He wanted to peel back the layers and examine what lay beneath. Professionally. Personally. "It's a temporary arrangement," Nick insisted. If Colleen agreed to go forward with a wedding, they certainly wouldn't be spending their honeymoon in his boyhood home. "Her work is much the same as mine." If aimed at private profit, not the public good. "On Anna's behalf, we will be working together. Closely. She refused to stay in her uncle's household, and a hotel is too public." For any number of reasons.

"I'm not interested in funding the Duke of Avesbury's secret missions," his father complained. "Or hosting additional spies." But he lifted his pen and signed a slip of paper authorizing his bank to transfer three thousand pounds to one Mr. Witherspoon, a virtual stranger. Anything for his daughter. "Be sure you fill out the paperwork for reimbursement."

"Of course." Nick rolled his eyes. There was little hope of a refund.

"Now, about your wedding. Your mother claims she knew you and Lady Stewart were destined for each other the first time she saw you share a dance."

Had she? His memory was somewhat different.

He'd been lurking in an alcove, awaiting the arrival of his contact, when a particularly persistent mother began drifting in his direction, her daughter in tow. He'd cursed—and a soft snicker emerged from even deeper in the shadows a moment before Lady Stewart stepped forward.

"May I offer the assistance of an escape dance?" She'd held out her gloved hand. "A brief waltz from here to there? I assure you, I've no interest in being trapped by Lady Delphinia's chatter."

"Most gratefully accepted, my lady." He'd swept her into his arms and onto the dance floor.

She'd been light on her feet, her silk- and boning-encased waist supple beneath his palm. He recalled drawing her closer than was strictly sanctioned, and the sly curve of her lips as she permitted it, a shared moment of mutual collaboration to antagonize their pursuers.

Perhaps he'd taken longer than necessary to traverse the room, but he'd deposited her midst a set of ferns and took his leave with a wink, unquestioning and oblivious to any further depth until they'd met again: at night, atop a roof and behind the concealing bulk of a chimney.

It did not, perhaps, speak well to his instincts as a spy.

"It's too soon to make plans." Though he had no qualms, a

bride who wished for a trial engagement wouldn't appreciate such assumptions. "I need Lady Stewart free to work." Whatever heat flared between them in their free moments was an entirely separate affair. "Not attending frivolous social events." He reached for the bank slip with the intent to snatch it and flee.

His father slid it out of reach. "I'll send it by special courier. The funds will be transferred in an hour, perhaps two." The viscount leaned forward. "Now, I don't care what arrangements you've made with your fiancée, you'll not be dragging our family's name through the mud. If she's to stay here, an announcement will be placed in the papers. I will procure a special license while your mother plans—dress fittings, guest lists, a wedding breakfast—all to be held here, with the ceremony in our London parlor, in a few days' time."

"I promised her more time," Nick objected. "And a wedding in Scotland." Would Colleen bolt the moment she learned of the viscount's conditions? She was not a woman to be kept. Such a prospect was as unlikely as keeping the cat sìth in a cage. Were anyone to attempt it, she would slip her tether and there would be hell to pay. "And I agreed to meet with her uncle. I know you don't trust Lord Maynard, but—"

"He wants something, and it's bound to be unpleasant."

Nick agreed, but for the sake of Colleen's relationship with her young aunt, he was willing to try. "Still, I'll meet with him. See what he has in mind."

"For aether's sake, don't agree to *anything* without first consulting me. He's too fond of leading people into legal quagmires. Do you have any idea how many lives he's ruined?"

"Too many to count." All the more reason to lend Colleen his assistance, even if she decided marriage was not to her taste. "I'll be careful. Did you discover anything irregular about the Laird of Craigieburn's will?"

"Nothing," his father admitted. Frustration simmered

beneath his carefully starched and ironed collar. "Though the prior Lord Maynard surgically cut his daughter from his life, the family rift was mended after his death. The current Lord Maynard re-established ties, lending his brother-in-law funds and arranging for his niece to have a London Season. My contacts have yet to discover what promises Lord Maynard extracted from *Lady* Stewart's father in exchange for such aid. But I've every confidence they will."

"Given Lord Maynard's sudden attempt to marry her to a business partner, one easily controlled, there must be something." While his father focused upon his youngest son's future, Nick wagered that he could pass along a task that, while necessary, might distract them from pursuing any leads their interrogation of Farquhar produced. "There is one agreed upon condition of my partnership, one separate from any wedding that may or may not occur. In addition to an agreed upon fee, our solicitors must collect all necessary paperwork and documents to return complete and total control of the Craigieburn estate and its properties to Lady Stewart upon her twenty-fifth birthday, two days hence."

"It is with pleasure that I shall rip such papers from her uncle's hands." Only then did his father smirk. "Work fast. Regardless of what we tell your mother, when she learns Lady Stewart possesses land *and* a castle her wedding plans will be in earnest." His voice dropped to a whisper of conspiracy, one that suggested his parents would—as always—be united in their goals. "Those yellow eyes? They bother me not a whit."

## CHAPTER ELEVEN

FAMILY BUSINESS attended to, Nick mounted the stairs. He'd take Colleen for a brief visit in the nursery. From there, they'd head upward to the aviary and wait for word from the constabulary or Mr. Witherspoon himself.

While he'd been contemplating how to court Colleen for months now, it was strange to realize how ready his family was to rush him to the proverbial altar. Not that he was opposed. Charles, his oldest brother, had already produced the next heir to the viscountcy and had another child on the way. James, a second son, had married a wealthy American and was the proud father of a sweet, little girl. Only Nick had resisted his mother's every effort to see him settled.

In the hallway, before the closed door of his room, a steambot rolled back and forth, spinning in circles upon the carpet, wielding a dust bin and broom like knights of old, while steam billowed from beneath her skirts. All in an effort to elude capture by the kitchen boy and reach the door handle.

"Sorry, sir." Robby jumped out of range to make a quick bow. "Hopsworth sent me to change her punch card, but Steam Mary is hardwired to clean your room at the top of the hour."

"There's a trick to these older models, if you you'll allow me?"

"Please, sir?"

Nick pulled a short length of hooked wire from his pocket.

"What's that for?" Robby asked.

"Watch." After a few more wild spins, Steam Mary's sensors registered that the path was clear. She lowered her arms and approached the door. "Beneath that ruff of lace and ribbon about where you'd expect a shoulder, lies the clavicular joint. When she reaches for the door handle…"

The steambot's clothing shifted and a chink in her iron housing appeared, exposing wires and tubing. With a strategic swipe, Nick hooked his wire beneath a thick cord of cable and tugged. Steam Mary froze.

The kitchen boy's eyes grew wide. "You broke her!"

"I did not. What kind of trick would that be? Now finish up. Change her programming."

Robby unpinned her apron, flipped open a panel upon her chest, and swapped one punch card for another.

"Now, while you're in there, look deeper." He handed Robby his decilamp. "That cable I yanked will have unplugged from its socket and should be dangling free. Do you see it?"

The boy bent over the steambot, peering into her illuminated innards. "I do!"

"Push it back into the empty receptacle, and she'll reset."

With a whistle, Steam Mary straightened, glanced at her dust bin and broom in confusion and moved on.

"Thank you, sir!" He bounced on his toes, holding out the decilamp.

"Keep it." Nick handed Robby the hooked wire as well. "But try to catch all the other steambots before you have to resort to sabotage."

"Sir! Yes, sir!" And Robby ran off, a grin stretched across his bright face.

His own grin fading, Nick stared at the door. He leaned closer, listening. All was silent. What had he expected to hear? The yowls of a wildcat? No, more like the sounds of a woman unpacking. Then again, she had but a single trunk in her possession. His lips curved. He could only hope it held a few scraps of red silk.

With a yank, he opened his own door, and all the air left his lungs in a single whoosh. For the space of a heartbeat, all he could do was stare at Colleen, lounging in his favorite chair reading by lamplight. Her skirts hiked up by silver chains to fall above her knees, legs dangling over its arm to cross at her booted ankles. She looked up from a thick journal propped upon her lap. But his eyes refused to focus on its title, preferring the hollow of her throat where a soft curl of hair brushed as she toyed with a long strand wrapped about her finger.

He closed the door behind him with a thud. Sorcha—who, peripheral vision informed him—lounged dead center in the middle of the bed, leg in the air, bathing with complete disregard for onlookers, certain she would not be disturbed. And she wouldn't be, for he had no interest in beginning their courtship upon a bed.

Perhaps the chair?

"The basic anatomy of the heart is simple enough." Colleen swung her feet to the ground with a soft thud and nodded at a nearby anatomy textbook. "But you neglected to mention that many of the facts you presented me with during your horseback lecture on heart physiology were drawn from experiments conducted upon the heart of an eel." She shuddered and pulled a face. "An *eel*, Nick."

Nick swallowed, finally realizing that she'd found and read the draft of an article submitted to the *Journal of Physiology* by J.A. MacWilliam in which the scientist detailed his studies conducted upon the heart of eels. "On the Structure and

Rhythm of the Heart in Fishes, with especial reference to the Heart of an Eel." He'd wondered where he'd mislaid it.

"It's a fascinating thought," she said. "If hard to wrap the mind about, to reconcile oneself with the idea that the heart is essentially autonomous, that various sections beat at their own pace, speeding or slowing in response to heat and cold."

"You've been busy." Impressive, her willingness and ability to throw herself into the topic at hand. All these years, she'd hidden a spectacular mind from the *ton*. Perhaps there were many such young ladies concealing their intelligence, but only one particular woman had disturbed his dreams last night, leaving his sheets tangled about his waist. He met her eyes. No barrier blocked their gaze, as she'd set aside her smoky glasses to read in the dim light of his room, and her golden eyes gleamed. "And now your grasp of cardiac electrophysiology easily surpasses that of many first year medical students."

"Only after a concerted effort to understand all matters of heart physiology pertaining to our particular case. Information as currency. We do have a galvanist to interview." Tossing aside the paper, Colleen arched her back, stretching her arms above her head before rising onto her feet. Lips curving upward, she stalked across the space separating them and rose up onto her toes, wrapping her arms about his neck. "Dr. MacWilliam seems to have left out one particular stimulus. Or perhaps eels don't possess them?"

"What's that?" Anticipation set his heart pounding as he dropped his hands to her hips.

"Emotions." Her soft breasts pressed against his chest as her fingertips toyed with the fringe of hair that brushed his collar.

Vague thoughts of leaving the room flitted about in his mind, then flew away altogether. His sister and skeet pigeons could wait. "He's a mind as sharp as a scalpel but, no, I don't think he's interested in theory of mind. MacWilliam has, however, begun a systematic investigation into the mammalian heart studying cardiac fibrillation and the possibility that a spark of electricity—carefully timed and applied—might help restore a normal heartbeat."

"Begun." She kissed the corner of his mouth. "But impatience compels you to chase after a scientist who might already have fabricated such a device."

"It does."

"How long until Dr. Farquhar awakens?"

"Another hour at least." He slipped his palms over the smooth satin encasing her waist, drawing her closer still. "We'll bring pen and paper. If he can't pinpoint the location of his device, a composition exercise detailing its features and functions might be in order." He skimmed his lips across the edge of her hairline.

He bent and caught her lips with his own, spinning her off her feet and pinning her against the door. All while plundering her soft, sweet mouth while she mewled her encouragement, wrapping her legs about his and tugging at his cravat.

Nick couldn't recall the last time a woman had driven him to such distraction that he stood on the knife's edge of losing control. Yet his mind constantly returned to a certain sturdy desk, the first time she'd offered herself to him—in a location that flirted with the possibility of discovery. Despite all public appearances, Colleen was a woman who enjoyed flirting with danger and discovery. Indulgences he'd be happy to provide.

He nipped her lower lip, then drew back, tucking a long, silky strand of her hair back into the coil at the base of her neck. "Not here," he murmured. "Someone might come looking for us, and it's too obvious a location."

"So it is." Her legs dropped to the ground, and she straightened his collar, all business, though her amber eyes were still dark with desire.

He swallowed. Hard. "Introduce me, formally, to Sorcha. Then we've things to do," he slid her a knowing glance and a smile, "before we can carve out a moment to play. Some place a bit more... exotic."

---

COLLEEN'S BREATH caught in her throat. She'd been smothering her disappointment that Nick had failed to do more than kiss her against the wall, but at his words, her pulse jumped anew. The sooner necessary tasks were behind them...

"Sorcha?" She approached the bed—hand extended—where the cat sìth sat, enthroned. "Might I?"

The feline returned Colleen's request with a long, steady gaze, then rose onto her feet, tail lifted, and approached, arching her back as Colleen stroked a palm down her soft, sleek pelt.

A quick scan of the shaved patch of skin upon her shoulder informed her that the small incision remained uninfected. Thank aether Dr. Farquhar hadn't had a chance to do further damage. "Allow me to present Mr. Torrington, the gentleman who led me to your prison."

"She's quite majestic." His lips quirked. "If the male of her species is a king, does this make her a queen?"

"On par with Queen Victoria herself, yes."

Smiling, he bowed. Then extended his own hand, fingers curled.

Sorcha sniffed, her whiskers twitching as she considered his offer of friendship, then accepted a brief chin scratch before padding to the head of the bed to select a pillow for her nap.

"Quite at home," Nick commented. He slid open a bedside table drawer, slipping something from its recesses into his pocket. "Much like you've made yourself."

"A compliment," Colleen replied, leaning backward against the thick and solid carved bedpost that reached toward the ceiling. "I love the darkness of your room. The rich wood, heavy curtains, worn leather and the whorls of vines that twist across the forest green wallpaper. So much better than the light, the airy, and the ruffled that's forever thrust upon women."

"The dark suits you."

She lifted her chin toward the window where raindrops pelted the panes and ran in rivulets down the glass. "Rain suits me as well, though it makes the rooftops treacherous."

"So it does." They shared a knowing glance, spy to burglar. "Come, let's stop by the nursery. We'll visit Anna and I'll introduce you to my niece, Clara."

He reached for her, tugging her from the room. Had a man ever held her hand in such a manner? She had no memory of anyone save her father, but that was years in the past. Every inch of her skin delighted in the feel of his palm sliding against her own with a roughness that came from gripping stone walls, drain pipes, and ropes. It created a delightful friction that she couldn't wait to feel brushed across the rest of her skin.

She blinked, then focused on the moment. "Your sister is among those family members who know?"

"That I'm a spy?" Nick closed the door behind him, then led her up a flight of stairs. "Yes. She and my parents are aware, not so much my brothers. It would have been impossible to hide my odd comings and goings from this house, given I often stay here when she's feeling poorly. Anna is fully aware that I've also been making more private inquiries on her behalf, but all of them know better than to press for details about the tasks I carry out for the Queen."

Carefully, quietly, Nick opened the door. Inside, Anna—a woman with the heart-shaped face of an angel—sat in a rocking chair beside a fire, cuddling an adorable baby. Three months? It had been years since Colleen had held an infant. Her heart gave a twist. The price of refusing to consider any London gentlemen. She glanced at Nick. What kind of father would he make?

"She rarely leaves my niece alone," he whispered. Colleen understood. With an uncertain lifespan, precious moments must be savored. "But both of them have an aid, should help be required." At the far end of the room, one nurse's face lifted from the sewing she held in her lap, while the other glanced up from a book. At Nick's wave, both nodded respectfully, then dropped their gazes back to their occupations.

"Shh." Anna held a finger to her lips. "Clara has only just fallen asleep."

They tiptoed across a soft carpet to Anna's side. The room was dim, but the low light hid nothing from Colleen's eyes. Behind Nick's sister, a large, disturbing machine hulked and hummed in the corner. Dials and buttons and switches covered its surface. A long wire extended—tentacle-like—from its side, its end screwed into a sharp, pointed metal rod. One designed to pierce the skin and touch the heart to deliver a life-saving bolt of electricity? A shudder of terror ran over Colleen. The thought of wielding such a device turned her insides to custard.

"Anna, allow me to introduce Lady Colleen Stewart," Nick whispered. "She'll be working as my partner while posing as my fiancée. We've unearthed some promising information about a new device."

They politely greeted each other with a nod.

"We've met, though briefly." Colleen kept her voice to a murmur.

"A fiancée?" Anna's eyebrows rose.

She felt awful, letting his family wonder about the depth of their involvement. "Your brother has proposed. I'm considering his offer but, like him, I also possess a flair for prying into affairs that men and women prefer to keep hidden."

From the corner of her eye, she saw Nick struggle to control his shock, followed by a subtle straightening of the shoulders as satisfaction settled upon them.

"Ah, I see." A knowing grin stretched his sister's face. "I won't turn down a miracle or a new sister-in-law. Either or both would be more than welcome."

Nick lifted the sleeping infant from his sister's arm with practiced expertise, and warmth spread through Colleen's chest at the sight. Gentleman, scientist, spy. Devoted brother. Quite probably he'd make a most excellent husband and father.

Marrying him would be the adventure of a lifetime, but it would also bind her to London. What of her responsibilities in Scotland? As laird, people depended upon her, and she'd been absent far too long.

He turned and passed the baby into Colleen's arms, smiling at her shocked expression. "If you don't mind. Anna has spoiled her. To the point she rarely sleeps unless held, and I want to listen to her mother's heart."

"Of course." Colleen gathered the precious bundle close, and found herself gently swaying. She pressed a kiss to the fine, silky curls upon the baby's head—inhaling her soft, sweet scent—and caught a small waving fist as she stirred, all while marveling at the perfect, tiny, pink bow of her lips.

When she thought to glance up, Nick—eyes closed—held a stethoscope to his sister's narrow chest. Only then did Colleen note the bluish tinge of Anna's fingertips and the heavy woolen rug draped over her knees despite the warmth of the room. She'd taken a risk, bearing a child, and regretted nothing. Impossible not to admire a woman who'd reached out and grabbed what she most desired despite all advice to the contrary. Colleen resolved to do the same.

"Are you still experiencing occasional numbness in your hands and face?" Nick asked, moving his fingers to Anna's wrist, taking note of her pulse. A careful blankness clung to his face. "A feeling of being out of breath? Damp palms?"

"Yes, yes, and yes," Anna answered. "Along with all the usual symptoms. Fatigue, chest pain, dizziness, and shortness of breath. But only one seizure in the past week."

As Nick straightened, pain and a hint of helplessness flickered in his eyes, but quickly resolved into steely determination.

No stone would be left unturned, no scientist left unquestioned. He shifted, impatient and keen to take action. "When Mother returns, do try to keep her contained."

His sister laughed softly. "You ask the impossible."

Resignation tightened his mouth, and he lifted his gaze to Colleen. "Time to visit the aviary. We've a message to send."

Indeed, Mr. Witherspoon could be counted upon to act quickly once funds reached him. "And one to watch for."

As she slid the swaddled baby back into her mother's arms—somewhat reluctant to part with the soft weight, Anna whispered, "I've been away from society, but don't think I never noticed the sparks that fly whenever the two of you are together. It's easy to see you've captured my brother's... regard and have the look of a woman about to lead him on an adventure. I heartily approve. He needs a partner..." She glanced at Colleen's skirt hikes, then gave her an impish wink. "And a distraction."

A slow burn crept across her cheeks. She'd certainly offered him one. Repeatedly. But the man was determined to torture her with searing kisses and teasing promises. He'd best deliver, and soon.

## CHAPTER TWELVE

HE NARROW, METAL staircase leading to the aviary folded back upon itself several times before it reached the roof. A hatch opened to reveal a low wall supporting an arch of iron and glass that protected the message-carrying skeet pigeons—and them—from the afternoon's soft, misty rain. At one end, a glass door. At the other, a square window—propped open—allowed the clockwork birds entry and exit. A corner of the space had been appropriated for more than birds. Warmed by the sun's occasional appearance, a small potted garden of purslane, rosemary and fennel thrived upon a low bench.

Steadying herself on the iron railing she climbed into a different world where, through grit and soot-smudged panes of glass, all of London stretched before her. High overhead, silver dirigibles dotted the sky. Slate roof-tiles glistened in the dim light while smoke rose in billows from thousands of chimneys. Thousands of windows glowed—some yellow with oil, some a brighter white with gas, and a few with the blue tinge of biolu-minescence.

Colleen pressed her palms against the cool glass. In this vast city, rooftops meant freedom. Exploring the possibilities that lay above London had saved her mind from the gloom that descended following the loss of her parents, of her forced relocation. "So breathtaking. Always." And in the raincloud-muted light, her spectacles were unnecessary. She tucked them away and turned to watch Nick.

He was all brisk business and impatience, examining the legs of the six skeet pigeons who perched upon the aviary's interior ledge. For years they'd circled each other—beneath both the glow of chandeliers and the twinkle of starlight—sharing casual flirtations. Light touches. Pointed, knowing glances. And details of their lives not meant for anyone else. Never quite daring to fully enter the other's orbit. Until now.

"No message yet from the constabulary," he reported, selecting a dispatch canister from a metal box and inserting a tightly rolled scroll. "Funds are being transferred to your employer as we speak. I assume you keep a punch card with his location near at hand?" He lifted a bird from its perch, fastening the canister to its ankle.

Mr. Witherspoon hadn't been pleased at her request. Though he'd agreed to reveal the buyer's name for a hefty sum, the skeet pigeon hadn't contained a return token. A clear message that— had she not retired—her employment would have been terminated. But Mr. Witherspoon knew Colleen kept a backup punch card, permitting her to contact him by bird one last time. Not that she wished to return to his employ. Not after what she'd found in that burnt-out shell of a laboratory.

Pushing all dark thoughts aside, she smiled. Nick would like this.

"I do." Lifting her fingers to the first button beneath her chin, she turned to face him as she unfastened her bodice, letting silk panels fall open to expose the lacy trim of her chemise.

His eyes brightened and the corner of his mouth lifted. Silent, but keenly attentive, Nick raised an eyebrow and waited.

With the edge of her underbust corset revealed—along with a generous bit of cleavage—she extracted a pen knife from the pouch at her waist and slit the half-dozen threads that held shut a tiny pocket sewn into its hem. She extracted a punched address card and pressed it into his palm. "It's my last token."

The pulse at his neck jumped. "Don't move." He pointed at her. "Not so much as a single extra button." With deft fingers, he slid the punch card into its slot, then quickly wound the skeet pigeon's mechanism. Wings flapping, Nick tossed the bird into the gray London sky before turning the full force of his intense gaze upon her.

"Does a rooftop aviary qualify as exotic?" She hoped so. For once they were alone with no one in pursuit and nowhere else they needed to be. A brief window of time open to them before a message arrived.

He glanced at her, swallowed, then flipped the hatch closed, kicking a bar across it to ensure there would be no interruptions from below. "Do you want it to?" Desire darkened his eyes as he closed the gap between them.

"Desperately." She tugged at his cravat, urging him closer.

He gripped the edge of her jaw, tipping her face upward, searching her eyes for any objection. "Anyone might catch a glimpse."

She shrugged a shoulder. "In this weather? Unlikely, but they *might*. Will that stop you?"

"Not a chance." The dam broke and his mouth crashed down upon hers. Their tongues tangled and plundered as spikes of pleasure zinged though her body. She tightened her hands upon his coat, anchoring herself upright as her world tilted off center and plunged her into a kiss so deep it stole her every last breath.

He pulled back, nipping at her lip. "More?"

"You need to ask?" Her voice was huff of frustration.

Impatient fingers fell upon the buttons of her bodice, finishing the task, pushing the silk from her shoulders and down her arms until the garment fell away. He tossed it over the railing, then froze. All his attention focused upon her as she tugged the drawstring of her chemise loose and slid the straps down her shoulders. The lacy-edges caught upon the swell of her breasts.

"All the way," he ordered, his voice hoarse.

"As you wish." A cold, damp breeze drifted across her bare breasts, peaking her nipples. She arched her back and dragged a fingertip over their swell, a clear invitation.

His eyes flashed, but he spun a finger in the air, denying her. "Turn around. Hands against the glass."

*This was new.* And most definitely exciting. She complied, bracing herself. In front of her, all of London glittered with light and swirled with fog. She might miss the countryside, but the city held such an interesting variety of secrets within its many nooks and crannies. Including—the corners of her mouth curved upward—rooftop trysts.

Hands skimmed over the boning at her waist, over the metal fastenings that held her corset closed. But made no effort to free them. Instead, his broad, warm palms moved upward, cupping and caressing her breasts as his mouth sank against the skin at the nape of her neck. A soft bite that spoke to primitive desires, electrifying every nerve ending and sending her heart racing.

"Is this what you want? A touch of danger?"

She rocked back against him—against the stiff evidence of his arousal—and groaned at the sensation. Need built to a fever pitch.

He nipped her earlobe. "Say it," he whispered over the skin beneath her ear.

"Yes," she breathed. "Don't stop." This moment—atop and apart—far exceeded anything her imagination had dared to conjure.

For too many years, she'd dreamed of ending their flirtatious dances by dragging him from the ballroom onto a dark balcony to steal a kiss. But with a reputation to maintain, propriety had always won. No more. At last he was hers, and she intended to make the most of it.

With a groan, he nudged her forward, pressing her bare breasts against the cool, smooth glass and her hips to the low, brick wall. His body was hot and hard at her back, crushing her with just the right pressure as his warm, demanding mouth explored the curve of her neck.

She let her head fall backward onto his shoulder. Every touch fanned the flames that licked across her skin as a wet heat gathered between her legs. Was this really her, tossing all inhibitions aside to give in to every wanton desire? It was. Her only regret was that they'd wasted so much time denying each other.

His fingers caught at her skirts, hiking them higher still, settling them about her hips. "Yes," she breathed, rocking her head sideways to nip at his neck. Waiting with sweet anticipation.

He eased back, giving himself room to touch her. To run his fingers across the top edge of her stocking, to discover she wore no knickers. Abandoned in his room, they lay among the last vestiges of her inclinations to follow society's rules. "Aether," he whispered. "I'd thought to find red silk."

"Last night you would have." She pushed backward. "Disappointed?"

"Not at all." His hand shifted and dipped between her legs to stroke her. Gentle yet firm, extracting the maximum of pleasure. Her hips flexed, eyes drifting shut as need coiled and twisted, tighter and tighter and—

Rough, calloused hands gripped her bare hips and spun her about, lifting her, propping her on the edge of the low wall. "Wait for me," he growled.

Feet dangling, she grabbed at his shoulders to brace herself. Her lungs dragged in a ragged breath. "Hurry."

"Foot on the railing behind me." He tore at his waistband, as desperate for her as she was for him.

He was going to take her—back to the glass—where discovery was a distant, but real possibility. No gentle, careful explorations in the dark. Rather a raw, primal coupling. Perfect. She lifted a leg, catching the heel of her boot upon the steel bar, watching as his cock fell free, thick and heavy.

"My turn to touch." She caught his length in her hand—smooth, hard, hot—and stroked from tip to base. Aether, she wanted him deep inside her.

From his coat pocket, he drew forth a wrapped sheath and pressed it into her palm. Another first. Never had a man placed so much control in her hands. Without letting go, she tore the paper with her teeth, covered him, then lifted her gaze to his.

Dark with arousal, his eyes stared down at her, hazy with lust and... something more. His gaze pierced straight through her heart. "Have you any idea how many times I've imagined this?" His voice was a growl. "At the end of a shadowy garden path. Behind a rooftop chimney?"

"Atop a sturdy desk in a stranger's study? I've lost count." She clawed at his cravat, pulling his lips down to hers. As his mouth devoured hers, she unfastened the buttons of his waist-coat, of his shirt. At last, the warm, firm skin of his chest and stomach met her hands. Skin she wanted to feel against her own. Wrapping hands about the mounds of his tight buttocks, she tugged him closer. "Stop wasting time."

Again, his hands slid up her thighs, shoving aside layers of skirts and parting her legs before him. He touched her center and—finding her wet and ready—entered her with one hard thrust. "Yes!" Lightning ran up her spine and shot through her limbs as he claimed her, and she gasped at the sensation of him filling her.

Slowly, he began to move, his long length sending darts of pleasure radiating through her. Heart pounding, she panted, digging the tips of her nails into his skin, urging him deeper still.

His intense thrusts came faster now. She closed her eyes and mewled her pleasure as the smooth glass at her back grew warm, as the rough brick beneath her dug into her soft flesh, as the rough scattering of hairs upon his chest brushed across the sensitive tips of her breasts. So many sensations, all of them building as he drove into her again and again and again pushing her ever closer to her peak.

"Nick!" The tension snapped and pleasure exploded in repeated waves of pleasure.

Once, twice more he plunged into her, stiffening as the spasms of his own release overtook him.

Braced against rough and smooth, Colleen wrapped her arms around his hot and heaving chest, hanging on as her world tilted, as she rearranged every expectation she'd ever had for a husband. Nick had shattered them all and the pieces no longer fit together. Worse, the tender feeling tugging at her heart would need to be ruthlessly leashed and caged, lest he glimpse the emotions roiling through her mind. She needed to think about this, about how—a mere two days from freedom—a man had managed to steal a piece of her soul.

She rested her head against his chest and listened to the steady beat of his heart.

WAS it possible to see stars in a cloud-covered sky? Nick closed his eyes and found the celestial bodies still dancing before them, a lingering euphoria unlike anything he'd ever experienced. In his arms, Colleen's soft curves melted against him, mere moments after she'd come apart, screaming his name. A wildcat in... well, not in bed. On a wall.

He grinned, entirely too self-satisfied for such a brief

encounter. With the pent-up passion of days, weeks, no, months of flirtation finally released, might they manage to take things slower next time?

*Next time.*

Hot and sweaty, their bodies were still fused. His skin touched hers at all the right points, and he was reluctant to part, to let so much as a thin layer of cool air rush between them. He'd been a fool not to act sooner.

He'd kept his past affairs simple, short and sweet. Much like their own flirtations had begun. But with each passing interaction, words shared between them had grown richer with meaning, as he'd caught glimpses inside her curious and exceptional mind. She'd wormed her way into his heart, and he could think of nothing he wanted more than to call one Lady Colleen Stewart his wife.

As her fingertips traced cords of muscle up and down his back beneath the linen of his shirt, an unsettling twist buried itself deep in his gut. He'd managed to make her his fiancée, but would two days be long enough to convince her they ought to stay together?

Fiancée. *Shit.* He'd meant to tell Colleen about the very real wedding plans that might even now be taking place several stories beneath their feet, but when she'd sliced that punch card from the edge of her corset, his mind had short circuited, leaving behind only the most basic of thoughts.

He would warn her. In a moment. After he'd stolen a few more seconds to revel in the glory of finally holding the only woman to ever steal his sleep and invade his dreams. He brushed his lips over the skin of her neck and felt her shiver beneath his touch. "Walls and desks and chairs are all well and good, but I want more." More than rooftop trysts. "I want to stretch you out fireside so that I might peel away and examine all your layers. Slowly. One by one."

Her head lifted and a cool rush of air invaded the space

between them. "Likewise." She pressed an open-mouthed kiss to the hollow of his throat. "But as we're trapped here on the roof, we might move to the bench and explore other options." Eyeing the rosy tips of her nipples, he stirred inside her, and she laughed, throaty and low. "Or we could stay here." She flexed her hips. "That works for me."

"Vixen." He caught her face in his hands and brushed a thumb over her swollen lips, grateful fate had landed them both on the same roof—chimney side—one particularly dark night.

Her fingers slid down his backside, urging him—

*Crack.*

A dull crunching sounded against a glass window pane. Their gazes caught, then turned toward the noise. A rusty skeet pigeon jerked and slipped upon the rooftop, dragging a broken wing as its internal programming insisted upon reaching the final, preprogrammed destination. Not far away, an overlarge black cat crouched, tail twitching.

"Is that... Sorcha?"

"It is." She sighed at the interruption. "It's rather a habit of hers, I'm afraid."

"That makes two wildcats on my roof." He grinned against her skin. "It appears we must postpone our activities. Work calls."

"Flaps," she amended, her lips curving upward as she tugged the two halves of his shirt together. "No worries about the message, she'll drag it inside in a moment."

He relaxed his grip on her hips, pulling free as he lowered her onto the rooftop and silently cursed the resilience of one particular mad scientist. "The constabulary prefers boots on the ground and the element of surprise—the better to read a guilty expression—and sees no reason to invest in maintaining a flock." A poor investment, his coin. The bobby had done no more than pocket it. "When forced to send a skeet pigeon, they snatch up the closest bird. One that is clearly no match for an interested feline." He tucked himself away as she drew her chemise back into place and reached for her bodice.

"Indeed. I, for one, want to look into Dr. Farquhar's eyes while I ask my questions." Anticipation lit a flame in her eyes. "Before we're done with him, I'll want to know who supplied him with a cat sìth. Fairy tale or not, such cats are rare and ought not be stolen away from their homes."

"Not only that, but I want to know who was funding his research. And why." He held her gaze, even when guilt urged him to look away. She needed to know. Now. "About our engagement—my father insisted upon a few slight alterations to our plans."

CHAPTER THIRTEEN

"SETTING A DATE IS not slight." Had her uncle known the Viscount Stafford would also insist upon a prompt ceremony? Without doubt. Foolish of her to act as if she would be free from society's expectations the moment she vacated her uncle's property. A touch of panic swirled in her stomach. Everything was happening so fast, and she was being pressured to make life-altering decisions without enough time to consider all the possible outcomes. A verbal promise was one thing, but a signature upon a marriage license? That was binding. "This is all very... rushed."

She tore her eyes away to focus upon the clockwork bird as it turned itself about and hopped toward the door of the aviary. Behind the skeet pigeon stalked Sorcha, alert and fully prepared to keep the contraption from taking wing. Colleen opened the door and snatched up the beady-eyed bird, focusing upon unfastening the message canister all while willing away the slight tremble of her fingers.

"I'm sorry." Nick took the still-twitching clockwork pigeon from her hands, smoothing its wing back into place and turning

411

it off before setting it beside the others. "If you'd prefer, I can escort you to a hotel."

Sorcha, with the skeet pigeon no longer an item of interest, turned her back upon them with an air of nonchalance and returned to watch for a new victim.

"No." She pushed her worries aside, focusing upon another emotion that thrummed though her body: yearning. "Your family only wants what's best for you. As they should." Her own parents would have guarded and protected her so. She missed it. "I'm staying."

Nick stroked a finger down the side of her cheek. "If you change your mind…"

"I'm not opposed." Her heart tripped as she spoke the words. "But I won't walk blindly into such a commitment. Might we discuss expectations later… fireside?"

"Done." He dipped his head and pressed a soft kiss to her lips. "Make a list of your demands." A provocative smile curved his lips. "I look forward to experiencing your persuasive techniques."

Did he mean… Her mind began to consider various possibilities, rendering her mute. And slow. For Nick snatched the paper scroll from her fingers with a laugh. "But don't think I won't exploit your every weakness in return."

Grinning, she smacked his arm, then leaned close. "That trick will only work once."

"We'll see." He read the note aloud, his voice sobering.

*Apologies, sir. Your man was removed from my custody without explanation. Carted away, while only semiconscious and muttering about hearts and worms. I objected and demanded an explanation from my supervisor, but was told the Queen's agents had no business interfering in private matters.*

"Damn it." Nick crumpled the message in his fist.

"Private matters?" Colleen's eyebrows drew together. "Might it be time for your long, complicated story about Queen's agent's business?"

He pinched the bridge of his nose. "He's the missing connection, Dr. Farquhar."

"Missing being the operative term." Colleen crossed her arms. Ice crystalized on her next words. "I can't help if I don't have all the relevant details."

"My hunt for the cardio-pacing device began when a stray comment crossed my path. A laboratory technician glanced at MacWilliam's paper."

"The one I read?"

"One and the same. Though the technician couldn't recall details, he remembered that the Lister Institute had once considered hiring someone whose work had reached similar conclusions. That there'd been talk of constructing a device that might supersede or alter the automatic pacing of a heart. But that nothing had come of it."

Colleen wrapped her hand about his fist and squeezed.

"I took my questions to Lord Aldridge, a board member of the Lister Institute."

She drew in a deep breath as all became clear. "*That's* why you were in his study in the dead of night?"

Another nod. "I've no proof he's involved in anything. Nothing but the slightest of hesitations when I inquired about past cardiac electrophysiology applicants."

Hesitations could mean something—or nothing. But Nick's instincts had pointed him in the direction of decidedly suspicious research activity. "And, like a cat with a mouse, you couldn't stop toying with the idea."

He threw her a twisted smile, then opened his fist and caught her hand in his, lifting it to his lips. His eyes were two deep pools that might hide any number of secrets. "Would a business partner and fiancée agree that any secrets a Queen's agent shares are sacrosanct?"

Warmth spread through her chest, driving back the frost. "She would. Tell me what this has to do with Sorcha."

"We're not old enough to remember when it began, but there was a time when biologists scoffed at the mention of such creatures as kraken and pteryformes, but now—"

"They darken our skies and choke the Thames."

"And cryptozoology is an established science." He took a deep breath. "There are rumors of a shadow committee known as CEAP, the Committee for the Exploration of Anthropomorphic Peculiarities."

"Anthropomorphic," she repeated. "Ascribing human characteristics to nonhuman creatures?" The ice crept back.

"Selkies, for example. Seals who can turn into humans. There have been reports of them on the northwest coast of Scotland."

Her eyes widened. "Are you telling me *selkies* are real?"

"No. But neither am I saying they aren't. Someone else is tracking down those sightings." He drew her hand to his heart and caught her gaze. "Within CEAP are individuals who are also interested in humans with animal characteristics. Men who would like nothing better than to capture and study such humans with an eye toward exploiting their unique skills. They've no interest in protecting even the most basic of individual rights and are not to be trusted."

*Humans with unique skills.* "Such as myself," she whispered. A woman who might once have been burned at the stake for suspicions of cavorting with the devil beneath the moonlight. Colleen struggled to keep her breathing steady. That mad scientist had stared at her, not with fear, but with amazement. And far too much interest.

"If you keep working with me, if a member of this CEAP committee is watching, it may well draw his attention to—"

"My distinctive eyes," she spoke on a soft exhalation. Caged within her ribs, her heart began to pace. "My uncanny athletic abilities. But it's too late. Dr. Farquhar has already taken note of my eyes. That explains his spellbound stare before he turned tail and ran."

Nick swore.

Precious few cat sìth roamed the woods of her family's Scottish estate. The same could be said of the men, women and children who also possessed golden eyes. Sorcha had been snatched from the streets of London, but now that Dr. Farquhar had made the link from the cat sìth to her, it was only a matter of time until someone connected her to Craigieburn and its unique occupants.

Knees weak, she sank to the floor, leaning against the low wall at her back.

Nick crouched beside her. "Colleen?" Concern filled his voice, but throughout it threaded a note of curiosity. "I have to ask. Are there any truths to the myths surrounding the cat sìth?"

"Truths?" She took a deep breath and looked into the eyes of the only man to ever treat her as an equal. "I've the eyes of a cat —as did my father and his mother before him. A number of families who live on or near my land can name at least one member—past or present—with eyes such as mine."

"A tapetum lucidum, a reflective layer of the retina allowing an animal—"

She winced.

"Or the rare human," he squeezed her hand, "to see in the dark."

"In low light," she corrected. "A candle. A spark. A thin ray of moonlight. But there must be at least a glimmer light for them to reflect, for me to see."

"And your spectacles?" Nick gathered her to his side.

"Bright light tends to blur my vision, hence the tinted lenses." She waved a hand at the arch of glass above them. The rain had stopped and rivulets no longer ran down the glass panes in long streams. "But fog, clouds, rain. Soot. Anything that turns London bleak and gray brings the world into sharp focus."

"Enhancing your nighttime prowling abilities." He kissed the tip of her nose. "And what of Sorcha's devotion, do you have a unique attachment to her?"

"My familiar?" The term once used with lighthearted humor had lost its appeal.

"I didn't mean—"

"But perhaps it's true. Cat sìth are rumored to be drawn to those who share my eyes." She shrugged. "We've an affinity of sorts, an ability to understand their thoughts when others sometimes struggle. Nothing unnatural, but I can easily deduce from the sound of their cries, the tension or position of their bodies, the intensity of their stares, what they want or need. More so than most. What seems a bit exceptional is that a cat sìth who has attached itself to a human will carry out tasks on their behalf. Sorcha occasionally assists me. Fetching an item from a top shelf, for example. Yowling if another prowler approaches while I'm working. And she's learned to carry messages home to Isabella, a precaution in the event I ever needed help extracting myself from a sticky situation."

"And has that ever happened?"

She smiled. "Not yet."

"Nonetheless, we have circled back to the cat sìth and the origin of one particular myth."

"Or, in other words, am I a witch with nine lives?" Her laugh was rueful. "If only. I can't shape-shift, and I assure you, were I to fall from a rooftop or lose my grip on the cornice, I might land on my feet, but the impact would kill me, same as it would you." Sadness swept through her. "Death, after all, stole away my father, as it did my mother and every other life on that ill-fated train."

She'd told him once of the Tay Bridge disaster, when a violent storm had caused the bridge to collapse as a train ran across it, plunging all aboard into the river. Over seventy lives lost that night and not one survivor.

His thumb brushed a tear from her cheek. "I'm sorry."

"It's five years in the past." And was a tragedy that had altered the course of her life, but did not define her. "It may have stolen away my parents and my home, but I intend to recover the latter. I won't sit idly by if there's a threat to those like me, to the cat sìth."

"Spoken like a woman with sharp claws."

"Who is ready to prowl."

They both laughed.

*Smack. Crunch.* Four soft paws dropped back onto the slate roof, and Sorcha proudly carried in a freshly crushed skeet pigeon. The thin, overlapping plates of the bird's irises stared blankly, all input terminated. The cat sìth deposited the newly arrived mechanical bird at Colleen's feet. A gift. Dropping onto her haunches, the cat awaited the praise that was her due.

"Thank ye." As Colleen stroked her hand down the feline's sleek back, Sorcha closed her eyes, quite pleased with herself. "Your assistance is noted and appreciated."

Beside her, Nick smothered a snort and reached for the message canister.

"My turn." She batted his hand away to unfurl this new scroll sent to them by none other than her former employer, Mr. Witherspoon. "Cornelius Pierpont," she read the scrawled name aloud. "It sounds familiar, but I can't quite place it. Is he anyone you know?"

"No. I am, however, curious to discover if one particular individual might find it familiar." Nick stood and held out a hand. "A steam carriage collects Lord Aldridge from the Lister Institute promptly every evening. The rain has stopped, and his house—with the mews behind it—is only a few rooftops away, while beneath us lies nothing but trouble."

She let him pull her to her feet. "In the form of dress fittings, guest lists and menus."

"And my mother." Nick tugged her close. "Who is certain to be overenthusiastic to the point where she might already have browbeaten my father into procuring a special license."

Colleen lifted an eyebrow. "Not much chance of stretching out before a fire to conduct our... discussion?"

"Not without interruption." He lowered his mouth to hers, savoring a slow and sultry kiss that ended all too soon. "We'll have better luck as the midnight hour approaches. I've climbed that trellis too many times to count. Leave the window open. In the meantime, shall we interrogate Lord Aldridge?"

CHAPTER FOURTEEN

From the roof of the mews, Nick kept his eyes on the activity of the stable hands in the alleyway below them, waiting for Lord Aldridge's distinctive steam carriage to emerge from the carriage house. Clockwork horses mixed with the living beasts, an increasing rarity in the city. Most vehicles housed in the stables that backed against the terraced homes of Mayfair were of the steam-driven variety, though a few crank-wagons were kept close for the sake of convenience.

"You're certain Lord Aldridge won't have us thrown behind bars?" Skirts hiked, Colleen crouched beside him. As did Sorcha. The cat sìth had followed them across the rooftops. Not closely, but behind them. Occasionally in full view, but the feline often disappeared behind rooflines and chimneys and aviaries.

It was all he could do not to let his gaze wander to Colleen's ankles, to admire the boots snugged against her calves, to note the shape of her stockinged knees. *Later.* There would be time later to contemplate how easily the woman he hoped to call his wife transformed from a lady into a thief. Perhaps he ought not feel so deeply satisfied that she hadn't so much as hesitated when he suggested they sidestep propriety to invade a gentleman's private conveyance and demand answers, yet he was nonetheless.

"For the minor transgression of a brief ride in his steam carriage?" Nick smirked. "He ought to appreciate the discretion with which we approach this matter. He was asked—directly— by a Queen's agent to provide information that would inform a course of action—"

"To be fair, you were prying into matters for personal gain, not in the service of the Crown." She rolled her eyes. "Are you not his employee?"

"Debatable. The Lister Institute's board supervises the medical school and all research conducted under its roof. Some of us, including Lord Aldridge, also answer to the Duke of Avesbury. His will supersedes all."

She cocked an eyebrow. "Does it now? There seems to be some debate about that, given his daughter, Lady Amanda, somehow managed to enroll in medical school. And I hear Lady Olivia was involved recently in some kind of scandal? Though both seem happily married now."

"Indeed." He wasn't privy to all the details, but the whispers he'd heard were fascinating. "Marry me, and I'll introduce you to them. Perhaps you can pry free their secrets."

She gave an amused snort. "Are you attempting to lure me to the altar with the promise of gossip?"

"Among other things. Have you ever thought of becoming a Queen's agent yourself? Not all of us are scientists." He winked. "I could be persuaded to put in a good word." She laughed, and it occurred to him he'd never asked. "What exactly precipitated your appearance in Lord Aldridge's study?"

"I snatched his daughter from the jaws of a harsh future. What?" She smacked his arm. "Don't look so disappointed. You know I worked to set wrongs to right, not to relieve the wealthy of their family jewels or stock holdings."

*True.* "An ethical sneak thief, so rare." He grinned. "You've never been tempted to snatch a necklace, a ring, stock certificates? By now you could have built a hoard that even a dragon would envy."

"Temptation at every turn. But no. None of my activities could ever be traced back to me."

"Ah, but they could," Nick disagreed. "If an interested party presented Mr. Witherspoon a number with enough zeros."

"With all I know?" Her lip curled. "I doubt it."

"Bedtime stories?" he teased.

"None that would lull you to sleep. The peerage, for all its talk of honor, has a dark underbelly."

That it did. "Not a problem," he said. "I've no real interest in using a bed for sleep. Not if you're in it."

Her cheeks flushed, and he debated teasing her with a few possibilities for passing the small hours of the night, but a belch of black smoke curled about the roof's edge, and a moment later, Lord Aldridge's steam carriage jerked and rattled onto the cobblestones. It was time.

"Ready?"

Her eyes—muted behind the dark lenses once again propped upon her nose—swept their surroundings once more. Satisfied, she nodded. "Let's go."

The scratch of a phosphorus match across the roof slate ignited a flame that he touched to the short wick of a loud firecracker. He lobbed it to the cobblestones below.

*Bang!*

A cloud of smoke billowed upward, and shouts rang out as stable hands turned about, searching for a miscreant guttersnipe who laughed at their expense. But he and Colleen had already leapt to the ground and slipped inside the earl's steam carriage.

None of them paid any attention to the cat who followed, disappearing beneath the vehicle, no doubt finding a handy cubby in which to secrete herself.

A well-appointed interior surrounded them. A Lucifer lamp for light. An iron box filled with hot coals for heat. And velvet upholstery for comfort. But even better was the view. Perched on the seat opposite him, Colleen unhooked her skirts from their hikes to smooth them over booted ankles. He squeezed his eyes shut and tried not to dwell on the memory of them wrapped about his hips, braced on the railing while he—

"Straighten that cravat of yours," she chided.

His eyes snapped open, the dream shattered.

Colleen's eyes glittered in the lamplight. She knew *exactly* where his mind had wandered. "And tuck in your shirt. Or Lord Aldridge will think we commandeered his carriage for entirely different purposes."

Such a plan inked itself onto his mind. A private carriage on the streets of London. He'd see it happen. And soon. "Not helping." His voice was strangled.

She laughed. "While I have to admit I rather like that hungry look on your face, you need to make yourself respectable."

While he did his best to repair his attire, his eyes were fixed upon Colleen's own transformation. It was like watching a butterfly crawl back into its cocoon. Loose locks of hair were ruthlessly pinned in place. Her spectacles adjusted upon the bridge of her nose. Elbow-length gloves—over which she carefully slid her ring—appeared from inside a pocket slit into her skirt. All of this followed by a small hat and a glinting hatpin to position it at a jaunty angle upon her sleek, dark hair. By the time the steam carriage jerked into motion, she looked every inch a lady while he—hatless, gloveless and rumpled—still very much resembled a profligate rogue.

"Tell me I'm the only one to ever watch such a transformation."

"The only *man*." She leaned forward to trail a single gloved fingertip down the edge of his face while the ghost of a tease clung to her lips. "Isabella, working to stall or divert my discovery, has caught glimpses."

Two days, he reflected as the steam carriage chuffed, clattered and swayed toward the Lister Institute, was not going to be enough time with this woman. He wanted to look into those golden eyes of hers and speak vows. "How set are you on returning to Scotland?"

She blinked at the sudden change in topics. "Extremely." Colleen glanced out the window, worrying the stone of the amber ring with her thumb. "I've long-neglected responsibilities to shoulder."

"The University of Aberdeen, complete with research facilities, is a short dirigible ride away from Craigieburn Castle," he answered, initiating negotiations.

"Are you offering to relocate?" She glanced at him from the corner of her eyes.

"I am. Not all Queen's agents are located in London year-round. If a position were to open, might there be any chance you would allow me to build a landing platform upon its roof?"

"Were there a roof to build upon." His mouth fell open while she recounted a story of irresponsible boys and a fiery crash—and the reason behind her participation in the obfuscation chain involving the rosewood box. "Now is the perfect time to incorporate such an upgrade. But are you certain you wish to leave London?"

"Do I detect a slight note of regret?" he asked. "Could it be you'll miss the city? Do you worry you might tire of land management and home repairs?"

She pressed her lips together. "It's true. The city, though overcrowded and grimy, is bursting with innovations and activity of all sorts."

An interesting tangle. "Married female agents are not unheard of. Many work on a case by case basis. Any interest?"

"You'd permit a wife of yours—"

He leapt across the space separating them to sit beside her. "Not permit." He growled in her ear before nipping the lobe. "Encourage."

Her breath caught. "Perhaps we could split our time between country and city."

"A perfect compromise." He nibbled at the corner of her jaw as he spoke.

Alas, the carriage chose that moment to rattle to a stop. Outside, there were thuds as feet landed upon the ground.

"I suppose that might depend upon the outcome of this interview. You might find yourself summarily dismissed from employ." She batted at his leg, and her voice took on a haughty tone. "Now place a respectable distance between us, that I might cling to the few remaining shreds of my reputation." As the carriage door swung open, Colleen folded her hands and dropped her gaze, once again assuming the mantle of the demure, lusterless young lady she was anything but.

Nick drew himself straighter. He was about to step onto thin ice with little knowledge of what clawed tentacles might lurk beneath, ready to snag his career at Lister Institute into an abyss from which he might not escape.

"Torrington?" Lord Aldridge gaped for a brief moment before his bushy eyebrows slammed down. He pointed a silver-capped walking stick at Nick. "What cause have you to invade my carriage? If it's about that—" He caught sight of Colleen and recoiled. "You."

Interesting.

"And you would criticize my manners?" Nick reproached. "May I presume a prior acquaintance with Lady Stewart?"

Lord Aldridge pressed his lips into a flat, bloodless line.

"Join us," Nick waved, inviting the man into his own vehicle. "We need to discuss the whereabouts of one Dr. Farquhar."

"Sir?" The guard holding the door—for that was his role despite his braid-embroidered livery—possessed an unusual amount of muscle. A single word from Lord Aldridge and he would empty the carriage of uninvited guests.

His graying mustache twitched. Lord Aldridge knew something. "No worries," he told his guard before climbing into the carriage. The ease of his movements suggested a wiry strength, identifying his walking stick as a weapon, not a support.

The door closed behind them and, a moment later, the carriage lurched into movement.

"The scientist is mad," Lord Aldridge stated. "His whereabouts do not concern me."

"And yet he might be the only hope of my sister surviving her third decade. Would you decline to answer my questions knowing that you might deprive an infant of her mother?"

"You'd let a mad man experiment upon your own sister?" Lord Aldridge growled back through clenched teeth. "Like as not, he'd kill her."

"Genius is often mistaken for insanity," Nick countered. "I *am* a trained physician and scientist, capable of evaluating any treatment he's developed. He was in custody not two hours ago. I'd prefer not to cause a scene at the local station house, but if he's my only lead…"

Not for the first time, Lord Aldridge's gaze darted to Colleen who sat still and silent beside him. "Is it?"

Telling, that glance. Had it to do with the reason she'd been in his study, a fact he didn't care to hear spoken aloud? Or was there yet more?

"I'm not here on behalf of Witherspoon and Associates, my lord. Blackmail is not a service he provides."

Nick snorted. He'd beg to disagree.

But Colleen's voice continued, eerily calm and professional. "I would, however, consider it a personal favor were you to provide us with information about Dr. Farquhar. A favor you might call upon should your—shall we say—willful daughter fall prey to any *further* indiscretions."

Oh? Was Lady Sophia not quite the demure debutant she appeared? Had she been caught with a man? Impressed with the currency Colleen offered, Nick watched the exchange, pride swelling in his chest.

"Done." The lord snapped up the bait all too quickly. Was anyone in the *ton* as they seemed? Certainly not Lady Sophia's father, for intensity darkened his gaze. "A few years past, the board offered Dr. Farquhar a research position despite my concerns about his mental stability." His gaze shifted to Nick. "Documents were drawn up. Laboratory space was assigned. But he declined in favor of private funding." Lord Aldridge narrowed his eyes. "He threw away a promising career to chase after feral cats."

Colleen stiffened, then carefully framed her question. "What have feral cats to do with studies of the heart?"

"An excellent question, Lady Stewart." Sarcasm laced his voice. "Some are rumored to have nine lives. Perhaps that makes them a more robust experimental subject?"

All vestiges of good humor burned away as Nick scowled. "You knew of his connection to a shadow board and said nothing? Knowing my role as a Queen's agent, knowing the smallest of connections sometimes matter most?"

"Your questions were of a personal bent. It was time you set aside your futile pursuits to focus on your career. And how dare you bring *her* into this," Lord Aldridge hissed. "Such information is only for the ears of—"

"I've also informed her about the existence of CEAP." Nick leaned forward. "Her involvement is directly relevant. My personal concerns and the Crown's interests are one and the same. Tell me—us—what you know." Had Lord Aldridge seen fit to share, Dr. Farquhar's activities might have been unearthed months ago.

Lord Aldridge turned his glare upon Colleen. "I always

wondered if your uncle's ostensible acceptance of you in his household possessed a mercenary bent."

Unhooking the wire of her spectacles from behind one ear, she tugged them free and tipped her chin upward in challenge. Her eyes caught the light of the Lucifer lamp affixed to the carriage wall and flashed a brilliant green-gold.

"Impressive, my dear," he commented, his voice bland, for after five years in London Colleen's unusual eyes surprised no one in the *ton*. "But I'm not prey to such superstitions. Animals shape-shifting to take human form is a ridiculous proposition. As is the reverse. Stuff and nonsense. Now, concerning your eyes, were one to propose a hypothesis involving descent with modification as an adaptation to a more nocturnal environment, we might be able to apply scientific reasoning to discuss the possibilities by which such an unusual feature might arise."

His words—highbrow and clipped—were betrayed by a white-knuckled grip upon his cane, as if he feared the docile Lady Stewart might lunge without warning. A claw to the cravat? A bite to the neck? Yes, she was entirely capable of such actions, but as her fiancé, he would have to insist she confine such activities to one man.

"Don't dodge the question," Nick said. "Did Dr. Farquhar's interests catch the attention of anyone suspected to be a member of CEAP?"

The gentleman's gaze did not waver, but stayed locked upon Colleen. "Despite efforts to uncover these reputed shadow committees, no such organizations have yet been found to exist. As to rogue scientists managing something resembling loose organization?" Lord Aldridge offered Colleen a smile brimming with pity. "When your uncle became your guardian, the trappings of his lifestyle improved. Tell me, how much do you know about the goings-on at your estate?"

"It's been some five years since I have set foot upon Scottish soil. I do, however, exchange frequent correspondence with my estate manager who—" Colleen's mouth snapped shut. Anger vibrated off her in waves.

Eyebrows lifted, Lord Aldridge finished. "Makes frequent requests for funds? My dear, it appears Lord Maynard has fashioned himself a villain while ostensibly acting as a guardian." He turned his attention back to Nick. "If you're looking to connect Dr. Farquhar, feral cats, and Lady Stewart to a purported shadow committee, may I offer advice as old as dirt? Follow the money." He raised his cane and thumped upon the roof, indicating their interview had reached an end. The steam carriage came to a stop. "Be careful not to misstep, Torrington. Lord Maynard has extensive connections."

Nick refused to be dismissed. "One last question."

Lord Aldridge sighed heavily. "One."

"We need to speak with one Cornelius Pierpont. Can you provide an introduction?"

"No. I've never heard of the man." The carriage door swung open. From the tone of his voice, Lord Aldridge was clearly at the end of his rope. "Out. Both of you."

# CHAPTER FIFTEEN

REELING FROM Lord Aldridge's revelations, Colleen gripped Nick's arm as they approached his family's townhome. Though she wished to storm her uncle's study and demand answers, unsubstantiated accusations and ravings about fairy cats would see her delivered to the mad house.

Had her uncle been abusing his position as her trustee to turn a profit? If so, then her estate manager, Watts, was corrupt. He'd been sending her reports for years, and it made her ill to think how many thousands of pounds she had transferred into his care. Had he pocketed the money? Funneled it back to her uncle? What was the true state of Craigieburn and its lands? Was the roof truly damaged, or was it a ruse designed to keep her dashing about the shadows of London, turning a profit with her skills? *Gah!* If so, then all these years he'd *known* she was a sneak thief.

Worse still, had he used those earnings to fund a mad man's research? Had her uncle himself placed Sorcha in Dr. Farquhar's hands? She recalled the charred bodies in the burned-out basement laboratory. Exactly how many other cat sìth had been sacrificed to this lunacy? Did cryptid hunters roam her land, unchallenged, collecting the cats to sell to others who believed them capable of magic? And what of those men, women and children who possessed golden eyes? Might such attention incite a modern witch hunt?

Bilious twistings escaped the pit of her stomach and spread upward, constricting her throat.

Not that the repercussions ended there. Though the imprisonment and torment of cat sìth made her blood boil, any good that might have come of it—a possible treatment for heart block—had slipped through her own fingers.

"I'm of a mind to gather a few supplies and head directly to your uncle's door," Nick said.

"As am I." Colleen entertained a brief fantasy of doing exactly that. With Nick at her side, they could— She shook her head. "But he won't tell you anything, and he certainly won't admit to any underhanded dealings." Her feet slowed. "There is, however, a dinner party he's attending this evening."

"You think he's involved."

"I do. In so many ways."

"And you want to break into his home, his study, and rifle through his papers for answers and evidence. Before we confront him about Dr. Farquhar's whereabouts. Properly, over tea and whisky. And perhaps the sights of my TTX pistol."

"You know me so well." She managed a faint smile. The brilliant orange sun hung low over London, casting the jagged line of rooftops into a dark profile and setting the low-hanging clouds aglow. Chimney pots spouted smoke, warming homes as the city quieted, hunkering down for the night. "I'll contact Isabella, make certain she and my uncle still plan to attend the dinner party. I'm certain they do. He'll want to keep up appearances."

His face was all business, yet she knew revenge and justice

lurked beneath the surface. "A few hours from now, then, we'll go. Together."

"Agreed." They stopped upon the pavement before the entrance of his family townhome. A few feet behind them, Sorcha brushed against a scrolled iron railing, watching. Lights blazed in every window. Not once had Colleen left by roof to return by door, lest she find herself floundering for an explanation before her uncle. Not, apparently, that it had mattered.

She pulled free her dark spectacles and perched them upon her nose.

"No worries." Nick led her up the stairs. "They're accustomed to my odd comings and goings. They'll adjust to the cat."

The door swung open. Hopsworth lifted haughty wire eyebrows, but said nothing as they entered the foyer, an over-large black cat trailing in their wake.

"Where have the two of you been?" Lady Stafford cried as she rushed down the staircase and past Hopsworth, the train of her shimmering gold tea gown rustling as it swept behind her. Ruffles edged in daring black lace framed her face, circled her wrists, and cascaded to the floor. "No—" She lifted a hand, palm outward. "I've changed my mind. *Do not* tell me what you've been about. It will only color my nightmares. Nicholas, you look a fright. Please change into more appropriate attire. Lady Stewart," the viscountess held out her arm, waggling her fingers, "do come with me. I managed to persuade the modiste with the loosest tongue in all of London to abandon her other clients and transport her wares to our parlor, but we must make haste if we're to have a gown ready in four days' time."

Colleen blinked at the rush of words.

"Mother—" Nick objected.

"I'm aware of the terms and conditions of your fiancée's presence, Nicholas," the viscountess said. "Wedding or not, maintaining appearances means providing society with the finer details of Lady Stewart's wedding preparations, down to the beads upon her bodice and the embroidery upon her sleeves. Invitations must be engraved. A wedding breakfast planned. And so on and so forth."

"Your mother is correct." Colleen found her voice. "A closely chaperoned young woman in the throes of frantic wedding plans is unlikely to have time for other pursuits." She cast him a significant glance. There were several hours before her uncle's house would grow quiet. "While we coo over silk and lace, you might best use the time to investigate the positions of other players upon the board."

Nick hesitated. Furrows of worry lined his brow. "There are individuals I must contact. You've no objections if I leave you in my mother's care?"

"None." On the contrary. Lady Stafford presented a curious mix of co-conspirator and managing mother, and Colleen was curious about which direction the balance tipped.

Within minutes, she stood upon a stool in her undergarments while a seamstress affecting a French accent poked, prodded and measured, calling orders to her two young assistants while eyeing Sorcha—who crouched before the fireplace, front paws tucked beneath the flare of white upon her chest— with deep mistrust. When cats and rustling cloth mixed, the fabric was always trounced.

"Is it possible to remove *le chat noir?*"

"Entirely possible," Colleen answered, stepping down. En route to the cat sìth, she snatched up a stray bit of string, tied three knots—a code—then looped it about Sorcha's neck as she carried the feline to the window. "Tae Isabella," Colleen whispered. *To Isabella.* Then cracked the window. "A sasser o cream fin ye return." *A saucer of cream when you return.*

With a twitch of her whiskers, the cat sìth leapt free.

She turned to find two partially finished gowns held up for

her approval. "Perhaps the silk moiré?" It rippled and flowed beautifully beneath the flickering gaslight.

"An excellent choice, my lady," the seamstress agreed. Pins and needles flew, securing swaths of heavy silk about her hips, slipping sleeves with raw edges over her arms while her assistant's needle flashed as she basted panels together. Moments later, a mirror was placed before her, and the modiste gathered her assistants and moved to the far end of the room, giving their patron and her future daughter-in-law a moment's privacy.

Lifting a shaking hand to her chest, Colleen touched a row of filigree-set amber buttons hastily tacked in place to embellish the simple, unfinished bodice. Sparks of light flashed off the stone inclusions embedded in the ancient resin.

"They match the ring." First an heirloom of sentimental value, now this. The thought and consideration Nick and his mother had showered upon her was almost too much. She blinked back the tears that threatened.

"And your eyes." Anna's voice was breathy. Waif-thin and pale, she made her way across the room. Behind her, an attendant wheeled the bulky, quietly-humming, yet truly terrifying machine into the room, doing her best to be unobtrusive. The name of the device, P.C. Hutchinson's Magneto-Shock Machine, was embossed across its side. Did Anna go nowhere without it? Anna and her mother shared a conspiratorial look. "What are the odds you'll stand with my brother before clergy?"

Colleen's mouth opened. Then closed. This was no hastily arranged fitting. It was a planned ambush.

"From the look upon her face?" Lady Stafford's smile was rather smug. "Higher than I'd hoped. Nicholas brought her home dusty and rumpled, but smiling. Given those boots laced to her knees and the knife they *almost* conceal, I think my son might finally have found his match."

"Agreed," Anna said. "Only a wife predisposed to similar clandestine activities will ever truly understand him."

Colleen's heart constricted. Never could she have predicted such a warm welcome. She'd reconciled herself to abandoning her career and returning alone to Craigieburn, but with Nick waving temptation before her in all its forms, she was reassessing her decision. Thoughts of becoming his wife, of becoming a member of his family filled her with warmth and happiness. "How long ago did he ask for his grandmother's ring?"

"Months ago, before his most recent, unexpected disappearance." Nick's mother clasped her hands to her chest. "I do hope you'll forgive our attempts to convince you to become a more permanent member of our family."

The modiste cleared her throat, impatient.

"Ah, we mustn't keep her waiting." The viscountess winked. "She's a gown to finish and rumors to spread."

Released from the heavy fabric and handed a robe, Colleen pulled Anna aside while the seamstress consulted with the Lady Stafford about details such as seed pearls and knife pleats and the necessity of trim. Choices she was happy to cede to another.

"I can't believe this is happening," Colleen murmured. It was a struggle to follow the various strings knotted together in her mind. A welcome marriage proposal. A quest to improve Anna's declining health. The discovery of a mad scientist with designs upon cat sìth. The manipulations and involvement of her uncle.

"And why not?" Anna pressed a hand to Colleen's arm. "Admittedly, I do not often attend *ton* events, but did you think I never noticed the dances you and my brother shared?"

"It could have been no more than pity for a dull wallflower in a plain vase set high upon a dusty shelf." Their first dance had been one shared for mutual convenience, an exercise in moving from one point to another in a manner least likely to draw comment.

"Perhaps at first." Anna tipped her head. "But I've long suspected you might share more than dances."

As they had. But only out of the public eye and well-hidden in the shadows. A blush crept across her cheeks.

"Ever since that first waltz, every woman we've pushed, shoved or dragged into his path has been summarily rejected. So if you think we'll let you escape without a fight—"

"There are, of course, complications," Colleen interrupted even as she fought back a smile. "I've my own responsibilities— and desires—that lay in Scotland. And your brother has his. To the Crown, to—"

"Me," Anna finished on a sigh. "He can be a fool, my brother. He drives himself too hard and neglects his own interests. I know very well he's on a quest to heal my heart, to fix what he did not break. I appreciate his efforts. I truly do, but he should not put the entirety of his life on hold."

"Listen," Colleen caught up Anna's cool, gaunt hands, unwilling to admit aloud that Nick's devotion to his sister might well drive a wedge between them no matter how hard they worked to find middle ground. Until they located Dr. Farquhar, Cornelius Pierpont and the contents of a certain rosewood box, deciding upon their future would have to wait.

"I can't and won't make you promises about the likelihood that the device we seek—one I've yet to lay eyes upon—will offer you any solutions. But we will find it." She thought of Sorcha locked in a cage. Of the morbid contents within the other wire cages of Dr. Farquhar's charred laboratory. Was it possible another cat sìth had undergone some kind of testing *and* *survived*? "If there's any hope of its success, we'll do our best to — Anna?"

Anna crumpled to the floor, and Colleen lunged, managing to catch her about the waist, softening an otherwise hard landing. "Help!" she cried.

"Anna!" The viscountess dropped a length of fabric as both

she and the attendant nurse rushed forward to drop to their knees besides Anna's convulsing form.

The nurse lifted her wrist. "Respiration steady. Pulse absent." Standing, the nurse pressed a pocket watch into Lady Stafford's hand. "Mark the time. Three minutes, no more." She hurried back toward P.C. Hutchinson's Magneto-Shock Machine, flipping a lever that made the contraption hum and crackle as she pushed it to Anna's side.

"Fifteen seconds." The viscountess encircled her daughter's wrist, searching for a pulse. A tear ran down her cheek.

In two minutes and forty-five seconds they would... what?

Her own heart hammering against her ribcage, Colleen cradled Anna's head while the nurse ripped open the loose bodice fitted about her narrow chest and swiftly unbuttoned the camisole that lay beneath, exposing the pale expanse of her torso to begin chest compressions.

"Thirty." The viscountess's breaths came in short bursts. Her face was ashen and bloodless as she detached a sharp and glinting probe from the instrument's side.

Every instinct screamed at Colleen to stop this madness. But Anna herself—and her mother and Nick—must approve, for they'd installed both the nurse and the device.

A treatment acceptable only in the face of certain death.

"Forty-five." A tear splashed onto the viscountess's cheek.

The whine from the device grew louder.

*Crack!* Colleen jumped as a blinding flash of white light arced between the point of the metal rod and the device itself. The machine fell silent. A puff of acrid smoke rose from its innards.

Lady Harrington let out a deep wail and began to frantically bang on the device, flipping switches and spinning dials. But to no avail.

WHILE COLLEEN WAS SWEPT up the stairs and into a room filled with flowing lengths of white silk, lace and other assorted trims, Nick fled into the study where he scratched out a quick note to Jackson requesting help. Friend and fellow agent, the man was tasked with keeping an eye on foreigners looking to turn a profit by absconding with British ingenuity. Perhaps Cornelius Pierpont was one such individual. Moreover, Jackson was a damned good agent. They'd worked together in the past and, given today's revelations, backup would be welcome, particularly if he and Colleen found hard evidence upon examining the contents of her uncle's safe. He dashed up the stairs to the aviary—his new favorite location—and sent the message on its way.

Task done, he tugged his pocket watch from his waistcoat. Seven o'clock. Given Colleen's presence, would his family insist upon a formal evening meal? Months of flirtation had crystalized into the oddest of courtships, and he hated to leave her in his family's clutches for even a short length of time while their future was still on uncertain ground. He didn't keep much clothing in his old wardrobe, but he'd make do rather than return to his bachelor quarters.

He started down the stairs toward his old room.

Distress at Lord Aldridge's revelations that her uncle and estate might well fund Dr. Farquhar's studies of the cat sìth had tensed Colleen's supple frame and stiffened her resolve to see their quest through to the finish line. Cryptid hunters were a blight upon their nation's natural resources and, if they'd been turned loose at Craigieburn, there was no telling the damage her uncle had wrought upon her inheritance and its inhabitants. The anger such thoughts engendered curled his hands into fists, ones which he'd like nothing better than to wrap around the man's throat. He would see the man pay. Any connection to CEAP needed to be severed and quickly, before men without inconvenient moral scruples used the existence of cat sìth as an excuse to study human oddities in the name of scientific advancement. With her reflective eyes, Colleen—and others like her—might well end up as unwilling research subjects. He'd not let that happen, not to any of them.

As his list of tasks grew longer, they'd begun to circle back upon each other, winding tighter with each revelation. Save his sister. Assist the woman he wished to marry. Locate a mad scientist and his device. Shut down a shadow committee by ripping control of his fiancée's estate from her guardian's hands. All while wondering at the ethics of employing a life-saving contraption that tainted money had financed.

Life had grown immeasurably complicated these past few days.

Screams echoed up the stairwell. Shouts followed. As he ran down the steps, he could feel the hum of electricity as P.C. Hutchinson's Magneto-Shock Machine came to life. A loud *pop* sounded and his mother cried out. He burst into the parlor, trampling silk in his rush to reach his sister's side where the nurse administered percussive pacing and chest compressions.

Anna's eyes flew open and she dragged in a great, horrible and stertorous breath. Her face flushed red as blood began to flow through her veins and arteries, her heart once again condescending to continue its labors.

"It happened again?" his sister whispered, staring up at her brother.

"It did, darling." His mother wrapped her arms about her daughter, ignoring the tears that still trickled over her cheeks. "For about one minute and thirty seconds."

The nurse nodded, confirming his worst fears. "And the device short-circuited. I'll send for the technician."

Colleen, eyes wide, looked at him.

"Longer than before." He answered her unspoken question as the sound of his own heartbeat thrashing in his ears faded.

"She'll recover?" Colleen's voice was a whisper.

He nodded. *This time.*

Only then did he glance at the Magneto-Shock Machine. A faint wisp of smoke rose from deep inside its mechanisms. So much for its usefulness. He was almost grateful, and yet, had his sister not revived, a functioning device—horrible though it was—might well have saved her.

"How are you feeling?" he asked, turning his attention to his sister, ever careful to maintain a calm, clinical pretense after each attack, watching closely as color returned to her face.

"Fine." She rubbed her chest. There would be bruises. "Mostly."

"Is there anything more that can be done?" Colleen pushed a loose lock of hair behind her ear with a shaking hand.

He shook his head. "These episodes come on without warning and don't seem to cluster, though she'll be watched closely."

"As always," Anna sighed. She threw Colleen a wan smile. "Privacy is in short supply when your heart can't be relied upon."

"It's necessary," he commented. "Come. I'll carry you to bed."

"In the nursery," Anna insisted.

Nick knew better than to argue that point. He scooped his sister into his arms and turned to leave the room. "Where you will let me listen to your heart." To be certain he could detect no further progression of the damage. He gave Colleen a speaking look. "Don't... take any actions without me."

"I'll wait," Colleen assured him. "In your—my—room."

Where there was a fire, a bed, and a few hours until they could take once more to the roofs.

Anna snickered softly. "Convenient," she muttered under her breath, just loud enough for her brother to hear.

He gave her arm a pinch. "Hush, lest I accidentally drop

you." He wouldn't, but light-hearted sibling sparring always brought a grin to her face.

"Let me see the modiste out." His mother pressed a kiss to Anna's cheek. "I'll be with you directly."

"Of course." As their mother hurried to the flustered dressmaker and her assistants, Anna dropped her head against Nick's chest. "I'll be fine. Well, as fine as I ever am. I'll feel even better if the 'actions' you have planned for tonight have to do with that miracle mentioned earlier?"

"They do." If they didn't find answers inside Lord Maynard's safe, he'd hunt the man down himself and drag forth the whereabouts of Dr. Farquhar in a most ungentlemanly manner. "We've a new lead to chase down."

"Progress?" Her eyes held a cautious hope.

"Perhaps," he warned.

"I won't keep him long." Anna caught Colleen by the sleeve of her dressing gown. "There's nothing he can do that my nurse isn't equally capable of—save hunt down whichever scientist is jealously guarding this secret you seek. Promise you'll come visit me tomorrow and tell stories about your toe-curling adventures?"

"They're more of a scandalous nature." Colleen gave his sister a wink. "I can't—and won't—tell you *all* the details, but you *might* ask me questions about the gossip rags, and we'll see what I can confirm or deny."

"Excellent." His sister's cheeks were pale, but maintaining a healthy glow. "I've a full year of missed ballroom scandals to inquire about." She released Colleen. "Let's go, brother."

Colleen turned away to gather her things, and Nick began the climb to the nursery. "I hate to leave you so soon after an attack."

"But you will," Anna answered him. "Go find this device you've been carrying on about and, while you're at it, convince

Lady Stewart to marry you. I'd like nothing more than to attend your wedding before—"

"Don't say it," Nick stopped her, frowning. "I've every confidence you will live to hold your grandchildren."

She slapped him lightly on the chest. "So long as it's not at the expense of being able to hold your own. You have an hour, no more, before I toss you from the nursery."

# CHAPTER SIXTEEN

COLLEEN ARRIVED at her—Nick's—door to find a small boy bent at the waist and peering through the keyhole while balancing a tray.

"Something of interest?" she asked.

He jumped backward, nearly upsetting the saucer of milk, and looked up at her with wide eyes. "That's a really large, *black* cat. Aren't black cats supposed to be bad luck?"

"Only if you treat them badly," she said. "But since you come bearing food, she'll likely be predisposed in your favor. Would you like to meet Sorcha?"

"It's yours?" The boy gaped.

"Some might say so, but one never *owns* a cat." Colleen opened the door while the child lifted the tray. "*She* chose *me*. Sorcha, meet—" She raised an eyebrow.

"Robby," the boy supplied, setting down the tray.

"Hold your hand out for her to sniff."

Tail held high, Sorcha strolled over. Though her attention was focused upon dinner, the feline recognized an in-house ally, permitting Robby to run his hand over her back as she lapped up the cream.

"There's a string about her neck," he said, examining the twine. "And a message!" His eyes blinked up at her. "You trained a *cat?*"

*Trained?* No. Frequently bribed was a more appropriate description. But none of the feral cats that prowled the streets of London could ever be coaxed to her aid, making the cat sìth a far superior species. "Sorcha is no ordinary feline." She held out her hand, and he dropped the paper scroll into her palm.

She unfurled Isabella's message.

*Our evening proceeds according to plan, but take every precaution. After your departure, your uncle was called away on urgent business. He returned white-faced and shaking with rage. I suffered a pointed stare of suspicion that bodes nothing but ill. Tonight, we most both walk upon eggshells.*

Had her uncle been the one to free Dr. Farquhar from his prison cell? Try as she might, Colleen could not imagine him passing down the halls of a station house. No, one of his minions would have been sent to fetch the mad scientist.

But he *would* know where the man had been deposited.

And might well know this Cornelius Pierpont. The name continued to niggle at her mind. She'd heard it before. Somewhere.

"Are you going to save Lady Anna?" Robby broke into her thoughts.

"We're going to do all we can, starting later tonight." She hesitated, then decided this interval of time must not be squandered. "Can I count upon you to wake me in two hours' time? With a tea tray fit for a human?"

He jumped up. "Anything to support the mission." Grinning, the boy exited the room.

Though her nerves were still wound tight—would she ever forget such a moment of watching a woman's heart stop... then start again as if nothing at all was amiss?—she could feel the edge of exhaustion dulling her mind, her reflexes. The rest of the household would be doting upon Anna, as they should. She looked at the mattress with longing. A short nap, a light tea, and she'd be ready to hunt down Cornelius Pierpont and the contents of a particular rosewood box. A task that needed to be accomplished tonight. Ferreting out Dr. Farquhar's location was another goal, though wading through his madness to extract the specifications of the device was a far less appealing—though potentially viable—option.

Alone, Colleen unlaced her boots and tugged them from her feet. There was no point in unlacing a corset only to struggle with it in a few hours. She pulled a few pins from her hair, letting it tumble free. Tossing the dressing gown aside, she crawled beneath the covers and lay her head down upon the soft pillow with a sigh.

Years of late nights had trained her to sink swiftly into a deep sleep. In moments sweet oblivion claimed her.

Some time later, the mattress shifted. A displacement of far more weight than that of an overlarge cat. Her heart slammed against her chest and her eyes flew open, every nerve ending alive and alert.

"Shh." Nick's voice was a whisper as he stretched out beside her atop the covers wearing nothing but his trousers and shirtsleeves. "Go back to sleep."

Unlikely. Not when the tips of her fingers were tingling with the desire to touch the rough stubble that had begun to shadow his face. Or while her elevated pulse flooded her body with heat and desire. Even his scent teased, leather and spice and something decidedly male.

With so many other bedrooms from which he might choose, he'd come to her. Her heart flipped in her chest, and her mind agreed: sleep was not what he had in mind. Still, she willed herself motionless for she'd not deprive Nick of his own chance for rest. Except his eyes didn't close. Instead, after several long minutes, they still stared at the ceiling while heavy thoughts weighed down his mind.

"How is your sister?" She rolled onto her side, propping her head upon her hand.

"Resting." He sighed. "Save for the trauma of the attack itself, there is little in the way of aftereffects, save a bit of fatigue."

"With little to be done save fret and worry about when the next will occur and what the outcome will be?" The clock upon the mantle informed her there was plenty of time yet before her aunt and uncle would depart from their townhome.

"In a nutshell." He rolled to face her, and a faint, suggestive gleam kindled in his eyes. "The door is locked." He winked. "And I've clean shirts in the wardrobe."

"Oh?" She let a knowing smile touch her lips. "And you wish for me to... help you dress?"

"I rather thought you might help me undress. It's such an inconvenience to work these small buttons of my shirt by myself. What with the door locked, there's no one else to assist."

Colleen pushed herself upright, tossed aside the covers, and reached to pop free the button directly beneath his chin. "Such troublesome things, buttons." Her mouth watered at the sight of the hollow of his neck. She freed another button and trailed a fingertip over the dark curls of hair she'd exposed before unfastening a third, a fourth.

A rumble of approval sounded deep in his chest. "They are."

"If I'm to set myself to such an onerous task, you must loosen my laces. I find this task takes my breath away." The last buttons fell free and she spread the placket wide. Leaning forward, she ran her palm over the firm muscles of his chest that flexed beneath her touch, then traced the trail of hair leading downward between the ridges of his stomach. Her finger caught at his waistband. "You're certain you only wish to change your shirt? These trousers?" She clucked, her hand hovering above the obvious bulge of his erection. "They're a bit… dirty."

"So they are." His hands fell on her shoulders and pulled, dropping her crosswise over his bare chest and crushing her breasts against him. Only a wisp of silk and an underbust corset separated them. Too much. She kissed the hollow of his throat while his frantic fingers worked the laces of her corset until it fell loose. "Sit back, Colleen, and extricate yourself from that garment so that I can see you breathe freely."

Laughing, she pushed back onto her knees to unhook the corset and toss it aside. "And?" She pulled her chemise over her head.

The look he gave her sent a shiver down her spine.

"Perfect." His hand ran up the side of her ribcage until it came to rest, cupping her breast. "In every way." His thumb brushed over its tip, slow and languid, sending a new flood of warmth between her legs. "But come closer. Finish what you proposed to start."

"Enjoying all the attention, are you?"

"And the view." His eyes filled with a gratifying, lust-crazed interest as his hands fell to her hips, urging her closer.

Bare, save for her stockings, she straddled him and leaned forward to lightly kiss his lips, dragging the sensitive tips of her nipples over the coarse hairs that sprinkled his chest. Her own breath caught as fire crawled across her skin.

He groaned and opened his mouth, inviting her in.

"Not yet." She nipped at his lip and backed away, swatting at his wandering hands to focus upon a task that grew more urgent by the minute. She caught at his waistband, unfastening its closure.

"Torture?" He all but strangled on the word. "Is that what you have planned?"

"A touch." Nick began to sit upright, but she pushed him

back onto the pillow. "This time, I'm in charge. Stay." Crawling backward, she dragged his trousers to his knees. A most impressive erection sprang free.

Reversing course, she slid her hands up the firm, strong muscles of his legs. As she reached their apex, she dipped her head to taste the hard length of his cock, reveling in the faint saltiness that met her tongue.

Nick's fingers threaded into her hair as if he would guide her to the very tip of his erection. She obliged, pulling as much of his length into her mouth as she could manage, toying with him, enjoying the groan that tore free from his lungs.

But this was not how she intended to finish what he'd started. Not today. Crawling back up the bed, she pulled open his bedside drawer, plucking forth a sheath and dropping it on his chest. "Suit up."

He grinned, tearing the paper and covering himself. "Caught that move earlier?"

"You'll find it's hard to hide anything from me." Once again, she straddled him, guiding the thick, blunt tip of his cock to her weeping entrance. Then, ever so slowly, she sank onto him, inch by sweet inch as he stretched her, filling her completely with a glorious pressure. "Aether," she breathed. He was so perfect. Too perfect.

He nudged upward, and she gasped as his hips pressed snug to hers.

She began to rock her hips, shifting him inside her ever so slightly as a delicious tension built while hundreds of thousands of nerves all cried out at the delightful friction. She met his gaze and saw wonder and lust and something she thought might be love all twisting and surging across his face.

Aether, she'd lost more than a small piece of her heart to this man.

"Kiss me, Colleen," Nick pleaded.

And she fell forward, dropping her hands to his shoulders

and sliding them beneath the linen of his shirt. Parting her lips, she tangled her tongue with his, all while the slow motion of their hips continued their sensual dance. Push, pull. Push, pull.

Until she needed more. His fingers tightened on her hips as he tore his mouth away, giving voice to the same thoughts that ran through her head. "Harder," he begged. "Please."

Colleen rose up onto her knees, letting him all but slip free. Then dropped as he rose, thrusting deep into her. She mewled her pleasure aloud as his fingers dug into her flesh pushing her away, then pulling her tight against his hips. "Is this what you want?"

"Yes," she cried, clutching his shoulders and spreading her thighs wider even as she rose for the next fall. "More!"

Nick thrust harder still.

Again and again their hips slapped together as coils of pleasure wound themselves tight. "Come for me, Colleen."

Already teetering on the edge, his words sent a frisson of electricity arcing through her body, and she threw her head backward, crying out her pleasure. Nick stiffened and surged upward, slamming into her as he yelled his own release.

As the world about them once again came into focus, she collapsed onto his chest. He wrapped his arms about her waist. "Next time," his voice was husky, "all the clothes come off."

"All," she promised, laughing softly against his neck as her stockinged feet brushed over his trouser-clad calves. Wondrously boneless, she rolled free.

<hr>

HOW HE COULD STILL MOVE AFTER SUCH amazing sex, Nick was uncertain. But he managed to clean himself, then shuck the remainder of his clothing before crawling back onto the bed and gathering Colleen close. He pulled the blanket over them both, wondering at how he'd managed to fall head over boots in love with such an amazing woman. "Now," he began, "about our future." He lifted her amber-clad hand to his mouth and pressed a kiss to the inside of her wrist. "Have you given any thought to becoming a Queen's agent? I've a contact, a married woman, who might provide you with insight that I cannot if you'd like to speak with her."

"I'd like that." Brushing a lock of hair from her face, Colleen drew breath. "While you were with Anna, Sorcha returned. About her neck—"

*Bang. Bang. Bang.*

Colleen froze.

He closed his eyes. *Dammit.* Ignoring *any* summons this evening was an impossibility.

*Bang. Bang. Bang.*

He lifted an eyebrow and tipped his head at the door. She *was* the only one who ought to be present in his room.

"Who is it?" Colleen called out. "I did ask for a light tea," she informed him under her breath.

"Robby, miss," the kitchen boy answered. "Is Mr. Torrington about?"

She pulled the sheet to her chin when an eyeball appeared at the keyhole. "Er."

Nick sighed. He'd have to speak with the boy about that bad habit. "Present," he called.

So much for a perception of privacy.

A brief moment of silence followed before Robby spoke again. "I've been sent to let you know there's a package, sir. One marked 'urgent'. Hopsworth placed it upon a table in the library. He's rather upset. It's leaking, sir."

"Leaking?" Colleen whispered. Her eyebrows drew together.

His thoughts echoed hers. "This can't be good." He forced himself to his feet. "I'll be down momentarily, Robby."

"Shall I bring that tea now, miss?"

"Yes," Colleen called, though feebly and with color high

upon her cheekbones. She glanced at him. "I've not eaten since breakfast."

"Nor have I. Save me a bite." He threw open the wardrobe and yanked out a clean shirt and a pair of trousers. A glance at the mantle clock informed him it was just past ten o'clock. A bit late for parcel deliveries.

Colleen also slid from the bed and began to dress, pulling on dark trousers, a shirt and a corded cincher—not a corset—to gather in the excess cloth. Clothing better suited to leaping across rooftops than her earlier skirts.

She caught his glance. "Don't worry. I won't leave without you. Go see about this package."

"So much for any pretense of propriety beneath my parents' roof." He pulled on a waistcoat, shrugged on his holster and TTX pistol and shoved his feet into his boots. "If Hopsworth knows we're both in here, the rest of the household is certain to have their suspicions as well." Perhaps they should have made an effort to muffle their cries, but he found it hard to regret her moans of pleasure.

Her lips parted, and Nick saw a hint of anxiety creep onto her face. "I can't—"

"I'm not pressuring you, merely pointing out the obvious." He tipped her chin up. "And the reason I'll not be bothering with the trellis in the future. Remember, it doesn't matter what my family wants. Or yours. What's between us is ours alone to decide." He dipped his head and kissed her, pouring devotion into it, hoping their dreams for the future would align. His heart gave a great thud when she rose onto her toes and returned the kiss with an equal amount of passion.

"Mr. Torrington?" This time the interruption was accompanied by a huff of impatience outside the door, then a light rapping began. Hopsworth himself had arrived outside their door. The matter must truly be urgent. "I intercepted the kitchen boy who insisted you ordered tea. I really must stress that this is a pressing matter, not one that can be addressed at leisure."

"A moment, Hopsworth," Nick called. With a sigh, he dropped his hand from her face and stepped back. "I'd best see what is wrong with this package before our steam butler begins to ding with impatience and stirs up the entire household."

"Please do," she said. "I'm not at all certain Hopsworth can be convinced to overlook our indiscretions or the presence of a cat sìth."

"If we marry, we'll be certain to acquire steam staff that can be customized to *our* specific and unique needs."

"Go." She swatted at him, but he caught the hint of a smile. "We'll speak about such things later. For now, we have work."

"HAS my father returned from his club?" Nick asked. They would need to take to the roofs within the hour, and he hated to leave his mother alone in the townhouse so soon after an attack. Not that there was anything to be done save to offer moral support by patting her hand while she sat by Anna's bedside in a silent vigil.

"He's been sent for, sir. Expected at any moment." Hopsworth rushed past Nick down the hall, wheels clacking, intent upon fulfilling his duties, lest the entire British hierarchy crumble because a gentleman opened a door before his butler. "Many, many apologies for the," gears grated in the steam butler's throat, "interruption. The package arrived by human courier. He insisted it be brought to your attention as a time sensitive issue."

"Let me know when my father returns," Nick said. "That will be all, Hopsworth."

The door closed softly behind him as he advanced, eyeing the paper-wrapped package bound up with coarse string upon the library's table. A dark stain spread outward from a lower corner. Not a promising sign. A tight band of dread wrapped about his chest, ratcheting tighter as he slid free the folded note tucked beneath its knotted bow.

The message was sealed with red wax and imprinted with a triangle. *No.* The Greek letter delta, the symbol for change. Had he been contacted by CEAP? Possible. *Someone* had taken note of his activities and wished to convey a message.

Bile crept into his throat as he broke the seal.

*Your interest in our organization has been brought to my attention. Though our methods are unorthodox, they facilitate the acquisition of knowledge that would otherwise remain shrouded by myth and dismissed as superstition.*

*One of our members has recently been demoted for failing to properly secure his research and findings. Should you accept this invitation to fill his position, you will be privy to the specifics of his work. Though a procedure still in the experimental phase, we have what you seek. Not a treatment, but a cure.*

*An interview, should you choose to proceed, has been arranged. A carriage awaits. Come alone. Come immediately. Tell no one.*

*Should you choose to decline, cease your inquiries. Outside interference is not tolerated.*

*Damn it.* He should never have trusted Dr. Farquhar to the constabulary. By snatching him off the street, he'd done nothing but hand him back to his vengeful overlords. The mad scientist *did* possess what Nick sought, what Anna needed.

A cure.

Was it not an electrical pacer the man had developed, but something more? Something better? Whatever discovery the mad scientist had made, at the heart of it were the cat sìth. What biological truth hid behind the myth of a shape-shifting feline said to possess nine lives? This shadow committee knew.

Dr. Farquhar knew. And presumably one Mr. Cornelius Pierpont knew.

Clenching his jaw, he pulled a penknife from his pocket and cut through the string. With the tip of his knife, he unwrapped the box and flipped open the lid.

Shock rippled through him at the stark warning that lay before him. A human heart rested on a bed of bloodied tissue paper. One freshly removed. Glistening dark red with bands of whitish fat, veins threaded across its surface, branching and wrapping across the muscular tissue on their—former—mission to deliver blood. At its crown, the attached blood vessels—the aortic and pulmonary trunks, the venae cavae—had been roughly cut, hacked from the chest of—

Dr. Farquhar? A cold sweat gathered between his shoulder blades. No. The note had mentioned outside interference. Did this heart belong to the man's wife?

Either way, this was a cold-blooded and calculated murder. The need to report this "warning" warred with the advice contained within its accompanying message. If he delivered this to his superiors, CEAP was certain to retaliate. Neither, however, could he contact the local authorities with ramblings about a scientific committee making inquiries into the possibilities of shape-shifting. He himself had been tasked with infiltrating this very sub-committee, and such suspicions were to remain confidential.

Shock shifted to anger, and blood began to pound and roar in his ears. All he wished to do was provide his sister with a better —and longer—life. To stop the exploitation of rare animals—and perhaps humans. He'd long known it would eventually require him to walk into the midst of a predatory community of individuals who had the temerity to call themselves scientists and who thought nothing of lives lost, rare animals poached, or patients denied access to secret medical advances.

Unacceptable.

The moment to act had finally arrived.

A scream rent the air.

Nick jerked his head up to stare at the heavily curtained window that faced the street, listening. A second outcry followed the first. More shouts, each joining the next, grew louder by the second. His stomach twisted. The timing could be no accident. Was the grisly parcel not enough?

With a curse, he dropped the lid and loosely wrapped the paper about the box. Yanking open the drawer of a nearby cabinet, he hid the stained package and message within, lest another member of the household stumble across it. He slammed the drawer shut at the very moment the library door banged open.

Steam billowed from under Hopsworth's collar as he rolled across the rug at a furious clip, flapping his articulated hands. "Sir, come quick!" He careened back toward the door. "A catastrophe of immense proportions has landed upon our doorstep!"

Nick ran past Hopsworth into the foyer and heaved open the front door. He froze at the sight before him. His second guess as to the origin of the heart had been on the mark.

A pool of light cast by the streetlamp highlighted what remained of Mrs. Farquhar impaled upon the iron spikes of the fence before his home. Back arched, arms out-flung, her sightless eyes stared upward. Gray skirts and long, dark hair fluttered in the wind, her chest a gaping, raw and *empty* cavity.

A bold and public statement drawing much unwanted attention to his family home… within which the woman's heart lay, wrapped and hidden.

*Shit. Shit. Shit.*

"…fell from the sky!"

"A dirigible…"

"…swooped low and someone shoved…"

His eyes swept the scene before him. The engines of steam carriages idled and the gears of crank hacks clacked as onlookers paused to stare, those on foot edging ever closer to the gruesome tableau before them. Crime the likes of which was never visited upon Mayfair. A well-dressed lady had collapsed upon the pavement at the sight, and her weeping daughter waved smelling salts beneath her nose. A gentleman brandished his cane in the air while yelling for the constabulary.

On the far side of the road sat a richly appointed clockwork horse-drawn carriage. The man perched upon the driver's seat boldly met Nick's stare, his expression expectant. A slight tip of his head was all the invitation Nick received.

The damning evidence in his possession was meant to make it impossible to decline. He returned the nod, lifted a finger, then turned to climb back into the house—a moment too late to spare his mother.

"Nicholas?" She appeared in the door, craning her neck to look behind him. "What is going—?" Her hands flew her mouth, stifling a scream.

Colleen, eyes wide, stood directly behind his mother. "Is that—?"

"It is." Arms wide, Nick forced them both back into the foyer. "Hopsworth," he called. "My coat and hat."

"Yes, sir!" Still wobbling on his wheels, the steam butler zipped off to the cloakroom.

He turned back to the women. "I need to leave. Immediately. Work calls."

"But there's a body!" His mother's hands flapped. "What am I supposed to *do*? Your father isn't home yet."

"He'll be here soon. In the meantime, cooperate fully with the police. Make my excuses. It will look bad, my absence, but it can't be helped. Invent a medical emergency." He kissed his mother's forehead. "I can't explain. But, please, for Anna's sake."

His mother's face grew stony, but she nodded.

"Work?" Colleen repeated flatly. "Has this anything to do with—"

"Yes." He cut her off, catching her wrist and tugging her aside. Fully dressed and geared up—though a dressing gown was strategically wrapped about her to conceal her non-traditional attire—she was ready to leap across rooftops to her uncle's home. He leaned close to whisper in her ear. "In the library is a cabinet filled with drawers. Third to the right, second from the bottom is a box that holds what can only be Mrs. Farquhar's heart along with the message accompanying it. Read it, then burn it." A risk to share such information, but she deserved to know.

The blood drained from her face. "CEAP?"

"Perhaps. Either way I've received an ultimatum." The clock ticked, counting each second that passed. How long would the driver wait? Another such opportunity would not present itself. "I'm not supposed to speak with anyone about it, but I need your help. Please dispose of the contents of that drawer; they cannot be found in my—or my family's—possession." Rifling through his pockets, he turned up a punch card and pressed it into her hand. "This is the address of a colleague, a Mr. Jackson. He's aware of my assignment. Write to him before you go... out," he added, for her face informed him she would not be waiting for his return. Her uncle's safe would be cracked open and searched this very night. It worried him, and yet such was the very reason he'd been so determined to win her hand. "Explain our situation. Stress the need for urgency." Not caring who watched, he dipped his head and caught her lips with a quick kiss. "Be careful."

Hopsworth was back, frowning. "Sir—"

But Nick had no time for protestations. He grabbed his hat and coat—and was gone.

CHAPTER SEVENTEEN

THE NOTE THAT LAY beside the blood-tinged box was written in her uncle's hand. Proof that he was mixed up in the group Nick sought to infiltrate. He might be the very man conducting this "interview".

Heart in her throat, she dashed to the window and flung the curtain aside, ready to throw open the sash and call a warning, but there was no trace of the carriage that had waited across the street for Nick, its driver noticeably detached from the frenzy upon the doorstep. Combined with Isabella's warning, it could mean only one thing.

Her uncle *knew* of their presence at the burned-out building. Had the scientist himself identified them? Had the body on the doorstep been his wife?

It didn't matter; her uncle's message was clear.

A cold frost settled over her. All these years, she'd known he was a merciless reptile, but she hadn't thought him so barbaric as to order a woman's heart ripped from her chest. For there was no chance a man who prized neatness and order had wielded the knife. A minion with no such misgivings had been set to the task of the woman's execution and disposal.

Who was her uncle to judge another when he'd spent the past few years stealing *her* hard-earned money, poaching upon *her* property, sacrificing the hapless cat sìth who roamed free in *her* woods all to fund Dr. Farquhar's research so that he might... what?

She glanced again at the note.

*A cure?* Her mind struggled with the concept. A cure implied there was a way to return Anna's heart to full working order. No device could accomplish that. Which meant that whatever was in that rosewood box was *not* an electrical pacing device. But what could restore a damaged heart's ability to beat? What exactly had she transported beneath her bustle?

Her mind recalled the broken, smoke-stained shards of glass that had littered the floor of the charred basement laboratory, the pools of liquid, the threadlike material that floated, curling and twisting within the liquid, and she shuddered. They'd missed a key clue, but she couldn't begin to fathom what it was.

Sorcha leapt onto the table and sniffed the distasteful package. She pulled back her lips and gave it a baleful stare.

"Agreed," Colleen said. "Tonight, we put an end to my uncle's crimes. And then there are others who must pay." The memory of scorched skulls lining the charred shelves of Dr. Farquhar's laboratory could never be erased. "We must also locate the mad scientist and drag forth answers." Perhaps some good might be yet salvaged on Anna's behalf. "After which we take back my lands and your forest. I'll not allow another cat sìth to be harmed to serve my uncle's selfishness and arrogance."

The Queen's agents might expect Nick to play the long game, to infiltrate this shadow committee and trace its many tentacles, but his sister was running out of time. Faster to break into her uncle's safe, retrieve any relevant papers that lay within —suspicious property deeds, accountings of funds paid to mysterious men, documents relevant to her inheritance—and drag them into the light of day before he had the chance to destroy any evidence linking him to illegal activities.

Tossing the letter into the small fire burning upon the grate, she scribbled a quick note to Mr. Jackson letting him know the particulars of their situation. Thinking of what Nick might face alone made her stomach churn, no matter how many times reason reminded her that he was a trained Queen's agent. She too would face risks creeping into her uncle's study. What if someone was stationed inside, waiting? But if he could trust her to handle herself alone, she could return the favor.

Wrapped in bloodstained paper and cardboard, the cold, still heart weighed heavily in her hands as she began to climb the stairs toward the aviary. She had to try. Tonight might be the only night such an opportunity presented itself. A man who would order the murder of another man's wife might easily turn upon his own, particularly now that her uncle had guessed—or at least suspected—his own wife's collusion. Isabella was no longer safe. There'd be no leaving London before this serpent had been slain. Time to breach her uncle's study and discover exactly what he was about before he slithered home.

Tucking away her tinted spectacles, she cracked open the hatch and climbed into the aviary, happy to have Sorcha shadowing her once more. She plucked a skeet pigeon from its roost and inserted the message into an ankle canister. *Snap*, the punch card with Mr. Jackson's address clicked into place. She wound the bird's mechanism and tossed it through the window, watching as it took to the night air.

She set aside the dressing gown and checked her tool belt one last time. Lock picks, Rapunzel rope, pouches of various other items, and her precious Keller stethoscope—audiologically enhanced at great personal expense—all securely hooked. She'd yet to lay fingers upon her uncle's personal safe, but she'd seen the strongbox delivered and knew precisely where it lay.

There was no more avoiding the horrid package. Sliding it

into a cloth sack, she tied it about her hips. She might have burned the letter, but she had other plans for Mrs. Farquhar's heart. Over her shoulder, she slung a map case, one she'd found in Nick's study that would allow her to carry away any important or incriminating documents. With her dirk in her boot and her hooded cape about her shoulders, it was time to take to the rooftops.

Overhead, a dark shadow passed—a hungry pteryform soaring toward the Thames, ready to fish out a kraken or two for breakfast, their preference for the cephalopods the only reason the city council did not launch an armed force to terminate their presence in the city. Stars struggled to shine through the haze that filled the nighttime London sky, and the running lights of several Sparrow-class personal dirigibles fared little better. Those who could afford them—like her uncle—risked their own safety to discreetly travel to evening activities.

Colleen stepped from the aviary onto the roof and slid her hands into a powder-filled pouch. She dusted her hands and lifted her face to the cool night air, sensing the direction of the gentle breeze that blew through London. Taking a deep breath, she stretched, reveling in the anticipation of freedom that always accompanied a long, complex rooftop run.

"Riggit?" she asked Sorcha. *Ready?*

The cat sìth crouched, braced to spring forward.

Colleen took off at a running start along the ridges of the roofs, leaping onto, over and around row after row of chimney pots that delineated one terraced home from the next. Tail held high, Sorcha shadowed her every move. A controlled slide down the sharp slope of a slate-tiled roof... a fast run along the edge... a dash past a heated rooftop greenhouse. Over and again until she reached a corner tower. Crouching, she gripped the eaves of the roof to drop onto a narrow balcony.

A deep breath. An assessment. Then she continued. Corbel to cornice to lintel, she dropped toward the street, jumping off the rounded finial of an iron fence onto the pavement. The cat sìth followed. Lifting her hood and dodging lamplight, Colleen darted through traffic with Sorcha at her heels. A few quick steps and she was down a narrow passageway—one with a drainpipe. She paused, letting Sorcha leap onto her shoulder before she began to climb. In seconds, both of them were safe upon the rooftops, once again leaping across slate tiles and clay chimney pots.

And finally arrived at her uncle's rooftop where the dirigible stood upon the landing pad. Wary, she crept closer and peered inside. A hasty attempt to wipe blood from the jump seat had been made, but there was no mistaking the rusty-brown stain that clung to the upholstery's stitching. Though she could prove nothing, there was no doubt in her mind that this very dirigible had been used to drop Mrs. Farquhar's body onto the Stafford's doorstep. Mr. Vanderburn might have piloted, but who had assisted? And did they now patrol the interior of her uncle's home?

Her stomach gave a slight twist. Never before had she taken a job where she might encounter deadly force. But, she reminded herself, Mr. Vanderburn—and his assistant—were employees of her uncle's. They wouldn't kill her simply for being caught in his home, would they? Still, she would take extra care.

There could be no creeping through its halls; she'd have to make a direct entry. Thankful her uncle's study faced the back of the house, she pulled on her leather gloves, then looped the Rapunzel rope about a chimney and secured its other end to her belt. Lowering herself onto her stomach, she slid—feet first— down the pitch of the roof, dangling from the eaves and waiting until Sorcha climbed onto her shoulders. Slowly, she dropped them both down the rope until they hung outside the window of her uncle's study. Smart, to have installed a lock, but it was no match for her picks, not even while she was hanging like a spider from a thread and working the lock one-handed. She pried open the window, glanced inside to be certain no one was about, then nodded to the cat sìth. Sorcha leapt into a room lit only by the fading glow of a single Lucifer lamp. Colleen swung in behind her, dropping noiselessly into a crouch upon the floor, listening.

The room was empty but for a mechanical brush—now with an overlarge feline riding upon it—that whirred its way back and forth across the room, grooming the carpet.

Reassured by Sorcha's nonchalance, she took a step forward, but the small hairs on the back of her neck lifted.

The house was eerily quiet.

Suspiciously quiet.

There ought to be a low-level hum of *human* activity, but all she heard was the *thrum* and *chuff* of the steam servants.

She sniffed the air and caught the faint scent of warm sugar and dried currants—spotted dick and custard—along with the fragrance of bergamot-laced tea, a favorite. Had the servants gathered in the kitchen for a late tea of their own volition? Or had they been confined there?

Likely the later, increasing the odds that Mr. Vanderburn walked a patrol by one hundred percent. Were this any other mission, she would have turned back, but she refused to leave. Not until she'd plundered her uncle's safe and dragged the proof of his misdeeds into the moonlight.

Not once had she entered this inner sanctum without a summons; she'd had no wish to tip her hand inside her own home. But all too often she'd been called to stand before his desk to be berated for her behavior or, of late, for her refusal to consider a particular suitor. Over the years, she'd taken note of wear patterns, observed which ornaments shifted upon her uncle's shelves. And which did not.

Though a relic of times long past, not once had the medieval helmet of a distant ancestor acquired the tiniest speck of dust.

She flipped up the visor and rolled her eyes at the predictable lever concealed within. Grasping it, she pulled... and the bookshelf swung open—silent upon well-oiled hinges—to reveal the Crypt Safe. A smile turned up the corners of her mouth. Advertised as unbreakable, not one had been breached. Or so they claimed. Colleen had cracked two.

Time to scour the depths of her uncle's safe.

She pressed the thin membrane stretched across the Keller stethoscope's bell to the cold, steel door and focused on the faint sounds of the lock wheels as they each clicked into place. Even with her many talents, catching and identifying all ten numbers in order was a challenge. But in the end, the safe gave up its secrets.

The heavy door swung open and there, in pride of place upon the top shelf, sat the rosewood box. Her jaw dropped. How was it possible? Had he tracked down the buyer himself to snatch back that which had been stolen from him?

Though her fingers itched to peer inside, piles of documents awaited. She forced herself to rifle through them, looking for cold, hard evidence of his wrongdoings. And she found it. A stack of papers signed by none other than Cornelius Pierpont agreeing to the sale of a cure for "sluggish hearts" to a number of prominent gentlemen.

But why would such documents be in her uncle's possession?

She squinted at the scrawled signature—and gasped. It was her uncle's handwriting.

If Lord Maynard and Cornelius Pierpont were one and the same, *that* meant he'd stolen from the very shadow committee he chaired, deliberately plotting to profit from the death and suffering of others. He'd bought the "cure" from the scientist's wife, framed her to take the blame, then conveniently murdered her to send a "message". All the while the "cure" sat securely within his own safe.

The betrayal struck her hard in the chest, making her heart-beat stumble and her lungs struggle for breath.

Over and over men had demonstrated there were profits to be made selling snake oil and sham cures to desperate individuals. But the value of a working cure selectively distributed only to those with deep pockets? Priceless. And therefore irresistible.

Her uncle was a despicable man.

She'd carried that rosewood box through a step on the obfuscation chain, all on his behalf. The thought that she'd aided her uncle burned with the heat of a thousand suns. How could Mr. Witherspoon have agreed to such a task? Had he not known? Did that excuse him from complicity? She'd consider the moral implications later for, as fast as righteous anger had flared, it quickly cooled, turning to terror. If her uncle was so quick to order murder, what might become of her, were she caught rifling through his safe?

She picked up her pace, locating the property deed to Craigieburn and the documents naming her uncle as guardian and trustee. Quickly, she rolled them together with the most damning of contracts signed in Pierpont's name and stuffed them into the map tube.

Then, unhooking the burlap sack from her belt, she swapped the blood-stained cardboard box for the one of carved rosewood. Like Pandora's box, it was impossible not to look inside. She lifted the lid. Upon a padded velvet cushion rested a glass vial filled with a clear fluid and a tangle of white threads.

No. Not threads. Threads didn't move.

She dropped the vial with a sharp yelp, then clamped her hand over her mouth as the last meal she'd eaten curdled in her stomach.

Worms. Her uncle was peddling *worms*?

How was this a cure for anything? She'd heard of tapeworm eggs swallowed by women unhappy with their girth, but never of the radical step producing positive results. If anything, reports were negative, when women found their bodily organs riddled with cysts.

Remembering the worms from the fire, she shuddered.

Somewhere in the bowels of the Lister Institute a parasitologist must exist, hunched over a microscope, studying distasteful organisms of all kinds. He—or she—would wish to study this.

Colleen took a deep breath. Swallowed. Then retrieved the vial, skin crawling, and dropped it into the burlap sack before tying it to her belt. She gave a shudder, thinking of the distasteful items she carried about this evening. Shoving the wriggling creatures from her mind, she reached for a velvet pouch that sat deep within the safe.

Sorcha hissed a warning and leapt from the carpet sweeper. Colleen was out of time. Slamming the safe closed, she spun the dial and yanked on the lever. As she turned to follow Sorcha to the window, the bookcase closed behind her.

The door banged open. "Stop right there, Colleen."

The cat sìth—fur standing on end—let out a yowl that scraped every nerve ending raw, then leapt to freedom.

*Mr. Glover?* Mr. Glover was her uncle's minion? Regrets and recriminations could wait until later. She didn't turn her head to look, but reached for the window frame, seconds from freedom, when—

*Bang!*

Sharp daggers of glass rained down upon her, and her hand slipped as a strange numbness washed over her right arm. She leapt onto the sill, pulling with her other arm, about to jump blindly, when a rough hand grabbed her hair and dragged her back into the study.

With a twist and a shove, he tossed her to the ground. There was a faint click. "Don't move." A revolver appeared before her face and, behind it, Mr. Glover's enraged face.

She clutched at her limp arm as a tight pressure built. She'd been shot by an ex-lover? *Aether.* She wouldn't have thought he had the nerve. But her burning arm, the hot and wet sleeve beneath her palm, informed her otherwise. She was bleeding. Bleeding badly.

"You wouldn't," she challenged, rolling onto her side and curling her knees to her chest. No need to feign the agony she felt. She slid the palm of her good arm over her trousers, wiping the blood free before reaching for the dirk concealed in her boot. Shaking fingers found its hilt and clutched at its leather-wrapped handle. Years had passed since her father trained her in its use, and she'd never before needed the blade. Excellent reflexes, keen senses and speed had kept her from any direct confrontations on the job. But she always wore the blade, because she'd be damned if men like Mr. Glover would ever win.

"Why not? It isn't as if I'd marry you now that you've welcomed another man into your bed."

"Fool." She slid the blade free and slashed his ankle. "Did you think you were the first?"

Mr. Glover screamed—anger or agony, she couldn't tell—as she scrambled onto her feet, but Colleen hadn't taken more than one step when he launched himself at her, bodily slamming her to the ground, knocking the air from her lungs and sending her dirk skittering across the floor.

She rolled, clawing at his eyes.

He caught her wrists and pinned them to the ground, holding her down with the weight of his body. "I should have been the last," he growled. "You were promised to me. All I had to do was—"

Another man, gasping, ran into the room. In his hand was a long, metal rod. It hummed. Ominously. "Enough!" he yelled, his eyes wild. A shock of white hair rose from his head. "We need her. Stick with the plan."

"You!" It was Dr. Farquhar, the man who'd tried to rip Sorcha's carrier from her hands. Her last lover might be a possessive, jealous man sewn together by a thin thread of incipient madness, but Dr. Farquhar had long ago fallen down the rabbit hole of insanity.

Grudgingly, Mr. Glover stood, yanking Colleen onto her feet. Blood dripped from her fingertips. So much blood. But she would fight to the end. And the stupid man had no idea how close they were to the shelves. Ignoring the pain, she reached behind her. A book met her hand. She smashed it into Mr. Glover's face, and his hand flew open, releasing her.

"Witch!" he yelled, lunging.

But she slipped away and lifted the tome over her head, struggling against the numbness. Blood ran down her wounded arm and dripped onto the rug as her heart pounded. Escape was impossible. Still, she had to try. Whatever the two of them had planned for her couldn't be pleasant. "Out of my way! Both of you!"

But the scientist only stared back at her, his head tipped. A demented light glittered in his eyes, and a shadow of a smile touched his lips. "Such spectacular eyes. All this time, he kept you from me. All of them did. Only when they witness it for themselves will they believe."

"Quit your rambling, old man!" Mr. Glover limped across the room and ripped the humming rod from the scientist's hands. "If you had married me, Colleen, I would have protected you from this."

"From what, exactly?" she spat. Her arm began to shake with the effort of holding the book aloft. She stood no chance against an electrified weapon.

"From becoming a laboratory rat." He pointed the strange rod directly at her.

Her eyebrows drew together, struggling to process his words. They intended to... Dr. Farquhar was to be allowed to... stop her heart? The room began to spin. If she could make the front door, fling herself into the street, perhaps the good will of strangers might save her. With a war cry worthy of Boudicca herself, Colleen heaved the book at Mr. Glover and ran for the door.

But as she passed, the humming weapon met her side and a loud buzzing filled her ears. Every muscle tensed, then she felt herself falling toward the floor.

## CHAPTER EIGHTEEN

*N*ICK GROUND HIS TEETH and muttered to himself as the carriage wound its way—slowly, painfully—though the chaos of humanity and technology that thronged the evening streets of London. Banging on the roof of the carriage had done nothing to quicken its pace, and he suspected the driver had been given specific orders not to arrive before an appointed hour. The vehicle came to a stop before a familiar passageway in Hatton Garden at precisely ten o'clock.

This was London's jewelry quarter, famous for its underground tunnels, vaults, and rooms. But in its darker recesses lurked other infamous locations. Tucked away down this particular dark, narrow and dimly lit path lay The Three-Eyed Bat. An outwardly respectable pub during business hours, it became a den of iniquity when the sun fell. Years ago, when he was a new, untried agent, he'd chased a man down this very alleyway nearly losing his life when the criminal turned on him with a knife, striking for his neck. If he looked, would there still be a gouge in the brick wall?

The door swung open, and Mr. Vanderburn stood before him,

blocking his exit. It gave Nick no pleasure to see his worst suspicions confirmed, that Lord Maynard did indeed control this shadow committee.

"Before we proceed, Mr. Torrington," the henchman said, "I have orders to confiscate your weapons."

Nick bristled. "Unacceptable."

"Very well," Vanderburn said, his voice flat. "The driver will see you home. I will convey your regrets to Miss Stewart. Best wishes for your sister's continued health." He began to close the door.

Nick thrust out his hand, holding it open. The cold wind blew shards of ice beneath his collar, freezing the air in his lungs. How was it possible? "Lady Stewart is here?"

"She is expected shortly." Vanderburn's dead eyes gave away nothing, but it was clear the man could read his. "You think to wait, but it will do you no good. They will divert her elsewhere."

His hackles rose. Duty might forbid he comply, but love insisted. He could no sooner leave Colleen to her uncle's schemes than he could stop breathing. Nor could he turn away from anything that might help heal his sister's heart. Gritting his teeth, he drew his TTX pistol from its holster and handed it over. Down this path lay disaster.

Vanderburn turned the unique weapon over in his hands before sliding it into his coat pocket. Nick caught a glimpse of a holster containing a standard revolver. "Blades as well."

He growled. One knife followed another, each clattering to the ground as a small pile grew at the henchman's feet. "Satisfied?"

"For now." Vanderburn made no attempt to collect them. "This way, Mr. Torrington." He turned.

Between the cobblestones beneath Nick's feet, a sluggish fluid oozed, glowing with a faint bluish light and leading the way to the old pub. There, small panes of wavy glass emitted the warm glow of oil lanterns and coal fires. A cast iron bracket held aloft the winged sign, as it flapped and creaked in the night wind. Every so often, the bat's gilded eyes caught a stray beam of light, flashing gold. His stomach tied itself another knot. Only for Colleen and his family would he violate every instinct that screamed "Trap!"

"If you'll take a seat, I'll let Lord Maynard know you've arrived." Vanderburn tugged on the worn, brass handle and waved Nick inside.

The dark, paneled room was filled with smoke and gentlemen of dubious morality. He ignored the server behind the bar, made his way to a heavy oak table near the fireplace, and sat beneath a low ceiling held up by rough-hewn beams. The pub was rumored to date to the reign of King George the First and, from appearances, had not once been updated. As he waited, the room closed in on him.

Colleen would have left immediately for the aviary, to send the message before leaping across roofs to reach her uncle's house. But it was a move her uncle had been expecting. Nick glared at the fire. The bloody package had been a diversion, designed to separate them. He should have anticipated such a move. Wrapped up in emotions from lust and love to disgust and fear, they'd both missed it. She'd been caught, and now an entirely different evening would unfold. This meeting was less interview than it was a hostage negotiation, and Nick wouldn't like the terms.

A gust of cold air set the flames dancing as Lord Maynard entered the pub. Vanderburn lurked beside the door while the earl joined Nick, lowering himself into a chair. His eyes were irritated, impatient and set in a face that appeared all too capable of plotting a woman's demise.

"Interesting gifts you've sent." Nick felt no need for pretense. Neither, however, could he afford to antagonize the gentleman now in control of both his fiancée and a potential cure for his sister. And so he suppressed his anger and kept his words benign. Any chance Nick had at convincing Maynard to admit him to the inner circle relied upon him keeping his personal feelings about the man and his project locked inside a chained box and buried fifty feet deep. "Original. Well-designed to catch the attention of a man you wish to offer employment."

"I thought as much." Colleen's uncle tapped his fingers on the table between them, sizing up the man before him. "Mrs. Farquhar failed the simplest of tests, betraying years of her husband's work for a sum that netted her very little in the way of funds. I considered letting her run free but, alas, she knew too much. It took her husband years to unearth the secret of those curious cats' longevity, and I won't chance that information falling into other hands."

*Failed a test.* Maynard himself had arranged the opportunity for his scientist's wife to betray herself? Were the earl and Pierpont one and the same? When Nick had stormed the man's office to lay claim to his niece, had he stood—as before—mere feet away from a particular rosewood box? He struggled to keep his face impassive. "Hence the warning that arrived with your offer of a position."

"Interview," Maynard reminded him. His eyes narrowed. "You were sighted at the scene of the fire, and yet are so much more than an inconvenient witness of which I might easily dispose."

"Trained in cardiophysiology. Sworn to uphold the law. Engaged to your niece." Nick leaned forward. "Hence your decision to recruit me."

"As we're being blunt, yes." Maynard smirked. "The fire, though distressing to a certain organization, presents me—and therefore you—with a unique opportunity to strike out on our own. I alone have access to the cure."

Did he? Colleen might have been captured in his study, but there was no chance the earl himself had captured her. Nor did Vanderburn have his fiancée in his grips. If she had managed to breach her uncle's safe before she was apprehended—and there was, as yet, no proof that she'd been caught—this purported cure might now be in another's hands. But whose? Two particular men came to mind. A mad scientist and the man who'd campaigned to marry Colleen, despite his obvious hatred of her.

"What about the minions who carry out your orders?"

"They answer to me. Like you, they've little option but to accept my terms." The earl's words were bold, but a tremor of uncertainty ran beneath them. Were the reins slipping from his fingers?

"Is that so?" It was time to begin negotiations, to lull the man into believing Nick was willing to collaborate for the right compensation. "Farquhar's work might be dependent upon your funds, but why would you expect Glover's continued loyalty? He expected to become family, to gain control of Craigieburn, of its lands… of its inhabitants. At last glimpse, he was not handling disappointment well."

Maynard's lips twisted. "There will be profit for all. If he cannot accept a new role…" *Then he'd be the next example.* No need to speak the words aloud. "Work with me, Torrington, and you'll be a rich man. No need to rely upon your father or," his lip curled, "a government position to pay your debts. You'd be surprised what a man will pay for an exclusive and limited remedy to keep his heart beating."

*Profiting on the sick and desperate. Lovely.*

"I have investments," Nick countered. "Money alone is insufficient inducement."

The earl glowered. "How many more heart seizures will your sister survive? Ten? Two? Or will the next one snuff out that fragile spark of life?"

Beneath the table, Nick balled his hand into a fist and resisted an urge to throttle the man. "Your scientist appears mad, attempting to rip your niece's pet cat from her arms. What could possibly induce me to allow him to lay a single finger upon my sister?"

"Ah, but the creature is so much more than a mere house cat." The earl cocked his head. "I'd no idea my sister had stumbled into such a windfall when she ran away with a Scottish laird." His lips pressed together. "Glover proved himself a sluggard when he chose to hand over Colleen's particular beast to Farquhar rather than make another trip north. But not wrong. Those cats hold the key."

Another reason to hate the man. "What could a cat possibly possess that would cure my sister?" Speaking the words aloud, watching the earl's face as he said them, was the confirmation he needed. There was no electrical pacer. The cure was biological. But what? And how?

Movement beyond the pub's windows caught Vanderburn's attention—and Nick's—but when the guard dismissed it with a glance and settled back to his post, Nick forced his full attention back to Maynard's arrogant face.

"I don't think so, Torrington." The earl puffed out his chest. "I'll not be sharing any details until we've reached an agreement. But wipe the doubts from your mind. Dr. Farquhar may dance at the edge of sanity, but he's proven his life-saving technique again and again. I witnessed one such experiment with my own eyes. It works."

"On cats?" Nick lifted an eyebrow in challenge. He hadn't missed the animal cages or their unfortunate contents.

"And dogs. We've also managed to revive a fox, a weasel and a badger. Most notably, a monkey acquired from the London Zoo. Human trials are the next logical step."

*Of course they were.* And a man who thought nothing of

murder and arson wouldn't let the question of medical consent stand in his way.

"But Farquhar needs closer supervision and direction. Of late, his mind has taken a maddening turn, veering from the scientific toward the realm of fantasy. I'm in need of a scientific-minded man with a clear head."

"Who has connections to the scientific and medical community." Nick crossed his arms, leaning back in his chair. "You're proposing a partnership?"

"No." Maynard's eyebrows slammed together. "The cure is in *my* possession, the knowledge under *my* control. It is *my* funds that will pay to establish and outfit a new laboratory."

"That may be," Nick said. "But recall that I am engaged to *your* niece. Not only will you and I soon be family, but in two days, she will control the Scottish property upon which you rely."

The man's eyes narrowed and his lips pressed into a thin line.

*Damnit.* The cure *was* reliant upon the cat sìth. "I expect convincing my future wife to look past your questionable land management will require much work on my part." It was an impossible task. "But for equal terms, I'm willing to convince her." He wasn't. "She might find it curious to learn her uncle is so keen to profit off her lands. Is the coffer nearly empty?"

Maynard glared at him.

Beyond the ripples of the pub's glass windows, two men passed carrying a large, rolled carpet upon their shoulders. One of a length and width that might accommodate the form of a woman. His heart began to pound. Was this how Colleen was *expected* to arrive?

Nick shoved his chair back and began to rise.

"Sit," Maynard commanded. "You'll not make it past the door."

A glance at the door informed him the earl was correct. In

Vanderburn's hand was Nick's TTX pistol. The man's eyes dared him to make a move.

"If she's injured…" Nick began, then realized his mistake.

"Care for her, do you?" The earl shook his head. "A shame you let that chink in the armor show. You ought to be more careful. Sentimentality is a weakness, and Colleen has been mine. A final tie to my sister that I ought to sever, but I've found it curious to observe her preternatural sight and reflexes as she's busied herself about London's nightscape, working to fund this very enterprise."

Nick held still, for a predator's stare was upon him. *Follow the money.* Lord Aldridge's speculation had had the precision of a kraken sharpshooter. If only they'd known her uncle ought to be considered a target.

"I find myself facing a curious dilemma," Maynard continued, annoyingly smug. "I can't have her marrying someone upright and honorable, someone who might take objection to my project. I'm not at all certain either of you can be controlled." The earl tapped his fingers on the table, then rose. Vanderburn crossed the room, snatched up a lantern, and disappeared into a room behind the bar. "But I'll give you one last chance to prove your worth. Follow my assistant."

---

THE CELLARS of The Three-Eyed Bat twisted beneath the ground, a labyrinthine tangle of corridors, stairways and storage vaults filled with stacks of barrels and crates, broken and discarded furniture, crockery and rusty machinery. Without breadcrumbs or string, Nick was quickly lost. Not that there would be any turning back, not with Maynard at his back.

Long minutes of following the bob and weave of Vanderburn's lantern led them to a room fitted with a rusty iron door and a strikingly shiny brass padlock. Not the best for keeping people out, but effective at keeping them *in*. The space was lined with riveted sheets of metal, and beneath the raised threshold ran two copper pipes. His eyes traced the path of those pipes down the hallway to a Linde's Ice Machine, a vapor-compression artificial refrigeration system. It squatted in the hallway, silent.

Activated, however, it would cool the space and turn the entire room into a refrigeration unit, into a cold storage room. Memories of the cat sìth beneath the fume hood and a bucket of water sprang to mind. Ice was used by cardiac electrophysiologists to slow—and stop—the heart.

Nothing good could happen here.

The door hung ajar.

Nick heard faint groan of pain, feminine and familiar. Any hope that Colleen's capture was a bluff disintegrated. An aching hollow took root inside his chest. He pushed past Vanderburn, yanking on the door, and found Colleen stretched out upon a carpet. Her dark shirt was torn and bloody, a rent in the garment exposing pale skin where a raw bullet wound to her upper arm oozed. Used rags littered the metal floor, and a bloody bullet rested in a bowl beside a pair of tweezers. Dr. Farquhar bent over her arm with a needle and thread, muttering to himself.

Glover stood over her, holding a voltaic prod, one that—turned to the highest setting—could drop a charging rhino. He leveled the humming weapon at Nick, but nodded to Colleen. "By all means, tend to your whore. Farquhar's a bit out of practice with his human doctoring skills. Too much time with the cats." Laughter with an edge of anger met Nick's ears. "Then again, maybe he's the perfect man for the job."

Rage gripped him as he rushed forward, dropping to his knees beside Colleen. He pushed the mad scientist's unsteady hands aside. Colleen's eyes were hazy and unfocused. Eyeing the color of her skin, he pressed his finders to the pulse at her wrist. Steady and strong, an excellent sign. No major blood vessel damage. "What did you give her?"

"Laudanum for the pain," Farquhar answered, his eyes filled with an awe that confused Nick. As did his next words. "I'm so very sorry, sir. Had I known why you sought to join us—"

Glover cuffed him. "Let the man work. On with it, Torrington."

"I *told* you not to hurt her," Maynard bellowed.

"It was necessary," Glover snapped. "She was too quiet, too fast. But even she couldn't outrun a bullet. We stopped her, but not before she broke into your safe."

"*My* safe?" Disbelief colored Maynard's voice. So many strongboxes advertised as uncrackable, but none of them truly were. Yet all the gentlemen believed.

"Colleen." Nick grasped her limp fingers. "It's me."

Her head rolled to meet his gaze. "It hurts."

Vanderburn hung his lamp from a hook fastened to the ceiling.

"I imagine so." And he would see Glover pay for it. "You've been shot in the arm. Can you squeeze my hand?" Her fingers flexed. "Harder. Ignore the pain. Crush my fingers like you're hanging from a ledge fifty feet above the ground."

She squeezed, crying out at the pain, but her fingers pressed against his with nearly full strength. Good, there was no nerve damage.

"You'll need a few stitches," he warned. "But you'll heal." Assuming he could find a way for them to escape this window-less, underground space. Not a soul—save those present—knew where they were. "I need alcohol to clean the wound."

"Er." Confused, Farquhar turned about as if he might find a bottle conveniently resting nearby in the empty room.

"We're beneath a pub!" Nick snapped. "Whisky. Vodka. Find some."

Vanderburn sighed and reached into his pocket. "Here." He held out a flask. "Vodka."

It would have to do. Nick splashed a measure over Colleen's

wound, over the needle and thread, then carefully drew the edges of her flesh back together.

"Your niece may be an unpleasant aberration," Glover said. "But she is talented. Came in the window of your study, not the door. We almost missed her. A minute later, and she'd have been out the window behind that damned cat." He shifted, and Nick noted the man favored his left leg. He hoped Colleen was the cause of his injury.

While they argued, Nick leaned close to Colleen's ear. He needed to ask even if questioning her while using a sharp implement to pierce her flesh felt akin to torture. "Did you find anything of note?"

"Worms," she half-gasped, half-whispered.

Though he'd known the answers wouldn't involve wires or batteries, any other words would have made more sense than... "Worms? The creeping invertebrates one digs out of the dirt?" Another stitch.

"More the wriggling kind that infest an animal's intestines. Threadlike and alive."

Revulsion twisted and writhed at the back of his throat. He resisted an urge to glare at Maynard. Cure? The man was as insane as Farquhar. The needle plunged, the thread pulled. "You found them... in the safe?"

Confusion tumbled inside her amber eyes as she nodded her confirmation while gritting her teeth against the pain. "In the rosewood box," she whispered. "Nothing else, save the vial in which they floated."

Around them, the argument grew heated. He tied a knot, snipped the thread, and quickly bandaged her arm.

"Fine!" Maynard barked. "It doesn't matter. We have her, and she'll serve as our first human test subject."

Ice ran through Nick's veins. "What? No!" He'd not allow these worms to...

"You will if you wish to leave this basement alive," the earl snarled. "As discussed, you'll oversee the transplant, accurately recording *human* data, all while ensuring my niece cooperates." He waved a hand at Farquhar. "I don't trust a man who mutters like a loon about transmutation."

"Both questions can be answered at once," Farquhar defended weakly.

"I don't think so," Glover barked back, ignoring the mad scientist. "Not after you let him," a hand slashed in Nick's direction, "waltz out your front door with *my* fiancée!"

"No!" Colleen's voice warbled as she struggled to sit up, to focus through an opium-laced haze. "I refuse."

Nick tensed, sweeping his gaze about the room, hunting for anything that would make a suitable weapon.

"Everyone settle down," Vanderburn said. He pointed Nick's own TTX pistol at him. "Back up. We've time enough to wait for the lady to recover."

Hands in the air, Nick complied.

"I care not who weds my niece," the earl barked.

"But I do!" Glover yelled back. "Whoever controls the property, controls the profits. That cat sìth is replaceable, as is the witch herself. What cannot be replicated are the legal documents, conveniently inked with your own hand, and the marriage certificate, valid but for her signature. Imagine how pleased I was to find such documents *and* a certain vial all in her possession."

Vanderburn met Nick's gaze and slowly shook his head. Between the TTX pistol and the voltaic prod that hummed and crackled in Glover's hands, Nick wouldn't stand a chance.

"Fine," the earl spat. "You marry her."

"I will," Glover said. "But I no longer trust you, a man who exploits his own niece's inheritance, offered my fiancée to another, and lured Farquhar's wife into stealing his hard-earned findings. All so you could quietly sell them for profit." His lips pulled back. "For there's no other explanation for the missing vial of worms in her possession, is there?"

"I meant to—"

"Betrayal after betrayal. Enough." Glover rushed at the earl, ramming the humming weapon he held into the man's stomach.

"Wha—" But the cry died in Maynard's throat with a crackle as the Galvanic prod discharged, sending bolts of electricity shooting through the earl's body and dropping him to the floor.

Colleen screamed and Nick grabbed the opportunity to kick out, landing a solid blow to Glover's damaged leg. The man screamed as he fell, and the Galvanic prod skittered across the floor, useless until it recharged.

"Stop!" Vanderburn squeezed the trigger of the TTX pistol, discharging all ammunition at once. *Crack! Ping! Thwack!* The first dart went wide, glancing off the metal wall, but the second and third caught Nick in the arm and wrist.

*Shit.* He had mere seconds before unconsciousness.

He yanked them out and threw them to the floor, hoping not all of the toxin had discharged, then fell on Glover with balled fists. An uppercut to the jaw made a satisfying crunch, whipping his head to the side. Blood erupted from Glover's mouth. But he felt nothing for his hand was already numb. A second punch to his abdomen doubled Glover over into a howling ball of pain.

*Bang!*

Nick twisted about.

"I said stop!" Smoke curled up from the standard revolver Vanderburn held in his hand, one now pointed at Nick. He froze, stunned. At his feet, the earl lay in a rapidly spreading pool of blood, a gunshot wound to his head. Dead. "A man wants to be protected, he should pay his employees. The way I see it, the less people involved, the more profit there will be to share. I'm willing to reserve judgment, Torrington, but I'm not at all certain you've anything to contribute to our project, so don't test me."

As if he could. The numbness spread up his arm and outward. Into his chest. Across his face. He swayed as his legs began to give out.

"Nick?" Colleen's distant voice was at his ear, but he couldn't answer her. He could barely feel her arms wrap about him as, together, they collapsed. The floor rushed up at him, but —completely numb—he never felt it hit.

# CHAPTER NINETEEN

"LET ME GO!" Colleen screamed and clawed at her uncle's henchman as he dragged her away from Nick. A desperate act, as the man's body was three times the size of hers and comprised of nothing but thick, ropy muscle.

Nick lay motionless on the cold, metal floor. His wide and unblinking eyes gave no indication that he could see her. But for the faint pulse at his throat and the shallow rise and fall of his chest, he appeared dead. And might well be if the toxin overtook him. How many darts had struck him? *Not enough to kill him.* And that thought alone gave her hope, one she clung to. A tear trickled down her cheek. For the thought of living in a world without him brought far too much pain. Had she fallen in love?

She'd loved her parents, and now Isabella. Her bond with Sorcha was deep and unbreakable. But Nick? He was a friend, a colleague, a lover... and so much more. Love and marriage were scary prospects, for his thoughts, opinions and decisions would —necessarily—influence hers. As hers would impact his. Was this a weakness or a strength? She rather thought it might be the latter. And she was tired of being so very, very alone.

One thing she knew with certainty: she'd never loved her

uncle. That cold, selfish, arrogant man was dead. Blood oozed from the hole in his forehead, spreading in a widening pool beneath his skull. Grotesque, horrifying, but she felt only detached relief. And a twinge of happiness. Not so much for her, but for Isabella. If Colleen didn't survive this, at least her aunt would be free.

Beaten and bloody, Mr. Glover rose from the floor. He pressed his hand to his mouth, checking for broken or loose teeth. She spat at his feet, happy to see Nick had managed to bloody Mr. Glover before he'd fallen. "I hope you've lost several. You're no better than the brutes you employ."

Mr. Vanderburn's hands tightened on her arms.

"And entirely capable of murder," Mr. Glover agreed, eyes narrow. "Keep that in mind." His nostrils flared as he glared at her. "Get what you need, Farquhar," he ordered. "Take this chance while you can, before I end her myself."

*Here?* This subterranean room was to serve as the man's laboratory? But how? There was no equipment, no instruments. Only the blood-stained rug beneath her feet and a doctor's bag that contained only the most basic of supplies.

"Yes, sir!" The mad scientist—who had pressed himself to the wall and cowered behind raised arms when the fighting broke out—tripped across the room, his steps too lively and cheerful midst the miasma of bloodshed and death. "A chair," he muttered. "A chair will do."

*A chair?*

"But first." Mr. Glover threw her a malicious grin, and Colleen was glad to note his jaw continued to swell and that he had at least one broken tooth. "About our wedding."

"I refuse." She lifted her chin.

"Do you?" Vicious rage contorted his face and, though a limp hitched his step, he managed to deliver a swift kick to Nick's ribcage. "Let me know when you change your mind. Quickly, if you wish to spare him a punctured lung." A second. A third.

"Stop!" Wretched despair twisted her heart. "I'll sign it! I'll sign it!" Did Nick still breathe?

She told herself a marriage certificate was as worthless as the tree pulp upon which it was printed, provided she could set a match to its corner before it was recorded at the registry. And if it saved Nick's life…

Dr. Farquhar returned with a chair and placed it upon the rug before her. Rope hung over his shoulder. "If you'll sit, my dear."

"In a moment," Mr. Glover snapped. "We've a few legalities to attend to first." He slid the horrid slip from her map case, a pen from his pocket, and slapped them both onto the chair before her. "Sign."

Tears ran down her cheeks as she struggled to lift her throbbing arm, to scrawl her name in ink. "There."

They were married. She snuck a glance at Nick and was relieved to see the gentle rise and fall of his chest.

"Again." Another sheet of paper dropped before her. "Don't even think of refusing. Remember, Torrington's life depends upon it, and forging your signature is always a possibility."

While Mr. Vanderburn kept a tight hand on her upper arm, she signed away control of Craigieburn and its lands. Then threw the pen at Mr. Glover's face. Ink spattered everywhere, mixing with the blood still drying upon his lips. "Satisfied?"

"Not even close." He folded the documents away, then pulled a handkerchief from his pocket and began to wipe away the streaks of blood and ink that marred his face. "Profits, however, those will make me very satisfied indeed. Bedding you, an abomination, was only a necessary exertion to be endured. An experience I doubt I'll be inclined to repeat even if you do survive." He looked over her shoulder and pointed at the chair. "You may proceed."

Mr. Vanderburn spun Colleen about, forcing her to sit.

"Survive?" she asked.

"Please," Mr. Glover said. "The cure must first be tested on a healthy individual. Preferably one that is expendable. But don't worry, Mr. Torrington's sister will be next."

Mr. Vanderburn's grip about her wrist was tight and, though she resisted, the laudanum had weakened her. The rough fibers of a rope bit into her skin as he bound her to the chair.

"I shouldn't worry too much," Mr. Glover went on. "His last few experiments have been wildly successful and, with all the traits you share with your familiar, I'm nearly certain this first test will proceed without incident. If not?" She recoiled as his hot breath brushed across her ear. "As your husband I'll inherit. Cryptid hunters will pay well for a cat sìth. One particular feline is sure to turn up eventually. We'll test the market with your very own familiar, witch."

"No!" She hated the pleading in her voice.

"No?" Mr. Glover shrugged, then gagged her with his bloody handkerchief by stuffing it into her mouth. "Well, then, we could always harvest the cure from its heart. Turn the pelt into a stole for you to wear about your neck. It did, after all, take Dr. Farquhar several cat sìth to suss out the reason for their longevity. Might as well make use of the remains."

Her outraged cry was muffled by the rag.

"Time to let Dr. Farquhar have his fun." He straightened. "Imagine if it works... We'd have to offer a package deal. One cat and one witch." His laughter raked knives down her back.

"I'm nearly certain it will be so." Dr. Farquhar approached with scissors. He cut through her shirt, peeling the linen away to bare her right shoulder while she swallowed back her tears, trying not to choke. "We can preserve your modesty for now, my dear," the doctor crooned in a sing-song voice. "Particularly as there's no need to shave the incision site." He swabbed her skin with cold alcohol. "Given conservation of mass, there must be an additional concept I'm missing. Perhaps energy? After we witness your transformation, I'll adjust my calculations."

Her stomach churned and bile rose into her throat. The scientist really was insane. She could not transform into a cat any more than a cat could turn human. What had addled his brain to believe so?

"It must be exothermic," he muttered, strapping surgical goggles to his forehead and adjusting the magnification. "Might be I should have attempted an endothermic reaction to shift the cat sìth into human form? But I expect cold would do the trick in this case. If not, I'll need to reconsider my approach."

"Enough blathering," Mr. Glover snapped. "Save it for your journal article. On with it."

Icy tentacles wrapped themselves about her spine and squeezed. Dr. Farquhar truly expected her to transform into a cat? Into a cat sìth? How?

*No!*

The room had metal walls and a metal floor. From the ceiling protruded a number of meat hooks and eye bolts. Giant sheets of iron riveted together—her lungs started to heave—it was one large refrigeration unit. Not running at the moment but—

She screamed into the gag and tensed her body against the ropes, ignoring the throbbing pain that was her arm. He intended to freeze her, to stop her heart? To jolt her back to life with... with what? Electricity? All she'd found in her uncle's safe were those... Worms?

"Hold still," the scientist huffed, tracing the path of her collarbone and tapping at the bare skin that lay beneath it. "A percutaneous approach to the subclavian vein is a different procedure for a human. Bipeds differ from quadrupeds, altering the angle. But it provides almost direct access to the right atrium." He glanced up at Vanderburn. "Hold her very, very still."

Mr. Vanderburn's hands pressed her shoulders tight against the chair. "It will go better if you cooperate," he said. "The animals that struggled were... worse off."

Dead, in other words. Tears streamed from her eyes.

It took her every effort to keep breathing slowly, steadily. If—when—she survived this, they would *all* pay. Nick would help her. She didn't dare turn her head to look at him. He'd been breathing. He was going to be fine. Absolutely fine.

Dr. Farquhar lifted a gleaming hollow needle—one that more resembled a tiny tube—with a sharp point before his eyes. "We begin with a blind puncture at the junction of the clavicle and the first rib."

A sharp pain pieced her chest and a warm rivulet of blood trickled down across her breast. She whimpered, but didn't dare move. Breathing also seemed ill-advised with such a sharp piece of metal implanted in her vein.

"Excellent," Dr. Farquhar congratulated himself. "And on the first try." The scientist's face disappeared. "The nematodes. Where are they?"

"Here," Mr. Glover held out the fluid-filled vial she'd found in the rosewood box.

She shuddered at the horror of it all. Aether, what was he thinking, sending infectious worms directly into her heart? How could this possibly be a cure for *anything*?

"Still!" Mr. Vanderburn commanded.

The mad scientist uncapped the vial, then reached into the glass tube with tweezers, delicately extracting a thin, threadlike strand some four inches long. A single worm wriggled and twisted, glistening as a drop of fluid ran down its body to coalesce and drip onto her shirt.

Mr. Glover made a noise of disgust and turned his face away.

Colleen gagged on the handkerchief.

"Such a lovely, delicate thing." Ever so slowly and carefully, Dr. Farquhar lowered his hand and, against her will, her gaze followed, straining the muscles of her eyes, of her neck, following his movement.

Terror battered her heart against her rib cage. The worm's head—for it must be—lifted. Could it sense blood?

"There you go, little one," the scientist's voice encouraged, as if helping a child to take its first steps. The tapered tip of the creature slid into the blood-slicked opening of the hollow needle, and fresh tears pooled and overflowed from her eyes. "Follow the pathway. Squirm your way home."

The worm disappeared into the tiny, metal tube. Into her vein. Propelled by the very pounding of her heart into the very structure it sought. But no matter the horror, she felt nothing. *Nothing.* The creature had slipped inside, taking up residence within her chest. Preparing to... What?

Tears slid down her cheeks, leaving salt-stained trails behind as they fell from her face, dripping onto her chest. Dark, damp patches upon her linen shirt spread ever wider as the mad scientist lifted another writhing creature from the vial and coaxed it to follow the first. Then another. Five worms in all slipped into her veins.

"Done!" Dr. Farquhar declared. He slipped the needle from her chest and pressed a ball of lint to the puncture wound.

Mr. Vanderburn's hands lifted from her shoulders, but he made no move to loosen the gag that muffled her moans.

"What now?" Mr. Glover asked.

"We wait." A distant, unfocused smile shaped itself onto Dr. Farquhar's face. "The worm is in its final stage of development, ready to implant. Cold speeds the process, encourages the nematode to settle in, to make itself at home. Then we proceed."

"Done," Mr. Glover said. "For now. We've other tasks to see to in the meantime."

"What of Torrington, sir?" Mr. Vanderburn asked, leaning over Nick. "He's still alive."

"Leave him." Mr. Glover's voice held an edge of malice. "He can play nurse to my wife, and I want Maynard's death linked to Mrs. Farquhar's partial evisceration, not his. Besides, if this works, we'll need him to *encourage* his sister to serve as our second patient. If we cure Lady Anna of her heart condition, all afflicted *ton* will beg us to take their money in hopes that such a treatment will reinvigorate their own hearts."

"And the witch might transform," Dr. Farquhar insisted, his focus sharpening. "You promised I could present such findings to the Royal Society."

"Just so." Mr. Glover rolled his eyes as he patted the madman on the shoulder. "Should that come to pass, we'll rearrange all our plans." He looked to Mr. Vanderburn.

"Grab the earl. Our night's not over yet. Decisions, decisions. Do we toss him to the kraken in the Thames? No, I suppose we need him found. We'll dump him on his doorstep, like a cat gifts a mouse. I've no doubt his wife will be glad of a corpse."

A smear of blood streaked across the floor as Mr. Vanderburn dragged her uncle by the collar from the room. Dr. Farquhar unhooked the overhead lamp, snatched up his bag and followed, mumbling about transformative powers of particulate matter. All while Mr. Glover limped away clutching documents to his chest that would twist her future to suit his purposes. All of them ignored her strangled cries.

The iron door clanged shut behind them, plunging the room into darkness.

# CHAPTER TWENTY

OUND AND GAGGED and left in the dark with parasites worming their way into her heart, Colleen's muffled cries tore at Nick's soul. He ached to offer her comfort, but all he could do was breathe. One inhalation after another while the increasing cold of the floor beneath his cheek, beneath the entirety of his body, seeped into his bones.

Time passed and Colleen's unsteady breaths smoothed as she fell into a drugged sleep. From time to time, she woke and fought against her bindings, dragging in panicky gasps of air about the gag. But inevitably, the drug dragged her under once more, leaving him alone with his thoughts.

The hellish scene he'd been forced to witness from the floor played out over and over in his mind. Colleen signing a slip of paper that legally bound her to Glover. Another that handed over her family's lands. A blind vein puncture. A vial of nematodes.

No electrical cardiac pacer existed. No specialized device that could monitor a heart, shocking it back to life when it stilled. Instead, threadlike nematodes—roundworms—would complete the task. But how? Would they burrow through the wall of her heart to lodge in the muscular tissue between the two ventricles? Were their primitive nerve cords capable of conducting an electrical impulse from the top of the heart to the bottom, from atria to ventricles and outwards?

Without evidence, it was impossible to know. Farquhar's mad ramblings about transformations made it impossible to believe any words that fell from his lips. And no proof that this might work existed—not even observational notes that another scientist might examine. All had been destroyed by the fire. Maynard claimed he'd witnessed success, but there would be no questioning the earl. Though it was impossible to mourn the horrid man, his cold-blooded avarice would have been preferable to the emotionally driven ravings of a spurned suitor who only wanted her for her lands, a crazed scientist who thought to turn his fiancée into a cat, and a mercenary guard.

Nick blamed himself for their situation. Distracted by a disembodied heart and certain Colleen would be safe upon the rooftops while her uncle attended a dinner party, he'd both failed to anticipate Maynard as the villain or to anticipate his trap. Keen to infiltrate the shadow committee, Nick had neglected to consider all the angles, including the possibility that she would make both the perfect hostage and the perfect human test subject.

Was there any hope of diverting the outcome of this madness?

His mind ran down a mental list of anti-helminthics that might kill the worm, but any and all vermicidal drugs that sprung to mind were either powerless to act outside the digestive tract or likely to kill a person if injected directly into the bloodstream. Not that it mattered. He could not foresee a future in which he laid his hands upon any such drugs before the creature was lodged in her heart.

At last the effects of the TTX poison began to ebb. Sooner than he'd dared hope, a testament to the thick wool of his coat sleeve and the reflexive instinct to yank the darts from his wrist and arm before the entirety of the toxin had discharged.

He heard Colleen wake with a gasp.

"Steady your breaths," he said with half-numb lips.

Her ragged inhalations steadied. Grew slower.

He filled his lungs again. "No more tears." The rag the bastards had stuffed into her mouth and bound with a length of linen would only become a threat if it began to slide down her throat. "My fingers are tingling. A few minutes more and I'll have you free." With the toxin flushing from his system, his own breaths came more easily.

Light. With Colleen's keen eyesight, the faintest of light would offer a measure of comfort. He flexed his wrist, his biceps, forcing his hand deep into his coat pocket to wrap tingling fingers about his decilamp. *Click.* A reddish light began to glow. He tossed the miniature light source a few feet from his face, casting a faint silhouette of her lithe form onto the far wall.

"I'll be at your side soon." Freeing her, wrapping his arms about her, took precedence above all else.

The room was empty, but for them, the carpet she'd arrived in, an old wooden chair, and the black shadow of pooled blood. When their captors had left, they'd carried away a body and every other loose item that might aid them.

"Look about, Colleen. Hunt for structural weaknesses."

He doubted she'd find any, but she needed a focus and every rivet, every seam must be examined. All they needed was to find a single fault in construction that might be exploited.

He pushed onto his elbows, then shoved himself onto hands and knees, and crawled to her side. Every movement taxed his strength, but his fingers found the rough fibers of the ropes about her booted ankles. The bindings fell away. As yet more strength returned, he lifted onto his knees and freed those about her wrists.

Her hands flew away, yanking the gag from her mouth. She dragged in a deep breath, then dropped onto the rug beside him.

"How bad is it?" he asked.

"The gunshot or puncture wound?" Her cool hands pressed against his cheek and her golden eyes flashed as she searched his face. "And I would ask the same of you."

"Both. And I'm fine. Or, rather, will be." He dropped his gaze to her bare shoulder. To the bandage inexpertly applied to the puncture wound. The men who had done this to her would pay. He'd see them dead or behind bars—or die trying. "But—"

"There's no retrieving them, is there?" She shuddered. "The worms?"

"No." He wished he had a different answer. "And no way to kill it without horrible side effects that would put your very life at risk."

"Perhaps it's not as awful as it seems." She shifted closer, leaning against his side as he wrapped an arm about her shoulder for both comfort and warmth. "The cat sìth are known for being difficult to kill. And there are legends of wild women with amber eyes like my own, known for living alone deep in the woods, women with lifespans that far exceed those that most humans are allotted. If this particular worm somehow resides within their hearts..."

"Nine lives." Nick considered the implications. "A cat with nine lives, and witches who can transform into them. You think the legends might have originated in your woods?"

"They came from somewhere." She shifted. "If there's a truth buried in the myths, what are the odds this could be a cure for your sister?"

"Roundworms do possess a nerve cord, musculature. Though such worms are usually parasitic, they might be able to live within a human in a mutualistic fashion, somehow regulating nerve impulses." He swallowed. "But it's impossible to know." Nick's gut twisted. He hated to offer her false hope. "Not without testing it."

"On a human," she finished. "In this scenario, me." Her face hardened. "Dr. Farquhar plans to stop my heart—much like he did to Sorcha, to all the cat sìth before her—to see if it will restart."

He'd reached the same conclusions. "Making it imperative that we escape. Even if you were willing to risk your life in such a trial, Colleen, I'd not allow it here in such primitive, unsanitary conditions beneath a pub."

"But in a hospital?" She licked her lips, then put on a brave face. "With colleagues that you trust?"

"No." He stilled. Did she think him capable of such an act? "There are no circumstances under which I would agree to test such a thing on an otherwise healthy, young woman."

Maybe over time, if he could independently verify Farquhar's findings and after much consideration of every possible risk such a procedure could involve, he *might* agree to allow a desperate, sick patient on the cusp of death—someone much like his sister—to insert the worms. But he'd never stop a human's heart on purpose, merely to see if such a cure was possible.

She rubbed her chest. "It appears I may have no choice in the matter."

"Unless we manage an escape." He traced a finger down the side of her face. When would he force the words past his lips if not now? "I love you, Lady Colleen Stewart of Craigieburn, and will do everything possible to prevent such an occurrence."

Her mouth fell open, but before she could answer, he kissed her. Was he that afraid of a rejection? Yes. Very much so. He needed to believe they would have a future. Together as man and wife.

Mindful of her bandaged arm, he teased her mouth until both of their hearts beat a rapid staccato. What he wouldn't give for a warm fire and a soft pile of blankets. Alas, there was nothing but cold metal, a stained rug, and a damp woolen coat. Never mind the frigid air. Letting the fantasy fade, he released her. Though still somewhat weakened by the various drugs and toxins that lingered in their veins, it was time to fully assess the grim situation of their current reality.

"Come." He stood and held out a hand, pulling Colleen to her feet.

"About the heart." Pride and concern wrapped about each other and cast a shadow over her face. "I almost made it out the window before they caught me. I found the rosewood box in my uncle's safe along with pages upon pages of signed contracts arranging to sell a 'cure' to a number of prominent gentlemen. Your agency would have a field day, except—"

"Glover tore them to shreds." With the intent to renegotiate. No doubt at a higher price point.

She nodded. "My uncle is—was—Cornelius Pierpont."

There it was. Confirmation. "He bought back his own," for lack of a better word, "product?"

"Worms." She swallowed. Hard. "I took the vial. Directly from that rosewood box. And left my own gift in return. Glover has no idea I left a human heart in my uncle's safe."

A laugh burst forth. "Clever woman." Not at all planned, but it would neatly tie the death of Mrs. Farquhar to the man who was soon to be found upon his own doorstep. Assuming they managed to both find and crack open Maynard's safe. The police would be utterly confounded, but at least no blame could be laid at the feet of his family.

Colleen read his mind. "I imagine when the police swarm my uncle's home, they'll find the incriminating blood stains inside his personal dirigible. Moreover, Dr. Farquhar will soon be a hunted man, and he'll waste no time pointing a finger at my uncle, a man who is conveniently dead." Shivering, she wrapped her arms across her chest and stomped her feet. "Was it so very cold when we first arrived?"

"No." He shrugged his coat from his shoulders and wrapped it about hers. It all but engulfed her. "No objections," he added, when her face told him she was about to do exactly that.

She snapped her mouth shut, then smiled. "Ever the gentleman. Thank you." She pressed her hand against the metal-paneled wall. "There's a faint vibration. And the walls are damp with condensation."

He picked up the decilamp and began to scan the riveted seams of the metal panels. "With the flick of a switch, our captors have activated a Linde's Ice Machine, a vapor-compression artificial refrigeration system, outside in the hallway."

"A refrigeration unit beneath a pub." Her nose wrinkled. "That explains why it smells like soured hops, jellied kraken, and boiled tripe."

"It also explains why they left us alone and unbound." He moved the beam of light along a row of rivets, testing each one in turn. Each and every one was distressingly sound. "Cold salt-water brine is circulating inside the metal panels of this wall through a network of pipes. I expect the temperature will continue to drop, eventually inducing mild hypothermia."

"Making us sluggish and easily controlled."

He nodded. "We need to escape—or disable the pipes—before they return. Our best hope is to find a weak point."

"Where in London, exactly, are we?"

Wounded, drugged and carried through the dank streets inside a rolled carpet, she wouldn't know. "In the labyrinth of storage rooms deep beneath The Three-Eyed Bat." He waited, trailing the faint light across the walls. Was she familiar with its reputation? Her muttered curse informed him she was indeed.

"There." Colleen grasped his wrist and angled the light to shine upon the far wall.

He had to cross the room to see what had caught her eye.

As moisture collected upon the walls, it ran in thin rivulets to form puddles upon the floor. But one particular stream had pooled and caught upon the rust-encrusted bolts of a perforated panel affixed to the wall.

He stepped closer. Holding out the palm of his hand, he detected the slightest air movement. "A ventilation shaft." The panel was only fifteen by eight inches. Not an exit for him, but for Colleen? At the very least, they might snag the attention of someone above it in the pub or on the street... "Is anyone there?" he called.

Silence.

Down this alleyway it surprised him not at all.

Colleen took the light from his hand and peered through the tiny holes. "It's an old coal chute." She winced, then drew in a deep breath. "I can fit through this opening and climb up the chute, but exiting? Standard coal holes come in two varieties. Twelve or fourteen inches in width. I can't fit through the smaller hole, but fourteen inches? That I can squeeze through."

"And find help." Street urchins managed such a maneuver on a regular basis when an unsuspecting homeowner failed to latch the metal plate after a coal delivery. But there was no chance that he, a grown man with wide shoulders, would be exiting from such a hole of any size. He hated the thought of her walking alone through London in the middle of the night, but said nothing. She'd done exactly that for years. "But only if we can remove this grating." He yanked a boot from his foot. "Let's have a try."

"Impressive." She smiled in the dim light as he pried off the heel of his boot to reveal a flat sheet of metal cut to serve as a number of tools.

He held it before the light, triumphant, pleased he had something to offer. Can opener, screwdriver, knife—but most importantly—wrench.

"Glover and Vanderburn were too obsessed with the obvious weapons and missed a few hidden tools," he explained. "I've a wire cord sewn into my waistband. Unfortunately, I should have worn a different coat, one with more options. A lesson to take to heart. You've never thought to hide any weapons within the seams of your clothing?"

"Only punch cards." She smiled. "A short-sighted mistake I intend to rectify." She joined him before the panel, rubbing her hands together.

He fitted the tool to a bolt, twisting. It moved, the slightest of fractions, but it was enough.

Over the next few hours, they took turns as one of them worked at the panel, while the other shouted into the grating or banged on the iron door. But to no avail. Progress was measured by the fall of bolts upon the floor. A few loosened and fell away with relative ease, but those that had rusted presented a greater challenge.

Teeth began to chatter as the temperature within the vault dropped. Slowly but steadily, the cold seeped through their clothing, their skin and into their very bones. The light of the fading decilamp illuminated the frost of their breath and their hands that grew stiff and numb and streaked with blood as they pried at the sharp edges of the panel. By the time the last bolt clattered to the floor, both shivered uncontrollably.

*Clang!*

The panel dropped to the floor.

CHAPTER TWENTY-ONE

THEY BOTH JUMPED back as the iron grille hit the floor, though not as quickly or as far as they ought. Reflexes and strength were ebbing. The only blessing of the cold was that it dulled the pain in her arm, though a gunshot wound seemed a trivial fact in the face of a greater horror should they fail to escape.

Colleen rubbed her arms, mindful that she wore Nick's coat, leaving him exposed to the chill radiating from the walls. His larger size could only keep him so warm for so long. Overcome by the cold, they were bound to be helpless to resist when Mr. Glover and Dr. Farquhar returned.

Fear and anxiety kept rearing their heads. Trapped, her mind repeated, over and over. As her parents had been when the wind blew their train carriage off the bridge, plunging it into the river below. Had they been killed instantly? Or had there been a frantic scramble to escape before the icy water rushed in? She'd never know.

But here, beneath The Three-Eyed Bat, she had the benefit of time.

And now, the possibility of escape. She dragged in a deep

breath and squared her shoulders. Nick loved her. *Her.* A senti-ment he'd demonstrated in both words and actions. And, though her heart insisted she felt the same, her mind resisted speaking the words in such a cold, dank space.

Directing the fading light of the decilamp inward, Nick stuck his head into the hole.

"Please," Colleen whispered on a breath of fog and ice. "Tell me there's an 'off' switch."

"Sadly, no. I see shadows of pipes to either side, but even if we managed to break one of them, we'd likely only flood the floor and worsen our sorry state." He stepped back and held out the decilamp. "As to the coal chute, I can make out the original brick wall of the cellars, but the light is too faint for my eyes as it disappears into the darkness above."

Afraid she might drop it, she gripped the light with more force than strictly necessary as she stuck her head into the void. Coal dust stained the narrowing ascent of the shaft. Easy enough to climb, but disappointment waited at the top. "A twelve-inch coal hole." *Not* an escape route. But still an opening onto a street. Buoyed by hope, her heart lifted. Men, women or children might—or might not—pass by, and might or might not be induced to summon help. She backed out. "I'll climb up and try to pass a message."

"Not to the managers of The Three-Eyed Bat," he warned. "At least not until all other options are exhausted. They saw me descend and haven't bothered to come looking. I expect Glover has ensured they've been paid well for the use of this space and their silence. Alerting them would likely only result in our captors' swift return."

"So noted." She shoved her hands deep into the pockets of Nick's coat. They'd stripped her of her belt and with it, all her supplies. "Please tell me you've paper and a pencil somewhere on your person."

With a half-smile, he produced said items from the cuff of

his sleeve and the hem of his trousers. The slip of paper was damp, but serviceable. "At your service."

She lifted an eyebrow. "I don't suppose they conveniently overlooked a skeet pigeon you've tucked inside a boot?"

A ghost of a smile touched his lips. "A small mechanical assistant would be quite handy at the moment. Alas, we will need to depend upon the goodwill of drunkards and street urchins. Send as many as you can. Promise them the moon." He blew on his hands and flexed his fingers before tearing the paper into thin strips. "What shall I write and to whom?"

"Begin with a message addressed to my aunt," she directed. "Sorcha might be hanging about in the shadows."

His hand stilled, and Nick lifted his gaze. "Really? Your familiar followed you?"

"She'll sometimes take to the streets on her own business, but when we're out working, not once has she ever left my side. She leapt out the window first, but would have waited. Despite the laudanum forced upon me before they rolled me inside that carpet, I caught glimpses of her trailing behind the crank hack."

"You'll pardon my disbelief, but Sorcha is mostly wild. And a feline. They're not known for being the most cooperative—or trainable—of creatures."

"Agreed." Colleen tore strips of cloth from her damaged sleeve, braiding them together to form a collar, twisting a wider length of the material to form a pouch. "But neither is she a fat house cat accustomed to a life of pampered indulgence. Which is why the promise of a tin of sardines never fails."

Nick made an amused noise.

A small smile twitched her lips. "Isabella and I trained Sorcha to carry messages home to warn my aunt of inevitable delays, so that she might conceal my absence." For all the good that had done. All that time her uncle had known what she was about. "We always knew there might come a day I found myself trapped. This situation certainly qualifies."

Colleen certainly wouldn't suggest they reach out to Mr. Witherspoon. Not after he'd hired her to work an obfuscation chain that helped her own uncle to double-cross his traitorous colleagues in a tangled web of betrayal. If—when—they survived this, she was of a mind to bang on his door and set his ears on fire with a few choice words.

"Worth a try." Nick began to scratch out a message. "I'm asking her to contact my father who, given the dead body dropped upon his stoop, will have noticed our sudden, and now prolonged, absence."

"We only have to pray Isabella is not overly beleaguered with the consequences of her husband's arrival upon the doorstep." By the arrival of constables and Runners. By the morbidly curious. But mostly, by relief. They needed Isabella to retreat to her room and find the cat sìth waiting in time to send help before Dr. Farquhar and Mr. Glover returned with plans for Colleen's death and resurrection.

Nick handed her the slip of paper, then began to compose a few more general pleas for help. Rolling the message into a tight tube, she tucked it into the cloth pouch and knotted it into place. Minutes later, the notes were written, addressed and stashed securely into her cincher.

She caught Nick by the lapel of his waistcoat and rose up on to her toes to press a kiss to his lips. "Thoughts of sitting hearthside with you have never been so appealing." Where she might find the courage to whisper her words of love.

"Sitting?" He forced levity into his tight voice as he caught her waist and let his gaze slide slowly over her ruined shirt and torn cincher. "There'll be no sitting. Not until we're old and gray. But the sooner we've a fire before us the better. Let me give you a boost."

The opening into the coal chute posed not the slightest problem. Nor—though her cold, raw and much-abused fingers smarted and her arm ached—did the passageway itself. As suspected from the gentle movement of air into the chamber below, the iron plate of the coal hole cover was perforated. Working the latch with frigid fingers proved a challenge, but after a few fumbles, she managed to pop it open. Like a fox emerging from its den, she lifted her head.

Fifty feet away lay the entrance to the pub. Over its dark, wooden door a sign flapped gently in the wind. Inky shadows clung to the street, but the wavy glass of the pub's windows gave off a soft yellow glow despite the hour. She could hear the soft clatter of late night traffic, but The Three-Eye Bat was at the end of a long alleyway, close yet removed from nearby busier streets, and foot traffic was regrettably light. "Sorcha!" she called softly, clicking her tongue against her teeth. "Are ye here?" A shadow detached itself from the gloom, wending its way along the buildings, padding cautiously in her direction upon silent feet. "Div nae worry." *Do not worry.* "It's me, Colleen."

In true feline form, the cat sìth approached in a cautious, roundabout manner. Sorcha sniffed at Colleen's mussed hair with disapproval.

"I'm in need o yer services, fairy cat. Grant me a boon?"

Sorcha sat back upon her haunches, as if contemplating Colleen's quandary. Slowly, she lowered herself back into the hole, hoping the cat sìth's curiosity would draw her closer. It did. The cat sìth peered down into the coal hole, whiskers twitching.

Colleen lifted the braided collar. "Might I?" When Sorcha did not back away, she tied the twisted neckband about the cat sìth's neck, an indignity suffered without complaint. "Ging hame," she said. *Go home.* "Tae Isabella." *To Isabella.*

The cat sìth blinked at Colleen, then turned about and darted across the cobblestones, melting into the shadows.

When she was certain Sorcha was beyond hearing, Colleen began to call for help. "Is anyone there?"

Long minutes passed while she shivered. So close to freedom, yet so very, very far. A drunkard or two staggered from the doors of the pub, oblivious to her beckoning calls. Not until an old, hunch-backed woman turned down the alleyway did a soul turn a face in her direction.

"What's this?" The old woman altered course and crept forward to peer down at Colleen. "In a bit of a pickle are you, young lady?"

"Quite." Colleen lifted a slip of paper beside her face. "I'm trapped inside The Three-Eyed Bat's cellars and desperately in need of help."

"I'd say," the old woman agreed, stroking her hairy chin.

"Please, will you carry a message for me?" Colleen pleaded. "The recipient will pay ten pounds."

"One hundred," she demanded, cackling.

Unease swirled in Colleen's stomach. "Done."

"And what guarantee have I that it will be paid?" The woman made no attempt to reach for the message.

"The recipient will be desperate for news. He holds a seat in Parliament."

"A lord?"

Colleen nodded. "He is."

The old woman took a step back. "What kind of fool do you take me for? A thousand pounds is no use to a dead woman. No one trapped in cellars beneath The Three-Eyed Bat is worth paying the price of drawing the attention of a peer." She straightened. "Now, they do pay their informants well, and that is an effort worth making." The old woman padded to the door of the pub and banged.

"No!" Colleen called. "Please! I'm begging you."

But as the door to the pub cracked open, Colleen ducked beneath the surface, pulling the iron coal hole cover closed and praying those inside The Three-Eyed Bat would dismiss the old woman's tale.

"What is it?" Nick called.

Heart pounding, she slid down the brick shaft. "No amount of money—or so I am informed—is sufficient to purchase assistance. I managed to send a message with Sorcha, but an old woman declined my offer in favor of alerting those inside the pub."

Nick's curses echoed her own thoughts.

She crouched at the bottom of the shaft beside the opening. "What do—"

*Bang. Bang. Bang.* The sound of a booted foot stomping upon the coal hole, her silent plea denied. "Is that you, Mrs. Glover? I gather the worm has brought about no ill-effects, though by now you ought to be feeling the cold. No? Shimmy back my way so that we might have a word."

"It's Mr. Glover," she hissed. Had he not left the pub? Or had he only just returned?

"Stay still," Nick whispered. "Let him wonder if the old woman lied."

"Quite a lot of trouble you've caused me of late," Mr. Glover called. "Perhaps we shouldn't have skipped so lightly over the marriage vows. I would enjoy hearing you promise obedience." There was a long pause. "Last chance, wife. My patience has grown thinner than a French whore's negligee."

Hatred burned in her chest. She refused to answer him.

"No witty reply?" Mr. Glover said. "Has the chill addled your mind? Excellent. Time to hasten our little experiment. Dr. Farquhar is most anxious to escape to Scotland. Between a burned house and an eviscerated wife, the Metropolitan Police are all too eager to speak with him."

A faint clang sounded above her, the sound of tin scrapping across stone. A second later a deluge of cold water poured down upon her, drenching her hair, her shirt and splashed off the brick, soaking through her trousers and pooling inside her boots. Her lungs dragged in a deep, shuddering breath, but the resulting scream froze in her throat as the entirety of her body began to shake uncontrollably.

"Colleen!" Nick yelled. His hands reached through the metal wall, tugging at her as a second bucket of water rained down.

She slid back into the frigid prison, as Mr. Glover called, his voice twisted by malice. "We won't be much longer, my dear. Inform your lover that if there is any resistance on his part, Lady Anna will not be granted the privilege of a cure while supervised by her most dedicated brother. We will instead dispose of him and consider a more compliant patient with more appreciative family members."

"Bastard!" Nick yelled.

Evil laughter filtered down. "Only a third son, like yourself, looking to secure a future."

CHAPTER TWENTY-TWO

ET AND DRIPPING, Colleen fell into his arms. Violent tremors shook her petite body. Not only had the water Glover poured down the coal chute soaked her to the skin, it had splashed onto his own clothes, drenching the front of his waistcoat and trousers. Hypothermia was now a given. At best, they could lessen its severity.

"Hang in there." Nick carried her to the chair as quickly as he could manage. With stiff fingers, he wrung out her long hair, then twisted it into a rough knot and pinned it in place with his pencil to keep the wet from the back of her neck.

"Your sister…" Her teeth chattered, clicking uncontrollably as she spoke. "Is it possible… he has her?"

The thought nagged at him. "Doubtful. She rarely leaves the house and forever has her attendant trailing behind her." And she was in bed. Sleeping deeply after her most recent syncopal episode. Police officers would be swarming the property. Glover could not possibly have Anna in his clutches.

Hanging his wet waistcoat from the back of the chair, he stripped away his coat, then Colleen's cincher and shirt. Tugging off his own shirt, he shoved her cold arms through its sleeves, fingers fumbling to fasten its buttons. Back on went his own waistcoat; when hypothermia threatened, damp clothing was better than no clothing at all.

"But... promise... of a cure."

"With a dead body on our doorstep, I would hope Anna and my parents would be more circumspect about miraculous offers." Off came her boots. He dumped the water pooled within onto the floor and forced her frigid feet back into the damp leather. Stockinged feet were not an option. Not on cold, wet metal. That way led nowhere but to frostbite.

He retrieved her wet shirt from the floor and knotted the garment at the wrist, gathering the bolts within the makeshift pouch. Another knot secured them in place. It was a crude weapon but useful when swung at an enemy. He set it along with the metal grating beside the door. When Glover and his minions arrived, Nick intended to be waiting. He only hoped he'd not be too cold to wield it when the opportunity arose.

*When. Not if.*

For the deluge of water spoke of impatience, of a desire to push the moment of the cruel experiment sooner.

Lifting Colleen from the chair, he lowered himself onto its seat and settled her upon his lap. Nick tucked her wet head beneath his chin and clasped her against his chest. Shared body heat was their best hope to slow their decent into hypothermia. There'd be no stopping it.

"How are you feeling?" He did his best to ignore the frosty air that billowed about their legs. If the cold drove the nematode into the cardiac muscle of the heart as Farquhar insisted, had it now lodged in her myocardium? "Has your heart skipped a beat? Any sensations of fluttering? Chest pain?"

"No... to all." She touched the bare skin of his arm—a sensation that barely registered. "I'm so cold, Nick. How much longer... before..." A tear slid down her cheek.

"We'll hold out as long as we can," he answered. "Remember, they wish us to live." Farquhar had a mad hypothesis to prove, but Glover only cared to the extent that their—temporary —survival might fill his coffers.

"When this… is over…" A shiver ran through her body, and Colleen tucked her hands beneath her arms. "Ask me again… to marry you. Properly. On one knee."

"Why? Have you finally come to your senses?" The levity in his voice was forced. He rubbed his hands up and down her body, hoping friction might warm her. He'd not win her, only to lose her. "When did you finally realize I was the only man for you?"

Her tremors subsided. Some. In a few moments, he'd insist they stand, move about in an attempt to keep blood flowing through their extremities. Soon. When his own shivering slowed.

She huffed a frosty laugh. "It wasn't one moment. More an accumulation of them. The waltz that first brought us too close. The night we passed an hour with our backs pressed to a chimney stack. Watching you slink through halls. Storm into a room. Seeing you care for your family. Working with you as a partner."

"Let's not forget that desktop kiss. Or time spent in a certain aviary."

"But a thief shouldn't angle for a Queen's agent." Her smile was faint, and if his decilamp could illuminate a full spectrum of colors, he had no doubt her lips would cast a faint blue.

"And yet she caught one." For he was well and truly hooked. "Tell me, if we marry, do I become a laird?" He refused to let morbid thoughts occupy space in his mind. They *would* survive this.

She laughed softly into his neck. "No. That title belongs to the landowner. While a wife is afforded a courtesy title, I do not believe the tradition extends to a husband. Does this third son find himself overly disappointed?"

"Not at all. I've never wished for a title and find myself happy to ponder a future in which I'm a kept man." He kissed her damp hair and tightened his arms about her. "Tell me again about Craigieburn Castle."

"It's styled after a tower house." Her voice grew wistful. "And looks like a miniature castle, stretching straight up toward the sky. No moats. No curtain wall surrounding a courtyard."

"So very disappointing, that. At least it's old."

"If you consider that it dates to the sixteenth century old." She laughed into his shoulder. "And before its heirs depleted the family coffers, they fussed with the architecture adding turrets and balustrades, corbeling and gargoyles."

"What's not to love about a scowling gargoyle?" But though she cherished the castle, he knew the inhabitants of its surrounding lands were ever at the forefront of her mind. "And the countryside?"

"Forests and fields. Most of those who farm the land can lay claim to at least one ancestor with golden eyes, and in the surrounding woods prowl the cat sìth." The faint smile upon her face faded away. "I'm the last Stewart. If I don't return—"

"You will, and I'll escort you there myself." He kissed her cool forehead. "Do tell me there's a massive fireplace in the great hall where we can stretch out before a fire."

"Upon piles of warm blankets woven in the clan tartan." She sighed as her eyelids fluttered shut.

"Such a tease," he quipped. But Colleen's sleepiness worried him. "Time to stand up." He pushed them to their booted feet. "We need to move. Circulate the blood. Frostbite is something potential brides and grooms ought to avoid before a wedding."

Side by side, they moved about the icebox, careful to avoid puddles—be they of blood or water—as they struggled against the deepening freeze.

Time passed. Minutes or hours, he no longer knew. Only when the decilamp flickered and died, only after shaking it failed to reinvigorate the bioluminescent bacteria within, did Nick notice the gray, feeble light filtering down the ventilation coal shaft from some six feet above.

Dawn had arrived. With it came the sounds of iron-shod hooves. Cart wheels clattering over cobblestones. Halloos of workers calling out to each other. Ought they themselves scream from the depths of their prison? Or would it earn them another bucket of water? Did it matter? Yes, they needed to try. Any minute they might succumb to hypothermia.

As their circuit once more drew them near the opening of the ventilation shaft, his ears caught a faint sound. Metal scraping against stone.

"Did you hear that?" Colleen's voice was a thready whisper. "It came from inside the coal chute."

"I did." With Herculean effort, he hastened their progress, but each step required far more effort than it ought and a horrible pounding had begun inside his skull. Each symptom attributable to the onset of hypothermia... save for the jump in his heart rate and an increasing shortness of breath. Something was dreadfully wrong.

Colleen leaned into the opening. "Copper pipe has been threaded through the grating of the coal hole cover." She sniffed. "There's a bite of vinegar and the air feels heavier somehow." Straightening, her eyebrows drew together. "Might they pump some kind of gas down the coal chute?"

All too slowly, his brain churned, and then he swore. "Hypercapnia." That would explain why the pulse at Colleen's throat beat at such a rapid pace. "Carbon dioxide. Easily produced by mixing vinegar and sodium bicarbonate, otherwise known as baking soda."

*Aether.* He glanced at the bolt-filled sleeve he'd left beside the door. Glover was smarter than Nick had credited him. Their captors wouldn't be entering their prison, not while the occupants were still conscious. Instead, they would send a silent, odorless gas to ease their entry. It was fast becoming a struggle to draw a satisfying breath.

"That sounds… medical. And chemical." She staggered sideways, then sagged against the wall. "Does it explain why the room has begun to spin?"

"Yes." On the floor lay Colleen's damp shirt, minus a sleeve. Snatching it up, he tore the other sleeve loose and pressed it into her hand. His ribs screamed in pain as intercostal muscles contracted with all their might, a futile attempt to provide enough oxygen. "You need to climb into the shaft, Colleen." His words were a desperate plea. "You need to plug the pipe." He pushed her toward the shaft, clumsy as she struggled to climb through the hole. "When its levels become elevated, our blood becomes too acidic. The central nervous system will shut down."

"Can't…" Her foot slipped off the wall, and she fell to the floor even as she reached again for the opening. "Too cold. Too tired."

"No giving up." Catching Colleen beneath her arms, Nick heaved. But she was dead weight and no longer shivering. Her eyelids fell shut. The rag tumbled from her limp fingers.

*Shit.* Hypothermia. Carbon dioxide poisoning. Both meant death. Air. Fresh air. Door. Crack. He grabbed the collar of her shirt and dragged Colleen across the room. His rib cage ached with the effort of pulling in air. Still, it wasn't enough. The door was tightly sealed.

He'd failed the woman he loved by involving her in this mess. By provoking Glover to such rash behavior. Nick would kill the man at the very first opportunity. As he collapsed beside her, he wrapped his fist about the bolt-filled sleeve, praying he might have a chance to use it. "Sorry. So sorry," he whispered.

A heartbeat before the gas stole the last of his vision, his hearing—both fading with every blink—the door slammed open and two men wearing gas masks burst into the room.

COLD. So very, very cold. Stiff rubber pressed against her face while warm air filled her lungs. Her body gave a great shudder. Pinpricks of pain needled her fingers and toes as feeling returned. Wet and damp, her clothes stuck to her skin. Soggy boots encased her toes and ankles. But she'd been lifted, transferred to a smooth surface. A table of sorts, the kind upon which a mad scientist might dissect his specimens.

Colleen pried open her frozen eyelids, blinking at the bright light that glared overhead. A shock of white hair rose above a beaked mask. Enormous circular eyes ringed in brass stared down at her. From beneath the pointed beak ran a hose, like a giant bird attempting to swallow an equally large worm.

Worm.

"No!" she screamed, her cries muffled as she kicked and thrashed against the iron bands that bound her wrists and ankles. Medical instruments upon a metal tray beside her rattled and shook. "No. NO. NO!"

Memory snapped back. Frozen and gassed, they'd been all but dead. But Mr. Glover and Dr. Farquhar wanted her alive, if only so they could snuff out the last of her life to prove the miracle worked as promised. Try as she might, she couldn't bring herself to believe in the resurrective powers of a heart worm.

Her heart gave a great twist. Nick. Was he still alive? Nick *had* to be alive. Her heart and soul insisted. He *was* still alive, her mind reasoned. Mr. Glover would save him, if only to hold him as a bargaining chip, as a lure to draw Anna into a similar trap.

Colleen fought against the rubber mask the giant avian creature held to her mouth and nose, turning her head.

*There!* On the floor. A long tube trailed behind another masked birdman, one who hunched over a collapsed form upon the metal floor. Nick. But instead of holding a mask to his mouth, the masked birdman snapped shackles about Nick's wrists and ankles, ones bound to each other via chains, a design used to prevent a convict from spreading his arms, from lifting his hands above his waist.

Which meant Nick was alive.

For now.

The masked man stood, tethering a length of chain to a metal eye loop affixed to the ceiling with a padlock. *Snap.* He turned, then reached behind his head to drag off his mask. Thick-necked and unrepentant, Mr. Vanderburn stared at her with dead eyes. "All secure," he called. "Air acceptable."

The man who stood over her pulled off his beaked mask and handed it to Mr. Vanderburn. "If you'll bring the rest of our supplies," Dr. Farquhar said, "I'd like to take advantage of her near hypothermic state to begin the procedure."

Gathering the masks and hoses, Mr. Vanderburn left the refrigeration unit as Mr. Glover strolled into the frigid chamber, wearing a fur-lined coat and a woolen muffler about his throat. "Rather Arctic in here, isn't it?" He gave a dramatic shiver and patted his arms. "One wonders that you've not already died a time or two, *wife.*" He tipped his head. "Or have you, without yet slipping into cat form?"

She growled into the rubber mask.

"No? Well, we'll have a few more tries regardless. We need firm evidence. To lose a Scottish woman with nothing but a courtesy title is one thing. More care must be taken with titled patients."

"Let us go now." Relief swept through her at the sound of Nick's voice. Chains clanged against the metal floor as he stirred. "And I'll consider letting you live. But if you touch Colleen again or dare to lay a finger on my sister…"

Mr. Glover snorted. "Ah, but that is precisely what I intend to do the very minute Farquhar here finishes working out a few pertinent details. Well, *I'll* not touch your precious sister, but the good doctor will. Take heart," he cackled, "the first step of the procedure appears to have done my wife no permanent harm." Mr. Glover turned back to her and patted her cheek. "Did it, wife?"

Colleen snapped her head to the side, dislodging the oxygen mask, and bit his bare hand. A salty tang touched her tongue. She'd drawn blood.

He yanked his hand away, cradling it against his chest. "Witch!"

Silent, she curved her lips into a feral smile. Let him worry what would happen when she survived.

There was a clatter, and Mr. Vanderburn reappeared pushing a machine before him, one that looked exactly like the one Anna's nurse had attempted to use, save this one's wires were not connected to a sharp metal probe. Instead, the leads attached to a jointed metal belt. Humiliation burned as Dr. Farquhar's cold, clinical hands unbuttoned the lower half of Nick's shirt and wrapped the device about her chest. A leather belt cinched it about her ribs, and a buckle held it firmly in place.

Her heart slammed into her ribcage, then took off like a runaway train. "Please," she begged. "Don't do this."

Dr. Farquhar leaned close, eyes dancing. "Know you make history, my dear, for in all the archives I've studied, only one man has witnessed such a forced transition of a witch, but—mired in his pagan belief of magic—failed to discover the scientific underpinnings of such a miracle. An element we will test today."

Swearing, Nick pushed to his knees. Chains clattered as he struggled to stand.

"Scientist or inquisitor, you be the judge." Mr. Glover rolled his eyes. "But know I've every interest in this procedure working and becoming a financial success. Not to mention a *living* wife would help certify the veracity of our marriage. Though, I'll remind you again, with the right solicitor, a grieving widower could easily take control of his lawful property." Mr. Glover tipped his head, uncaring of Nick's attempts to stand. "Torrington, however, presents a problem. For now he lives, but..." A shrug. "I've no qualms about disposing of your lover. We *will* need to point a finger at someone to explain your uncle's death. A thwarted suitor would do nicely." He gave her a sharp, toothy grin. "In the end, it might be the best course of action, allowing me to focus entirely upon you."

"And all I possess," she snapped. With any luck, the bite to his hand would grow septic and bring him the death he so richly deserved.

"All *I* possess," he corrected. "I'm done dancing to your whims. To your uncle's. I did everything he asked of me and more. What did I receive for my troubles? Nothing but contempt and a callous dismissal. From both of you. There will be no bargaining, no deals."

Mr. Vanderburn was back wheeling a new cart stacked tall with bulging oil cloth bags tied with coarse string, and a bucket of ice. Tucked within the bucket, as if a bottle of fine wine, was a glass bottle filled with a clear liquid.

Mr. Glover stepped back. "Today you'll die," he waggled his hand, "eight times? Or just once, if Dr. Farquhar's postulates prove false. I suppose there is also the possibility that you will transform into a fairy cat, in which case there will be much to rethink. Survive," his face contorted into that of a madman as he cackled, "and I shall suffer a witch to live."

"A quick test." Dr. Farquhar fiddled with the knobs and dials of the Magneto-Shock Machine, then pushed a button.

"Ow!" She jumped as a buzz of electricity zipped through her. Or would have jumped, but for the restraints.

"Excellent. The machine appears to be in good working order." Dr. Farquhar cinched the belt tighter still.

"Stop! This is madness." She twisted, trying to loosen the electrical belt. "Shape-shifting is a physical impossibility."

"Maybe. Maybe not. We shall see." Dr. Farquhar's wild eyes danced. "Behind all myths and legends lie core truths. The cat sìth are special, this is true, but I have established that they do not metamorphose into a human form."

"How many?" she demanded, seething. "How many fairy cats have met their end beneath your hands?"

"A dozen, maybe more?" Dr. Farquhar answered as if her question was a request for facts, not a furious attempt to point out the harm he'd wrought. "It may well be the felines I've been provided are witches forced into a ninth and final transformation, fated to live the remainder of their lives in cat form."

She gaped, unable to form a response to such insanity.

"You and yours may bear the name Stewart, but in my clan, those with eyes like yours once bore the Kellas name," he rambled on as if recalling the bedtime stories told to him as a small boy, ones he'd now twisted into a bizarre hypothesis requiring experimental proof. "All but lost now. Finding you was a stroke of luck. All that remains is to test the stories, to determine if—when your life spark flickers and dies—your body will shift into the configuration of a cat. A black cat, I expect, with no white patch of innocence upon your chest."

"Stop this now, Glover." Nick stood upright, though he leaned against the wall for support. "Or you'll end this day in a grave."

"Ah, Torrington." Glover shrugged. "A man in chains is not much of a threat, is he?"

Mr. Vanderburn picked up an oilcloth bag and lifted an eyebrow.

"Stack them upon her hips, waist, and chest. We need to drop her core temperature yet further." Dr. Farquhar plucked a glass bottle with a nozzle from the ice bucket and hung it from the overhead hook by means of a leather strap before connecting it to a long rubber tube.

When the first bag of ice landed upon her, all the breath left her lungs in one giant rush. Cold. So cold. Another bag of ice landed upon her. And another. The warmth that had begun to seep back into her veins retreated once more. "Please." Tears streamed down her face.

A vision of her own skull placed upon a laboratory shelf beside those of the cat sìth flashed through her mind. All of them cooled until their hearts stopped, never again to prowl the night.

"It's true, I've been labeled insane by my colleagues, but see here?" He waved a hand at the Magneto-Shock Machine. "I took the precaution of insisting they locate and drag this device through the streets of London. Should my hypothesis prove false, should your heart not leap back to life, I will do my best to restart it." He smiled down at her with benevolence in his eyes.

Did he expect her to *thank* him?

Her teeth chattered. She was sinking faster this time, unable to resist the pull of hypothermia. "I love you," she called to Nick, her voice faint. The words wouldn't console him, but she needed to say them nonetheless. Not at all the circumstances under which she'd wished to speak, but at least he would know. Should the worst happen. And she rather thought it might.

She didn't want to die. Not now. Not when everything she'd ever wanted lay within reach. Marriage to the man who had stolen her heart and had done it without demanding she surrender possession or control of Craigieburn or its lands. Nights spent prowling the streets of London together, working side by side on behalf of their country. And, eventually, the possibility of welcoming a child of their own into this world.

"No!" Nick yanked against the iron chains that bound him in a futile struggle to reach her. "Stop this insanity!"

Dr. Farquhar tied a length of rubber tubing about her upper

arm, then tapped along the inside of her elbow, hunting for a vein that had not collapsed in fear. "I don't suppose you'll cooperate and hold a thermometer in your mouth, my dear? No. It wouldn't do to have the glass shatter between your clenched teeth. I suppose we'll do without. Hypothermia *is* imminent, but the heart will not cease beating until it reaches approximately seventy degrees Fahrenheit. Chilled saline will hasten internal cooling and speed this process." A ball of cold wet cotton swept across her arm a moment before he produced a needle from the instrument tray beside her. "Mr. Vanderburn, I require precision and our subject refuses to hold her arm perfectly still. Your assistance, please."

Uncaring hands clamped down upon her arms, and the doctor slid the needle into Colleen's arm. The scientist worked quickly, connecting the tube to the needle. Icy fluid burned a path through her veins, and she screamed.

# CHAPTER TWENTY-THREE

"Excellent. She's slipped into unconsciousness." Dr. Farquhar released Colleen's wrist to slide a thermometer between her lips. "Her heart and respiratory rates are dropping quickly as is her core temperature. A few minutes more and we'll have our answer."

*Was that frost on her eyelashes? Aether, her fingernails were blue.* After watching it fail during one of his sister's attacks, Nick had little confidence in P.C. Hutchinson's Magneto-Shock Machine, less still in Farquhar's heart worm.

Frantic, his breath hung on the air as he yanked yet again on the chain that tethered him to the ceiling. The eye bolt shifted. Intent on Colleen and ignoring his frantic yells, their captors hadn't noticed Nick's efforts at escape. Losing her wasn't an option, not when he finally *knew* he'd won her heart.

Unable to reach his makeshift weapon, Nick focused his every effort on pulling free. The mortar crumbled, sending another puff of fine dust floating downward, yet still refusing to release the metal ring that held the chain. *Dammit.* But if he couldn't break free, perhaps he could entice a villain closer?

"You lily-livered dowry thief." Nick's jeer sent a bolt of lightning straightening Glover's spine. "Are you so impotent that you must resort to kidnapping and torture to snare a wife?"

The man spun around. Glaring at Nick, he waved a bloody hand, the one into which Colleen had fiercely sunk her teeth. "Gag him," Glover ordered Vanderburn. "We can't have him distracting Dr. Farquhar, and I weary of his blather."

The henchman snatched up a scrap of cloth and stalked toward Nick.

*Perfect.* He braced his legs.

"Cooperate," Vanderburn said. "Or we do this the hard way."

Sneering, Nick curled a finger, inviting the man to try his worst. "What have I to lose?"

"The hard way it is."

Nick feinted right then jabbed with his left, but the thick-necked guard side-stepped the attack. But Vanderburn had lifted his chin, a faint flinch. Even bound and manacled, the henchman believed Nick had a chance. "Scared?"

"Only that I'll kill you. The boss wants you alive. Me?" He shrugged. "I'm still not convinced of your value."

Nick wrapped his fingers about the chains that bound his wrists together. Readying himself. "More than yours. Hired muscle is cheap and replaceable. It's brains that command a premium."

With a low growl, Vanderburn stomped forward, eyes slitted.

The moment he drew close, Nick jumped, yanking with all his might on the overhead chain, lifting himself into the air as he kicked his feet forward and slammed his boots into the man's chest with a satisfying thud.

Vanderburn staggered backward. "Good try."

Fingers curled into fists, he rushed at Nick, delivering a solid upward blow to his stomach, to his solar plexus, and knocking the wind from his lungs. The pain was awful, the inability to draw breath much worse. For a long moment, his diaphragm spasmed, leaving him groaning in an unmanly manner.

"Not so helpful now, are they, brains?"

Slowly, the ability to draw breath returned, but Nick couldn't take much more.

"For the love of aether," Glover called. "*What* is the problem? He's bound in chains. Use the voltaic prod if you must."

Nick hung from the chain, gasping in great gulps of icy air as he spun, letting his body weight twist the chain. "Weapons? To fight. Me?" His limp body was the very picture of defeat. Poisoned. Frozen. Gassed. He was close. Electrical shock? He would recover, but by then Colleen might no longer be alive. He needed to lure Vanderburn close once more. To make one final—

The bolt screeched and dropped a half inch. He planted his feet beneath him and yanked. Plaster crumbled and the iron ring gave way. With a whoosh and a clatter, the chain fell to the floor. With no time to lose, Nick didn't wait to gauge his attacker's reaction. He wrapped a fist about the chain and, bent double, lurched forward to ram his head into Vanderburn's stomach as he swung the chain upward.

*Thwack!* Nick struck the guard on the side of his face.

Vanderburn spun sideways, raising a hand to his jaw. A trickle of blood seeped from between his lips. Anger—the only emotion the henchman knew—flared in his eyes, and he rushed at Nick again, fists raised.

Nick swung the loose chain behind the man's legs and caught the free end with his other hand and pulled. Vanderburn toppled like a telegraph pole, straight and stiff. With a sickening crunch, the back of his head slammed against the cold, hard floor and he fell still. With any luck, the man was dead.

Crouching, reduced to functioning like a feral animal, Nick spun the length of iron chain and pivoted toward Glover, ready to forever alter the function of his knee joints.

*Click.* A pistol's hammer latched into firing position. Slowly, Nick lifted his gaze. Glover held a gun pressed to Colleen's temple.

Glover's irritated voice echoed inside the metal icebox. "Move another inch and I'll end this experiment now."

Farquhar howled. "Absolutely not! We're so very close. Two degrees more and her heart will stop! Shoot *him* instead!" The mad scientist fiddled with the dials of P.C. Hutchinson's Magneto-Shock Machine. Its humming grew louder.

"Don't. Farquhar is right." Nick took a step forward, letting the chain fall slack in his hand, lulling Glover into a false sense of security. "I'm the one you want to shoot." There was a chance Colleen might survive. Slim, but a chance. He'd not steal that from her. Not in exchange for his own life.

Behind him, Vanderburn groaned. "I will kill you, Torrington."

*Dammit*. Nick couldn't seem to catch a break. Threats before *and* behind him.

"No." The barrel of the gun didn't waver. Glover's response demonstrated more intelligence than Nick would have credited him. "She dies. I inherit. There are more like her we can experiment upon. Your sister, for example."

"You're not going to inherit anything," Nick snarled. "Your death is a foregone conclusion."

"Last warning. Don't take another step forward."

"Success!" Farquhar yelled, clapping his hands. "Her heart has stopped! The moment of truth is upon us!"

Distracted, Glover glanced at Colleen. This would be Nick's last and only chance. He leapt on the opportunity with a feral roar, rushing at Glover, praying the man would turn his weapon back toward Nick.

He did.

*Bang! Bang! Bang!*

The bullets missed, zinging past Nick's shoulder to strike the metal wall behind him.

Nick slammed into Glover, knocking him to the ground and

smashing the iron manacles about his wrists into the man's head. Again and again and again.

Bloody and battered, Glover lay still. Perhaps dead. Nick didn't care.

Behind him, the henchman growled.

As the leather soles of the guard's shoes pounded behind him, Nick snatched up the pistol and rolled, firing a bullet into Vanderburn's head. The henchman dropped to the floor, this time most certainly dead.

Nick staggered onto his feet and turned the weapon on Farquhar. Colleen's chest no longer rose and fell. "Bring her back. Activate the Magneto-Shock Machine."

"She'll turn," the scientist insisted without giving Nick a second glance. "Any second. We must have patience."

"Now!" Nick bellowed. Had the madman not noticed the two men—one dead—at his feet?

Colleen's eyes flew open. A horrible sound—a great and prolonged gasp—ripped from her throat. She was alive!

"Failure!" Farquhar moaned, pressing his hands to either side of his head. His fingers curled into his wild hair, taking hold as if he might rip it from its roots. "I was so very certain it would work." His wide eyes met Nick's gaze, unaware or uncaring of the death that surrounded him. "Perhaps transformation only happens on the final death? On the ninth and final round?" He blinked. "We'll need more ice."

There would be no reasoning with the scientist. They might, however, still have need of him later. Assuming anything logical could be dragged forth from his brain. Nick stalked toward Farquhar and smashed the butt of the pistol into the side of his head, turning away as the man crumpled to the floor.

Colleen's eyes fluttered shut as she sank once more toward cardiopulmonary arrest. She needed warmth, and she needed it now.

Nick shoved the wet, dripping ice bags from her body, then

clamped the tubing that fed ice-cold saline into her veins and cut the tubing. He bent, digging through the mad doctor's pockets, yanking out the keys to unlock the iron bands binding her to the metal gurney.

"There'll be a fire upstairs." His fingers felt thick and clumsy and they fumbled his first attempt with the lock. The key nearly jammed with the force of his second effort, but it turned inside the keyhole. *Clang.* The iron band fell to the ground. The second was in his hand.

*Yeowl!*

The cry of a demon split the air.

*Sorcha?*

Snatching up the pistol, Nick spun.

Blood dripped from raw gashes upon Glover's face. He'd not had the courtesy to die. Instead, he'd managed to crawl across the floor to retrieve the galvanic prod. It hummed in his hands.

A black shape darted across the room, swiping at Glover's ankles.

Cursing, the man kicked at the cat sìth, then he lowered the galvanic prod, pointing it at Nick.

Their eyes locked.

"Don't." It wasn't a warning. It was a command. Nick hadn't the strength to wrestle Glover, to win control of the galvanic prod. Nor the inclination. Not only would he gladly see the man dead, Colleen needed warmth *now*.

Beside him, Sorcha hissed, arching her back.

But Glover was far beyond reason. His nostrils flared as he rushed forward.

*Hiss!*

Sorcha slashed at Glover's pant leg as he ran past.

*Bang!*

Nick fired the last bullet into Glover's chest. Shock and surprise rippled across the man's features. Then he fell. Dead.

Nick felt no remorse. Not the faintest inkling.

He threw aside the weapon and turned back to Colleen. Once her wrists and ankles were free, he yanked off the metal belt, shoved the keys into his pocket and scooped her into his arms. His own shackles could wait.

"Yeowl!" Sorcha looked at him, then ran into the hall.

Nick staggered behind, trailing the cat through the twists and turns of the subterranean cellars of The Three-Eyed Bat, blindly trusting the ever-loyal creature to lead her human to warmth, to safety.

Curled against his chest, Nick could feel the rise and fall of Colleen's chest, the faint thud as her heart beat slowly. Then, without warning, they both stopped.

"No, Colleen." He gave her a great shake, ready to drop to the ground, to pound her upon her chest and insist she revive. "Stay with me!"

Another horrible intake of breath rattled her chest as her heart jolted back to life once more. The heart worm? Could Farquhar have been right about the electrical pulses the nematode could deliver, if not the shape-shifting?

The cat sìth yowled again, looking at Nick insistently.

The distant sound of people yelling met his years. A woman's voice—two—rose above a deeper rumbling. Both warmth and assistance were close at hand.

The feline had not let them down.

Ignoring the snap and groan of his cold joints, Nick struggled onward behind Sorcha who paused at each corner, glancing behind to ensure he followed. A moment later, they arrived at the stairs that led upward into the tavern.

He lifted his foot and heaved them both upward. But Nick's adrenaline-fueled efforts to knock down—kill—their captors had weakened him, making each step a struggle to climb. One. Two. "Help!" he yelled.

A third step.

The voices quieted, then began shouting all at once. "Here!"

he called.

A pale face appeared at the top of the stairs. Lady Isabella Maynard peered down the dim staircase. "I found them!"

Footsteps thundered in his direction.

Agent Jackson rushed down the stairs and took Colleen from his arms.

"Fire," Nick ordered. "She needs as much warmth as possible. Immediately."

Jackson nodded. "Of course." He turned and rushed up the stairs.

Another man grasped Nick beneath his arms, pulled him upward and into the warm, fire-lit pub.

***

COLLEEN SHIFTED, burrowing closer to the glorious heat that pressed against her. A soft blanket slipped across her shoulders. Across *bare* shoulders. Beneath one ear was warm skin and the steady thump of a heartbeat. Listening to the soft crackle of a nearby fire, she slid her palm across the rough curls of hair that dusted Nick's chest as they gathered and trailed down his stomach. He'd made good on his promise. A smile formed on her lips —then froze.

*Froze.*

This wasn't right. She had no memory of—

"Wake up, Colleen," Nick's voice pleaded. His rough hands rubbed up and down her arms beneath the blanket. "Please wake up. We're safe now, I promise."

Her eyes snapped open, and her gaze darted about in confusion. "Where are we?"

"Thank aether." He pressed a kiss to the top of her head. "Upstairs in the pub. Sorcha reached your aunt, and Isabella mobilized the cavalry, including a number of Queen's agents.

When they arrived en masse, everyone but the owner turned tail and fled."

"We're still in The Three-Eyed Bat?" Were she not so chilled, a blush would have crept up onto her cheeks. "We're naked?" The low murmur of nearby voices met her ears. "In a public tavern?"

"Nearly naked. We've a blanket." A low laugh rumbled through his chest. "But no worries, we're not on display." He tipped his head toward a privacy screen that hid them from general view. "Well, except for Sorcha who refuses to let you out of her sight."

She shifted and found the cat sìth seated upon the hearth. "Ach, sweetie," Colleen crooned, slipping a hand from beneath the blanket to stroke her hand down the feline's back. "Thank ye."

Sorcha blinked her two golden eyes slowly. Satisfied her human had rallied, she sank down onto her front feet, tucking them beneath her chest, ever watchful. If the cat sìth wasn't worried, Colleen too could relax.

"What happened? How did we escape? The last thing I can recall is the pain of cold fluid burning through my veins."

"You died," he whispered.

Her jaw dropped as Nick recounted Vanderburn's attack, a pistol held to her head, a mad scientist knocked unconscious, and her miraculous return to the world of the living. "Sorcha, extraordinary creature that she is, arrived in time to alert me of Glover's recovery, of his intent to attack." Nick clenched his jaw. "He didn't survive the second attempt."

"Good." And she meant it. Betrayal had left her bloodthirsty. "I never thought I'd be so happy to find myself a widow."

Nick huffed a laugh. "Sorcha made it back to the pub before our other rescuers, slipping down into the tunnels beneath the building. It was she who led us out through the underground maze while everyone else was above, arguing with the proprietors and organizing a search." Nick squeezed her tight. "You died. At least three times before we reached this room."

"The worms?" She shuddered.

"I suspect they saved your life. Not that it would have needed saving, but for your greedy uncle, a malevolent suitor, and one persistent mad scientist." He slipped his hand from beneath the blanket. Circling his small finger was the amber ring. "My sister found this on the dressing table."

"It catches the light." She reached for her engagement ring. "I didn't want to risk—"

"Shh. You told me to ask again." A gleam lit Nick's eyes from within, and her heart gave a great leap of joy. "I love you, Lady Colleen Stewart of Craigieburn. London or Scotland, running across roofs or restoring family estates, I would be by your side. Will you do me the great honor of becoming my wife?"

"Yes." A tear of happiness escaped the corner of her eye as she took his ring and slid it back onto her finger where it belonged. "Only one man has ever stolen my heart." The corner of her mouth kicked up. "How convenient that I find myself a widow when a date is already set." He opened his mouth, but she pressed a finger to his lips. "And it's fortunate you work for a secret government agency, is it not? I imagine the Duke of Avesbury might be able to make those official papers in Mr. Glover's possession disappear."

"Please," Nick rolled his eyes. "So little faith. While you slept, I dispatched Agent Harrison to Glover's home. He found those pages. So certain of his success, the fool hadn't bothered to secure them, but dropped them atop his desk. The touch of a match to dry paper, and a moment later you were once again an unwed heiress. I'd tell you to abandon your black clothing, but—"

She grinned and kissed his nose. "I've been promised rooftops."

"And I'll see them provided."

"Colleen?" Eyes wide, Isabella peeked around the paneled screen. Her hand was pressed to her chest as if afraid to hope that Colleen had truly rallied. "You're awake! It's been hours. How do you feel?"

"I'm fine. Really." She looked to Nick. "Hours?"

He nodded. "We've all been worried."

Isabella disappeared a moment, then was back, rounding the divider with a tea tray in hand. Depositing it upon the nearest table, she hastily poured a cup of steaming liquid, adding far more sugar than Colleen preferred. "No arguing. You need both the energy and hot liquids."

Dutifully, Colleen cradled the warm cup and sipped.

"After your cryptic note, you can imagine my concern when I returned from the dinner party to find my husband on our doorstep, surrounded by police. A most gruesome sight." Isabella shuddered. "One of those horrid newspaper reporters was dancing about the edge of the crowd, whipped into a frenzy by an earlier death that occurred on—above?—Viscount Stafford's property. All of them firing questions and demanding immediate answers." Her hand fell against her lower abdomen. "Already, like hyenas, they're circling demanding answers. They want to know..."

"Who will inherit," Colleen finished. The watch would be on. Should Isabella's child be male, he would become the next Lord Maynard. Otherwise, a cousin would claim the honorific. But at least her aunt was free.

"I will, of course, wear black, but my husband will not be missed." Her face was tight. "Not by me and certainly not by you. But the burden of his misdeeds will take time to sort, to set to rights. Particularly given what was discovered on the premises. Don't think I didn't see you, Mr. Torrington, passing secrets along to one Mr. Jackson. Soon after, an expert locksmith was sent to my house." She lowered her voice to a whisper. "I'm informed they found a human heart inside the safe!"

"Leave such problems to the Queen's agents," Nick said. "I'll see it sorted."

"Gladly." She glanced from him to Colleen. "In any case, I had to pretend a faint before the police would allow me to rest in my room. Not one minute after I opened that sardine tin, Sorcha was on my window sill and, well," Isabella lifted a hand, "you see the rest."

"I hear voices." Anna rounded the privacy screen and dropped into a free chair. "Receiving guests, are you?" She held up a hand, forestalling Colleen's question. "Yes, they tried to stop me from coming, but I have a vested interest in the outcome of tonight's events." She eyed the ring on Colleen's finger, then glanced at Isabella. "*Is* there to be a wedding after all?"

"Well," her aunt huffed. "It won't be postponed on account of mourning for a murderous, traitorous relative, that's for certain."

"Would a small one disappoint your mother?" Colleen asked.

Anna clapped. "A private ceremony will thrill our mother. She's utterly convinced Nicholas will scare you away before he manages to slip a wedding band on your finger."

"Will you be up to it, Colleen?" Isabella asked. "Lest we forget the trauma of all you've been through this past night."

"There's nothing to be done," Nick added, "but watch and wait."

Colleen snatched up his hand and pressed it to her heart. "I feel absolutely fine. But if you want to delay the wedding..."

"Absolutely not." The sultry look on his face told her everything she needed to know.

"Then all that's left to sort," Anna's haunted face searched Colleen's, "is the matter of... an unconventional treatment for my heart block."

"Anna." Nick's voice warned, though his voice cracked. Desperation warred with logic as he weighed the risks. In the past, charlatans and their false cures had raised the hopes of Anna and her family, one disappointment following another. "It's unproven. There are tests I need to run. People I need to consult, including Dr. Farquhar himself. When they took him into custody, he was spouting all sorts of nonsense. Sorting fact from fantasy will take some time." He pinched the bridge of his nose. "In the meantime, deliberately infecting someone with parasitic nematodes. I—"

"While you were missing," Anna interrupted, her voice soft but firm. The dark shadows beneath her eyes intensified. "I had another attack. Twice in one week. I don't expect to live long enough to watch Clara crawl, to walk, let alone speak her first word. I might not even survive to welcome my husband home."

"Anna," Nick warned. Pain crept over his face.

"It may well be commensal," Colleen reminded him, intent on championing Anna's case. "The cat sìth show no ill effects, but rather live long lives. Remember the women who live in my woods are among the eldest of all Scotland." She tapped his chest. "Three times you watched me revive. With no side effects. If Anna understands the risks, why not let her take the chance? Those creatures won't survive in a vial indefinitely. If we wait to be certain, they might be all dead—and collecting more? Well, we can hunt for them in the forest, but there's no promise we will we be able to find another infected cat sìth. And if we do, can cysts be acquired from the blood? Or must we examine their very hearts?" It would break hers to face such a choice.

"Please," Anna begged. "No better alternative exists."

Nick's lips pressed together. "You're right," he conceded with a great sigh. "But we do this carefully, in a sterile environment and—as numerous physicians from the Lister Institute will be involved—there will be endless tests involving much poking and prodding."

Anna clasped her hands to her chest as a tear ran down her cheek. "Thank you."

Isabella handed Colleen a fresh cup of tea, then tugged gently at Anna's sleeve. "Let's give them a few more moments of peace. Mr. Torrington? Agent Jackson would have me inform you that there is a duke with many questions. He finds my husband's connection to a 'shadow committee' of some concern. I imagine," she eyed Colleen, "he also requires an explanation for the human remains found in a certain safe. You're both to report to him as soon as possible."

Colleen dropped her head back onto Nick's shoulder, pulling the blanket to their chins. "The Duke of Avesbury himself?" she whispered once they were alone.

"He'll want to know about how you came to be involved." He slid his hand behind her head and kissed her. A long moment later, he added, "There will be no hiding anything from him, but once he hears our story, the duke will realize what a fine Queen's agent you'd make." She closed her eyes as his hand skimmed down her spine, coming to rest upon the small of her back. "Think of all the secrets we could uncover together."

So much had changed in the mere space of two days. "You do realize this is not at all the hearthside encounter you promised me? Next time, I will expect much better."

Nick trailed his fingers along the edge of her jaw, then pressed a soft kiss to her lips. "Recover, sneak thief. As soon as all is settled here in London, we head north to Craigieburn Castle where, a certain laird has assured me, a massive and *private* fireplace is under her command."

EPILOGUE

"DID YOU EVER THINK you'd call a castle home?" Colleen walked beneath the raised portcullis to slide the great iron key into the rusty lock of the large oak door, the last barrier between her and her childhood home. She had to use both hands to force the mechanism to give way.

*Clank.* The lock popped free.

"Never. Especially one with a list of repairs longer than the kraken-infested Thames." Nick winked, then gave the great nail-studded door a shove. It creaked upon rusty hinges as it opened.

The journey to Scotland had been a long one—beginning with a steam train and ending with a clockwork horse-drawn carriage—during which they'd taken every advantage of the private compartments.

Only minutes ago they'd traveled the length of the tree-lined drive, slowly bringing Craigieburn into view. At first, only its turrets peaked above the snow-dusted branches, but then the castle emerged in all its glory, towering above the landscape. A sight she'd yearned to see for far too many years. As they drew closer, her mind grew more critical, noting crumbled plaster, missing shingles and… She squinted. Was that a broken window pane?

The driver of their carriage had dropped them before the castle door and set their trunks beside them. He'd watched Colleen set the cat sìth free, then lifted his gaze to her golden eyes and smiled. "It's a relief to have you return, Lady…" He hesitated, uncertain how to address her now that she'd married. "Will you be staying?"

"Aye," she'd said. "And I'll be setting things to rights, you can count on that."

"Will there be anything else?"

She'd shaken her head. "Nothing. My new husband and I would like to spend the night alone, but let the villagers know that I'll be looking to hire help tomorrow."

Her estate manager, Watts, had indeed been in her uncle's employ. Though not so much as a shilling of her hard-earned money had been invested in caring for Craigieburn or its surroundings, the dirigible crash and resulting fire had been fictitious. All told, simple neglect accounted for the physical damage done to her ancestral estate. Nothing that couldn't be fixed with sufficient funds.

But the cat sìth and those humans in possession of amber eyes? They'd melted into the countryside. Convincing them to return would require quite some effort. Perhaps when news of The Much Honored Colleen Stewart of Craigieburn's home-coming—with a husband, no less—spread through the country-side, a slow and cautious return would begin.

Doffing his hat, the driver had hurried away. Colleen expected that tomorrow would be a very busy day.

Several weeks had passed since their ordeal, ones filled with the joy of their wedding, the anxiety of Anna's treatment, and endless meetings with the Queen's agents, all while a confusion of solicitors dug through the layers of her uncle's misdeeds.

Garbed in the elaborate white gown with amber buttons,

Colleen had stood beside Nick in his front parlor and spoken vows. The small and intimate ceremony, however, was followed by a well-attended wedding breakfast. One from which the newlyweds had soon slipped away, discarding their finery to tumble into the solid behemoth that was Nick's bed.

Later, the heart worm had slipped into Anna's vein, taking up residence, and within a day, her heart rate had increased from a worrisome forty beats per minute to over sixty. Her pale cheeks grew pink and her hands warm. Not a single seizure had transpired since. Cured. But the parasitologists of Lister Institute were left mystified, for soon after Anna's treatment, the roundworms extracted from the vial had indeed died.

Impressed, the Duke of Avesbury offered Colleen contract work, a chance to assist the Crown on a case by case basis. Her primary task? To restore her family's lands, ensuring the health and well-being of the cat sìth within its woods. Nick, content to relinquish his position with the laboratories, would accompany her, directing an attempt to locate a source of the nematodes that could be collected without endangering the wildcats while keeping a sharp eye out for cryptid hunters.

Isabella—a widow whose wealth depended upon the outcome of her child's delivery and the Crown's investigation into Lord Maynard's illicit activities—had waved away Colleen's invitation to accompany them. "Such nonsense. Go enjoy your honeymoon while I adjust to widowhood. I have much to do, even if it is under the watchful stare of that rat-faced cousin who hopes to lay claim to the title." Concerned, Colleen had agreed to travel to Scotland for the coming spring only after both Isabella herself and Lady Stafford promised to send regular reports. "I'll return in plenty of time for the delivery," she'd promised, not caring for the hint of purple tinging the skin beneath her aunt's eyes. "Or sooner, if you have any difficulties. Any at all."

For now, she stepped into the cobwebbed wonder that was

the Craigieburn's entryway, then led her husband up the stairway and into the great hall. "Behold, the enormous fireplace I promised." A long-forgotten bed of wood lay, waiting. Drying for years upon the andirons and requiring no more than the touch of a match. "Shall we light the fire, or explore?"

Nick winked and held a burning match aloft. "I do believe the intent was to do both at the same time."

She laughed as he tossed it onto the tinder. The flames caught and in minutes, a fire crackled, chasing the chill from the hall. Without a soul to disturb them, they stretched out before the hearth upon a pile of tartan blankets and set about finding new ways to drive each other to distraction.

# ABOUT THE AUTHOR

Though USA TODAY bestselling author Anne Renwick holds a Ph.D. in biology and greatly enjoyed tormenting the overburdened undergraduates who were her students, fiction has always been her first love. Today, she writes steampunk romance, placing a new kind of biotech in the hands of mad scientists, proper young ladies and determined villains.

Anne brings an unusual perspective to steampunk. A number of years spent locked inside the bowels of a biological research facility left her permanently altered. In her steampunk world, the Victorian fascination with all things anatomical led to a number of alarming biotechnological advances. Ones that the enemies of Britain would dearly love to possess.

You can connect with Anne on Facebook at https://www.facebook.com/AnneRenwickAuthor/. Or join her in the Facebook group the Department of Cryptobiology: https://www.facebook.com/groups/1732211897016353 .

For email updates, sneak peaks, new releases and giveaways, sign up for her newsletter at https://www.annerenwick.com/